"WHAT DO YOU WANT?"

"What do I want?" Leith repeated slowly, still smiling. He stood with his legs braced wide apart, arms casually crossed over his chest. "Why, I want ye."

"Me?" Adrianna might have lived in a convent for most of her life, but she could hardly misinterpret his meaning, or fail to understand the danger gleaming hotly in his eyes. Dazedly she noticed that his shirt was unlaced, revealing dark tendrils of hair in sharp relief against the fine white lawn. "You—you don't mean that," she whispered, clutching the arms of her chair even more tightly as the room began to whirl in a slow dizzying circle.

"Oh, but I do, my sweet Sassenach," he said. "Ye're my prize, and I've come to claim ye."

BOOK YOUR PLACE ON OUR WEBSITE AND MAKE THE READING CONNECTION!

We've created a customized website just for our very special readers, where you can get the inside scoop on everything that's going on with Zebra, Pinnacle and Kensington books.

When you come online, you'll have the exciting opportunity to:

- View covers of upcoming books
- Read sample chapters
- Learn about our future publishing schedule (listed by publication month *and author*)
- Find out when your favorite authors will be visiting a city near you
- Search for and order backlist books from our online catalog
- Check out author bios and background information
- Send e-mail to your favorite authors
- Meet the Kensington staff online
- Join us in weekly chats with authors, readers and other guests
- Get writing guidelines
- AND MUCH MORE!

**Visit our website at
http://www.zebrabooks.com**

THE PRIZE

MARTINE BERNE

Zebra Books
Kensington Publishing Corp.

http://www.zebrabooks.com

For B., who is my prize

O Caledonia! Stern and wild
Meet nurse for a poetic child!
Land of brown heath and shaggy wood
Land of the mountain and the flood,
Land of my sires! what mortal hand
Can e'er untie the filial band,
That knits me to thy rugged strand!

—from Sir Walter Scott's *O Caledonia!*

CHAPTER 1

Carlisle, England
1580

"You've grown into a comely girl, my dear sister," drawled Giles, the new Earl of Westbrook. With studied elegance he lowered his lanky frame into what had been their father's favorite chair. Made of mellow oak, it had a high, intricately carved back and had once been richly upholstered; the soft burgundy velvet was threadbare now. Giles' doublet, crafted of a peacock-blue silk trimmed with soft calfskin, was nearly as shabby, and the linen ruff about his neck was edged in a white lace which had obviously been darned by an inexpert hand.

"Yes," Giles continued musingly, pushing back a lock of yellow hair from his thin face, "you're quite comely indeed."

Adrianna clenched her fingers together in her lap, resisting the nervous temptation to clutch the rough material of her skirts, so different from the delicate woolen lovingly woven by the nuns. "I wouldn't know," she replied coolly, trying to quell her inner agitation. This was the first time her brother had spoken more than two words to her since her return home a fortnight ago, and she misliked the avid gleam she saw in his pale blue eyes. What did he want, this older brother who was now a virtual stranger to her? And why did his servants, unkempt and insolent, look at her with such unpleasant speculation?

Oh, how she longed to return to the life she had known, to its peaceful routines, useful work, and affectionate camaraderie! Here she was kept to an enforced idleness that weighed upon her spirits and haunted her dreams with uneasy specters. She might have been born in this castle but all it held for her were the distant, hazy memories of childhood. She asked herself for the thousandth time, why had Giles sent for her? Even during the last weeks of his illness her father had not done so, perhaps because he had been reluctant to bring her back to a house filled with discord and animosity.

Lord Robert had been a celebrated military man, forceful and direct, and while he had not been one for cosseting and caressing, Adrianna had known despite his frequent, extended absences that he had cared for her. How disappointed he must have been to have sired first a dissolute wastrel in Giles, and then a weak and helpless female!

Adrianna had only learned of Lord Robert's death when the outriders from Crestfield had come for her, demanding that she return with them immediately. She had barely had time to say her farewells to her beloved Mother Superior and to the nuns . . .

Of their own volition her fingers went to touch the tiny gold cross that hung about her neck. Removing the delicate gold chain from underneath the starched, pure-white collar of her habit, Mother had given it to her just before

Adrianna had climbed into the carriage. *I could not have loved you more had you been my own daughter,* she had said softly. *Take my love with you wherever you go.*

Adrianna saw that Giles was still gazing at her, his arched brows raised, and she added quickly, "In the convent we never discussed such worldly matters as one's appearance."

Giles' thin lips curved into a wolflike smile that failed to reach his eyes. "What a dull place it must be," he said, sipping at the glass of wine he held in his slim, pale fingers. "Really, Adrianna, you should be thanking me for having you removed from such infernal boredom."

"I had planned to spend my life at Rosings, among the good sisters," Adrianna said quietly. "In six months' time I too was to become a nun."

"Why, what a waste of prime flesh," Giles returned, his smile widening to show yellowed teeth.

An angry heat suffused Adrianna's cheeks. She bit down hard on her lower lip to keep from blurting out her mortification and disdain, some sixth sense urgently informing her that to do so would be unwise. *Patience, my child,* Mother Superior had told her time and again, her gray-blue eyes warm and full of wisdom. *Patience and a steady heart will win the day.*

"I see I have made you blush, dear sister," Giles said smoothly. "Pray forgive me. You will of course recall what a horseman I am; being amongst those low peasant grooms has, I suppose, corrupted my tongue."

With an effort Adrianna met his gaze. "Indeed, I scarcely know you, Giles," she said, attempting to keep her tone pleasant even as she pushed aside recollections of Giles' hatefulness toward her when they had played together in their nursery. Four years older than herself, and considerably stronger, Giles had bullied her and stolen her toys and tugged upon her braids until she had cried. Their mother's gentle remonstrations had done nothing to palliate Giles' volatile temper, nor to bend him toward his studies, and Adrianna saw now in the harsh lines of his face how a life of unchecked self-indulgence had marked him.

"As you know," Adrianna went on, as steadily as she could, "Father sent me to Rosings when I was but a child of six, some twelve years ago."

"Can it really be twelve years?" Giles marveled, sipping at his wine. "Well, it is high time you were back at Crestfield, isn't it?"

Adrianna again clenched her fingers together, even more tightly than before. "Father knew that I intended to stay at Rosings."

"Well, Father is gone, and I am master now," her brother said with a casual arrogance that sent a chill down her spine. "I've plans for you, my dear, that have nothing to do with a nunnery."

"And . . . and what might those plans be?" Adrianna's voice wavered a little as inside, a part of her cried out at having been so rudely wrenched from her quiet, untroubled life at Rosings. It was a small convent tucked away in the woods of northeastern England, remote and with an income so mean as to have escaped the royal edict demanding the dissolution of monasteries and convents which had been put into effect by the queen's late father, King Henry VIII, nearly fifty years ago, in 1535. To Adrianna, Rosings, despite its meager accommodations and sometimes limited fare, had quickly become more than a shelter and a school.

I want to go home, she thought desperately. *I want to go home. There must be a way I can go back to Rosings.*

Giles eyed her sharply across the expanse of the massive oak desk which dominated the library. This had been Adrianna's favorite room in the entire castle, with its large casement windows generously letting in sunlight and its row upon row of books stretching high up to the ceiling. As a child she had loved to play here while her father, on his rare visits home, pored over the maps and globes, planning strategies of war on the queen's behalf. Adrianna had known little of battles and campaigns, of course, but she had enjoyed gazing wonderingly into the glass-encased cabinets displaying the curiosities Lord Robert had brought home from his travels and quietly watching as he sat at his desk consulting his books or furiously scribbling dispatches. She had not minded that he had paid little attention to her save the occasional smile; she was content merely to be near him.

For a few moments Adrianna let her mind slip back into the pleasant innocence of childhood, when all she had had to do was to play, and wander about the castle grounds, and cajole her nurse into giving her another sweetmeat . . .

Her wistful reverie was interrupted by the sound of a fist crashing down upon solid oak. "God's blood!" Giles shouted. "How dare you ignore me, you foolish wench?"

"My—my pardon," Adrianna hastily apologized, stammering as fear coiled through her. "I was—I was remembering how much I liked this room as a little girl."

Giles glanced contemptuously around him. "Oh, yes, Father's precious books and mementos," he said with a sneer. "I couldn't sell the lot at a price to justify the effort of hauling it away."

"Sell it?" Adrianna asked, astonished. "Why would you want to do such a thing?"

Giles gave a humorless bark of laughter. "Your ignorance, dear sister, is charming," he said with a spurious sweetness. His outburst over, his temper had subsided again, leaving him suave and controlled once more.

Adrianna didn't know which mood she found more discomfiting. "You—you were telling me of your plans," she said quickly.

"I was, wasn't I?" His eyes gleaming, Giles took another swallow of wine, stood, and came around the desk to stand behind her chair, where he bent down and drew his fingers along the exposed skin of her collarbone. "Yes. My plans."

Adrianna stiffened, her flesh crawling with revulsion, and stared straight ahead. *Dear God,* she prayed, *give me strength.*

"We may be one of the proudest, most esteemed noble families in England, but we are not one of the richest," Giles said softly into her ear. "In fact, it would not be going too far to say that we are . . . impoverished. Having you enter into a carefully chosen alliance would be most helpful to me."

Adrianna felt her breathing become shallow. "I do not wish to marry, Giles. I would like to return to Rosings, if you please."

"I do *not* please," Giles replied in a low, cold voice. His fingers slipped up to her slender throat and encircled it lightly. "Sir Roger Penroy has informed me that he is willing to overlook your pitiably small dowry and make you his wife without delay."

Horror surged through her. Sir Roger, a contemporary of her father's whom she only dimly remembered from childhood, had supped with them two days ago. Giles had made a great fuss about his visit and had even gone so far as to have the village seamstress come to Crestfield to sew a new gown for Adrianna. His generosity hadn't extended to the fine wool or damask that was considered appropriate for a highborn lady, however, and old Janey Miller was ordered to use a cheap frieze material. She was wearing the dress now; of a plain, muted gray, it was the only garment she possessed that was suitable for life outside of a convent.

As for Sir Roger himself, Adrianna winced at the memory. He was scarcely as tall as she, yet he outweighed her by several stone, his gluttonous table manners amply demonstrating how he came to be that way. Sparse gray hair fell about a round, coarse face whose most prominent feature was a bulbous blue-veined nose. He had chucked her under the chin and patted her on the arm and paid her many unwelcome compliments; she had endured him out of civility and because he had been the old earl's friend. Now she recalled that he had buried two wives and was the father of three ill-favored girls older than she herself was, all spinsters and reputed to be possessed of nasty, spiteful tempers.

With supreme effort Adrianna remained motionless in her chair. "Please, Giles," she said, unable to keep the note of pleading from her voice, "I do not wish to marry Sir Roger. Indeed, I do not wish to marry anyone."

The fingers around her neck tightened cruelly for a moment, and Adrianna gave an involuntary gasp of terror, then shuddered as Giles bent down and delicately drew his tongue along the curve of her ear. "Sir Roger is rich, and he is eager. Do not make me angry, dear sister, for when I am inflamed I do things that ... I occasionally regret later." Without warning Giles plunged his hand down the bodice of her gown and grasped her breast, squeezing it hard.

With an angry cry Adrianna wrenched herself free and, whirling to her feet, slapped her hand across his face. "How *dare* you?"

Giles straightened and gingerly pressed his palm against his scarlet cheek, all traces of affability gone from his expression. "Do not cross me, my dear sister," he said heavily. "I am lord and master now."

Adrianna stared at him, her fingers pressed tightly against her bodice. She could feel her heart pounding frantically, like a small bird desperate to escape. "I do not wish to displease you, Giles," she said, hating the way her voice trembled, "but I cannot—*will not*—marry."

Giles' pale blue eyes were as cold as ice. "You will obey me!" he snapped. "Or I'll make you rue the day you were born!" He showed his teeth in a savage mockery of a smile, then turned on his heel and stalked out of the library, slamming the door hard behind him.

Alone in the room that had once been beloved to her and now seemed nothing less than a prison, Adrianna sank back down onto her chair, a fear unlike any she had known taking hold of her in a hard, merciless grip.

"Heaven help me," she whispered aloud. "Heaven help me."

CHAPTER 2

"Are ye ready then, Colin?" Leith Campbell asked in a low voice.

"Aye, laird," Colin whispered in the darkness whose only relief was the faint light of the moon. He gripped the coil of rope slung across one brawny shoulder.

"Good," Leith responded softly. "Noo remember— Hugh's book is most likely concealed somewhere within the room. I ha' no doubt the auld bastard was canny enough tae hide the evidence o' his disgrace." He looked to Dougal and went on softly, "Keep yer eyes open and yer wits aboot ye, lad. We'll return the instant we ha' the book in hand."

"I'll no' fail ye, laird," Dougal promised fervently.

"I knoo ye willna," Leith said, then gripped his shoulder in rough farewell. "Come then, Colin. And quietly!"

He held out his hand for the rope, which Colin swiftly gave to him. With silent, graceful skill he tossed the end of the rope up high, angling it so that it slithered through the massive iron bracket supporting a primitive balcony and pitched downward into his waiting grasp. He tied a sturdy knot and thrust it into Dougal's hand, then took hold of the rope. He tested his weight, nodded to Colin, and rapidly began his ascent, climbing methodically hand over hand.

Leith could feel Colin following him a few feet down, but his mind had moved on from the logistics of scaling the castle wall and was focusing on the search just ahead of them when they would enter the room. A loquacious servant, slatternly and half-starved, had been persuaded by a few coins to reveal that the late earl had kept all of his trophies of war in his library, and that the new earl had not yet disturbed his father's possessions, instead contenting himself with rapidly depleting the contents of the castle's wine cellar.

It was rumored that the poverty-stricken old earl had died a slow and painful death from dropsy, and that the old harridan, Queen Elizabeth, despite Lord Robert's many years of faithful service to the crown, had failed to offer him either monetary assistance or to send one of her own highly skilled physicians to him.

Ach, the bloody Sassenachs, Leith thought grimly. They could rot in hell, every single last one of them, for all he cared!

For a brief moment Leith was flooded with the emotions he had forcefully pushed aside so that he could concentrate on what he needed to do. Instantly a haunting image of Hugh's beloved face—so like his own, yet so different in its youthful, merry insouciance—rose before Leith's eyes. Then came the inevitable wave of sadness, heavy and black, which was swallowed up by burning anger. *Damn them, damn them—*

Leith gave a little shake of his head and compelled cool, calculating rationality to take over again. He had planned his restitution for too long to let himself be distracted now. His moment—and Hugh's—was finally at hand . . .

Leith reached the bracket beneath the balcony, took firm hold of it, and peered upwards in the gloom. The balcony, he saw, was made of a stone different from that which made up the thick walls of the castle. It had clearly been an afterthought, no doubt inspired by the French craze for such fripperies, and thanks to its shoddy workmanship, its construction was uneven.

He would have to swing himself up in a single motion and gain some kind of purchase on the balcony's underbelly, then scrabble higher to reach the smooth stone lip and haul himself to safety. It would all have to be executed without a stumble or slip, else he'd plummet to the ground and meet certain death.

"Wait until I've reached the balcony," he instructed Colin in a whisper, and when the other signaled his understanding with a nod he returned his gaze to the challenge above him. He was still for a few moments more, his eyes searching the stonework, and then with a powerful thrust of his arm he was up onto the balcony's underside, his fingers and toes digging into the rough surface.

He ignored the sickening sensation of instability, instead pushing himself higher until his questing fingers caught hold of the cold stone lip of the balcony and he was able to propel himself up and over the edge, landing quietly on the safety of the balcony's floor.

Swiftly he leaned down and held out his hand to Colin, who had been waiting below with his fingers curled around the iron bracket. Colin shoved himself upwards, caught Leith's hand, and in another moment was hauled onto the balcony.

"Good man," Leith murmured, then turned to the casement windows barring their entrance. He ran his fingers along the center edges, and by their roughness could tell that much-needed repairs had not been done. A few quick slashes with his knife and the interior latch gave way.

Leith restored the knife to his belt, pulled open the iron-framed glass panels, and stepped into the library, scanning the darkness for signs of movement, his ears alert to any noises from within.

All was silent and still, and he gestured for Colin to come inside and follow him to the hearth where embers from the day's fire still flickered. They each pulled a candle from their breeches pocket and touched the wick to glowing embers.

As the candles softly flared, a dim light suffused the room and Leith's glance rapidly took in the many rows of books, the glass cabinets scattered about, an enormous desk, a motley assortment of chairs.

"There's sae many books, laird," Colin whispered in dismay. "We'll no' find Hugh's amidst sae many!"

"We can and we will," Leith answered in a low, determined voice. "The auld earl wouldna ha' put it aboot for all tae see, remember. Look for false shelves while I search through his desk."

"Aye, laird," replied Colin, then moved away to begin gently pressing against the shelves to test their solidity.

Leith in turn went to the desk and tried opening its drawers, but found them all locked. He pulled out his knife again and used its sharp, narrow tip to force open a lock. Quickly he slid open the drawer and examined its contents. Voluminous correspondence from the queen's men, William Cecil, Sir Francis Walsingham, Sir Ralph Sadler . . . as Hugh had many a time pointed out, all notorious opponents of the captive Queen Mary.

But no Book of Hours—Hugh's own Bible, handwritten and exquisitely illustrated by Scotland's finest artists, a gift from their parents upon his tenth birthday.

The book that he carried with him everywhere, long after the old laird and his lady were gone to their rest.

The book which he had taken with him seven years ago to join the lairds of Lethington and Kirkcaldy in Edinburgh Castle, in their valiant fight for the cause of Queen Mary.

But the fight had turned into a deadly siege for the Scots, when Queen Elizabeth had sent English troops and artillery.

Lord Robert had been one of the English generals masterminding the campaign. It was he who had killed Leith's younger brother Hugh Campbell in the hand-to-hand combat that had ended the siege in a disastrous loss for the Scots.

It was Lord Robert who, blatantly unmindful of the sanctity of death, had plundered Hugh's corpse and stolen the Bible that had been sacred to him.

And was therefore sacred to the Campbell clan.

Hugh's few remaining men, already taken captive and being forcibly removed from the field, had been powerless to prevent Lord Robert from carrying out his evil deed. They could only watch, and then wait until Leith was able to ransom them, and finally report to him what they had seen.

The entire clan Campbell had mourned the loss of Leith's gallant, much-loved brother. Impetuous and headstrong, idealistic and with a heart as big as the Highlands themselves, Hugh was an ardent supporter of Queen Mary and had gone off to war against Leith's advice. Himself a man without political passions—kings and queens came and went, was his cynically pragmatic view, while the clan would always remain his first priority—Leith had nonetheless burned to seek retribution for Hugh.

But seven years had passed in which the volatile instability sweeping across Scotland had made it impossible for him to leave Inveraray, make the long journey across the

Lowlands, and slip across the English border into Carlisle, all the while leaving the clan without leadership. It was a risk he could not take until recently.

And as bad luck would have it, even as he and his men made their way south, the old earl had disobliged him by dying.

Well, Leith couldn't personally revenge himself upon Lord Robert, but he could bring back Hugh's precious Bible and restore his honor.

But first he had to find it.

Leith forced a second lock and pulled open the drawer. More correspondence, some discarded quills, and, at the very bottom, two small, linked miniatures in delicate oval frames.

Leith peered at them more closely. One was a tiny portrait of a thin-faced young woman with light brown hair, blue eyes, and a wistful smile. The other was of a bonny little lass who couldn't have been more than four years old, an angelic-looking creature with luminous blue eyes, rosy cheeks, and thick, straight, golden-blond hair pulled back from a heart-shaped face.

No doubt these were members of the old earl's family. Leith stared into the soft blue eyes of the little girl and had every reason to believe that Lord Robert had loved the woman and child.

Perhaps as much as Leith had loved Hugh.

His lips twisting bitterly, Leith slid the miniatures into his pocket. It was a foolish act, he knew, taking such a small token when the old man was dead and could no longer feel its loss, but some imp of a demon was driving him on.

Leith glanced over at Colin, who was still patiently tapping at the shelves, and he forced the lock of yet another drawer. It held several rolled-up maps, a spyglass, and a crumpled linen toque embroidered with an elaborate R.

Leith ground his teeth in frustration. God's blood, where was Hugh's book?

Savagely he broke open a low, narrow drawer and crouched down to better examine what lay within. A pair of small, soft gloves with long flaring cuffs. A battered piece of parchment bearing the name *Robert* written in a flowing feminine script. And underneath the parchment . . .

Leith felt his heart quicken.

Yes.

There it was—a Book of Hours, its simple black leather cover much the worse for wear. Hugh's Bible!

Leith grasped it reverently, his fingers caressing the smooth leather, and rose jubilantly to his feet.

"Colin!" he said softly. "I've found it!"

Colin turned, and even in the dimness of the library Leith could see his answering grin.

"Thanks be!" Colin's voice was low but resonant with emotion. "Thanks be tae heaven and—"

Colin broke off as Leith abruptly raised his hand, his body tensing. The sound of a hushed footfall outside the library could be heard, and Leith blew out his candle, slid Hugh's book into his breeches pocket, and swiftly withdrew against the musty velvet curtains to the side of the casement windows; at the same time Colin snuffed out his own candle and flattened himself against the wall. Both men turned their heads toward the door as it was gently opened.

A slim figure clothed in dull gray came quietly into the room.

Leith's nerves were taut, his every sense alert. They could not afford detection; their escape down to the ground again and to the safety of a small copse of nearby trees where their horses awaited them was too bold, too complicated, and needed to be made without anyone in the castle being the wiser for it to be successfully carried off.

Who was this person—a female clothed in what looked

to be the drab garments of a servant—that she bore no candle to light the darkness? On what mysterious errand was she bound? Was she here to steal something of the earl's?

Slowly she drifted toward the casement windows, as if hesitant yet compelled by a force beyond her control.

Their unwelcome guest seemed oblivious to the smoky scent of extinguished candles, but in a moment, Leith saw, she would doubtless perceive that the casement had been tampered with and would of course sound an alarm.

Leith swore silently. He'd come too far, and gambled too much, to let tonight's enterprise be jeopardized.

As the servant girl came abreast to him in her slow, unsure approach to the windows, Leith didn't hesitate. Under the inky concealment of night, he moved with the deadly speed and silence of a panther descending upon its unsuspecting prey.

Adrianna moved toward the balcony of her father's library as if in a dream. Numb with despair and unable to sleep, she had remained in her room, still fully dressed, until the deep, dark hours of the night had cast the world around her into blackness and she had made her decision.

She would return to Rosings.

It was a long walk indeed, and dangerous for a penniless young woman on her own, but Adrianna knew she could not remain in this house and hope to keep mind and body intact.

She gathered up her few meager belongings—a simply made brush for her hair, a linen nightshift, a much-darned pair of woolen stockings, and a few coarse rolls she had managed at supper to slip into the folds of her gown and spirit upstairs—and then she made a bundle with the nightshift, using the long sleeves to fasten it securely.

She had crept along the chilly, drafty corridor to the landing overlooking the great hall. There she had paused. All was as still as a tomb. Then, almost without knowing why, she'd continued down the corridor to the library.

Just a last, swift look around a room she had once loved. A final farewell.

She'd opened the door and slipped inside. A familiar musty smell of old books and ancient velvet teased her nostrils. There were curtains on either side of the casement windows; as a little girl she had enjoyed rubbing her cheek against their plush burgundy softness. And through the tall windows was a balcony, which she vaguely remembered her mother having ordered built for her father, despite his protests that castles did not need such architectural foolishness.

You spend so much time in the library, my love, Adrianna recalled hearing her mother say affectionately. *If you were to step out into the fresh air now and again, it would gladden my heart.* And Lord Robert had gruffly assented, unable to resist the sweet coaxing of his wife. Whose death, when Adrianna was but five, had nearly driven him mad with grief.

Adrianna blinked, thinking she saw something behind her, nearly out of the range of her eyesight, move slightly. Doubtless it was only her imagination.

Yet why did an eerie prickle run up her spine?

She shook her head slightly, as if to clear it, then looked again toward the balcony. It was a mild spring evening and the valley would be beautiful from such a vantage, bathed in silvery moonlight. One glance and then she would go.

She reached the windows and had just extended her arm to open the casement when suddenly she felt herself snatched up against a big, powerful body, felt her mouth implacably covered by a warm hand as she tried to scream and to free herself. Her bundle fell unnoticed to the floor.

Adrianna frantically twisted against the firmly muscled arm holding her captive, but all her efforts were for naught.

Who was this intruder? And why was he here in her father's library in the middle of the night?

Certainly his presence augured ill, and cold terror pumped uncontrollably through her veins.

"Cease yer struggles, lass," the man holding her said softly, grimly, his voice deep and smooth and lilting with the inflection of the Scots, and Adrianna, her fright intensifying to hear it, redoubled her efforts to free herself.

A Scotsman. Dear God.

Her father had hated the Scottish people, she knew, in large part because he attributed his wife's death to the shock she had suffered, while a month shy of giving birth to her third child, during a border raid gone especially violent.

Some ten or fifteen of Lord Robert's men had died, which was bad enough, but Lady Katherine had gone into disastrously early labor and neither she nor the babe survived. A few weeks later, Adrianna had been packed off to Rosings. For her own safety, she remembered her father saying gravely, his gaunt face seeming to have aged overnight.

And now, to find herself at the mercy of a barbarous Scotsman! Everyone knew they were a treacherous, backwards race who lived in a wretched and desolate country, cheek to jowl with the dirt of their own swine.

Adrianna twisted violently, and, feeling the arm about her tighten inexorably—dear Lord, was the man made of pure iron?—she panicked and bit down hard on the hand covering her lips.

The man cursed under his breath and the sickly-sweet taste of his blood filled her mouth as he kept his hand firmly in place, continuing to prevent her from crying out.

"Colin!" he said quietly, and a dark form materialized from across the library to approach them.

Wide-eyed with fear, Adrianna watched the burly Scotsman draw near. He was scowling at her, his hamlike fists clenched, and she felt herself cringing away from him . . . into the rock-hard resistance of her captor.

"Take her," the man at her back growled. "Hold her while I bind her and stop up her damned mouth!"

"Strangle her instead," suggested the other. "She's just a worthless Sassenach!"

"Do as I say," her captor said, in a steely voice that brooked no dissent.

"Aye, laird," came the meek reply, and before she could even lash out with an arm or a leg, Adrianna found herself transferred with savage efficiency to the man called Colin.

A candle illuminated the darkness, and Adrianna was able for the first time to look into the face of the one who had snatched her up.

Her breath caught in her throat as she gazed at him, and for a dizzying moment she forgot where she was, who she was.

Surely he was a god from ancient times.

He had to be one of the tallest men she had ever seen. But it wasn't merely his height that made her heart pound harder in her breast. His face was one that, once seen, could never be forgotten.

He wasn't exactly handsome, but his dark, deep-set eyes, straight, proud nose, and sensuous lips together created an impression of fierce, quick intelligence, indomitable authority . . . and a bold, passionate nature.

Her mind timidly shied away from that thought even as she hastily pulled her eyes away from that curiously attractive mouth to touch upon the rich dark hair tied carelessly back, then couldn't prevent herself from taking in with a covert glance the broad shoulders, the deep, strong chest that narrowed to lean hips and long, muscular legs encased in rough breeches and boots.

"God's blood, lass, ha' ye never seen a man before?" came a mocking voice, and Adrianna's gaze rose in startled mortification to his. Those arresting features were twisted into an expression of amused derision. "Though if ye've only seen the English all yer life, then I suppose ye never *ha'* seen a man before!"

The burly man at her back chuckled, and Adrianna's temper rose, dissipating some of the paralyzing fear that had been clutching at her.

"In point of fact," she said coolly to the majestic Scotsman who stood but a few feet away, towering over her, "I have *not* seen many men in my life. I'm a nun." Even as she said the words she prayed that God would forgive her for her dissembling.

"A nun?" echoed the Scotsman. "I think no', lass, ye're hardly dressed like one." His eyes roamed lazily over her in the soft haze of candlelight, seeming to penetrate the awkward stuff of her dress, and Adrianna flushed hotly.

"Nor are ye the servant girl I took ye tae be," he went on, reaching out to slide a length of her long, straight hair between his fingers. "Yer voice is that of a highborn lass, though ye're dressed most poorly in that mouse-colored sack."

Adrianna repressed a ridiculous stirring of hurt vanity, and retorted, "I'll have you know I'm very nearly a nun! That is, I would have been, if ... Oh, never mind! Will you kindly let go of my hair?"

He had been staring at the silken strand as if struck by a startling thought. Now his intent eyes went to her face, and a slow smile curved his sensuous mouth as he released the strand and let it drift back to rejoin the heavy weight of her hair, which had escaped from her coif during her struggles and now tumbled loose across her shoulders.

Adrianna was not reassured to see that smile, nor could she keep from quivering as once again his gaze roamed over her, as intimate and shocking as a caress. Never had she felt such a sharp awareness of her own femininity. For a moment his expression was one of male hunger, raw and primordial—for her? she wondered, fear and confusion tightening her stomach even as a curious warmth suffused her limbs—and then his face was cold and shuttered once more.

"Well, well," he said softly. "Colin, ye'll be pleased tae knoo we've captured a fine prize for ourselves this night. This saucy lass is none other than Lord Robert's own daughter."

"His daughter, laird?" the man behind her responded in obvious astonishment. "How come ye tae knoo that?"

Instead of answering the Scotsman looked at Adrianna mockingly. "I'm waiting for ye tae deny it, lass."

Adrianna bit her lip, alarm rising again. "Yes, I'm Lord Robert's daughter," she admitted. "But I'm no prize to be captured!"

"Oh, but ye are, lass," he contradicted her with such gentleness that she felt her knees weaken in dread. "Ye're a fine, fine prize."

"My brother!" she burst out. "He'll come after you! He'll . . ." She faltered and fell silent; she hardly knew herself what Giles would do but she strongly doubted it would be in her best interests.

"Let him then," the Scotsman said silkily. "If he's no' too busy wi' the auld earl's wine!" Without waiting for her reply he knelt down and ripped off the wide hem of her gown, restraining her efforts to kick at him with such ease that Adrianna felt more helpless than she ever had in her life.

He straightened and with his knife he made two quick slits in the frieze and tore it into three long swaths. "Ye knoo, lass, I canna help but think that ye should be grateful tae us," he said conversationally as he worked.

"Grateful?" Adrianna repeated, dumbfounded.

He nodded at her little bundle on the floor. "Obviously ye're of a mind tae travel. Who's tae say we didna come along at just the right moment?"

A memory of her safe, narrow little cot at the convent flashed across her mind. "Please!" she said desperately. "Can you not let me go on my way? I swear I'll not tell anyone of our encounter!"

Those fine dark eyes rested on her face again, and for a moment Adrianna thought that they softened. But then an expression of harsh bitterness settled across his features.

"Enough talking," he said roughly, and bound the first swath of frieze around her mouth with swift efficiency, silencing her; the second and third strips he used to lash her wrists and ankles.

Adrianna felt her throat constrict with thick tears of despair. What dreadful fate awaited her as a captive of this merciless barbarian? Her thoughts raced ahead to images too awful to contemplate, recalling a hysterical outburst of her nurse after a border raid. *They beat their prisoners,* Winifred declared, nodding her head vehemently. *Torture them like the ungodly beasts that they are. And as for the women, they'll have their way with them and laugh as they do it! Then toss them away like broken dolls!*

To a child Winifred's agitated whispers meant little, but now they took on a terrible significance. Truly her lot would be worse than death.

He'll not take me like some lamb to the slaughter, she told herself. *I will find a way.*

"Pick her up, Colin, and follow me," the Scotsman said as he stooped to grasp her pathetic little bundle. He looped the ends of her nightshift sleeves about his belt, tied them securely, and stepped to the casement windows, opening them wide.

The man called Colin complied, slinging Adrianna over his shoulder as if she were a sack of coal, but said doubtfully, "Surely ye dinna mean tae take her wi' us, laird! We ha' the book, after all."

"The auld earl took something he shouldna ha'," the Scotsman answered grimly. "Noo *I'm* taking something o' his, and deem it a fair enough bargain."

"Aye, laird," Colin said obediently, and moved forward with her to the balcony. "How are we tae get her down?"

From her awkward perch atop the brawny Colin's shoulder Adrianna caught a glimpse of the ground far below them. A cool night breeze washed across her, but colder still was an icy numbness overtaking her. And in the far reaches of her mind she also wondered how the masterful Scotsman planned to spirit her away with them.

"Give her tae me when I call for ye tae do sae," came the assured reply. "Wait until I've gotten all the way down tae follow. Ye'll see how I do it—sae watch noo!"

She heard him softly call out to someone below. "Swing the rope oot, Dougal, and hold it there, lad, sae that I can grasp it. Aye, that's it!"

Adrianna craned her neck and watched in disbelief as the Scotsman jumped lightly onto the edge of the balcony, crouched down, then dove into space as if he were standing on the edge of a placid pond. Did he think he could fly? Was he mad? Or—a magician?

But no, for then, miraculously, she heard him just below the balcony. "Lower her down tae me, Colin, when I give ye the word."

Somehow, with almost superhuman strength and skill, he had managed to grab hold of the iron underpinnings of the balcony, Adrianna guessed. Well, he was resourceful, she had no doubt of that.

But she was resourceful too. And she had no intention of being carried off by a savage Scotsman, to be his pawn in some mysterious game of revenge. There would be no life ahead of her if she were to submit to his ruthless machinations . . . just as there was no life for her here if she remained to do Giles' bidding.

There was but one choice left to her.

God save her soul.

Purposefully Adrianna went limp as Colin moved to the edge of the balcony.

"Aye, that's it," he muttered. "Fight me and I'll drop ye."

It was an idle threat, of course. The man obviously lived to obey the commands of his lord. Fortunately, however, she had a better plan . . .

Faces of those she had cherished flashed across her benumbed consciousness. Her sweet mother, dimly recalled. Her father, stern but kind in his way. Indulgent, fluttery Winifred. And Mother Superior, benevolent and wise, with never a harsh word for anyone. Adrianna had loved them all.

The Scotsman's deep, lilting voice shattered her reverie.

"Noo, Colin."

As Colin held her tightly under her arms and lowered her down, Adrianna saw that the Scotsman was gripping the iron bracket beneath the balcony with one hand, and with his other a rope fed through the bracket. Did he intend to catch her with his feet? she wondered coolly.

Her knees were level with his face when Colin could lower her no more; Adrianna sensed the strain in his sturdy hands.

"Laird!" he whispered urgently.

"Drop her," was the unhesitating reply, and Adrianna knew that the Scotsman was going to take hold of her with one powerful arm. Calmly she held herself still and relaxed as Colin's fingers loosened and let go.

For the briefest moment she was floating in the air, and then the Scotsman's arm had caught her securely about her waist, bringing her against his hard-muscled body.

She had known he would succeed.

His face was so close to hers. Dark, intense eyes blazed into her own, afire with—triumph? Or something else, something hungry and sensual?

But no, she didn't dare dwell on such thoughts. They were distracting, wicked . . . and inviting.

Adrianna took in a shallow breath of air as best she could through her gag.

And then she twisted violently in his grasp, like a captured fish in its last, desperate throes.

She surprised him, evidently, for his hold slackened and she slipped free of him.

She was falling.

CHAPTER 3

Quick as lightning, Leith loosened his hold on the rope and for a few wild moments he too was falling through space. But only long enough to catch her once more against him, at the same time grabbing the rope with his free hand.

They swung in a wide, crazy arc and it took every ounce of Leith's strength to retain his grip on the rope as slowly the arc diminished into stillness once again.

"God's blood!" he growled, his breath coming fast as he stared into the cornflower-blue eyes looking defiantly into his own. "What the devil were ye trying tae do, lass, *kill* yerself?"

Her slender body was tensed, held close against him. Through the cheap material of her gown Leith could feel every curve and hollow of her body . . . the soft swell of her breasts, the flat plane of her stomach, even the slim, firm lengths of her legs against his own.

Unbidden, the heat of desire snaked through him. If he

hadn't been suspended perilously high above the ground he would have laughed at himself for reacting in such a primal male way at such a moment—especially given that the female in question was the daughter of the man who had killed Hugh.

Immediately a wave of self-disgust swamped the siren pull of attraction. What in God's name was he about, to feel such a thing for a misbegotten Sassenach?

"Try something again," he warned her fiercely, "and I *will* let ye fall."

The unblinking steadiness of her regard convinced him that she truly did intend to plummet to her death—the ultimate escape. As a master strategist himself, Leith could not but admire the steely courage she displayed. No empty-headed lass was this one!

A faint, pleasing scent of herbs drifted up from her thick blond hair and Leith had to force himself to repress an unwelcome urge to bury his face against those silken tresses.

"Laird," Colin whispered anxiously from above. "We must make haste!"

Leith cursed under his breath and brought his wayward attention back to where it needed to be focused.

He relaxed his grip on the rope just slightly, ignoring the burning sensation to his palm, and lowered them smoothly down to the ground. Quickly he signaled to Colin, who, as soon as Dougal held out the rope for him, jumped from the balcony's edge, caught the rope in his massive hands, and descended with more speed than grace.

The instant Colin's feet touched the earth, Leith thrust the girl into his arms, drew his knife, and slashed through the rope, which then slithered softly down to fall in a soft heap.

"Gather it up, lad," Leith told Dougal, who stood staring at the girl in round-eyed wonder.

"Aye, laird," Dougal replied, seeming to shake himself before swiftly doing as Leith bade him. When the rope was coiled over Dougal's shoulder Leith gave a nod and said:

"Let's gae. Carry her, Colin."

Colin unceremoniously picked up the girl and slung her roughly over his shoulder. A protesting moan escaped through her gag, and Leith could see in every line of her rigid body the painful indignity of her position.

Without understanding why he did so, he said curtly, "Put her down again."

Looking surprised, Colin obeyed, and Leith stepped over to them, took the girl's chin roughly in his hand, and said to her, "No screaming, then. Do I ha' yer word on it?"

Those enormous, thickly lashed blue eyes stared up into his. She glanced over at the castle and seemed to make up her mind, for she quickly nodded.

Leith used his knife to sever her bonds and then he pulled off her gag, tossing it onto the ground. "Come!" he said to them all, and took the girl's soft white hand in a firm grip.

Rapidly he led them across the open grassy field that surrounded the castle. The girl's fingers were unresisting entwined with his own; he shot a suspicious glance at her and saw in her alabaster profile taut determination. Planning her next escape, was she? A wry smile had barely crossed his lips when, just as they were about to reach the safety of the copse of trees where Malcolm and Jock and their horses awaited them, a panicked shout went up from the castle. Some tardily alert watchman, no doubt.

"Damn," Leith muttered under his breath. "Why couldna the bastard ha' slept a few minutes more?"

"He probably would have," the girl said in a monotone, "except that the guard changes at four o'clock."

"Thank ye for the information," Leith said sarcastically, pulling her into the dense copse and whistling shrilly.

Within moments came the sound of pounding hoof-beats, and then first Malcolm rode into view, holding the reins of Leith's horse Thunder, followed hard upon his heels by Jock who gripped the reins of Colin's and Dougal's mounts.

"Laird!" Malcolm exclaimed, pulling up his horse. "I heard the alarm!"

"Aye," Leith replied. "Let's waste no time, lads." He held out his hand and Malcolm promptly gave him Thunder's reins. Leith turned to the girl, grasped her about her slim waist, and lifted her up onto Thunder's broad back, setting her sideways. Then he swung himself up behind her, wrapping an arm around her and roughly pulling her close, steeling himself against the soft, seductive feel of that lissome body. She held herself stiffly against him, the straightness of her spine telling him more clearly than any words could have that silently she was rebelling against such enforced intimacy.

Too bad, little nun, for I'm keeping my eyes close upon ye, he thought, digging his heels into Thunder's flanks. Together he and his men rode quickly into the concealing shelter of the trees. Carlisle was but a league or two from the border, and a few hours' hard riding would bring them into the safety of Scotland and the Lowlands.

Behind them, from the castle grounds, he could hear the sounds of shouts and hoofbeats. "They're going north, my lord!" someone called out, and then another voice, cultured and aristocratic, shouted harshly, "Find them! Or by God, I'll have your heads!"

The girl shivered against him, and Leith glanced down at her in the burgeoning light of dawn. Her face was half-shielded by her shining gold hair which she made no attempt to brush back, but he could almost feel her terror.

That was her brother leading the charge, no doubt. And sounding a most unpleasant fellow to boot.

"Laird," Jock shouted, urging his horse alongside Leith's, "ye ha' the book?"

"Aye!" Leith returned.

Jock gave a jubilant laugh. "Well done, laird! Well done!"

Malcolm whooped victoriously as Colin and the Scotsman grinned, flashing white teeth, and Adrianna could not but wonder at their merriment in the midst of a life-or-death chase. Surely they knew that should they be caught by Giles' men, they would suffer painful, ignominious deaths. Yet they rode along as blithely as if they were merely going for a pleasant gallop through the woods.

"Laird," Malcolm, wiry and carroty-haired, called as his horse sailed over a fallen log, "who's the lass?"

"Ach, she's a gift from the auld earl," the Scotsman replied cheerfully, and Adrianna gritted her teeth. She would have preferred riding with the oafish Colin! It was torture having the Scotsman's broad, muscled chest pressed so familiarly against her back, those strong arms holding her so warmly . . . so securely . . .

Adrianna jerked herself upright. Mother of God, what unclean thoughts were these?

"Laird," Malcolm went on curiously, "what'll we do wi' a bloody Sassenach?"

Adrianna waited tensely for the Scotsman's reply, but from behind them came the sounds of their pursuers, louder now. "Hurry, you fools!" Giles yelled.

"They're gaining on us!" Colin shouted.

A vision of Giles' cruel face and of Sir Roger Penroy, fat and slobbering, flashed through Adrianna's mind. "Take that path to the left!" she blurted. "I remember it from my childhood. It's a shortcut to the flatlands leading north."

Could he trust her? Leith thought, his brain working

furiously. Or was this a trick? It was clear, however, that if they didn't make a tactical move soon, they'd be hunted down like hares; the Sassenachs knew the intricate maze of the forest far better than he. But if he and his men could make it to the flatlands, their fleet-footed mounts, born and bred to the thin Highland air, would have no trouble outdistancing the enemy.

"Gae left, lads, gae left!" Leith called out, a light touch to Thunder's reins causing him to veer toward the path Adrianna had indicated.

Jock, Colin, Malcolm, and Dougal quickly followed suit. It was a small, faintly marked trail leading them through the densely wooded forest, meandering seemingly without purpose. Yet, just as Leith was beginning to think that the girl had betrayed them, they emerged onto the flat, grassy terrain that led directly to the border and to safety.

"Thanks be!" Jock cried, spurring on his mount to even greater speed.

Leith leaned close to the golden-haired girl before him, relief washing over him. "See, lass, didn't I say ye were meant tae travel?" he remarked.

She twisted around to look up at him, her lovely blue eyes pleading again. "Please, won't you release me now that I've helped you?" she asked urgently. "I'll find my way to where I need to go."

"What, wi' that brute of a brother at yer back?" he replied sardonically. "Nay, lass, I feel it my duty tae protect ye from him."

"I can take care of myself," she said, scowling.

He laughed, not unkindly. "Ye're a poor wee lamb."

"Lamb!" she sputtered. "I'm a woman grown!"

"Ye're a poor wee lamb," he repeated firmly, still smiling, "and I'll no' let ye gae."

"You're a callous brute!" she snapped. "But what else should I expect from a *Scotsman*?"

She said the word with such contempt that Leith stiffened. What in God's name had compelled him to let his guard down, to let himself speak so playfully? She was his prisoner, his enemy—a Sassenach! "And what might ye knoo o' my kind?" he said bluntly.

"More than I'd ever want to know!" she retorted, her pale skin flushing angrily. "And I suppose you want to keep me with you to tend the pigs you keep in your bed!"

Leith's mouth set in a grim line. "Mayhap I want ye in my bed, little nun, but no' tae tend tae pigs," he said silkily. He saw her flinch and his scowl deepened. Did the girl find the thought of being touched by a Scotsman so repugnant? he brooded. Or was it himself she found abhorrent? She was clearly doing everything she could to keep their bodies from touching. God's blood! He was not such a one as to be rejected by a woman!

Leith searched his memory for an instance when he had not been welcomed into a lass' bed with open arms, and failed to recall a single episode. In fact, he'd had more bold-faced invitations for dalliance than he could possibly accept. It was a pleasant state of affairs he'd long taken for granted. So . . . what in God's name was the little nun's problem?

Once again, the sweet herbal scent of her rose up to tantalize his senses. What would that shining cascade of golden hair look like spread across his pillows? And that slender, delicately curvaceous body naked and white beneath him?

Enough o' this foolishness, Leith ordered himself curtly. *Ye sound like a callow lad whose young blood runs too high.* With a last glance at the forest behind them, he touched his heels to Thunder's sides, coaxing him ever onward.

* * *

Adrianna felt, rather than saw, the Scotsman twist around to look behind them, and couldn't resist a quick peep over her shoulder. Far in the distance, Giles and his men had just emerged from the forest and had pulled up their horses, bringing them to a halt. It was obvious that the Scots party was beyond their grasp.

"Well done, lads!" the Scotsman said, and his men gave a loud, victorious cheer.

Adrianna's mind was whirling confusedly as they rode along. The sun had come up and it was a beautiful morning, with but a few white puffs of clouds to mar the pristine blue beauty of the sky. She was free of Giles and his wicked plan; she should be glad for that.

But now her fate lay in the hands of the arrogant, unnerving Scotsman at her back—a fate utterly, completely unknown.

And therefore terrifying.

Had she done the right thing by telling them about the shortcut?

Once again she thought of Sir Roger Penroy. His round, heavy body and lecherous, mud-colored eyes. His too-obvious flattery and the caressing pats to her arm that made her want to shake him off as if she'd come in contact with a toad. She tried to imagine what her life might have been like being wed to such a man, and her mind recoiled in distaste.

And then, sensuously, like a cat winding pleasurably around its owner's ankles, an image of the Scotsman presented itself. His dark hair, waving and rich, gleaming with sun-kissed auburn glints. His flashing white teeth. His body, big and warm and alive with masculine power.

Mayhap I want ye in my bed, little nun.

Surely *his* touch would be preferable to that of Sir Roger Penroy. She could not help glancing at those strong, long-fingered hands so capably holding the reins.

Oh, God, what was she thinking?

Would he . . . have her?

No, more like he'd throw her to his men, like a rabbit loosed before a pack of hungry dogs. She'd seen the sidelong glances of his men.

As for the women, her nurse Winifred's hysterical voice blared in her memory, *they'll have their way with them and laugh as they do it! Then toss them away like broken dolls!*

She must escape. She must escape. Adrianna repeated the words over and over in her mind, in rhythm to the pounding of the horses' hooves, until she lost track of time and gave in to her terrible fatigue, slipping in and out of a light, troubled doze.

She came fully awake when the Scotsman called out triumphantly, "There's the border, lads! Just a few minutes more tae the River Liddel, and we'll rest the horses there."

Groggily Adrianna glanced up at the sky; the sun was high overhead. Clearly they had been traveling for some hours. Carlisle was far behind them, and she was in Scotland now. The grins among the Scots told her this without needing to hear their words of confirmation.

It wasn't long before the river glistened before them, a gentle, shallow tributary that was easy for their horses to splash through.

It was a welcome sight. Leith drew in a deep appreciative breath of fresh Scottish air.

He was in his homeland again.

With Hugh's book in hand.

And his murderer's daughter sitting before him.

Leith recalled the moment in the library when he had seen her face in the candlelight and had realized that she was the wee lass in the miniature he'd taken from the old earl's desk.

She had indeed fulfilled the promise of that early beauty, for she had grown into a stunningly lovely woman. Her face was still heart-shaped, her eyes still a vivid blue, thickly fringed by black lashes. But her body—ah, it wasn't the body of a child. Even the cheap, poorly made gown couldn't disguise the slender waist flaring gently into trim yet feminine hips. The pert, firm breasts. The rosy, sweetly sculpted lips that were made for kissing . . .

A kind of wild blindness had overtaken him. His all-consuming quest for Hugh's retribution, his bitterness and his anger had been joined by a fiery, unwelcome, uncontrollable surge of desire. It had been like flame to dry tinder and he had known that nothing—no one—could have dissuaded him from taking her.

This had not been part of his plan. He had come to Carlisle only to retrieve Hugh's book.

Yet with a will as hard and fixed as iron, he had taken the girl as his captive.

The question was, what was he to do with her?

He knew his men were wondering precisely the same thing. Their looks were inquisitive, speculative, frankly dubious.

He'd ignored those looks and kept riding.

They reached the opposite shore of the River Liddel and Leith gave the command to dismount. Their tired horses needed water, and a chance to rest and graze on the lush sweet grass growing around them in such abundance.

He swung himself down to the ground and held out his hands to the girl. With obvious reluctance she placed her fingers in his and allowed herself to be lifted down, and would doubtless have preferred to turn her back to him but for the fact that her legs were plainly rubbery; she'd have fallen were it not for his quick arm about her waist.

"Thank you," she said stiffly, not meeting his eyes. "I— I believe I'm fine now. I'd like to walk about a bit."

He withdrew his arm, frowning, feeling her rebuff like

a lash. "Colin," he said, "watch her. I'll take yer horse tae drink."

"Aye, laird," Colin replied, giving him the reins of his mount. He stood with his arms folded across his massive chest and stared fiercely at the girl as she slowly paced back and forth.

While letting the horses have their fill of the cool river water, Leith watched the girl from the corner of his eye. Her spine was as straight as ever, her head held high. If it hadn't been for the slight trembling of her hands as she paused to smooth her shining hair underneath her rumpled coif, it would have been easy to mistake her for a country girl out for a lazy stroll. Still, despite that betraying quiver, Leith marveled at her poise.

When the horses were finished drinking, Leith let them graze amongst the grass. The girl was sitting on a tree stump, hands folded in her lap. All around her, his men had spread out their cloaks to sit upon, leather sacks from their saddles opened beside them, voraciously eating the cheese and coarse bread they'd carried, and taking great swallows of ale from their wineskins. Colin, he noted, still gazed watchfully at the girl as he ate and drank.

"Lovely manners, lads," he said sarcastically as he came among them. "Did it ever occur tae ye louts that our guest might like something tae eat?"

"Our *guest,* laird?" Colin echoed in disbelief, his mouth full as he spoke. "She's naught but a Sassenach."

Leith scowled. "I believe even Sassenachs feel hunger and thirst." He went over to his horse and untied from his saddle the finely crafted leather sack and the tartan cloak lashed to a strap, then approached the girl and offered her a hunk of bread and cheese.

"Here," he said roughly, "ye must eat."

Her hands remained in her lap. "I have some rolls in my bundle," she said, her eyes downcast. "I will have those."

His temper, already frayed from the events of the day, flared and he placed an imperative hand under her chin and forced it up until their gazes met and clashed. "Ye'll take this and eat it," he said with gritted teeth, "or I'll force it down yer throat. I dinna want ye passing oot from hunger while we're riding."

Blue eyes warred with brown, until finally she said in a thin tight voice, "Very well." Ungraciously she accepted the cheese and bread and began nibbling upon it.

Satisfied, Leith spread his cloak upon the ground and started in on his portion. He ate with the concentration of someone long accustomed to arduous, fast-paced journeys through the Highlands, when the respites for meals were brief. He had just finished his last chunk of bread when she said quietly:

"It's very good. Thank you."

He looked up at her. She had eaten everything he had given her. Silently he passed her his wineskin of ale; she took it awkwardly, obviously unused to handling such a flexible container, and spilled some as she drank.

Leith watched in fascination as she brushed at the dark wetness on her bodice. He'd have liked to press his lips there, taste the bittersweet tang of the ale, let her feel the burning heat of his mouth through the fabric . . .

She gave him back the wineskin. "Thank you."

"Ye're welcome." He took a long swallow. "Ye like our Highland ale?"

She looked at him guardedly. "Yes. It's different from what I'm used to, but . . . it's pleasant."

"We brew our own at Inveraray," he told her proudly, "using a recipe that's been among the Campbells for ten generations or more."

"What is Inveraray?"

"Why, Inveraray is my home, lass—built on a Highlands promontory overlooking Loch Fyne."

"I do not know where that is," she said. "I have never studied the geography of Scotland."

"Yer loss," he said, and meant it.

She brushed some crumbs from her skirt. "And—and your name is Campbell?"

"Aye. Leith Campbell. And ye are?"

"Adrianna."

"Adrianna," he repeated. "A pretty name."

"Thank you."

"It suits ye," he added.

"Thank you," she said again, and for the first time, Leith saw those soft, rosy lips curve tentatively upwards. He grinned. By God, she was even more beautiful when she smiled!

He tore his eyes away from her at the sound of a throat being cleared. Colin was standing near him, his bristling black brows drawn close together.

"Laird," Colin said with pointed politeness, "might I ha' a word wi' ye?"

"O' course," Leith answered. "What is it?"

"In private, laird." Colin glowered at the girl Adrianna.

Leith rose to his feet, grumbling, and walked with Colin some paces away. "What are ye glunching aboot noo, Colin?"

Colin shifted uneasily from one booted foot to the other. "Wi' all respect, laird, it seems tae us that ye're acting like a lad in love, no' like a man wi' a prisoner. A *Scotsman* wi' a prisoner," he added emphatically.

Anger, hot and raw, curled in Leith's gut, making his hands clench into fists. "What in the name o' God are ye talking aboot?" he snapped.

Urgently Colin gripped his arm. "Laird," he said, "that bonny Sassenach is the daughter o' the man who killed our Hugh. Ha' ye forgotten that in the midst o' yer flirtation?"

Leith wrathfully flung off the other's hand. "Flirtation?" he growled.

"Laird, think for a moment," Colin pleaded. "Think o' Hugh, cut down in the prime o' his youth by that bloody marauding Sassenach. That lass' father!"

Leith shot a quick look at Adrianna. She was still sitting ramrod-straight on the tree stump, her hands again folded primly in her lap. She looked the picture of innocence, but it could not be denied that she had sprung from the loins of a most despicable man, one who would savagely plunder a corpse and carry off his prize, to have it join the many other trophies of war scattered about his library. And truly, Leith reflected grimly, how far *could* an apple fall from the tree? A Sassenach she was, and would remain so till she died! What kind of bloody fool was he to be swayed by a pretty smile? His resentful ire at Colin's critical words was swamped by a tidal wave of self-disgust so strong it left him feeling sickened.

Hugh.

His beloved brother Hugh.

How could he have for a single moment forgotten about him?

Leith looked soberly at Colin. "Ye're right," he said heavily. "I'm a damned *sumph.*"

"Ye're neither stupid nor soft," protested Colin. "It can be easy tae forget yer purpose when ye're staring intae a pair o' bewitchingly lovely eyes. And that," he said grudgingly, "I'll grant she has."

Leith shrugged. "It doesna make me any less of a *sumph.* Get up, lads," he shouted, his voice steely, "and let's be on our way tae Dumfries." Tensely he walked back to the girl. "Come," he said curtly, "let's gae."

Adrianna gazed up at the Scotsman, Leith, in bemused wonderment. A few moments ago, when they had been talking together, he had seemed nearly—human. Yet after a brief, charged conversation with the burly Colin, he was once again the remote, brusque captor of before, and Adrianna could almost feel the blood chilling in her veins. Damn the man for his arrogance!

"Where is Dumfries?" she asked as she stood.

"Ye'll find oot soon enough," he answered harshly, and walked toward his horse.

"I was merely trying to improve my Scottish geography!" she said irritably to his broad back, trailing a few paces behind. "Churl!"

He turned on her, hostility in every line of his tall, magnificent frame. "I say we shall ha' no more talking, Sassenach!"

Adrianna felt it best not to dignify his outburst with a reply, and with her chin tilted high in defiance permitted herself to be lifted up onto the saddle again. "Churl," she muttered under her breath when he swung himself up behind her, and pretended to ignore the roughness of his grasp as he wrapped an arm about her waist.

Yet despite her best efforts her spirits sank again after several hours of riding without pause. She managed to doze in fitful starts, but somehow awakened each time more exhausted than before. In her daze she took little note of her surroundings, aware only of endless sheep tracks, rolling green hills, and a vast blue sky. The rest was a blur.

It was nearly dusk when they rode into a tiny village. To Adrianna's bleary eyes it looked very much like the hamlet of Carlisle, with its cobblestone streets and whitewashed cottages—most of them with steeply pitched roofs and tiny windows—set closely together. Here the common people went barefoot, just as they did in Carlisle.

Leith led his party past the market cross and the well, in the town's center, and then a few minutes later stopped before a simple two-storied house with a sturdy external staircase and a slate roof. He had barely touched foot to the ground before the door burst open and out flew a short, round woman wearing a neat white kirtle and an overgown of immaculate forest-green linen.

"If it isn't Leith Campbell himself!" she cried in warmly welcoming tones, her bright black eyes fairly snapping with pleasure. "And his braw men! Ye're just in time tae sup wi' me!" She stopped abruptly as she caught sight of Adrianna, and her voice softened as she came forward.

"And who might this bonny bairn be?" she asked. "Ach, but she looks tired enough tae drop off the horse, she does!"

"She's my prisoner, Cecily," Leith told her dryly. "A Sassenach."

Cecily recoiled as if she had been struck. "A Sassenach?" Her black eyes lit with anger and disgust.

"Aye," Colin put in as he dismounted, "her father, God rot his soul, was the bastard who murdered Hugh at Edinburgh Castle."

To Adrianna's horror the woman spat at her and then whirled on Leith. Numbly she looked at the drops of spittle on the torn hem of her gown, her mind working tiredly. Who was Hugh? And was it true that Lord Robert had killed him? He had been a soldier, yes, but had he been a murderer?

"Why," Cecily was fiercely demanding, "why in the name o' God ha' ye brought this *taupie* tae my house, Leith?"

"We need a place tae sleep and break our fast in the morning," Leith replied matter-of-factly. "Ye've never been one tae stint on yer hospitality before."

"And I won't noo," Cecily said. "I'll do it for ye and the love I bear for all yer family. But what am I tae do wi' *her*?"

"Leave her tae me," he answered indifferently, not even bothering to glance in Adrianna's direction.

They discuss me as if I were some dumb, onerous beast, she thought, a terrible shame weighing heavily upon her heart.

"I do not wish to be a burden to you, mistress," she said quietly to the hostile Scotswoman. "I ask only that I might lie down somewhere to sleep."

At her soft words Leith did turn to her, his fine dark eyes glacial. "Ye'll eat first," he said shortly.

Adrianna was too tired to argue, and it wasn't long before she found herself seated inside the cottage at a rough trestle table, before her a platter heaped high with roasted capon, leeks and turnips, and a round loaf of fragrant brown bread twice the size of her fist.

"This is far too much food, mistress," she protested, and Cecily bristled.

"Let no one say Cecily MacBean doesn't knoo how tae dish oot a proper supper," she snapped, plump arms held akimbo.

"Thank you, it looks delicious," Adrianna murmured, and, much to her surprise, she found that at the first bite of tender capon her appetite revived. Still, the men around her had long finished their meal by the time she made her way through fully half the bird and a goodly portion of the vegetables and bread. Only Leith remained at the table, conversing with Cecily and catching up on the news in Dumfries.

Adrianna gathered that Cecily was a widow distantly related to the clan Campbell, and whose four grown children and numerous grandchildren were her chief interest in life, for she spoke of them frequently and with great affection.

"And wee Christina—she's Reginald's youngest—has

taken tae walking as if tae the manor born," Cecily told Leith proudly.

" 'Tis been many years since I've seen Reginald." Leith drank from his mug of ale. "Is he still trading yarn and cow's hides wi' the Irish?"

"Aye, and dealing wi' them most prosperously."

"I'm glad tae hear it. A fine man, is yer Reginald."

Cecily smiled broadly. "He is at that," she agreed. "And as for young Kenneth, he—ach, look at the lass over there," she added sharply.

They both glanced in Adrianna's direction; quickly she said, "The food truly was superb, mistress."

Scowling, Cecily eyed Adrianna's platter as Leith said, "Ye did give her enough for two men. Ye ha' tae admit she did it justice."

"I suppose," Cecily said grudgingly. Then, after a moment, she said to Adrianna: "Ye're aboot tae fall asleep wi' yer head on the table, aren't ye? Come, ye can sleep in my bedchamber, there's a trestle bed there."

Leith's brows went up. "Aren't ye afraid she'll murder ye in yer sleep?" he said sardonically. "She *is* a Sassenach, after all."

"Ach, she's fagged tae death, poor thing," Cecily replied briskly, rising. "I doubt she'd hurt a fly. Come, lass," she said to Adrianna, her tone almost motherly, "and I'll take ye upstairs."

Adrianna stood, nearly wavering on her feet with exhaustion. "You're very good, mistress."

"Call me Cecily," the other woman said, and with an arm about Adrianna's waist swept her out of the kitchen and toward the stairs.

Leith stared after them, torn between amusement and exasperation. *Women!* he thought wryly, taking another swallow of ale. *As changeable as the Highland winds!*

* * *

Adrianna's head had barely touched Cecily's soft goosedown pillow before she had fallen into a heavy, dreamless sleep. Cecily had woken her at dawn, informing her that Leith and his men were already awake and eating their porridge, and that she'd best make haste to ensure that she had her bowlful, too, as they were eager to be off and on their way.

The hearty oats porridge, rich with butter and milk, was surprisingly good, and Adrianna, by dint of eating faster than she had ever done in her life, managed to finish it all just as Leith came back inside the house.

"Let's gae," he said shortly, then turned to Cecily and enfolded her in a hearty hug. "Our thanks tae ye," he said, his handsome features briefly softening in a smile. "It's no wonder ye're renowned in the Lowlands for yer gracious hospitality."

"Pooh," Cecily retorted, but looked pleased nonetheless. "Ye're always welcome here, ye knoo that, Leith Campbell." Then she went to Adrianna with her usual vigorous step and quickly embraced her. "Ye're a good lass," she said gruffly, "even if ye are a Sassenach. A body'd ha' tae be a fool no' tae see that."

"Th-thank you," Adrianna managed to reply, astonished.

Cecily held a corner of her crisp white kirtle to her eyes and said a little unsteadily, "Ach, ye remind me o' my own dear Joan, taken away from me these ten years and more by the good Lord."

Adrianna placed a gentle hand on Cecily's arm. "I'm very sorry," she said softly.

Cecily gave a ferocious sniff, patted Adrianna's hand, and then looked to Leith, visibly straightening her shoulders. "Ach," she said bracingly, "here I am, nattering on, and ye're anxious tae be gone. Fare ye well, then!"

She followed Leith and Adrianna to the threshold of her tidy little house and waved at them until they rounded a bend in the cobblestoned street and she disappeared from sight.

"Making friends everywhere ye gae," Leith said sarcastically into Adrianna's ear.

How like the man to denigrate such a tender farewell! "Mistress MacBean has a kind nature," Adrianna said, refusing to be drawn into another argument with him.

His arm tightened around her like a vise. "Unlike myself?" he retorted harshly.

"I was not making a comparison," she said with as much patience as she could summon, and then, to change the subject, she asked, "Where do we go today?"

He was silent for a moment, as if debating whether or not to civilly answer, and then he said reluctantly, "We'll continue riding northwest, along the River Nith. We'll stop the night at Greenock."

"Will we reach Inveraray tomorrow?" she asked, a tiny, involuntary shiver of trepidation running through her.

"Nay. No' for two days more."

"It's that far away?" she said, her voice wavering a little.

"Aye, lass, ye'll be quite a ways from England, in case ye were planning tae escape and walk back."

She ignored his jibe. "Have—have you decided what you are going to do with me?" she asked in a low voice.

"Pig-tending, I think," he said carelessly, and then he lightly pressed his heels into his horse's side, urging him to break into a canter. Obviously the conversation was over, and Adrianna was left to ponder the significance of his answer in silence.

She had plenty of time in which to do so, as Leith rode his magnificent black horse, Thunder, on and on without so much as addressing a single remark to her aside from directives about mounting, dismounting, eating, and sleeping. They reached the bustling lakeside port of Greenock by nightfall, and by dawn of the following day they were on a roughly constructed ferry manned by a dozen brawny men wielding long wooden poles. Adrianna watched in fascination as with their massive muscles straining, the men soon had the ferry gliding across the smooth, deep-green waters of Loch Long.

Then it was back onto their horses again. Adrianna didn't dare complain about being stiff and sore from so much riding; she knew any such remarks would fall on deaf ears. Even though her body was in intimate contact with Leith's for hours at a time, he had absented himself from her as profoundly as if he were miles away. Those handsome, deep-set brown eyes of his were as cold as ice and impenetrably remote.

She attempted to distract herself from the questions weighing so heavily in her thoughts by studying the landscape around her. The flatlands of Carlisle were far, far behind them now, and the rolling hills she had noted when first they'd crossed the border into Scotland had been surpassed by jagged mountains rising imperiously into the slate-blue sky. They were in the Highlands now. It was a rough, untamed country, unmarked by roads of any kind, and Adrianna knew she should find it coarse and frightening. Yet it struck her as oddly beautiful, with its majestic headlands, fast-flowing rivers, and fathomless lochs. Inquisitive brown hares stopped to watch their progress, and hawks circled lazily overhead.

Into her mind drifted some verses the poet John Skelton had written some few years ago about the Scots, which had been vastly popular in England and passed around on crudely printed handsheets.

For ye be false each one
False and false again,
Never true or plain,
But fleer, flatter and feign
And ever to remain
In wretched beggary
And mangy misery,
In lousy loathsomeness
And scabbed scurfiness
And in abomination
Of all manner of nation,
Nation most in hate,
Proud, and poor of state.

Mother Superior had been scandalized when she'd come upon Adrianna reading the handsheet which one of the servants had brought into the convent. Mother had enjoined Adrianna to be more tolerant, but it had been impossible for her to dismiss her father's feelings about the Scottish people . . . or to forget her memories of how her mother had died.

Now, as Adrianna stared about her in awe, it was easy to understand why the Highland lords were famous for holding the power of life and death over their subjects, with little regard for the authority of their sovereign. They were very nearly inaccessible in their distant domains.

Still, nothing had truly prepared her for the sight that awaited her toward the end of their third day. It had been an afternoon of intermittent sun and rain, and the grass beneath their horses' hooves had been soggy and interlaced with mud as higher and higher they climbed, following the shoreline of the deep, calm waters of Loch Fyne. They gained the summit of one particularly steep hill, and there before them, framed by ominous gray clouds, was a massive stone fortress.

Turrets, high chimneys, and a single lone tower dominated its imposing roofline, and the many arrow slits circling its thick-walled exterior made for a vivid impression of invulnerability. Its enormous drawbridge was open, and people streamed in and out, some of them tending to the sheep that grazed upon the rich green grasses that seemed to stretch on for leagues.

One of the shepherds saw them and began waving wildly. "The laird has returned!" he shouted. "Laird! Thanks be tae God!"

Leith lifted a hand in reply and pulled up his horse as they drew near the drawbridge. A number of the castle's inhabitants were running toward them, waving their hands wildly in greeting.

"We're home at last, lads," Leith said to his men, deep satisfaction evident in his voice. And then he leaned close to Adrianna and spoke softly into her ear.

"Welcome tae Inveraray, little nun."

To Adrianna, the words sounded nothing less than sinister.

CHAPTER 4

As Leith rode across the drawbridge, surrounded by his jubilant clan, he was conscious of an overwhelming feeling of pride. Inveraray had housed the clan Campbell for more generations than anyone could count, and still it stood, sturdy and magnificent, seemingly oblivious to the ravages of time as it reached upward into the sky. He looked around the bailey and its bustling courtyard, at the smiling faces, young and old, that were as familiar to him as his own.

Home.

He was home at last, united with his people once again.

This was where he belonged, leading the clan as they joined together in the age-old routines of tending the land and raising the animals, the rituals of harvest and renewal, the ancient, eternal rhythms of life . . .

With a piercing intensity that nearly took his breath away, Leith was suddenly aware again of the presence of the girl, Adrianna, who sat before him, her back straight and her head held high. She couldn't help but be aware of the many curious eyes upon her, yet she conducted herself with all the dignity of a queen.

Aye, she was a brave one, Leith thought, admiration for her courage stirring unbidden within him. As did another, warmer sensation, seductively heating his blood as he took in her delicate profile, the long, slender neck, the womanly swell of breast beneath the drab gray gown.

As if sensing his gaze upon her, she turned her head to meet his eyes and Leith felt as if he was drowning in twin pools of blue, as deep and as lovely as Loch Fyne on a hot summer's day. Thick dark lashes blinked once, twice, and then those rosy lips parted, revealing a glimpse of small, straight white teeth.

God's blood, she was beautiful. Desirable. More desirable than any woman had a right to be. Could she hear his heart hammering in his chest? As if compelled by a force so strong as to be irresistible, Leith leaned forward. She was so close, her soft, tempting mouth a mere hairsbreadth away.

"Laird!" someone called, and Leith jerked backward, feeling as if he had just been doused with a bucketful of icy-cold water. He looked down to see young James, one of the crofters' sons, running alongside Thunder and vigorously waving his arms.

"Laird!" James called again. "Did ye get Hugh's book?"

"Aye, lad, that I did," Leith replied.

A great cheer went up, and then it was Wallace, the castle's blacksmith, raising his voice. "Laird," he shouted, "who's the pretty lass? Ha' ye taken a bride at last?"

Bride. Adrianna's breath caught in her throat, and her brain whirled madly. She was meant to be a nun. Chaste for all her years, bride to no man. Yet a tiny voice inside her whispered defiantly, *What woman wouldn't relish being held against that broad chest?*

Her eyes flew to the Scotsman's face, where she saw the

look of shock there. For the merest moment she thought an arrested expression crossed his features, and then there was nothing to betray what he might be thinking.

"Nay, Wallace," Leith answered coolly. "She's but a prisoner I've brought wi' me."

"A prisoner, laird?" a dozen voices queried.

"Aye," he said briefly, his mouth set in a grim line.

"She's the daughter o' him that murdered our Hugh," Colin supplied loudly. "A Sassenach *taupie!*"

"That's enough!" Leith snapped, and Colin's craggy face turned a bright red as he mumbled an apology. In the silence that followed, Adrianna felt the crowd's astonishment and revulsion as clearly as if they had thrown stones at her, and, summoning all her pride, she lifted her chin as they continued to ride into the great courtyard of the castle. The Scotsman's arms, encircling her as he held the horse's reins, were taut, yet he said nothing further, and Adrianna felt a trembling fear overtake her.

What was going to happen to her?

Even in England prisoners' fates could be harsh ones— she had heard many tales of captives suffering long, slow deaths, chained in dank cells without food or water—and here she was among the barbarous Scots, hardly known for their civilized ways.

Dear God, she prayed silently, *give me strength to endure whatever comes.*

A loud, raucous squawk of a chicken made her start, and for the first time since entering the bailey she found herself taking in her surroundings.

They were in a courtyard of immense proportions. All around them rose the thick stone wall of the castle, a vast circle edged on high with battlements that would permit the guards to survey the country for miles. Far across the bailey she spied an untended herb garden, thickly choked with weeds. To the left were the stables; to the right was a row of solidly built, thatched-roof lean-tos housing a cooper's workshop, as well as that of a shoemaker, a blacksmith, a tanner, and a weaver of rushes. These were signs of considerable prosperity, yet the ground below them, muddy from rain, was littered with straw, refuse, feathers, odd scraps of food and cloth. Milling about in aimless disorder were dogs, pigs, chickens, and even a cow or two. And as for the people themselves . . .

Adrianna looked around her and saw men clad in the distinctively Scottish garment she'd heard called the kilt, which left the owner's knees startlingly bare. Several among the men wore a woolen cloth, woven with lines of brilliant, crisscrossing red, green, and dark blue, draped on a bold diagonal across one shoulder to the hip. No one, she saw, wore ruffs, and the women's gowns lacked the fashionable farthingale, their skirts instead following the more natural curve of hip and petticoat.

It all seemed alien, yet Adrianna saw faces she might easily have encountered at Rosings, or in Carlisle, or anywhere in England for that matter. Scots they might be, rough in their dress and skins smudged with dirt, yet they hardly sported the savage's rags credited them back in England.

But Adrianna could not have fooled herself for a moment that she was in her homeland, for these faces scarcely presented to her a warm welcome. Hostility gleamed in every eye, even among the children as they trotted beside their chieftain's horse.

"Sassenach!" someone hissed.

"Taupie!" came another whisper, and then, more loudly: "Murderess!"

Adrianna flinched, and at her waist saw the Scotsman's long, powerful fingers clench upon the reins.

"Be still!" he growled, and once again, the people were silent.

Leith drew up his horse, tossed the reins to a young lad standing at its head, then swung himself to the ground, the grace and power of his movements undiminished by the many weary miles they had traveled. He glanced at her, those dark, deeply set eyes beneath strongly marked black brows unfathomable, and said over his shoulder:

"Colin, bring her in wi' ye." Leith turned and walked up the broad stone steps leading into the castle keep. He heard her soft voice saying hastily, "I'll let myself down," and Colin's gruff reply.

"As ye please, Sassenach."

It took all of Leith's fortitude to not to turn back, to take that white hand and lead her into the keep. Violent emotions were warring within him, making him feel as if he was a helpless ship being tossed on a stormy sea. It was not an experience he enjoyed. It was not one he was accustomed to.

For many years his focus had been direct and single-minded: first, to keep his clan safe and whole while people elsewhere in the kingdom, less remote than the Highlanders, were considerably more affected by the volatile affairs of state, more closely involved in the religious conflicts raging throughout Britain. And in the midst of all this lofty turmoil, many went hungry as little was done to improve the lot of the common folk. But he had labored without ceasing to ensure that the farms were diligently worked, the animals properly cared for, and that his people were fed.

Then Hugh had died, and he had waited with an eerie patience fueled by hatred, until the time was right for him to go in search of his revenge.

And when he had finally gained that revenge, standing in the dead Englishman's library, he had foolishly let himself be blinded by the extraordinary beauty of the lass who'd slipped mysteriously into the room—and into his life.

Now he had the Englishman's daughter, a delectable prize snatched from the hostile bosom of his foe.

What was he going to do with her?

A part of him wanted to shield her from the clan's enmity, to keep her within the protective circle of his arms where no harm could befall her.

But another, darker part of him fully entered into the emotions of his people. She was of the enemy, therefore she *was* the enemy.

Wasn't she?

With her pale creamy skin, her thick gold hair gleaming even in the rain-dampened gray of late afternoon, her supple, shapely body sweetly crafted for a man's touch . . .

Leith swore viciously under his breath and stalked into the great hall. A fire was burning damply in the vast stone hearth, sending puffs of bitter, stinging smoke into the air. His deerhounds were lying in a lazy heap before the fire, then leaped as one to their feet and ran to greet him, long tapered tails wagging madly, snouts thrust wetly into his palms.

"Andrew!" he roared.

His steward promptly emerged from the kitchen that was located just off the great hall, his plump face red and damp with sweat. "Laird!" he cried, beaming as he bustled forward. "Welcome home! We've begun the preparations for yer feast tonight. We've fresh goat, and oxen roasting—"

"It's smoking like the devil in here," Leith interrupted, frowning.

Andrew looked surprised. "It always does, laird."

"Well, fix it then." Leith glared at him.

"Aye, laird." Andrew scuttled off to the kitchen, calling loudly for his assistants.

Leith bent to stroke the head of the most persistent of his dogs, Mac, who enthusiastically licked his hand, when into his line of vision came a pair of soft black slippers, trim ankles in lavishly embroidered stockings, and the swirling hem of a russet gown.

"Laird," came a husky, breathless voice. "Leith."

Leith straightened, his gaze traveling up the gown to its low neckline that seemed barely able to contain the generous bosom that rapidly rose and fell in a blatant display of lightly freckled flesh.

"Fiona," he said. "Well met."

Fiona Grant smiled and tossed her dusky brown curls. "I ran all the way downstairs from the solar tae see ye," she said, then spread her fingers wide against the exposed skin above her tightly laced bodice. "I'm still oot o' breath."

"I can see that," Leith answered wryly, knowing that he should have found her coy gesture enticing. A few months ago it would have sent his thoughts winging heatedly toward his bedchamber. During the cold winter months prior to his departure for England, Fiona had many nights joined him in his bed. He had offered her no false promises, making it very clear indeed that their amorous interludes were that and nothing more. But Fiona hadn't seemed put off in the least, proving herself so fervent and capable a mistress that it was plain she had acquired considerable experience in other men's arms. He hadn't cared; it was merely a convenient arrangement that allowed him to slake his body's needs.

Coquettishly Fiona twitched her skirts about her ankles. "Do ye like my new gown, Leith? I had it made in honor o' yer return."

He could hardly say if he liked it or not, given that its daringly low, square neckline offered a most riveting focal point. He was spared the necessity of a reply by a commotion at the entrance to the great hall. Adrianna came slowly inside, Colin close beside her, scowling, one meaty hand grasping her by her upper arm. Even at this distance Leith could tell that Colin held her too tightly for comfort, yet her expression was controlled, composed. Once again he felt that same, unwilling admiration for her bravery.

Behind Adrianna and Colin came some twenty or thirty of the clan, crowding into the great hall, obviously eager to see what their laird had in mind for his captive.

Mac, pressed up against Leith's thigh, barked.

"Quiet," Leith ordered him sternly, then watched in astonishment as Mac, normally standoffish with newcomers, sprinted across the rush-strewn floor to sniff at Adrianna's skirts, wagging his tail.

She held out her free hand, palm up. "Hello," she said softly, permitting Mac to lick her fingers. A small smile curved her mouth, and Leith's heart twisted bitterly in his chest.

For so many years his purpose had been as clear as fine-blown glass.

Now he found himself wavering, uncertain.

Afraid of the emotions roiling within him.

This maddeningly alluring Sassenach girl was turning his life upside down.

He didn't need this.

Didn't need her.

Damn her.

"Mac!" he said sharply, pointing toward the hearth. Obediently Mac trotted past him, followed by the other dogs, who retreated to their spot before the fire and lay down.

Fiona curled her fingers around his forearm. "Who's this, Leith?"

"She's a prisoner," he said brusquely.

"Aye?" The sharp-tipped fingers tightened. "That and nothing more?"

Adrianna saw the freckled hand clenched around Leith's arm, heard the accusatory note in the brown-haired young woman's words, then raised her gaze to find Leith's dark eyes boring into her own.

Without looking away Leith stepped forward, causing the girl to relinquish her grip upon him. Green eyes flashed, subtly painted lips thinned, but Leith ignored her. "Colin, let gae o' the lass," he said curtly. "Ye're bruising her, I've no doubt. Maudie," he went on, without raising his voice, "come here. The rest o' ye, if ye've no business within the keep, I suggest ye take yer leave noo."

Adrianna felt her arm being freed from Colin's punishing grasp, and though she wanted to rub the throbbing pain he had inflicted, she remained motionless, caught in the night-sky intensity of Leith's gaze. Her breathing was labored and her knees began to tremble. Behind her she could hear the clanspeople filing out of the great hall, and then came a gravelly burr of a voice.

"Ye wanted me, laird?"

With an effort Adrianna blinked and tore her eyes away from Leith's to see a gray-haired old woman, clad in heavy brown wool, step past her and approach Leith.

"Maudie," Leith said, his tone flat, "ye'll be tending tae the Sassenach. Tell the grooms tae give ye the bundle she brought wi' her, and mind that she has sufficient food and drink. Colin, escort the lass tae the tower room."

"Aye, laird." Colin reached for her again and involuntarily Adrianna recoiled.

"Leave her be," Leith said. "Touch her only if she's sae foolish as tae try tae run."

"Might I ask—" Adrianna stopped to clear her throat and to will her unruly legs to hold her steady. "Might I ask what you intend to do with me?"

Leith was silent for a moment, and then he turned away from her, his face set and still. "Gae on then, Colin," he said stonily. "Take her away from here."

"Come, Sassenach," Colin ordered, and Adrianna had no choice but to comply. She began following him up the wide stone staircase, her heart sinking lower with every step she ascended.

"A wee bit of oxen stew, laird?" someone asked, and Leith looked up from the pewter goblet into which he had been staring moodily.

"Nay," he said, shaking his head, and the boy bowed and moved on with his tureen down the table where Colin, Dougal, Malcolm, and Jock sat, triumphant amidst the many hand-clasps and back-slapping from the men and being fussed over extravagantly by the womenfolk.

It was a festive evening in the great hall. Andrew had outdone himself, as had Betty the cook; the long wooden table groaned under the rich array of platters and bowls set out upon it. Among the dishes were fish, goat, two varieties of stew, cheeses, turnips and cabbages and leeks, and great fragrant loaves of wheaten bread infused with dark grains of rye.

A lute-player and a piper plied their instruments boisterously at the far end of the table, and gathered about them was a knot of laughing children who jigged and clapped their hands in time to the music.

His dogs, caught up in the merrymaking, rolled and frolicked and bared their teeth in mock-fights as they dashed in wild abandon about the hall.

Ordinarily Leith would have found their antics amusing, but tonight he was unmoved.

He felt separate, detached from the clan, watching their revelry as if from a great distance.

He sipped again at his whiskey, and felt the liquid warmth seeping pleasantly along his chest and arms.

Another goblet or two, and then, perhaps, his riotous thoughts might subside, leaving him with a welcome modicum of peace.

A movement from the staircase caught his eye and he saw Maudie descending the final steps. He signaled to her, and she made her way to the head of the table where he sat.

"Well, Maudie?" he said. "How fares the Sassenach?" He was eager to hear news of her, and, disgusted at himself for it, spoke more roughly than he had intended.

"I brought her supper, laird, and some ale," Maudie replied. "She thanked me and took the tray, and then I left her."

"Is the room adequately furnished for her comfort?" Leith said, hating himself even as he uttered the words.

"There's a bed and a chair, laird, and an auld cupboard."

"Is that all?" he said with a frown.

Maudie glanced at him curiously. "What else might a prisoner need, laird?"

Gritting his teeth, Leith pushed away a desolate image of Adrianna alone in the bare, stark tower room.

"Aye," he echoed in a growl, "what else might a prisoner need? Gae and eat, Maudie, and tell young Stephen I'm in need o' more whiskey."

"Aye, laird." Maudie dipped a curtsy and went down the table where she met with the serving boy, who promptly hurried over to Leith and refilled his goblet.

Leith drank deeply, then closed his eyes, savoring the lulling heat of the mellow, nicely aged whiskey. He could almost feel the tortured workings of his mind slowing, calming.

A soft touch to his shoulder brought his eyes open in an instant.

Fiona stood close to him, so near that he could smell the cloyingly sweet scent of the pomade she used to burnish her brown curls. "Laird," Fiona said with a sweet, confident smile, "may I join ye?" Her breasts were nearly at a level with his face, and Leith could not help but view the round, ripe bounty of them nearly spilling over the bodice of her russet gown.

Had he really found such fleshy abundance appealing? Leith turned his head away. "If that is what ye wish."

"Aye, Leith, that I do." Fiona spread her skirts wide and sat on the oaken bench next to his chair. Surveying the table, she said brightly, " 'Tis a wonderful feast they've made for ye."

Leith sipped at his whiskey. "Aye."

"We're all glad ye're home," Fiona told him, her green eyes fixed intently on his. "But there's no one more glad than I."

"Aye?" he said, noncommittally.

"Aye, laird," she said, then leaned forward. "Noo that ye've returned, we can . . . ." She pursed her lips and trailed off, lowering her gaze in a maidenly show of modesty.

"We can what?" he said, a hard note in his voice.

"Why, finish what we started."

Leith emptied his goblet and waved Stephen over to him. When the goblet was full again, he nodded his thanks to the boy and drank. "Perhaps ye might make yerself clear, Fiona."

She flushed. "Noo that ye're home," she began carefully, "and ye've accomplished what ye set oot tae do, ye can turn yer attention tae other . . . responsibilities."

He narrowed his eyes. "What kind o' responsibilities?"

"Ye're the leader o' the clan," Fiona said, "and as such, ye owe it tae the clan tae marry, and tae ha' children. Tae continue the Campbell line. Ye're a man o' thirty, Leith, and noo it is time. Can ye deny it is sae?" she demanded.

The whiskey was beginning to produce more than a pleasantly mild warmth in him. It was a tingling heat now that was burning along his arms and legs, in his head and in his groin, fiery and urgent. A vision of the Sassenach's slim white body and heavy golden hair flashed across his mind's eye and he shifted restlessly in his chair. "Nay," he answered at last. " 'Tis my duty tae marry."

Fiona smiled, catlike and complacent. "Well then," she said, as if the matter was settled. "We'll finish what we began."

He stared at her. Her brown ringlets, the bright green eyes and lips carefully reddened by the paint pot seemed to waver in the muted light of the wall sconces. "Aren't ye supposed tae wait for the man tae ask?" he said sardonically.

She shrugged and toyed with a curl that had fallen over her shoulder. "I thought it was understood between us."

"There was no understanding, and well ye knew it," he said harshly. "Dinna pretend we talked o' love or o' marriage."

"What had love tae do wi' it?" Fiona said, her voice sharpening. "I knew ye'd need a wife, and I was merely giving ye a . . . taste o' what was tae come."

"How businesslike o' ye," he retorted. "And I thought ye'd fallen for my charms."

The catlike smile was back. "Oh, ye've ample charms, Leith." She laid a freckled hand on his thigh and squeezed. Scowling, he pushed away her hand and her thin, arched brows drew together. "Let's no' play games wi' each other," she said, lacing her fingers together in her lap. "Ye need a wife, and that's why I gave myself tae ye."

"Why, a right clever campaign," he said, tonelessly.

" 'Tis a pity ye're no' a man, Fiona. Ye'd ha' made a worthy general."

She eyed him uncertainly for a moment, then her face relaxed. "Ye're teasing me, I see. Well, like a general who's won the battle, I can be generous." She rose to her feet, her petticoats rustling softly. "I'll come tae yer bedchamber tonight, Leith." Red lips parted in a wide smile. "I won't make ye wait until we're wed."

Leith looked up at her, feeling his heart thud slowly and heavily within his chest. He was aware of a cold anger mingling with the whiskey-heat suffusing his entire body, yet he didn't quite seem to have control over the sensations. Sounds from the great hall echoed weirdly back to him: a child's laugh, deep-voiced exclamations among the men, an excited yip from one of his dogs. His eyes focused hazily on Fiona as he pondered her invitation. A few months ago he would have gladly welcomed her into his bed, for she'd satisfied his carnal needs well enough.

But now all her wiles evoked nothing in him.

Now all he could think about was the Sassenach girl.

Her lithe form. White skin as smooth as the finest satin. Her delicate yet sensual mouth that he ached to plunder with his tongue, until she cried out in pleasure—

He shook his head, as if to clear it, then raked a hand through his hair.

"Leith?" Fiona whispered seductively. "When shall I come tae ye?"

"Dinna come," he said, slowly, deliberately. "I dinna want ye in my bed."

"What?" she said, whitening. "What did ye say?"

"I dinna want ye, Fiona. No' this night, no' ever." He drained his goblet and let it fall carelessly onto the tabletop. He stood, swaying a little, and began moving toward the wide, stone-inlaid staircase. A tiny seed of an idea was forming in his mind, crystallizing brilliantly with his every footfall.

"Bastard," Fiona hissed. Voices from the table called to him, but he scarcely registered any of them, so riveted was he.

Why shouldn't he simply take the Sassenach girl?

She was his prisoner, after all—his to use as he pleased.

One night, and he'd purge himself once and for all of the cravings she aroused in him.

Then he would be free.

Free of the terrible distractions she created with her presence.

His life could continue on as before.

"Aye," he breathed, climbing the stairs to the tower room. One night to slake his passion, and he'd be free.

Adrianna sat very still in the tower room's only chair. It was a rickety, uncomfortable affair, made of pine and crudely fashioned, yet it was, she supposed, preferable to sitting on the floor. Eventually she would have to climb onto the bed—whose wood frame supported a woven lattice of rope topped with a none too fresh straw mat—but while the sounds of revelry from the great hall floated up to her, she preferred to remain upright in the chair.

She had already explored every inch of the room. It hadn't taken long. Besides the chair and the bed there was only an ancient pine cupboard, its doors opening to reveal three shelves and two small drawers side by side. On the shelves she had found two tattered linen sheets, a moth-eaten blanket, and a lumpy pillow prickly with goose feathers; now the cupboard also contained the meager contents of her bundle: her hairbrush, her nightshift, and a pair of woolen stockings.

After she had supped Adrianna had dragged the chair

next to the round, high-ceilinged room's only window, which was tall and so narrow she could barely pass her hand through it. A warm breeze drifted inside, and she inhaled the mild spring air in deep, steady lungfuls, focusing on the rhythm of her breathing to keep her terror at bay.

A great burst of riotous laughter assailed her ears, and Adrianna shuddered. She fixed her eyes on the squat tallow candle which stood in its dish next to the bed, flickering eerily as it cast a weak, uncertain light. She had begged Maudie to bring her a candle, and the pinched-face old Scotswoman had ungraciously complied.

Adrianna had never been one to fear the dark, but here, captive and utterly alone, she dreaded the moment when the little hump of tallow finally sputtered and died. Rather than fumble around in the blackness of night, soon she would need to make up the bed, but she was putting it off for as long as she could.

Breathe, she told herself, *breathe.*

From below a pipe shrilled gaily, and Adrianna found herself envisioning the festivities in the great hall. There would be food and drink, of course. Music. Dancing, perhaps. What was Leith doing? Mingling amongst the clan, accepting the congratulations of the men, flirting with the women? Was he even now sitting close to the brown-haired beauty Adrianna had seen earlier, whispering sweet words of love?

Stop these foolish thoughts, she ordered herself sternly. Of their own volition, her fingers rose to touch the cool, comforting gold of the cross that hung around her neck.

Oh, Mother, help me.

But of course there was no one who could help her now.

Adrianna raised her hand to dash across her wet eyes, then paused.

What was that noise?

She strained her ears.

Footsteps.

But not the light, brisk step of the old Scotswoman.

These were boots coming up the stairs, firmly and decisively.

Heavy, masculine boots.

One of Leith's men?

Adrianna clenched her fingers on the arms of the chair, her knuckles going white, and lifted her chin.

Mother—

A hand fumbled at the lock, and then the door was slammed open.

O help me—

Leith strode into the tower room, seeming to fill it so pervasively with his dark presence that Adrianna could hardly breathe. Those deep-set eyes were glittering with an unholy light and his rich sable hair had come loose from its riband, reaching nearly to his shoulders.

"Still awake, little nun?" White teeth flashed in the shadowy gloom.

Adrianna swallowed convulsively. "What—what do you want?"

"What do I want?" he repeated slowly, still smiling. He stood with his legs braced wide apart, arms casually crossed over that massive chest. "Why, I want ye."

"Me?" She might have lived in a convent for most of her life, but Adrianna could hardly misinterpret his meaning, or fail to understand the danger gleaming hotly in his eyes. Dazedly she noticed that his shirt was unlaced, revealing dark tendrils of hair in sharp relief against the fine white lawn. "You—you don't mean that," she whispered, clutching the arms of her chair even more tightly as the room began to whirl in a slow, dizzying circle.

"Oh, but I do, my sweet Sassenach," he said. "Ye're my prize, and I've come tae claim ye."

"I'll scream," Adrianna said raggedly. "I swear I will."

He gave a mocking laugh. "Gae ahead," he said. "Do ye think anyone here will stop me?"

No, no one would stop their lord and master from carrying out his will, no matter how loudly she cried out. Adrianna could only stare helplessly at him and bite down hard on her lower lip to still its trembling.

"Dinna do that," he said, and in two strides he was before her, taking her chin in his hand, his long, strong fingers surprisingly gentle. "Dinna ravage that pretty mouth."

Adrianna shrank back in her chair and he let out an angry oath.

"Enough o' this talking," he growled. "It's time for bed, little nun." And with that, he picked her up in his arms as if she were hardly more than a child's doll and began walking swiftly to the door.

"No," Adrianna gasped. "No!" Frantically she pushed at his chest but all her strength seemed to have been drained from her. The room spun dizzily, and Adrianna felt her head loll back against his shoulder as suddenly the world went black and she was plunged into utter darkness.

CHAPTER 5

She had fainted. Leith paused for a moment on the threshold of the tower room and gazed down into the pale, still face of the girl he held in his arms. She looked so completely vulnerable with her lashes shielding her closed eyes, their silken, curling lengths stark against the ivory whiteness of her cheeks.

A gentleman, he knew, would turn on his heel, lay her down on the straw mat of the bed, and leave.

And he was a gentleman, wasn't he?

He was a Campbell, a Highlander, laird of mighty Inveraray Castle.

You're a callous brute, she had said scornfully as they rode away from Carlisle. *But what else should I expect from a Scotsman?*

She obviously didn't think him a gentleman.

No, in her eyes he was a low, coarse Scotsman.

His lip curled. Why then shouldn't he fulfill her expectations?

Rapidly Leith continued on his way down the spiral stairs. When they reached the landing of the floor above the great hall, she stirred and gave a soft moan. Her eyes fluttered open. In their azure depths Leith saw first a blankness and then bewilderment, and watched as they were flooded with alarm as she looked up into his face.

"No," she whispered, begging, "please—"

"Hush," Leith said, inexorably striding down the long dim hallway, and felt her tremble. His own heart was pounding hard in anticipation, and in his ears was a roaring excitement. The feel of her slender body, cradled against him, was arousing him to a fever pitch of hard, aching need.

Soon, he told himself, *soon . . .*

They passed the chapel, the private apartments of the west wing, the solar, then came upon the top of the stairs leading up from the great hall. Some half a dozen of the clan clustered there, their faces alight with mingled worry and curiosity.

"Is all well wi' ye, laird?" Maudie asked tremulously.

Leith gave a loud shout of laughter, tightening his arms as the girl stiffened. "Aye, Maudie, aye," he replied, grinning. "All's well, as ye can plainly see." He saw young Stephen hovering behind his steward Andrew and said, "Run and fetch me some wine, lad, and quickly too."

"Aye, laird," Stephen responded, looking a little scared, and immediately set off down the stairs.

Colin stepped forward, bristling black brows furrowed. "Laird," he said uncertainly, then stopped, his beefy arms hanging limply at his sides.

"Cat got yer tongue, Colin?" Leith said jovially, then added in a voice heavy with amused sarcasm, "I thank ye all for yer concern, but I must inform ye that ye're no' invited tae the festivities in my bedchamber. Gae on back down noo."

Maudie, her averted face scarlet with embarrassment, hurried down the stairs with the rest of the group hard on her heels. They soon reached the bottom and Leith caught sight of Fiona standing with one slipper on the first stair, her nails digging into the skirt of her gown, her green eyes hard as rock as she stared up at him.

A sardonic smile curled Leith's mouth as he took in that overbright gaze. Somewhere in the back of his mind the biblical adage *The ear of jealousy heareth all things* floated hazily past, and then Stephen was dashing up the steps, clutching a dark brown bottle and two delicate long-stemmed glasses.

"Good lad," Leith said, gripping the bottle with the hand that was tucked under the girl's knees, then added to her, "I dinna suppose ye'd carry the glasses noo, would ye?" He grinned at her tense face and said, "Nay, I didna think sae. Off wi' ye then, young Stephen."

"Aye, laird."

The boy hastily retraced his steps and Leith turned away, dismissing all thoughts of the clan and of Fiona. Swiftly he walked into the east wing, an agonizing impatience now burning fiercely within him.

He kicked open the door to his bedchamber and strode inside. Without ceremony he dumped her rigid body on the luxuriously worked silk coverlet atop his bed, then returned to the door which he shut and locked.

"And noo, little nun," he drawled, pivoting on the heel of his boot and dangling the wine bottle between his fingers. "Noo . . ."

He had thought to find her still supine on the coverlet, but in this he was mistaken. Instead she stood some feet from the bed, her spine straight and her head held high in that proud, queenly way he was coming to recognize.

"You must—you must listen to me." Her voice shook but she met his gaze squarely. "Please."

Leith strolled across the room and leaned against the carved bedpost. His blood ran so hot he could scarcely bear it, but if she wanted to play a little game of cat and mouse, he would indulge her . . . for a short while. "Talk all ye like," he invited. He uncorked the bottle of wine and drank deeply.

Adrianna gulped a shallow breath of air. For all his air of indolence as he stood there, he fairly radiated an animal energy barely leashed. Instinctively she sensed that his control could give way at any moment and desperately she cast about for a way to fend him off. Words were her only weapon; her strength measured against his was laughable.

"You don't want to do this," she said at last, knowing it was a pathetically feeble attempt at dissuading him.

That sensuous mouth smiled. "I'm desolated tae contradict a lady," he answered lightly, "but I do want tae—er, do this."

"You're drunk," she accused him, trying another tack.

He laughed, and drank again. "Ye think sae?"

"You're not yourself," Adrianna said as firmly as she could. "You'll feel differently about this in the morning."

Another saturnine bark of laughter. "I hope sae, lass."

"Surely there are others who would welcome your . . . affection." Lamely, Adrianna forged onward. "That—that young lady I saw you with this afternoon. She seems quite . . . enamored of you."

Leith waved the bottle carelessly. It nearly slipped from between his fingers. "Feh," he said amiably. "She canna hold a candle tae ye, my sweet."

She was getting nowhere. He was toying with her, and they both knew it. Adrianna took another gulp of air. "But I'm your enemy," she said, bracing herself for the inevitable reaction. "You hated my father."

At once the smile was wiped off his face, to be replaced

by a hard expression that caused Adrianna's insides to twist in fear.

He took a slow step toward her. "Aye, ye *are* my enemy," he agreed in a deceptively soft voice.

"Then—then return me to the tower room," Adrianna pleaded. "I'll bother no one there."

"Nay," he said coolly, shaking his head, taking another step forward. "I think no'." He leaned down and with exaggerated precision put the wine bottle on the floor.

Perhaps she could create in him a disgust for her, Adrianna thought wildly, grasping at straws. "Why would you want to ... touch your enemy?" she blurted, feeling a blush creep across her face.

"Because ye're very beautiful," he replied, coming closer still, his dark eyes gleaming.

"I'm not beautiful," Adrianna denied, hurriedly beginning to retreat, and she thought that she knew now how it was to be a hunted doe.

"Ye are," he muttered, almost angrily, and then Adrianna's back touched a wall and he was framing her body with his own big one, his hands against the wall on either side of her face. Adrianna felt the raw masculine heat of him, felt the iron-hard muscles in his chest against her palms as she sought to keep him at bay.

"Don't," she whispered, but he was implacable. That dark head lowered and before Adrianna could utter another word her mouth was covered by his firm, fever-hot one.

He kissed her savagely, without restraint, parting her lips with an insistent tongue as one hand slid behind her neck to grip her head.

Oh God no.

Please—

Oh God—

Adrianna's eyes drifted shut of their own accord and

her legs began shaking violently. His kiss was a devastating explosion of sensations unlike any she had ever experienced: the wet heat of his mouth, with its pleasantly tart taste of wine, and the seductive play of his tongue were turning her to jelly.

This was wrong, she knew it was wrong. Her destiny wasn't that of ordinary women who could enjoy the carnal pleasures. Her body was dedicated to a higher cause; it was merely a vessel for the spirit . . . But even as her mind screamed out its frightened protest, her willful body betrayed her.

One of Leith's hands brushed lightly against her breast, cupping the softly rounded flesh, and a little murmur escaped her throat as her frantic thoughts were drowned by a tidal wave of sensual awareness. Again came that feathery caress, this time trailing down the curve of her waist and lingering there.

How could such a simple stroke of long, sure fingers make her feel so utterly female? Every particle of her being was focused on Leith, his skillful mouth, the rasp of his breathing; there was no room for fear, or questions, or doubts.

As if in a trance she felt her hands relax upon the soft lawn of his shirt, then tighten again as a sweet, urgent ache began throbbing low in her belly. Until she had met this rugged Scottish laird, she had never dreamed of what it might be like to be held in a man's arms, never imagined that she could feel as if her limbs, her skin, the very core of her were on fire.

Leith groaned and gathered her fully to him, deepening the kiss, and Adrianna's senses reeled anew at being held so tightly against his tall, powerful body. The tips of her breasts, crushed against his broad chest, tingled with a voluptuous sensitivity; with a dizzying new recognition she felt the hard proof of his desire for her as his fingers, splayed now upon the small of her back, pressed her hips against his.

"Yes," Adrianna murmured huskily, hardly recognizing her own voice as she gripped his shirt even more needfully. This was all a dream, and surely this was some other Adrianna who reveled so wantonly in the Scotsman's wicked embrace. A crazy, delicious dream she never wanted to wake up from . . .

Leith lifted his head slightly and gazed at Adrianna. Her eyes were closed as if in rapture, her cheeks flushed, her lips red and swollen from his kisses. Her slim body was pliant against his, and she was clutching him as if she would never let go. She was alight with passion, passion *he* had ignited in her.

He felt a heady rush of masculine pride, and with it, an eagerness to raise her to even greater heights of pleasure.

"Come," he said hoarsely, lifting her up in his arms. This time she did not struggle; instead she opened her eyes, heavy-lidded and as brilliant as sapphires, and smiled at him.

His heart nearly stopped in his chest at that smile.

God's blood, but she was lovely.

And he wanted her as he'd never wanted another woman.

He carried her across the room, only the slightest bit unsteady on his feet, and laid her upon his bed. He was beside her in the next moment, kissing her ravenously, one hand at her jaw. But she did not resist him now; her lips parted willingly, and her tongue met his questing one, shyly at first, then with greater boldness.

"My God, lass," Leith said, his voice strangled, "do ye ha' any idea what ye're doing tae me?"

"No," she whispered. "Show me." One white hand reached up to smooth back a lock of his dark hair that tumbled across his brow, and Leith was lost. His mouth came down upon hers, hard, and he ripped off her prim coif to bury his fingers in the heavy gold of her hair. It felt like silk between his fingers, exactly as he had fantasized. He gripped her hair and tilted back her head, baring that creamy throat, and he moved his lips down it, biting softly as he went.

She moaned and flung an arm around him, her fingertips digging into the flesh of his shoulder. Leith kissed her breasts through the rough material of her gown, his breath warm and wet, and felt her nipples stiffen in response. His fingers unsteady now, he grasped the laces of her bodice, then paused.

Slowly, lad, slowly, Leith warned himself. It was a selfish lover who went too quickly. He took a breath, then turned on his side, propping himself up by one elbow.

"What . . . ?" she murmured protestingly, trying with the hand that clutched his shoulder to draw him to her again.

In answer he reached down to slide up the hem of her gown and with an exquisite languidness stroked his fingers along her bare thighs.

Adrianna shuddered with pleasure and felt the sweet, fierce ache between her legs intensify until she thought she might go mad unless it was assuaged.

"Please," she whispered, hardly knowing what she was saying. Only Leith could help her, only Leith knew what to do . . .

"Aye, lass, aye," he whispered, low and hoarse, and then those magician's fingers of his were there at the very heart of her, playing among her blonde nether curls, just barely caressing her damp flesh.

"Oh, please," Adrianna whispered again, and desperately lifted her hips to his touch. Now his hand was fully upon her, upon a hard little nubbin which he rhythmically fondled, sending shock waves of pleasure throughout her entire body. A delicious pressure was building inside her, intensifying with every knowing, deliberate stroke.

Adrianna whimpered, her head tossing restlessly on the soft coverlet, one hand clenched tightly on his shoulder. Panting, she strained toward her release, flowing on a rippling river that approached a great waterfall . . . If she could just drop over the edge . . .

"Aye, lass, that's it," he whispered, never stopping what he was doing.

Yes.

Yes.

Oh God—

She must have cried the words aloud, but Adrianna hardly noticed as she seemed to shatter into a thousand shards of spiraling bliss. She'd never known the cataclysmic force of her own body. She was a flower now, blooming in a heartbeat of time, she was flying like an angel high above the earth . . .

When at last the dazzling tension drained from her, Adrianna turned to Leith. "I—I—thank you," she stammered softly, then saw that the raging hunger in his eyes was unabated. He wanted her, and badly too, she thought in wonderment, yet he had put her gratification above his own. Passion flared anew in her, stunning her with its instantaneous ferocity, and she reached out for him. He ground his mouth against hers and she reveled in the sensual onslaught, winding her arms around his neck to bring him even closer.

Finally he broke the kiss and raised his head. "Noo then," he said, his breathing rough, "are ye ready for me, lass?"

She remembered the hard, aroused feel of his hips against hers and nodded, half in fear, half in anticipation. "Yes," she breathed.

Nearly delirious with need, Leith caught her arms which

twined around him and pulled them down to her sides. She was so beautiful with her skin flushed with excitement, her golden hair in glorious disarray, her skirts tumbled about her.

Yes, she was ready.

A good thing too, as he knew he couldn't wait much longer.

He was about to explode with wanting her.

"Ye've too many clothes on," he muttered. Obediently her fingers went to her bodice but he pushed them away. "Let me," he said, his hands first cupping her breasts, molding their firm, round contours before moving on to her laces.

In mere moments she would be bare to his gaze, bare to his touch and to his tongue. He ached to stroke her smooth flesh, suckle at those firm, responsive nipples until she begged him to take her and at last he could sheathe himself in the silken, heated velvet of her.

He had waited for so long.

For a lifetime, it seemed.

He wanted her, he *needed* her.

Leith tugged at the laces without gentleness, rapidly pulling them free of their eyelets, then pulled her bodice wide. He was rewarded by a glimpse of naked white skin, beautiful soft mounds tipped with rosebuds . . . and a flash of gold.

Distracted, Leith paused and reached out to take hold of the glinting metal. It was a small gold cross that hung about her neck.

A gold cross.

The symbol of her vocation.

This girl was meant to be a nun.

The realization, the remembrance, slammed him with the velocity of a blow.

She might tremble in his arms, and cry out as he brought

her to the peak of fulfillment, and willingly open her body to the intimate invasion of his own, but this girl was a nun.

He might not be a gentleman, but he wasn't a despoiler of innocent virgins bound for the convent.

In a single cruel instant all the fire of his passion was extinguished by an overpowering shame. He had drunk too much, that was it. It was the whiskey, and then the wine, that had driven him to these base lengths.

"Leith?" she whispered. She was looking up at him, her blue eyes wide and questioning.

He dropped the cross as if it scalded him and rose swiftly from the bed, raking his hands through his hair. Never had he felt such disgust with himself, such black self-hatred.

What kind of man was he, to use her so abominably?

His fingers clenched into fists, Leith stared down at the floor. There, a mere arm's length away, was the dark brown bottle of wine.

"Bastard!" he muttered under his breath.

Then kicked the bottle with a vicious snap of his boot.

The glass broke, and deep red wine spilled across the floor like a bleeding wound.

Leith heard her sharp intake of breath but did not turn around. Instead he went to the wardrobe and snatched a cloak off one of the pegs, then crossed to the door which he unlocked and opened.

"Leith?" Her voice was alarmed now, and this time he half-turned to see her sitting up in his bed, her slim fingers holding her bodice together over those soft white breasts. "Where are you going?"

"None o' yer business, my little Sassenach," he answered curtly. "Sleep well." He went out of his bedchamber without another glance and locked the door behind him.

The last thing he wanted was to have her attempting to escape and stumbling amongst the men who were doubtless sleeping off the excesses of the evening on the sodden rushes in the great hall. He trusted his men, but it was foolish to expect that they would be able to restrain themselves with her comely self in their midst. He didn't want a rape on his conscience in addition to his other sins.

When the sound of his rapid footfalls had died away, Adrianna fumbled dazedly at her laces, joining the two pieces of her bodice together again, and then lay back down upon the rumpled coverlet. She was limp, and confused, and exhausted now.

Why had Leith so abruptly withdrawn from her? Had she said or done something to displease him? Did he not find her sufficiently alluring?

He had *seemed* to find her desirable; every newly awakened female instinct had told her that.

Then again, she was so utterly new to the ways of men.

Perhaps her very ignorance had ultimately given him a distaste for her.

Did men prefer more knowledgeable women? Women who knew how to touch them, how to please them?

An image of the voluptuous brown-haired young woman who had been gripping Leith's arm so possessively flashed across her mind.

Surely *there* was a female who knew precisely what to do.

It was written in every line of that full-lipped face, in her every enticing curve.

Adrianna sighed, then stiffened as an ugly thought occurred to her.

Had Leith left her to seek out the brunette temptress?

Her cheeks burned in humiliation at the idea of it and she pressed her palms to them, startled at the coolness of her hands. It was cold in this vast room, she thought. Perhaps she hadn't noticed with the heat of Leith's presence to keep her warm.

Adrianna pulled up the coverlet and blankets, then tucked them around her. They were luxuriously soft and warm, but they brought her no comfort. Where was Leith at this very moment? And with whom?

There were no answers for her.

She was alone again and, now, lonely.

She curled onto her side in a tight ball of misery, and prayed for sleep.

CHAPTER 6

It was difficult to breathe. His pillow kept moving, rising and falling in a steady, snuffling cadence. And something was draped across his ankles, a soft, warm mass that too rose and fell rhythmically.

His back hurt and his head was pounding.

And what was that smell?

It wasn't bad, precisely, though it did make his nose prickle uneasily. It was just too close for comfort, this warm, earthy smell of . . .

Dog.

Leith's eyes shot open, and he winced at the morning light that was streaming like daggers directly into his eyes.

He was, he perceived groggily, lying near the hearth of the great hall. On the floor. With Mac lying across his ankles and his head resting on the stomach of Mac's brother Willy.

He had never noticed that Willy snored.

Doubtless because he had never used Willy for a pillow before.

Arduously Leith turned his head and saw that his heavy cloak lay in a heap next to him. Another of Mac's brothers, Charlie, lay cozily atop it, sleeping soundly.

"Hey there!" Leith croaked in protest, and Charlie opened his intelligent brown eyes and looked at him brightly. Then he gave an indolent stretch and yawned, his pink tongue curling lazily.

"Ye insolent whelp," Leith muttered bitterly, then raised himself up on his elbows and looked around, squinting.

The great hall was crowded with the sleeping bodies of his men. They rested on the floor, on benches, even on the long trestle table; some slumped uncomfortably in chairs, their heads tilted to one side and mouths hanging open. Refuse from the previous night's festivities was strewn everywhere: empty bottles that had held wine, over-turned jugs for whiskey and ale, trenchers heaped high with bones and scraps of food. No doubt his dogs had helped themselves until they'd nearly been ready to burst, Leith reflected morosely, and were now sleeping off the effects of their unwontedly rich meal.

Just as *he* had slept off the effects of his unusual indulgence in spirits. Leith closed his eyes again as memories, as vivid as if etched in glass, flooded him.

He remembered the feel of Adrianna in his arms and how she brought him to a frenzy of desire.

He remembered how she had panted and cried out, and his own pleasure in the giving of it.

He remembered his foolish vow to take her and then forget her.

As if he could.

Even now, with his back stiff and his skull throbbing as if the devil himself was using it for an anvil, he still felt his passion for Adrianna coursing hotly in his veins.

He was a fool, Leith thought darkly, a damned fool.

This was no Highland lass to dally with, with whom to enjoy an evening's romp and part casually.

No, this girl was a lady, a Sassenach, a would-be nun—and his enemy, he reminded himself for the hundredth time.

But so very lovely. So very arousing.

Leith clutched his aching head between his palms. God's blood, he would go mad with these torturous swings of the pendulum!

There was a rustling sound and Leith opened his eyes again. Maudie was tiptoeing across the sodden, filthy rushes toward him, her expression such a palpable mixture of worry and curiosity that in other circumstances he might have laughed.

"Laird," Maudie whispered in her gravelly burr, "I'm sorry tae disturb ye, but the Sassenach lass isna in the tower room. I thought ... well ... that is, might she be ... ?" She trailed off awkwardly and looked anywhere but at him.

"In my bedchamber?" Leith finished, taking pity on her. "Aye. But why didna ye gae there tae find oot for yerself?"

"I saw ye here on my way up the stairs," Maudie replied apologetically. "Ye looked sae peaceful I didna wish tae wake ye."

"Maudie, I didna knoo ye possessed such delicacy o' mind," Leith remarked. With an effort he drew himself up to a sitting position, jostling Mac who woke, raised his silky head, and eyed him reproachfully.

"I'm bothering ye, am I?" Leith said to him. "Ha' ye no' used my legs all the night long? Ye're an ungrateful beast, ye are."

Mac climbed to his feet, arched his back in a sleepy stretch, then padded over to Leith and tried to lick his face.

"No, ye wretch, leave me be," Leith said sternly, though he caressed the rough coat of Mac's flank before he stood up. He was all too conscious of his rumpled state and he ran a critical hand along the stubble of his jaw.

"Maudie, I'm parched," he said. "Can ye bring me a tankard of ale?"

"And something tae break yer fast, laird?" Maudie asked.

Leith felt his stomach lurch at the idea of it and shook his head. "I thank ye, no."

Maudie curtsied and hurried off to the kitchen, lifting the hem of her brown wool skirt high to avoid the rubbish scattered on the rushes.

Mother of a whoreson, what a mess, Leith thought gloomily, surveying the great hall as if for the first time. The great stone mantel over the fireplace was littered with chunks of wood, arrow tips, mismatched hunting gloves, someone's hat, a rotting half-eaten apple—all of it dirty and coated with dust. A wooden set of children's blocks, brightly painted, lay tumbled underneath the table, and elaborate spiders' webs dangled high overhead. Dog hair was everywhere. Was the castle always in such sordid disarray?

Leith stalked over to the immobile lump of disheveled hair and stained clothes that was Jock and prodded him with the toe of his boot. "Get up, ye lazy sod," he said sharply. When Jock groaned and stirred, Leith raised his voice and shouted: "Wake up, all o' ye lazy bastards! Ye're nothing better than swine in a pigsty!"

There were more groans. Yawns. Scratching of rumpled heads. Red, bleary eyes gazed penitently at Leith, who stood watching them sourly, arms crossed over his chest. If they looked *this* wretched, he could only guess at his own sorry appearance.

"Good morning, laird," ventured Malcolm, attempting,

without much success, to smooth his fiery reddish-orange mane.

"Is it?" he answered coldly.

Rubbing sleep from his eyes, Jock asked politely, "Did ye pass a pleasant evening, laird?" Someone snickered and he reddened, his expression self-conscious. "I mean—that is—a restful—"

Leith glared at them all. "That's enough oot o' ye!" he snapped. "Another word, and I'll—"

"Yer ale, laird," Maudie said from behind him.

Leith whirled to face her. "What do ye mean by sneaking up on me?" he snarled.

"Sneaking up on ye, laird?" Maudie echoed in bewilderment. "I merely brought yer ale, as ye requested." She held out the tankard.

Leith grasped it and took a long swallow of the refreshing brew. "Aye, well," he grumbled ungraciously, "just dinna do it again."

A knowing half-smile flitted across Maudie's wrinkled face before she curtsied demurely. "Ale for everyone, laird?" she inquired.

Leith, already feeling the better for having drunk half a tankard, saw the hopeful looks of his men and nodded. "And breakfast for those that ha' the stomach for it," he added.

Several of those present in the great hall blanched and Leith could not repress a grin. "I'm in the same boat as ye," he confessed.

"At this moment I'd gladly die," Dougal put in ruefully, rubbing the back of his neck. "I swear I'll never touch whiskey again!"

Malcolm laughed. "Ye said that the last time, lad."

There was laughter all around, and more good-natured raillery. Maudie and a pair of serving boys arrived with loaded trays and passed among the men, dispensing the tankards. When Maudie's tray was empty, she approached Leith again.

"Laird," she said, "shall I take breakfast up tae the Sassenach?"

The Sassenach. Adrianna. He'd actually forgotten about her. Leith's mood, which had lightened thanks to the bracing effects of ale and the camaraderie of his men, turned stormy in an instant. He had managed, for a few blessed moments, to free himself of the disturbingly powerful, almost magnetic pull she exerted over him.

He scowled at Maudie, but was forestalled from answering her when into the great hall burst one of his couriers, young Glen Morrison, and behind him, Colin, hot on his heels.

"Laird," Glen gasped, "yer presence is much needed at Strome Ferry, an it please ye tae come!"

"What's afoot?" Leith dropped his empty tankard on Maudie's tray and strode forward to meet Glen, his mind already working swiftly. "Another dispute between the Frasers and the Munros?"

Glen nodded, his wispy brown hair flying wildly about his thin face. "Aye, laird, and it's no' just a few sheep spirited intae someone else's pasture," he reported agitatedly. "This time they're threatening tae destroy each other's crops, and there's talk o' setting fire tae the crofters' huts. It's bad, laird, very bad."

"The fools!" Leith said irritably. "Did I no' help them negotiate a truce just last autumn?"

"They're hotheaded, they are," Glen replied, then added anxiously, "But will ye come, laird?"

"I knoo ye number among the Frasers some cousins and friends," Leith said, clapping the young man reassuringly on the shoulder. "O' course I'll come, withoot delay. We want no bloodshed among them."

Glen grinned in relief. "Thank ye, laird!"

Leith glanced to his men, who now all stood alertly listening to the conversation, bodies tensed and poised for action. It warmed Leith's heart to see it. Good men, all! "Let's gae, lads," he said briskly. "We've work tae do." He turned to leave, but stopped when Maudie sidled up to him and said in a low, nervous voice:

"Is the Sassenach tae remain in yer bedchamber, laird, or should I bring her back tae the tower room?"

Leith's temper flared. "God's blood, woman, will ye ever cease pestering me?" he growled, then turned on his heel and marched out of the great hall to the stables, trailed closely by the others. Secretly he marveled that he would actually be welcoming another tedious, difficult border dispute so that he could leave Inveraray.

Leave Adrianna.

Leave all the thorny doubts and questions she raised in him.

It was curious, Leith mused, how tending to a little war could, perhaps, bring him a little peace.

She was in Leith's arms again. He was kissing her, his mouth warm and hard on hers, and she was yielding to him in the sweetest surrender, her body arching up to meet his, her fingers gripping those bare, powerfully muscled arms as he moved above her—

"Wake up, then," said a gravelly voice. "Can ye hear me? Wake up!"

"What?" Gasping, Adrianna sat bolt upright and looked wildly around her. She had been dreaming, she realized. She was in Leith's bed. Maudie, the surly old Scotswoman, stood by the door with a tray in her hands, her face set in stern lines of disapproval.

"Ye're a heavy sleeper, aren't ye?" she said dourly. "I've brought ye some oatmeal."

"Thank you," Adrianna replied, wondering just how tangled her hair was and how rumpled her gown. She knew, with painful certainty, that she must look the complete slattern. "It's very kind of you."

Maudie sniffed. "I'm merely following the laird's orders, that's all." Her gaze fell upon the broken bottle and the pool of blood-red wine that surrounded it, and her frown deepened. "I'll bring some rags and clean that up."

It was useless trying to explain, Adrianna told herself, or to protest her innocence. What did it matter what Maudie thought of her in any event? "I'll do it," she said. Maudie glanced at her incredulously and she added, "I like to be useful."

"Suit yerself," Maudie responded with a shrug. She moved further into the room and placed the tray on a round table that was set near the fireplace. Its dark surface, beautifully inlaid with cherrywood, was obviously the product of meticulous craftsmanship. Two wide, high-backed chairs sat around the table, their seats embellished with charmingly worked cushions.

Quickly Adrianna looked around her and saw that the entire bedchamber was furnished with similar elegance, from the handsomely appointed bed with its high carved bedposts to a tall oaken cupboard, a large, heavy, masculine-looking desk, and the massive tapestry adorning one entire wall. All in all, it was a large, comfortable room . . . but it was Leith's.

And Leith meant danger. Even the penetratingly bright light of day couldn't banish the clinging memories of what had happened last night between her and Leith. Nor would her traitorous body let her forget. Her lips felt a little tender, her breasts still a bit tingly.

As for her own all too willing participation—culminating in that shattering, spiraling release as she shuddered against Leith's long, warm body—Adrianna could only cringe in guilty dismay. What would her dear Mother Superior think if she only knew of Adrianna's appalling behavior?

It was all, she instructed herself firmly, best forgotten and put behind her.

Still, how could she, ensconced in Leith's bedchamber, surrounded by his things?

"I thought perhaps you came to return me to the tower room?" she said hopefully to Maudie.

"I've had no instructions from the laird," Maudie answered crossly, "and since he's gone, here ye'll stay until he tells me otherwise."

"Gone?" Adrianna said quickly. "Gone where?"

"There's a border dispute north o' here," was the reply. "All o' the clans hereaboots rely upon the laird tae assist them in such difficulties."

"How long will he be gone?" Adrianna hardly knew whether to hope for his swift return or to pray that he would be many days away.

"I dinna knoo. I'll bring the rags." With that terse statement, Maudie went to the door with her brisk step.

"Mistress," Adrianna said, "could I trouble you to bring me as well the brush for my hair? It's in the cupboard in the tower room."

Aye, ye need it, too, said Maudie's eloquent expression before she gave a brusque nod and whisked herself out of the room, locking the door behind her.

Leith drew his horse alongside Colin's as they rode north. "Ye're looking in fine trim this morning," he remarked. "Ye've bathed and changed yer clothes from last night."

Colin glanced at him cautiously. "Aye. Is that a problem, laird?"

"Went back tae yer quarters instead o' sleeping in the hall wi' the rest o' the lads, did ye?" Leith asked conversationally.

Now Colin's face flushed a vivid crimson. "No' exactly," he hedged.

Leith laughed. "Ye look like a schoolboy caught in the pantry," he said. "Wi' a lass, weren't ye?"

"Aye," Colin replied, still looking sheepish.

"Dinna worry, man, I won't ask ye for her name," Leith chided him jovially.

"And how went *yer* night?" Colin said, pointedly changing the subject. "Consorting wi' the enemy and all."

Leith felt his smile harden. "Why, if I didna knoo better, I'd say ye disapprove o' me, auld friend."

" 'Tis no' my place tae judge yer actions," Colin returned stiffly.

"But ye are," Leith insisted. "Because ye think I'm setting up the Sassenach as my mistress?"

Colin shrugged. "I was there when ye carried her off tae yer bedchamber."

This barbed exchange with Colin was stirring up everything he had been hoping to put aside, Leith thought angrily. So much for the peace of mind he craved!

"Think what ye like then!" he snarled, pressing his heels into Thunder's sides. In a matter of seconds he had outpaced Colin's mount, and he continued to gallop until they were far ahead of the rest of the group and he could brood in silence.

Three whole days, Adrianna thought, pacing the floor for perhaps the hundredth time that morning. Leith had been gone for three whole days, and still she resided in his bedchamber.

What was going to happen to her? What did the danger-

ously attractive Scottish lord intend to do with her upon
his return? *He called me a prize,* Adrianna mused. Was not
a prize something to be cherished? Or was Leith thinking
only of pursuit and gain in men's deadly games of war?
Was she merely a captured chess piece to him, a helpless
pawn to be won and discarded?

And yet there were those sweet, fiery moments she had
shared with Leith but three nights ago in this very chamber . . . in that very bed . . . Did they mean nothing to him?

Adrianna knew she should feel guilt, shame, abhorrence
at the insidiously pleasurable memories of that evening,
but instead she found herself drawn into wickedly alluring
daydreams in which *she* kissed Leith, touched him and
caressed his tall, powerful body until he cried out with the
same ecstasy she had found in his arms.

Surely such radiant, all-consuming bliss could not be
wrong? But nothing in her life's experience in the convent
had taught her to welcome the idea of a man's embrace,
so she tried, instead, to focus on the desperation of her
circumstances. She was alone, far from her native country,
a prisoner in an enemy stronghold.

Somehow, she told herself, she must escape. But how?
The door to Leith's bedchamber was locked from the outside at all times. If she could somehow persuade the taciturn Maudie to release her from this room, to permit her
to stroll in the bailey, perhaps . . . What then would she
do, surrounded by dozens of hostile Scots? She could
hardly steal a horse from the stables and make a dash for
the border.

No, it was hopeless. There was naught for her to do save
sternly attempt to keep her unruly brain from slipping
back into thoughts of Leith . . . sinful, sensual thoughts . . .

To distract herself, she had spent most of the first two
days of her imprisonment tending to the chamber in which
she was isolated. Its furnishings were certainly luxurious,

but a closer examination had revealed that they were covered in dust and in a pitiful state of neglect. So she had asked Maudie, when that lady had returned with the promised rags and her hairbrush, for other cleaning materials, as well as a needle and thread.

Maudie's small dark eyes had been bright with suspicion, but she had grudgingly complied with Adrianna's request.

Time had then passed reasonably quickly, for Adrianna preferred to be engaged in useful occupations, but finally there was little else for her to do.

So she paced, her churning dark thoughts full of Leith despite her own best intentions otherwise. She halted only when there was a knock on the door and Maudie entered with the midday meal.

Adrianna went to meet her, and to take the tray from her hands. "It smells wonderful," she said.

" 'Tis mutton stew," Maudie informed her, sounding even more taciturn than usual. "And some fresh butter wi' yer bread."

"Thank you, mistress," Adrianna said, then looked more closely at Maudie. The old woman's eyes were red, and her expression was strained.

"What is it?" she said, placing the tray aside. "Something troubles you."

"Nay, 'tis nothing," Maudie muttered. "I'll leave ye tae yer meal." She turned to go, but Adrianna stopped her with a light touch to her shoulder.

"Please," she said gently. "I would like to help, if I can."

Maudie's eyes filled with tears. Blinking rapidly, she said in her gruffest voice, "No one can help. There's nothing tae be done."

"About what?" Adrianna prodded. "Please tell me, mistress."

The old Scotswoman stared hard at Adrianna, as if debating within herself, and then finally she said, " 'Tis my grandson, little John Ogilvy. He's very ill."

"What is his sickness?" Adrianna asked. When Maudie remained silent, she urged, "I have some experience in healing. Perhaps I can—"

"We think 'tis the plague!" Maudie blurted out. "My poor wee John tosses and turns, wi' the sweat pouring off him in buckets!" Tears spilled down her cheeks and she raised shaking hands to dab at them. "And if it *is* the plague, soon we'll all be dead, every last one o' us!" she wailed.

"It may not be the plague," Adrianna said soothingly. "There are sicknesses which manifest themselves similarly but are indeed very different."

Maudie sniffled but looked unconvinced.

"Won't you take me to him?" No thoughts of escape flew through Adrianna's mind; there was only concern for Maudie's young kinsman. "I would like to see him."

"Aren't ye afraid o' catching it?" Maudie asked disbelievingly. "Ye a Sassenach, and he a Scot?"

"Oh, what does it matter what our nationalities are?" Adrianna said impatiently. "He's a sick little boy, and I'd like to help him!"

"If ye're no' worried aboot contagion, then," the other woman said slowly, then suddenly shook her head. "Nay," she went on, "the laird gave no orders for ye tae leave this room. I canna let ye gae oot."

"Bring a guard to escort me," Adrianna said urgently. "For the love of God, mistress, there may be something I can do to help your grandson!"

Maudie's brow wrinkled as she mulled it over, and then she straightened decisively. "If the laird wishes tae punish me for my disobedience, sae be it then," she declared. "I'll gae get Ross tae come wi' us." She hurried to the door, then paused. "But dinna ye wish tae eat first?"

"Hang eating!" Adrianna fairly screamed at her. "Go get Ross!"

Inside the low-hanging crofter's hut, young John Ogilvy writhed on his sweat-soaked pallet. His angular little face was flushed an alarming shade of red and he was muttering unintelligibly through cracked lips.

Adrianna knelt next to the boy and placed a hand on his brow, though she knew she would find it burningly hot. She glanced around the croft. In the hearth bright yellow flames licked eagerly at the large pile of burning embers it contained, and nearby were stacked many lengths of wood to sustain the conflagration.

"Nay!" the lad croaked. "Mam! Mam! Why is my bed on fire? Make it stop, *please!*"

Mistress Ogilvy, a worn-looking woman with large, soft eyes and a tremulous mouth, wrung her hands. "Ach, Johnny," she murmured in anguish. "My poor boy!" She swallowed a sob and glanced at her big, burly husband who stood next to her; he patted her shoulder but said nothing, looking helpless. Behind them clustered the four other Ogilvy children, their dirty faces frightened, eyes wide with alarm as they peered around their mother's soiled skirts.

Everyone—including Maudie and the lanky, loose-limbed Ross—stared at Adrianna as she bent over the boy, pressing her ear to his chest and listening intently to the rapid movement of his lungs. He was breathing hard, but there wasn't any indication of congestion, she noted with relief.

She straightened and looked at Mistress Ogilvy. "Has he asked for food or water?"

"He wants no food, mistress, but begs for something tae

drink," Mistress Ogilvy answered in a shaky voice. "But when we give him water or ale, he brings it right up again."

"And does he complain of aching in his bones or joints?"

Mistress Ogilvy nodded. "Aye, mistress, that he does."

"Has he had the bloody flux?" Adrianna went on. "Are there sores anywhere on his body?"

"Nay, mistress."

"Does he say that he feels cold, even though his fever is high?"

"Aye, mistress. First he's hot, and then he's cold again, shivering like it was the dead o' winter. And then he says he's hot."

"It's not the plague, then," Adrianna told them. As relief washed over the tense faces of those in the room, she lifted her hand in warning. "But I believe he has the ague. There is much yet to be done." She looked at Master Ogilvy. "Tamp down the fire, if you please, sir. The season is still mild and the intense heat of the fire does not help the boy."

"We thought he needed tae sweat oot his sickness," Master Ogilvy responded, looking doubtful. "Everyone says that's best."

"Not with the ague," Adrianna replied gently. "He alternates between feeling too hot and too cold. When he says he's cold, he needs blankets. But when he says he's warm, he shouldn't suffocate with the heat and the blankets. Please, tamp down the fire."

There was a long silence as the Ogilvies glanced uncertainly at each other. Then Mistress Ogilvy tugged at her husband's sleeve.

"Listen tae the lass," she said quietly. "Our Johnny hasn't got much left in him, and she's our only hope."

Master Ogilvy gazed at Adrianna with desperation in his tired hazel eyes, then went to the hearth to do as she had bade him.

"Thank you," Adrianna said. She pulled off three of the four heavy wool blankets draped over the boy and laid them on a nearby stool. "Have you any dry blankets?"

"It's all we've got," Mistress Ogilvy said, but Maudie interposed, "Ye can ha' mine, Gracie. Fergus, will ye gae?"

"Aye, Mam," Master Ogilvy replied, and immediately hurried from the hut.

"We need to give Johnny some liquid, and ensure that he keeps it down," Adrianna said. "Have you any chamomile?"

"Chamomile?" Mistress Ogilvy echoed. "We use that tae dye our fabric yellow."

"Yes, but do you have some of it available?" Adrianna persisted. "As an infusion—a tea—it will soothe his stomach and keep him from retching it up."

"I'm—I'm no' sure," Mistress Ogilvy faltered, wringing her hands again.

Adrianna turned to Maudie. "What about the herb garden I saw in the bailey?" she asked.

Maudie's eyes brightened. "Aye, that might do. It's no' been worked for an age, but I knoo there used tae be chamomile . . . I'll gae right away."

Adrianna stroked the boy's hot brow. With the fire nearly put out, already it was more comfortable in the croft. Soon they would have dry blankets, and, hopefully, the tea she had asked for. After that . . .

After that, all that was left was to pray.

CHAPTER 7

Gently Leith drew his horse to a halt, and sat in the saddle for a moment, simply looking at the massive stone walls and soaring tower of Inveraray.

He had been gone ten days. Most of his time in Strome Ferry had been spent deep in discussion with the chieftains of the clans Munro and Fraser, who initially had been more interested in describing their plans for the other's annihilation than formulating the possible means to an amicable resolution to their conflict.

But Leith had patiently listened to their grievances, restrained them when they were on the verge of blows, soothed their ruffled feathers, sat with them nursing a mug of ale as they attempted to drink each other under the table, and finally persuaded them to resume the terms of the agreement he had helped them hammer out the previous fall. This morning he had left Roderick Fraser and Hamish Munro practically embracing each other, so full were they of renewed goodwill and brotherly affection.

How long it would last would remain to be seen, but for now, at least, Leith could take satisfaction in the knowledge that he had averted another long, costly, perhaps murderous border dispute.

Nor had he been too fully occupied with the affairs of the neighboring clans to devote some time to contemplation of his own problems.

Namely, Adrianna.

He had been wrong, he'd decided, to spirit her away with him. After the many long, grueling years of waiting for his chance to restore Hugh's honor, he had forsaken his own in a blinding drive for revenge.

And then he had been broadsided by the dazzling beauty of the slim golden-haired lass. His normally cool, rational brain had been overpowered by the lustful promptings of another part of his anatomy.

All in all, it was an unfortunate state of affairs.

But he was man enough to admit to his own errors in judgment, and to make reparations.

When he and Colin had encountered Adrianna in her father's library, she had confessed that she was about to embark on a journey. It had occurred to Leith during his time in Strome Ferry that she must have been planning to make her way to a convent.

Well, he would let her go then.

He would send her with two of his most trusted men to accompany her, for as far into England as they could safely go. He would give Adrianna a fat purse filled with gold so that she could then hire a conveyance and outriders to take her on the remainder of her journey.

It was the right thing to do, Leith said firmly to himself, as he had done so time and time again during the past week.

Why then had he still not been restored to the tranquillity he yearned for?

It was an issue he did not wish to pursue.

"It's *right,*" he muttered, then urged Thunder forward. The rest of the party—Colin and the other men—followed him up the easy, grassy slope to the castle.

As they approached the open drawbridge, Leith sensed that all was not well at Inveraray. He couldn't have said how he knew it was so, but more than a decade of experience as clan leader had honed his intuition to a razor-sharp point.

Had something happened to Adrianna?

He felt a stab of fearful agony at the thought, and knew that if it was true, then he would be to blame, for he had fled Inveraray—glad for the excuse to do so—without first ensuring that in his absence she would be carefully guarded from harm.

Leith rode quickly into the bailey and a dozen clan members hurried toward him, their faces pale and anxious.

"What is it?" Leith demanded urgently, dismounting. "What has happened?"

Wallace, the blacksmith, stepped forward. He had lost some of his bulk during the time Leith had been gone; even his big, normally jolly face looked less round. "It's the ague, laird," he said tiredly.

That explained why so few had come to meet him. "How bad is it?" he asked, bracing himself for the worst. When these sicknesses swept across the country the toll was usually devastatingly high. "How many ha' we lost? Forty people? Fifty?" *And was Adrianna among them?*

"Nay, laird," Wallace answered. "Only auld Barbara Mackay was taken, and two o' the Glammis children."

Relief—for the clan, for Adrianna—swept through Leith. Sadness for the three losses would come later. "It's a miracle, then!" he said.

Wallace exchanged glances with his neighbor. "Some say that," he responded slowly. "Others say . . ."

"Others say what?" Leith prompted him.

By now more people had straggled into the bailey, and when Wallace did not answer, someone in the back of the crowd piped up:

"Some say 'tis the witch!"

"Witch?" Leith echoed sharply. "What do ye mean, witch?"

"The Sassenach, laird!" Georgie, one of the grooms, said boldly. "There's some that say she's a witch, the way she cured sae many o' the ill!"

"Wi' her potions and herbs!" added Judith, a kitchen maid, shuddering dramatically. " 'Twas the devil's own medicine, I vow!"

Leith held up an imperative hand. "Are ye telling me," he said, "that the Sassenach lass went among ye and helped heal ye o' yer sickness?"

"Aye, laird," Georgie replied. "For fully a week, until the cursed ague had left us."

"I see," Leith said. It wasn't difficult to picture Adrianna as a ministering angel. He knew she was compassionate; he had seen how her soft words had comforted Cecily MacBean, when that damsel had spoken mournfully of the death of a daughter.

Adrianna was full of surprises, it seemed. First had come the stunning discovery the night of the feast of her astonishingly sensual, responsive nature. And now he learned that she was skilled in the uses of medicinal plants.

How next would she amaze him?

Ach, these were foolish thoughts, Leith chided himself. As soon as he could, he would arrange for her departure from Inveraray . . .

Someone was speaking to him. Leith blinked and realized that Ralph, the tanner, was looking up at him earnestly.

" . . . do ye no' think sae, laird?"

"Aboot what?" Leith said blankly.

"That since the Sassenach is a witch, she should be burned."

Incredulously Leith saw that several among the clan assembled before him were nodding in agreement. Then he saw Fiona Grant stroll into the bailey, a smugly feline smile on her pretty face. She whispered to one of the crofter's wives, Lisbeth, who in the next moment called out in a high shrill voice:

"She should be burned *at the stake!*"

Leith glared at Fiona. Her bright green eyes were fixed on a point behind him but he didn't bother to turn around to see what or who she was gazing at. "Ha' I got this right?" Leith said in a loud, sarcastic voice. "The Sassenach lass risks her own life tae cure ye, then ye wish tae reward her by having her burned as a witch?"

Wallace cleared his throat. "We ask ourselves," he explained nervously, "how she has helped sae many when in the past sae many ha' died."

"Did it ever occur tae ye that she might ha' skills as a healer?" Leith said witheringly. "That she's no' a witch but a healer?"

There were uneasy murmurs in the crowd, and many hung their heads and looked ashamed.

"But she's a Sassenach," someone objected.

"I dinna care if she's a savage from the New World," Leith answered harshly. "If the lass has saved my clan from harm, then it's grateful I am tae her."

There was a profound silence, and then:

"*I'm* grateful for what she's done," Mabel, a seamstress, said shyly. "Saved my poor wee bairns, she did."

"Aye, mine too," someone else put in, and another voice added, "My mam was very bad, but the Sassenach stayed wi' her all night long 'til she took a turn for the better."

"Well then," Leith said decisively, "enough o' this foolish talk. Gae on noo—and *thank* the Sassenach lass the

next time ye see her.'' Obediently, the clanspeople began
to disperse. Leith turned to Colin to ask him to oversee
the stabling of the horses, but found that the other's attention was elsewhere, directed past Leith's shoulder.

"Colin,'' Leith said loudly.

Colin started and looked to Leith, the dreamy half-smile
erased from his lips. If Leith hadn't been in such haste to
go seek out Adrianna, he would have interrogated Colin
about the unmistakably guilty expression on his craggy
black-browed face as his eyes met Leith's. As it was, he
merely directed Colin to accompany Georgie to the stables
and have the men assist there as needed.

Colin nodded, and then Leith had given into his hand
Thunder's reins, made his way into the great hall, and
began taking the steps to the tower room three at a time.

His heart was beating hard when he came to the top,
but it was only from the exertion of hurrying up the stairs,
he told himself, lifting his hand to knock upon the door.

Surely it wasn't because he was looking forward to seeing
her again.

Adrianna slid lower into Leith's wooden bathtub and
luxuriously dipped her just-washed hair into the warm,
scented water, rinsing it. It felt so good to soak her weary
body, and better yet to have found some of her favorite
herbs—lavender, calendula, chamomile—in the bailey
garden to add to her bath.

The fire in the hearth, before which the big tub was set,
crackled cozily and Adrianna leaned her head back, letting
her eyes drift shut. It was so comfortable, she thought
drowsily, so peaceful ... All troubling thoughts of the
future were magically dispersed amidst this soothing, soli-
tary indulgence.

The door to Leith's bedchamber opened and Adrianna

waited to hear Maudie's gravelly voice, announcing the arrival of the noon meal. When there was only silence, Adrianna opened her eyes and gasped. It wasn't Maudie who stood but a few arm's lengths from her, but Leith— tall, magnificent, every inch the warrior chieftain from the gleaming dark hair tied back with a riband to the heavy, sturdily crafted boots on his feet. On his handsome visage was an expression of mute shock.

His dark eyes gazed hungrily at her face, then dipped lower, and Adrianna knew she should protest in outraged modesty. Instead she felt a tantalizing heat suffuse her body that had nothing to do with the warm bathwater, and an intoxicating sense of her womanly power. "Good day," she said softly, surprising herself with her own composure.

"Ye're here," Leith said awkwardly, finding his tongue at last. "I went tae look for ye in the tower room."

"But you gave no orders for my return to the tower," Adrianna reminded him sweetly. "So here I remained. And have made use of your tub," she added mischievously. "As you can see."

His glance went again to the white curve of her breasts just visible below the water, lingered there, and then he dragged his eyes away. "Ye're welcome tae the use of it," he muttered, flushing.

"Perhaps you'd like to bathe as well?" she suggested.

"Pardon?" he said, startled.

"A bath is refreshing after a journey," she explained demurely. "Don't you find that to be true?"

He shifted uneasily on his feet. "Aye."

"Why, you could have yours now," she went on, "for I've finished with mine." Hardly able to believe her own boldness, yet reveling in it, she began to rise and hastily Leith turned his back on her

"Later, mayhap," he said in an overloud voice to the room before him.

Adrianna wrung the water from her long rope of wet hair, then stepped from the bath and began to rub herself dry with a large square of soft linen. She peeked at Leith's rigid back and smiled. He *did* want her after all. She hadn't imagined the passion in his eyes the night of the feast, for today she had seen it burning there again, hot and bright.

She reached for the clean white linen chemise that lay draped over a chair and slipped it over her head, followed by three fresh linen petticoats, the hems of which had been gaily embroidered with bright threads of yellow and red, and a simply cut moss-green gown. All had been loaned to her by Maudie's daughter Gracie while her own bedraggled gray dress and petticoats were being laundered. Fortunately she and Gracie were much of a size, Adrianna thought gratefully as she laced up the bodice. Quickly she combed her fingers through her hair and wound it into a knot at the nape of her neck, aware of an excited anticipation curling in the pit of her stomach. Would Leith kiss her? Hold her? Perhaps even take her to his bed again? Her breath caught in her throat and she forced herself to concentrate as she rolled her stockings onto her feet and fastened them with their knit wool garters at the narrow place between her knee and upper calf. The skin there was exquisitely sensitive and she found herself wondering what it would feel like for Leith to kiss her there. Her heart pounding at the thought, she slid her feet into her rough leather slippers and straightened.

A little breathlessly she said, "I am dressed now."

Slowly Leith turned around. Those fine dark eyes were intense, brilliant, as he took in her appearance and he said, "A new gown?"

"Gracie Ogilvy has lent it to me," she replied.

He nodded. "The color becomes ye."

Adrianna felt herself blushing with pleasure and she

smoothed her hands along the green material at her waist. "I'm glad you like it," she whispered.

There was a silence. The very air between them seemed to vibrate with words neither dared speak aloud, and Adrianna was acutely conscious that she and Leith were standing as still as statues as they gazed at each other.

Finally Leith cleared his throat. "Ye've done something tae the room," he said. "I canna tell for sure what it is, but it looks . . . better. Ha' ye changed the furniture around?"

"I cleaned it," she said.

"Oh, aye? Thank ye," he said lamely. "Ye didna need tae do sae."

"I . . . didn't mind."

Another tingling silence descended. After what seemed like an eternity, Leith took a hesitant step toward her, then abruptly stopped when someone tapped lightly on the door and it was pushed open.

"I've brought yer meal, Mistress Adrianna, and a surprise," Maudie said cheerfully, coming into the room with a tray in her hands. She froze in her tracks at the sight of Leith. "Laird!" she stammered. "Good day tae ye! I didna knoo ye were returned!"

"Aye, well, here I am," Leith responded, looking nearly as taken aback as Maudie herself.

"Did—did all gae well for ye at Strome Ferry, laird?" she went on.

"Aye, that it did."

" 'Tis glad I am," she said, then her gaze alighted on Adrianna and her gray brows drew together. "Ach, lass, ye canna be standing aboot wi' yer hair wet! What were ye thinking, laird?" she scolded Leith, bustling forward and thrusting the tray into his hands. "She'll catch her death o' cold, the poor wee thing!"

Clucking, she hurried to Adrianna, marched her over

to a chair, and began vigorously rubbing her hair with a linen cloth. Adrianna watched Leith as he stood awkwardly with the tray, then shook his head as if clearing it and placed the tray on the cherry-inlaid table. He stood observing Maudie's ministrations, looking bemused.

After a few minutes Maudie fluffed Adrianna's now-dry hair and expertly wove it into a single thick braid. "The herbs ye used smell lovely," she commented as she fastened a green silk ribbon at the end of the plait.

"Thank you, Maudie." Adrianna twisted around in her chair and smiled at her. "What was the surprise you mentioned?"

A look of comical dismay crossed Maudie's face. "Bless me, I very near forgot!" she chided herself, then called out, "John! Johnny! Come in, lad, and show Mistress Adrianna how well ye're doing!"

Young John Ogilvy poked his black-haired head inside the bedchamber and then shyly entered. Although he was still not quite fully recovered from his terrible experience with the ague, he was much better now; the ghastly dark circles underneath his eyes were gone, and even his cheekbones didn't protrude with such frightening sharpness.

"Come in, lad," Maudie instructed him, and added to Adrianna in a stage whisper, "There's something he's been wanting tae say tae ye."

Johnny advanced timidly toward Adrianna. She smiled and said gently, "I'm so happy to see you looking better. Has your mother been preparing the soup I told her about? The one with beef and eggs, and spring greens?"

He nodded. "It tastes nice, mistress," he said softly, and allowed her to clasp his little hand between her own. "Grandmam brought me here because I—" He paused and looked up at Maudie, who gave him an encouraging smile. He took a deep breath, then blurted out, "She brought me here because I been wanting tae thank ye, mistress, for all ye've done!"

Tears filled Adrianna's eyes and she blinked to keep them from falling. "You're very welcome, Johnny," she said. "I am glad that I was able to be of service."

"I would like tae thank ye too," came Leith's deep, lilting voice, and Adrianna turned her head to look at him. He stood near the foot of his bed, his arms at his sides, and on his face was an expression more serious than any Adrianna had yet seen there.

"Well, we'll leave ye two tae yer discussion," Maudie said briskly. "Come then, Johnny, ye'll see Mistress Adrianna again when she comes tae visit the croft. Say farewell tae the laird on yer way oot noo."

She took Johnny by the hand, and as they passed Leith he tugged politely at his forelock with his free one. Leith nodded at him, and watched as they left the bedchamber and closed the door behind them. Then he turned to Adrianna again, his heart leaden within his chest. How could he say the words that would send her away from him forever, no matter how just their intent?

But first things first.

"Ye ha' done a great deal for my people," he told her gravely. "I hardly knoo how tae thank ye properly."

Her lovely blue eyes were soft as she looked at him. "God was good to us," she replied quietly. "Most of those afflicted did live."

He half-smiled. "I suspect ye're no' giving yerself credit for all ye did."

"You're kind to say so." She smiled back at him. "I was glad to do whatever I could."

Merciful God, could it be that she had gotten even more comely than when he had left her? She sat, upright as always, in her chair before the fire, her slender white hands folded primly in her lap. No one would guess, looking at her, that she was capable of unbridled, unreasoning passion . . . But *he* knew, and that knowledge was the sweetest torture imaginable. It was all he could do to keep from carrying her off to his bed, stripping her of those borrowed clothes, and making love to her in the full light of day.

Then a stern little voice in his head reminded him, *Tell her ye're letting her gae. Tell her noo.*

Leith clenched his teeth and instead said at random, "Maudie's become quite the mother hen tae ye, I see."

"Rightly or wrongly, she believes I saved her grandson," Adrianna returned. "Does it bother you to see her manner toward me so changed?"

"Nay," he said truthfully, then cast about for another topic of conversation. "Sae," he said, "ye went abroad freely then, as ye tended tae the ill?"

"No," she answered cautiously. "Maudie had Ross Sinclair act as a guard whenever I left this room. I trust that meets with your approval?"

"Aye," he said with an effort. Inside him a fierce battle was being waged as his sense of honor warred with a fiery desire to make this beautiful Sassenach lass his own.

He felt his hands ball into tight fists and watched the flicker of alarm on her face as he did so. God's blood, how could he choose between his honor and his heart?

He was a Campbell. There was nothing more sacred to the clan Campbell than honor.

To sacrifice his own would be to shame his proud heritage.

How cowardly was it to put off the inevitable?

"Noo that I ha' returned, ye canna remain here in my bedchamber," he said stiffly. "I will see that ye're moved tae a private apartment in the west wing. Ye'll be more comfortable there. Ross will continue tae guard ye whenever ye leave yer room," he went on, "in order tae protect yer safety."

She raised her brows and he thought back to his exchange with the clansfolk this morning in the bailey. "While there's many that are grateful for the healing ye ha' provided," he told her carefully, "others . . . fear ye."

"They think I'm a witch," she said matter-of-factly.

"See ye knoo then," he said. "Their fear and their hostility are childish, and I must apologize for them."

"Don't," she said earnestly. "I am a foreigner to them, after all, with foreign ways that seem strange to them."

Her compassion, her willingness to forgive the uncouth intolerance shown her, nearly floored Leith. She was a shining example of all that was good, while he . . .

He basely kept himself from saying the words he knew he must.

"I can hardly blame them," Adrianna continued quietly. "Until I came here I, like many Englishmen, thought that all Scots were savages."

"And noo?" he said, feeling his entire body tense as he waited for her answer.

"Now I know differently," she said simply. Her cornflower-blue eyes were fixed on his, lambent with what he would have sworn was naked longing.

Leith cursed silently. By all the saints, he wanted her, wanted her so badly it hurt, but—

Honor.

Desire.

His duty.

His heart.

He must have shown something of his agony in his expression, for her own was puzzled now, confused; but he could not speak for the powerful emotions crashing within him, like waves pounding the shore in a mighty storm. One word, one gesture from her and he was afraid he would be swept away on a tide of passion, and would take her with him, never to let her go.

"I'll ha' Maudie come tae see ye installed in a new chamber," he said abruptly, then turned and left the room, his steps as heavy as his heart.

Her ear pressed to the keyhole, Fiona Grant heard Leith's footsteps approaching the door to his bedchamber. She scuttled down the hallway and just barely made it into the solar before she heard the sound of the door opening and then the crisp noise of his booted feet as he descended the stairs into the great hall.

Fiona leaned against the wall, breathing heavily from her frantic dash to the solar. It had been a narrow escape. She shuddered to think what Leith's wrath might have been had he chanced upon her at the keyhole, but it was a risk she had to take.

When Leith had gone striding into the hall after speaking to the clan, Fiona's feminine instincts told her that he had gone in search of the Sassenach, Adrianna. It was common knowledge that Adrianna had continued to stay in Leith's chamber during his absence and soon, Fiona had thought darkly, Leith would find out too.

She had secretively trailed Maudie and her grandson up the staircase to the second floor, then went into the west wing's solar and covertly watched them as they proceeded into the east wing, to Leith's bedchamber, and saw them, too, as they'd returned downstairs some ten minutes later.

It was then she had seized her opportunity. She *had* to know what passed between Leith and Adrianna. She'd run lightly down the hall and crouched next to the keyhole.

Her worst fears were confirmed.

No words of love had been exchanged, nor plans for a clandestine tryst, but Fiona, her ears jealously alert, had gathered much from intonation, from awkward pauses, from what *wasn't* said. No one among the clan knew exactly what had transpired the night Leith had carried Adrianna off to his bedchamber, but it was clear to Fiona as she listened that ten days' absence had failed to restore his attitude to that of merely jailer.

What was wrong with Leith?

Didn't he see that he belonged to her, Fiona?

He was *hers*.

Fiona straightened and raised her knuckles to her mouth, gnawing upon them viciously.

Only when Adrianna was gone would Leith be freed of his inexplicable obsession for the Sassenach girl. Only then would Fiona once again be invited into his bed.

The marriage bed.

While the ague had raged all through Inveraray, she had thought to rid herself of her rival by methodically planting rumors that the Sassenach was a witch.

The gullible ones, the superstitious ones, had believed it, and had talked wildly of punishment. Naturally she had encouraged such gabble.

And had taken comfort in the vision of Adrianna writhing in agony, tied to a stake, as flames consumed her.

But this morning in the bailey, Leith had quickly and efficiently allayed the clan's fears—a nervous dread that had taken her a full week to carefully cultivate.

Now she needed another plan.

Something a little more direct.

A little more straightforward.

A little more deadly.

CHAPTER 8

"There," Adrianna said, affectionately rumpling John Ogilvy's black hair. "I'm through poking and prodding you, Johnny."

He grinned and sat up on his pallet. "It didna hurt, mistress," he assured her.

"Well, Mistress Adrianna?" Gracie Ogilvy asked anxiously as she stood stirring the contents of a large iron pot suspended on chains over the hearth. "How is he?"

"I pronounce him cured," Adrianna said smilingly, and Gracie's expression relaxed. "He's ready to help his father in the fields again. And," she added, "to play and *skinkit* with his friends. Have I got that right?"

"Close, mistress," Gracie answered. "It's *skirtit.*"

"*Skirtit,*" Adrianna repeated carefully. "To run."

"Mam," Johnny put in, sniffing the air appreciatively, "what's that ye're cooking? Can I ha' some?"

" 'Tis another o' the soups Mistress Adrianna told me

aboot." Gracie smiled at Adrianna. "It's lovely tae see his appetite returned! Can I offer ye some, mistress?"

"No, thank you," Adrianna replied. "It's almost noon, and I know Maudie will have had something prepared for me at the castle." She watched as Gracie filled a bowl with the steaming golden soup, rich with onions, carrots, parsley, and bits of chicken, and placed it on the pallet in front of Johnny, warning, "Wait a bit for it tae cool, love."

Johnny nodded, then looked up at Adrianna. "Mistress," he said, "can I ask ye a question?"

"Of course, Johnny."

"Is it true that in England ye eat children for breakfast?"

"Johnny!" his mother said, looking shocked. "How dare ye insult Mistress Adrianna sae?"

But Adrianna only laughed. "Don't scold him, Gracie. We were told the same thing about the Scots!"

Gracie swathed her hands in coarse towels and lifted the iron pot from the hearth, placing it onto a large iron trivet atop the pinewood trestle table. "We Scots hate the English, and the English despise us in turn," she said, shaking her head. "It's all a lot o' nonsense, if ye ask me. Why, I canna count the number o' people I've told that ye're no'—" She stopped, looking embarrassed.

"Me too!" Johnny piped up, his bowl at his lips. "I tell everyone that ye're no' a witch!"

Gracie cast a mortified look at Johnny and then busied herself with setting bowls out along the table, her face flushed red.

"Don't feel badly, Gracie," Adrianna told the other woman gently. "I know what some of the clan think of me. It's to be expected, I suppose. People fear what they do not know."

"And after all the good ye've done here!" Gracie said. "It makes me angry enough tae spit, it does! But mistress," she went on, "remember, there are those of us who *do* speak up for ye, ye knoo."

"Thank you," Adrianna said. "Both of you," she added with a smile, then rose to her feet. "I can see you're nearly ready for your meal, so I'll bid you farewell."

"Will ye come again, mistress?" Johnny said, his dark eyes worried. "Even though I'm better noo?"

"Yes, I will," Adrianna promised, and Johnny went back to his soup, looking satisfied. She smiled at Gracie and left the croft, ducking her head so as not to bang it on the low-set lintel.

Ross Sinclair sat on a crude bench placed next to the door, whittling a birch stick, but stood promptly when he saw Adrianna.

"Shall we return to the castle?" she asked.

Ross nodded, pocketing his knife and stick, and fell into step a pace behind her. No matter how hard she tried to convince him to walk alongside her, his mute stubbornness prevailed. Adrianna didn't know if he felt uncomfortable being so close to his Sassenach prisoner, or if he believed he could do a better job by keeping his distance. It was unlikely she'd ever learn the truth, she mused, for gangly young Ross was quite possibly the least talkative person she had ever met.

They passed a series of small, neatly tended crofts, each with its own two- or three-room cottage, animal sheds and pens, and vegetable garden. Some had outbuildings for storage of tools and provisions, a small brewhouse or dairy, perhaps an orchard or colorful beds of flowers.

They encountered several clanspeople along the way. Some nodded at Adrianna, and greeted her politely; others hurried past her, eyes downcast, or shot her suspicious glares from within the safe confines of their croft.

"Good day, mistress," old Alan Graham called out as

he knelt plucking weeds from the vegetable patch in front of his tiny cottage.

"Good day," she replied, and walked on smiling. Three weeks ago the elderly crofter had seemed terrified of her when she'd come, at the height of the contagion, to give his wife a small linen pouch of dried chamomile; she could take comfort in the fact that he, and others, seemed slowly to begin accepting her presence among them.

Every day came one or two of the clan, tapping timidly on the door of her bedchamber, asking for her help. Seventeen-year-old Mary, whose monthly courses gave her such discomfort she could hardly stand; were there any herbs she could take? Angus Brown, the castle's brawny carpenter, with a painful splinter wedged deep into his forearm. Mistress Betty, the cook, wondering if Adrianna knew of spices which could preserve meat more tastily.

Yes, there were small signs from the clan.

But not, Adrianna thought with a sigh, from their chieftain.

Days would pass in which she wouldn't even see Leith. He scrupulously avoided her; of that she had no doubt. On the rare occasions when they encountered each other—in the great hall, perhaps, or in the bailey somewhere—he would glance at her, his eyes burning with some emotion Adrianna couldn't identify, and swiftly move on, or leave the room if he had to.

What was going on in his mind? Adrianna wondered for the hundredth time. What were his intentions? Why did he go to such pains to keep apart from her? Could he have forgotten the night when passion had joined them so profoundly, one to the other?

He didn't give her a chance to even ask the questions.

But even though Leith denied her his company, everywhere she went she came face-to-face with his influence among the clan. Every day her respect and her admiration for him grew.

He was a just leader, she gleaned from her conversations with the clan, meting out punishments all deemed appropriate and fair, yet was as ready to offer advice or assistance to those in need.

He could discuss methods of crop rotation as readily as he'd exchange a joke or two.

He knew the names of all the clansfolk.

No one went hungry at Inveraray, she'd learned in amazement. Each shared with his neighbor, in lean times and in prosperity. During her years at Rosings, it was not uncommon for the sisters, the servants, and herself to subsist on coarse bread and thin barley gruel for days at a time, while in a nearby manor its inhabitants feasted richly.

But the laird of Inveraray made it his business to see that his clan's trenchers were filled.

Adrianna had never heard of a nobleman taking such an interest in the day-to-day welfare of his dependents, and was much impressed.

The people, in turn, swore an undying loyalty for their laird, a passionate fealty and a love that went too deep for words.

Adrianna was beginning to understand that love.

Now that she had been at Inveraray for some weeks, she could see how a clan would bond so closely with its chieftain.

She could also see how a woman might love such a man.

Surely Leith was the embodiment of every girl's dream.

He was tall and darkly handsome, with those penetrating, deep-set eyes and that sensuous mouth.

He was strong, a skilled horseman, and, she had been told, an expert swordsman.

He was capable and just, fearsome in battle and revered in peace.

It would not be difficult, Adrianna told herself, for a woman to fall in love with Leith Campbell.

A woman, yes. But not a woman who was a nun.

A great pain seemed to claw at her.

She was not meant to be in the world, but apart from it.

A witness to, but not participating in, the joys and sorrows of everyday life.

Leith might as well be perched on the highest mountain in Britain for all that he was accessible to her.

She knew this.

But why did her wayward heart, her willful body draw her toward him, as surely as a bird seeks out nectar?

And why had she removed the delicate golden cross from around her neck, carefully wrapped it in a handkerchief, and placed it on a shelf in her bedchamber's cupboard?

Was it, perhaps, because she no longer felt the call of her vocation?

A flash of vivid color caught her eye and Adrianna, grateful for the reprieve from her troubling thoughts, paused to admire a bank of woodland wildflowers. Violets, anemones, and hyacinths bloomed brilliantly amidst the tall, lush grasses.

"They're beautiful, aren't they?" she said to Ross, who merely grunted.

Adrianna sighed again and continued walking. Soon they had crossed the drawbridge and were in the bailey, which was astir with its usual chaotic activity. She lifted her skirts to keep the hems from dragging in the feather- and refuse-strewn mud.

At the gatehouse, two of Leith's men were engaged in greasing the winding gear of the portcullis, the hinges of the huge iron-reinforced doors, and the drawbridge runners.

The mason was up on the battlements, replacing some stonework; Angus Brown, the carpenter, and his young apprentice were repairing the roof of the buttery.

Three washerwomen were spreading out linen sheets to dry, and a pair of sturdy milkmaids, on their way back from the meadow that lay outside the castle walls, had rested their pails on the ground and were flirting with a groom who lingered with a broom in his hand.

The miller's cart, laden with sacks of flour, rattled into the bailey, and half a dozen dogs chased after it, barking playfully.

A cow lumbered across her path, and Adrianna wondered if Leith's steward, Andrew, would be receptive to the suggestion that farm animals be penned within the bailey.

Or at the very least, she thought, wrinkling her nose as she held her skirts even higher, to the request that the bailey yard be raked clean every once in a while.

"Ha' ye done it then?" Fiona whispered.

"Aye," Colin said uneasily. "But . . ."

"But what?" Fiona's voice was sharp in the chill dimness of the storeroom. "Didna ye want tae rid Inveraray o' the Sassenach as much as I?"

"Aye," Colin replied slowly. "But tae kill her, and in such a way . . ."

"Ach, ye're as soft as a woman," jeered Fiona. "What could be more simple? And no one would ever think tae blame ye for it, too."

" 'Ye'?" Colin repeated, his voice hardening. "Are we no' in this together, lass? Am I no' doing this for ye?"

Fiona wound her arms around Colin's neck and pressed

herself against his burly form. "Oh, aye," she murmured. "Ye knoo I love ye, sweeting." She ran her tongue across his lower lip, and he groaned, grasping her buttocks in his large, meaty hands.

"Let me ha' ye, lass," he begged. "Ye've made me wait over a month since—"

Fiona nipped at his fleshy earlobe with her sharp teeth. "Later, sweeting," she whispered huskily. "Tell me aboot the Sassenach. I want tae hear aboot that brother o' hers, and the castle she lived in, and everything aboot her."

"Again?" Colin growled. "I've told ye everything I knoo, ten times over. Why do ye care sae much aboot her past?"

"Because," Fiona purred, sliding a purposeful hand into his breeches, "a body . . . should always . . . ha' another plan."

"Aye then," Colin sighed as her clever fingers commenced their work, and began again to recite the story.

The fire was smoking again, Leith thought sourly. He glared at Andrew who sat on a low oaken bench at Leith's right. People bustled in and out of the great hall's open door, up and down the stairs, in and out of the kitchen. Others stood patiently waiting for Leith's attention, anxious to discuss a problem, make a request, or transact a matter of estate business.

"Sae we've had three hundred and twenty lambs born this spring?" Andrew was saying to the reeve, Walter Chisholm, a grizzled man of sixty who had been superintending the Inveraray farms for as long as Leith could remember.

"Aye," replied Walter, "and nearly all o' them healthy, too."

" 'Tis bonny news," Andrew said with a smile, then seemed to feel the weight of Leith's stare for he quickly turned to him. "Aye, laird?"

"The fire," Leith said irritably.

Andrew looked dejected. "It smokes again?"

"Canna ye smell it like the rest of us?" Leith snapped, then relapsed into brooding silence as Andrew rushed off to the kitchen and returned a few minutes later.

"Too much peat," he ventured, gingerly taking his seat again. "The lads swear they'll be more careful next time, laird."

Leith only raised an eyebrow, and after a moment's pause Andrew resumed his discussion with Walter.

Even that worthy's auspicious report concerning the progress of the spring crops did nothing to lighten Leith's dark mood.

He was feeling the weight of the world upon his shoulders.

It was a heavy burden.

It had been three weeks since he had returned from Strome Ferry, and still he had failed to inform Adrianna that he was sending her home.

Every morning when he woke, he vowed to say the words.

And every night when he fell asleep, he promised himself again.

During the day he found himself eluding her, in this way also escaping the harsh demands of his conscience.

Slowly the weeks passed as he played this absurd game with himself.

How could he say the words when he never saw her?

It was a spell, an incantation he chanted to himself. His own foolish method of staving off what he knew must come.

It was like asking the sun not to rise, or the moon to keep away from the starry skies.

Tell her. Tell her.

I'm sending ye back tae England.

'Tis for the best.

He had never thought himself craven, yet he could not bring himself to utter those few simple phrases.

In his dreams, he did begin to speak, but the words wouldn't come out right.

I . . . I want ye, he would say to the dream Adrianna.

I need ye.

I love ye.

The dream Adrianna would smile, and hold out her arms to him, her smile so radiant, so joyful that it was hard to believe it wasn't real.

But then Adrianna's outline would begin to shimmer, and her body become hazy, and the next thing he knew he was looking into his brother Hugh's somber face.

Hugh would shake his head sadly.

How could ye, braithair? I gave my life for honor, while ye are prepared tae toss it away as if it meant nothing . . .

Leith would reach out to Hugh, desperate to explain, to excuse his cowardice, but as he drew close, Hugh would abruptly vanish into thin air.

And Leith would be alone, lost in a dark forest bristling with trees too dense for him to ever hope to find his way free . . .

He'd wake then, tangled in sweat-soaked linen sheets, and shakily reach for a candle to light the blackness of his empty bedchamber.

Yesterday he had gone to the memorial they had constructed for Hugh in the churchyard that lay sheltered behind the keep.

A tall ringed cross, fashioned from a single slab of gray marble, was set amongst the verdant grass. Celtic in design, the cross had been carved in bas-relief with the traditional braid motifs, which symbolized the bonds of mortality no man could hope to escape.

Or perhaps, Leith had mused, staring at the cross, they

represented the bonds of human love, which even death could not sever.

Aye, he loved Hugh still. No matter that his brother had been dead and buried over seven years ago.

There were others he had loved as well, he'd thought, his gaze traveling to the graves of his parents.

Two younger brothers who had died in their infancy.

Uncles, aunts, cousins, grandparents.

His doting nurse.

A tutor he had much admired.

A crofter's daughter he had fallen head over heels in love with at age seventeen, who had broken his heart by marrying a cooper in Greenock. He had recovered, of course, and gone on to other infatuations, other flirtations. He had heard that Dolly succumbed to childbirth fever five years ago.

They're dead, Leith had thought defiantly as he stood in the churchyard, *and I am alive. Surely I ha' a right tae find happiness in this life?*

Aye, he could almost hear Hugh's voice replying somberly, *and yer honor be damned.*

Then Leith had cried out in his agony, dropping to his knees on the damp grass. He felt the wetness of it seeping through his breeches, cold and clammy, but still he did not move. How long could he go on, shunning Adrianna yet remaining achingly aware of her presence, her whereabouts, and all that she did for the clan out of the goodness of her heart? How long could he continue, steadfastly keeping his counsel despite the rampant curiosity, the inquiring looks from his people, so obviously wondering what he planned to do with the Sassenach in their midst?

There was no way out for him. None between heaven and hell . . .

"—meet wi' yer approval, laird?"

"Eh?" Leith jerked back to attention. Andrew was speaking to him. "What did ye say?"

Andrew gestured to a slender man with a shock of red hair who now stood in Walter Chisholm's place. "This is Patrick Doyle, laird," he said, so patiently that Leith knew he was repeating himself. "He's an Irishman, from Belfast." The red-haired man bowed low and Andrew continued. "He would like tae return in a month's time wi' his wagon o' goods tae sell and trade."

"I'll bring fine cloth, needles and thread, lovely yarns, and sturdy pots," Patrick Doyle promised. "Silver trinkets for the ladies, and oranges, too, from Spain!"

"Oranges," Andrew said interestedly. "Very good. Ha' ye any—what is they're called?—potatoes, too?"

"Indeed I do!" the Irishman answered. "I'll bring a few bushels then."

"Do that," said Andrew, then looked to Leith. "That is, if it pleases ye tae ha' Master Doyle return, laird?"

"Fine," Leith said indifferently.

The Irishman bowed again and backed away, and Terrence Shepherd, a young crofter, stepped forward, clearing his throat.

"Good day, laird," he said.

Leith nodded. "What brings ye here, Terrence?"

"I ask yer permission tae gae tae Ballachulish, laird," Terrence replied, blushing fierily. "My bride awaits me there wi' her family, and I'm wanting tae bring her home."

At least someone could be happy, Leith thought, trying to ignore a searing flare of envy. "Aye, Terrence," he answered, "ye ha' my blessing."

"Thank ye, laird," Terrence said, beaming. "I will leave this very afternoon!" He turned and quickly left the great hall, where he nearly bumped into Adrianna as she came inside, saying a soft word or two to Ross Sinclair who went off to the table to await the serving of the meal.

Leith froze.

Their eyes met.

Her breath tight in her chest, Adrianna halted just inside the entrance to the great hall. She could not help but see the suddenly set expression on Leith's face, the tension in his big, muscular body where he sat in his chair holding audience.

Why could he not smile, and invite her to join him at table for the noon meal? Perhaps then they could talk, oh, of trivial, everyday things. The gawky, frisky new foal in the stables. The progress she had made in the bailey's herb garden. The beauty of the blue sky, and how warmly the sun shone today . . .

But Leith turned away from her, and nodded at the next man who stood waiting for his attention.

"Good day, Owen," he said.

Adrianna's heart sank, and slowly she began walking to the steps leading to the second floor, to the handsome bedchamber Leith had assigned her. It held every luxury, far surpassing the stark, threadbare furnishings of the tower room, yet she found herself missing the peculiar comfort she had known in Leith's chamber. She had become so intimately familiar with everything in it as she had scrubbed, swept, sewn, polished . . . and wondered about the man who resided there.

Lost in her wistful reverie, Adrianna jumped as a hand touched her arm. Standing before her was the pretty green-eyed girl she'd seen with Leith that first day at Inveraray.

Fiona Grant, her name was.

Mistress Betty, the cook, had informed Adrianna that Fiona was supposed to oversee the bailey's dairy, yet was rarely seen at her duties. *Why, sometimes I've had tae churn the butter myself!* Betty had reported in some annoyance. *Says she's in the solar at her needlework but I've yet tae see a mended cloth or a tapestry she's made! And how,* she'd added darkly, *the lass has sae much pocket money is a mystery tae us all!*

"Good day," Fiona said pleasantly. Her smile was sweet, yet Adrianna had to restrain herself from stepping back a pace.

"Good day," she answered cautiously.

"On yer way upstairs?" asked Fiona. "Tae the chapel, mayhap, tae pray?"

"There is a chapel on the second floor?" Adrianna said, surprised.

"Oh, aye, at the very end o' the west wing."

"No one told me."

Fiona shrugged. " 'Tis no' been used for an age, no' since the laird's brother passed away."

"Hugh?" Adrianna asked sharply.

"Aye. The laird seemed tae take it hard. He sent the minister away, which 'twas a pity." Red lips pouted. "He was a right handsome man."

Here, perhaps, was her chance to learn more about the brother she knew so little about. Eagerly Adrianna said, "Please, can you tell me what happened to—"

"Ach, here I am, keeping ye from yer business," the other girl interrupted. "Ye were no' going tae the chapel then?"

"No," Adrianna murmured, frustrated, "to my room."

"Dinna let me keep ye then!" Fiona said, her green eyes bright. "Besides, 'tis nearly time for our meal, and I must find my place at the table!" She leaned closer. "The laird likes me tae sit close by," she said in a confiding voice, "and I wouldna like tae disappoint him."

"Of course," Adrianna said woodenly, and began walking up the stairs. Once she'd gained the landing, she halted, and, without knowing why, she turned. There, still standing at the base of the stairs, was Fiona Grant, smiling up at her.

A chill danced down Adrianna's spine and quickly she continued along the hallway to her bedchamber. The door was slightly ajar; one of the washerwomen had come to make up her bed with clean sheets, perhaps, or a maid-servant had brought a fresh jug of water for her basin.

Adrianna stepped inside, closed the door, and after a moment of indecision she went to the bed whose neatly embroidered curtains were opened invitingly. Suddenly she was so very tired. She'd rest for a little while, until Maudie came with her meal.

Adrianna sank onto the silken softness of the coverlet, turned onto her side, and let her heavy eyelids drift shut.

She could not have said how long she slept, but it surely wasn't but a few minutes later that her eyes came slowly open again. For a drowsy moment she did not know what had wakened her. A rustle of some kind, a movement . . . ? Or was it merely a dream?

No, for there it came again. Another quiet rustle.

Then Adrianna's eyes opened wide as something warm and smooth slithered across her outstretched arm and her heart flew into her throat, threatening to choke her.

It was a snake. Black and green and red, with little, shining black eyes of pure evil.

CHAPTER 9

Leith held out his hands and a serving boy poured water from his jug over them. Another serving boy held a basin to catch the water, and a third was ready with a linen towel.

As Leith was drying his fingers he saw Colin taking a seat near the end of the long table. "Colin," he called out. "Come and bear me company."

Awkwardly Colin stood up again and made his way to the table's head where Leith sat, and perched himself on an oaken bench. "Good day, laird," he said, busying himself with the hand-washing.

Young Stephen came by with his jug of ale, filling tankards, and Leith nodded to still another serving boy, who filled his plate with a wedge of steaming mutton pie and several stalks of asparagus. He tore off a chunk of fresh bread that sat on a wooden board before him, then turned to Colin who had already begun eating.

"Slow down, man, ye'll choke yerself," he said. "What's yer hurry?"

Colin swallowed and said rapidly, "I've much tae do this day."

"Aye?" Leith raised his tankard to his mouth. "What is it that's keeping ye sae busy? I've scarcely seen ye these last weeks."

"The—the horses' saddles, and their bridles, too. They've been sore neglected o' late."

"Dinna think ye can fool me," Leith said lightly, and watched as Colin's face was flooded with color.

"What—what do ye mean, laird?" he stammered.

Leith smiled. "Did ye think I forgot aboot the lass ye mentioned on our way tae Strome Ferry? I've no doubt *she's* what's keeping ye occupied, and nicely too."

Colin lifted his tankard and drained it in three long gulps. "Aye," he said to Leith, a little breathless. "That's it."

Leith glanced down the table and saw that every seat was filled. Serving boys circulated quickly, refilling tankards and replenishing plates. Andrew was sitting at the table's foot, keeping a sharp eye on the servants as he ate, and near him was Fiona, her eyes fixed demurely on her mutton pie as she listened to one of the washerwomen talking.

Leith knit his brows slightly. He hadn't failed to notice Fiona's conversation with Adrianna near the staircase, and now he wondered at it. Surely they had little in common. What in God's name had they spoken about?

Suddenly, to his ears came a thin, faint noise from upstairs. It sounded like . . .

A call, a cry . . .

A woman's scream.

Adrianna!

Jumping to his feet, Leith pushed back his chair with such force that it crashed to the floor, startling the dogs, who hastily scrambled to safety. Moving more swiftly than he ever had in his life, he ran across the great hall, vaulted up the stairs, and then he had bolted down the hallway and pushed open her door.

Silent now, she lay perfectly still on her bed, on her side, unmoving, her slender back to him.

"Adrianna," he rasped. "What is it, lass?"

"Help me," she whispered. "Oh, God, Leith, help me."

Rapidly, but carefully, he approached the bed, and as he came around the side of it he saw what held her fast.

It was a deadly wood snake. It had wound itself over her arm and close to her breast, its small flat head poised and ready to strike her vulnerable white throat.

"Dinna move, lass," he said quietly, his voice betraying none of the fearful horror that pumped through his veins.

"I . . . won't," she whispered back, the pupils of her blue eyes so dilated they appeared to be black. "Please . . . help me."

Leith crept closer to the bed. Later he would ask himself how a wood snake—a creature that avoided men and their domiciles, preferring its own secretive domain deep in the forest—had made its way into Adrianna's bedchamber. For now, he needed to focus, focus with every fiber of his being, for Adrianna was in mortal peril.

He had not prayed in years, yet Leith found himself lifting up a silent, desperate voice to heaven. *O God, dinna let her die! Give me the cunning, the agility I need!*

He went as near to her as he dared, not wanting to agitate the snake. He took a deep breath and then, quick as lightning, he reached out, snatched the snake from her arm, and flung it to the floor where he ground the slithering black form under the heel of his boot. There was a sickening crunch as the spinal cord was severed, and then the snake lay still.

Shaking a little, Leith turned to Adrianna. Her lovely

face was drained of color; even her normally rosy lips looked bloodless. "Is it gone?" she whispered.

"Aye," Leith answered. "It's dead, lass."

"Thank God," she said, and began to cry softly.

Without thinking Leith reached down to her, scooped her up in his arms, and carried her away from the bed. Ferociously she gripped the material of his shirt with trembling fingers and buried her face against his neck. "I—I tried to be brave," she whispered tremulously. "But I hate snakes, I'm so very afraid of them!"

"And well ye might hate this one," he said somberly. "Its venom kills within minutes o' its strike."

"Kills?" she echoed, then gave a hysterical laugh. "It bore the colors of your clan's tartan, did you see? Green and red! How fitting! They want me dead, don't they? *All* the clan!"

"Nay, sweeting," he murmured against her bright hair. "Hush noo, I'll no' let anyone harm ye."

She sobbed outright then, and he tightened his arms around her. It felt so right to hold her, to keep her close against him. God's blood, but he had missed this.

Missed *her*.

A muffled noise from the doorway made him glance up. Crowded on the threshold were half the clan from downstairs, their eyes wide and their mouths gaping open. From behind there was an angry sputtering, a gravelly voice demanding, "Let me through, ye louts!" and then the group parted reluctantly to let Maudie push her way to the front.

"Laird!" she gasped in astonishment. "What has happened? Has Mistress Adrianna taken ill?"

"Nay, Maudie, the lass is all right," he replied. "But perhaps ye can be o' some service tae her."

He moved to a comfortable-looking chair set next to the fireplace and gently began to lower Adrianna into it. She surprised him by clinging fiercely to him and whispering, "Don't let me go."

"I'll be right here," he replied softly. "Let Maudie tend tae ye, noo there's a good lass." He placed her onto the chair, as delicately as if she were made of the finest china, and jerked his chin at Maudie who hurried forward and took Adrianna's limp hand between hers and began vigorously chafing it.

"Dinna just stand there, Andrew," she snapped at the steward who remained frozen just inside the doorway, goggling helplessly. "Bring me a cup o' water from the jug on the table, ye clunch!"

Andrew started, as if waking from a dream, and bustled to obey. Maudie coaxed Adrianna to take a few sips, and Leith was relieved to see some color returning to her cheeks.

"You are so good to me, Maudie," she murmured, reaching up to grasp the gnarled old hand and press the back of it to her cheek. "Thank you."

"Ach, lass," Maudie protested, "dinna say sae." And then her eyes brimmed with tears, and she said no more.

" 'S blood," breathed an awed voice.

Leith turned to see that Humphrey, one of the serving boys, had ventured closer to the bed and seen the mangled remains of the snake. "How did a wood snake come intae the castle, laird?" he asked incredulously. "I've never seen one but in the forest!"

"Well ye might inquire, lad," Leith said grimly. "I want everyone assembled in the great hall. *Noo.*"

As he watched the clan silently file downstairs, he clenched his fists, struggling to control his rage. Then he looked to Adrianna and spoke as gently as he could.

"Can ye come tae the great hall as well, lass?"

"Yes," Adrianna said, gallantly rising to her feet and

taking the arm Andrew offered. "I'm feeling better now. I'm sorry to be such a trouble to you all," she added.

At that Leith did frown. "Dinna talk such foolishness, lass," he said gruffly, then waited until she, Andrew, and Maudie, who was hovering solicitously, had left the bedchamber to follow them out.

If he had lingered in the hallway, Leith might have seen Fiona dart out from the solar and slip noiselessly inside Adrianna's room.

"An act has today been committed which shames us all." Leith paused and looked around the great hall which was filled to capacity with the members of the clan. "Whatever yer feelings toward . . . toward the Sassenach lass, ye had no right tae endanger her life."

Adrianna felt the burning wrath in Leith's glance where she sat, head bowed, hands clasped loosely in her lap. He had placed her in a chair next to him where he stood, facing the clan.

Adrianna had seen Leith angry before, but never had she witnessed such absolute fury as she did now. His body was as taut as a bowstring, and the muscular cords in his neck stood out sharply. It was obvious that he was keeping himself in check only through superhuman self-restraint.

His voice was heavy and deliberate as he said, "Come forward and declare yerself. If ye dinna, I will gae among ye, one by one, until I ha' found ye oot." His eyes glittered blackly. "Ye knoo me well enough tae believe that I will do it, too. Ye willna escape me. If it takes a hundred years, I will find ye oot!"

Adrianna shivered in the ghastly silence that followed, and saw out of the corner of her eye that Leith's dogs were cowering under the table. Someone coughed nervously, and a child whimpered piteously in his mother's arms.

Then:

"I did it."

There were shocked gasps from the crowd as Colin stepped forward, his craggy visage as hard as stone as he confronted Leith.

"I put the snake in the Sassenach's bed," he said without a trace of remorse in his voice.

Agitated whispers filled the room, and Maudie was heard to mutter bitterly, *"Clootie!"*

Devil.

As Leith gazed down on Colin, Adrianna could see that some of his terrible anger had drained away, to be replaced by a ponderous sorrow that made her ache for him. "Why?" he asked simply.

Now Colin flushed a little, and looked away. "We dinna want a foreigner among us," he answered roughly. "And surely no' the daughter o' him that killed our Hugh!"

"God's blood, man, leave off wi' that!" Leith said harshly. "If that's anyone's business, surely 'tis mine! I'll thank ye tae permit me tae tend tae my own affairs, and no' gae aboot putting snakes in people's beds because ye think ye're acting on my behalf!"

"I didna mean tae overstep my bounds," Colin said sullenly.

"Overstep yer bounds?" Leith echoed. "Colin, ye tried tae murder an innocent lass!" He closed his eyes for a moment, as if he could scarcely believe the enormity of it, then said quietly, "I thought ye were my friend."

At this Colin did look ashamed, and hang his great head. "I ha' wronged ye, laird," he said slowly, "and I'll take my punishment as ye deem fit."

"It's no' me that ye wronged most grievously," Leith replied sternly, "but Adrianna. And it seems tae me that a fitting punishment is one that's appropriate tae the crime."

A hand at her throat, Adrianna stared at Leith dumb-founded. Surely he didn't mean to condemn Colin to death?

"Ye wanted the Sassenach lass gone from here? Well then, Colin MacCrae, as o' this moment ye are banished," Leith said. "Ye must leave Inveraray and the Highlands, never tae return."

"Nay!" Colin howled, and dropped to his knees. "Nay, laird, kill me first, but dinna banish me from my home— from the clan!" he begged.

Leith looked at him with cold revulsion in his face. "What did ye expect, man?" he said savagely. "Death would be too good for ye."

"Nay!" Colin gibbered, clutching at Leith's boots. "Dinna do it, laird! Please!"

Adrianna had never thought to see the competent, self-possessed Colin so unmanned. She knew she should feel anger at what he had done, hatred even, but she could not find it in her. Instead she felt sorry for him, that he would have committed such a vile deed because of his prejudice, his long-held rancor that ate away at him like an acid.

She stood and went to Leith, and gently touched his arm. "I ask for your mercy," she said.

Leith's dark brows drew together. "What are ye saying, lass?"

"I am saying that I do not wish Colin banished because of me."

"He tried tae kill ye!" Leith said brutally. "Dinna ye realize that?"

Aware that every eye was upon her now, Adrianna nod-ded. "Yes. But if I can forgive him," she said, "will not you?" She came still closer to Leith and went on softly, gathering all her courage. "He loves this land, his people . . .

and you. I ... can understand such a love, and to be wrenched away from it would indeed be worse than death."

Leith stared at her, his expression unreadable, and Adrianna held her breath, feeling as if a swarm of butterflies had taken possession of her stomach. Finally he turned to Colin and said, "Do I ha' yer word that ye'll no' harm Adrianna?"

"Aye," Colin said fervently, hope shining feverishly in his eyes. "Oh, aye!"

Leith stared hard at Colin for a long moment. "Stand up, then, for ye are no longer banished," he said. "And ye ha' Adrianna tae thank for it."

Colin rose to his feet, went to Adrianna, and awkwardly bowed low before her. He straightened, towering over her, and said humbly, "I dinna deserve yer clemency, mistress, but I'm grateful tae ye for it, and am wholly in yer debt."

"There is no debt," she replied, "but perhaps ... perhaps we can begin to understand each other a little better now?"

He nodded soberly. "Aye, lass," he said. "Aye."

"Good enough," Leith said, and Adrianna turned to see that same inscrutable look on his face. "Ye can gae back tae the table and finish yer meal," he said to the clan, then added to Adrianna, "And if ye like ye may join them there."

She blinked in amazement, but had no chance to reply for he glanced at Andrew and ordered curtly, "Tell one o' the grooms tae gae up tae the lass' room and remove the snake, then ha' a maidservant clean the floor and change the linens."

"Aye, laird," Andrew said. "But aren't ye going tae ha' the rest o' yer meal as well?"

Leith was already halfway to the door. "Nay," he called over his shoulder. "I'm of a mind tae gae falconing. Dinna keep supper waiting for me, either."

And with that, he was gone. Adrianna gazed after him, a crushing disappointment assailing her. Here, then, had been their opportunity to sit together, to converse, to look into each other's eyes—

"Come, lass." It was Maudie taking her by the arm, and gently leading her to the table. "I'll find ye a place by me."

There was a compassionate note in her gravelly voice that made Adrianna wonder uncomfortably exactly how much those wise old eyes had seen.

In the end it had all been surprisingly easy. Fiona leaned back against the coach's tattered squabs and smiled to herself as she watched the landscape lurch past, oblivious to the discomfort of being crammed four to a seat.

How clever she had been to formulate another strategy in the event the wood snake did not find its target!

On that fateful day Fiona had left the table like the rest of the clan and gone hurrying up the stairs in Leith's wake to Adrianna's chamber. There she had witnessed the spectacular failure of her plan.

She should have guessed Colin would somehow manage to botch it.

But she knew what she had to do next.

It would take a good deal of effort on her part for it to come off successfully. But as the days had rolled by and she had watched how Adrianna was slowly ingratiating herself with the clan, slowly insinuating herself into Leith's affections—oh, yes, *she* saw how Leith looked at the other girl!—Fiona's enmity had steadily grown stronger, and deeper, and more intense, until now there was nothing she would not do to be free of the Sassenach girl.

And so, when everyone had gone back downstairs, she

had hidden in the solar and waited until the hallway was empty, then whisked herself into Adrianna's room.

A diligent search among the Sassenach's pitifully few possessions had yielded the crucial item she needed to ensure that her new scheme prospered.

The gold necklace with its simple little cross, which for some unknown reason Adrianna no longer wore.

The necklace was cold against her skin as she dropped it down her bodice, and for a moment Fiona had hesitated, feeling a flicker of superstitious unease.

Then her resolve had firmed again, and she crept back out into the hallway, crouching behind the stone banister until the unexpected rapprochement between the Sassenach and that ham-handed fool, Colin, was over, Leith had stalked out, and people were milling excitedly about the great hall. Amidst all the confusion she had slipped down the stairs, mingled casually, and taken her place again at the table with no one the wiser.

A few days later she had gone to Leith as he sat in the great hall holding audience, and asked that she be permitted to go to Dunadd to visit her grandmother.

Leith had looked at her sharply, and for a crazy, terrified moment Fiona was sure that he was peering into her soul and reading her true intentions. But then he had given his consent, and had even directed Andrew to see that she was presented with a few gold coins with which to purchase a gift for her grandmother. As if she *would* have bought something for that mean-spirited old hag, much less willingly gone to visit her where she was watched night and day and barely let out of the house!

Nonetheless the money was useful, for otherwise she would have had to steal it from Mistress Betty the cook or the kitchen maids. It was just enough to pay for her passage to Glasgow and back.

The sleeping woman next to her, a fat, overdressed dam-

sel of uncertain years, snored loudly as her head drooped
down onto Fiona's shoulder.

"Get off me, ye auld sow!" Fiona hissed, pushing her
away, and the woman started awake, straightening herself
with an indignant tug to her lavishly feathered bonnet.

"Well!" she said testily to no one in particular. "The
manners o' today's young people!"

Fiona made a rude face at her, settled back into her
corner, and closed her eyes. Soon, she thought dreamily,
soon the Sassenach would be gone from Inveraray forever,
and Leith would be hers again.

Fiona let her mind drift back to those winter evenings in
Leith's bed. She had never much cared for what occurred
between a man and a woman; it held little interest for her.
But she had discovered at an early age that her ripening
body gave her a great power over men, and that she found
very interesting indeed. She had made it her business to
learn what men liked and how to coax a few coins out of
them afterward. It was quite simple, actually; with most she
merely had to lie there and let them paw at her and pound
away until they collapsed on top of her, groaning like a
dying animal.

Leith, however, had actually made her *work* at seeming
to enjoy it, for he insisted on giving her pleasure in return.
It was very dull to have to writhe, and pant, and moan,
but she entertained herself by imagining what it would be
like as mistress of Inveraray.

She would have all the pretty dresses she wanted.

Beautiful jewelry, and fine shoes.

Maidservants to obey her every whim, and that snobbish
Mistress Betty in the kitchen would *have* to listen to her
then!

Oh, it would be glorious. She could hardly wait.

"Glasgow!" the driver bellowed from his perch outside
the coach, and pulled his tired team of horses into the

yard of the Raven's Nest Inn. Several coaches were already
there, either waiting for a change of horses or for dawdling
passengers to emerge from the inn. Drivers yelled and
cursed, postboys dashed wildly about, horses restlessly
stamped their hooves, and hungry-looking dogs sat patiently by the Raven's Nest front door, hoping for a scrap
tossed away by someone hurrying to his coach.

Despite the chaos Fiona looked calmly about her, as-
sessing the situation as she stood poised on the steps one
of the postboys had let down. Behind her one of her fellow
travelers—was it the fat woman with the ridiculous hat?—
huffed indignantly at the delay, but Fiona stood her
ground.

"Can I help ye, mistress?" a shy voice said, and Fiona
turned to see a tall young man, dressed in the sturdy
breeches and boots of a groom, standing next to the steps.

"Ach, ye're a strapping lad," she murmured appreciatively, and saw how his faintly pocked cheeks blushed vividly. "What's yer name?" she asked, smiling sweetly into
brown eyes opened childishly wide.

"Cedric," he stammered. "Cedric Murray."

"I'm Fiona Grant," she said, regally holding out her
hand. Awkwardly he grasped her fingers, then seemed not
to know what to do next.

"Ye may kiss it," she said demurely, and Cedric, his
blushes redoubling, did so, clumsily brushing his lips across
the back of her hand. His mouth was wet, his breath hot,
but Fiona determinedly ignored the unpleasant sensation.
He was a gawky lout, but he was strongly built, impression-
able, chivalrous. Not overburdened with intelligence. And
he had access to horses. Yes, he might just be the one she
needed . . .

"Well, 'tis lovely how ye're both getting along oot there,"
came an exasperated female voice from within the coach,
"but some o' us would like tae get oot o' this rattletrap!"

"I'd like nothing more than tae oblige ye, mistress," Fiona said in a sugary tone over her shoulder, "but it's just that there's sae much mud, and I've these new slippers . . ." She turned back to Cedric, smiling helplessly. "I wonder if ye would be sae kind as tae . . ." She hesitated with all the appearance of maidenly modesty. "Would ye mind *terribly* if I asked ye tae carry me tae the inn?"

Cedric gulped, his Adam's apple bobbing agitatedly. "Aye . . . I mean nay . . . I'd be glad tae, Mistress Fiona."

"How very gallant," Fiona sighed as he carefully lifted her into his nicely muscled arms. "Thank ye sae much. I knoo I must be such an awful burden . . ."

"Ye hardly weigh more than a feather," he denied, walking toward the two-story wood building that housed the Raven's Nest's taproom, private parlors, and bedchambers. "Why, I've carried sheep that weighed more than ye."

Fiona resisted the urge to roll her eyes and instead called out gaily to the driver, "Dinna forget my bandbox! It's sitting right behind ye on top—the red one!"

The driver glared at her, but said nothing as he went sullenly to obey.

Cedric came to the doorway of the inn, where, perhaps because he was unused to carrying pretty young ladies in his arms, he miscalculated his angle of approach and caught Fiona's ankles square against the wooden door frame.

"I'm sorry!" he gasped, twisting about and clumsily maneuvering her inside to the taproom.

Fiona's eyes were watering painfully but she managed to paste a complaisant expression on her face as Cedric lowered her to her feet. " 'Tis nothing," she lied.

"Ach, Mistress Fiona, I canna believe I used ye sae ill!" he said remorsefully. "What can I do? Can I bring ye a mug of ale, or wine? Would ye like tae sit down?" He was nearly jigging up and down in his mortification.

"I think there *might* be something ye can do tae make

it up tae me," Fiona said, tilting her head to one side and eyeing him soulfully.

"Aye! Aye! Anything!"

Casually she unknotted the light woolen shawl tied across her bosom and let the ends fall free. Cedric's eyes went swiftly to the expanse of bare flesh revealed above her bodice and he licked his upper lip; inwardly Fiona smiled. Aloud she said haltingly, "I was wondering . . . if perhaps . . . ye could take me in tae dine. I'm sae *very* hungry."

"Aye," Cedric breathed, his homely face lighting up. "Oh, aye, Mistress Fiona, I'd be honored tae! And I've plenty o' money, for we just got paid our wages today!" he added naively, holding out his arm.

"How nice," Fiona murmured sweetly, and allowed him to escort her into the taproom.

CHAPTER 10

It wasn't there.

Adrianna stared in consternation at the empty white handkerchief.

Her necklace was gone.

Quickly she looked on the other shelves of the cupboard and searched through the drawers, but did not find it.

Her brow furrowed, she went to sit on the chair by the fireplace. She was sure she had not misplaced the necklace; with loving care she had wrapped it in the handkerchief and placed it in a corner of the shelf next to her nightshift.

That left only one other possibility.

It had been stolen.

But by whom?

One of the maidservants? A washerwoman?

Adrianna bit her lip. It could have been anyone, really, for she was gone from her chamber for hours at a time and people freely came and went in the castle.

It was a painful blow to lose the necklace, for it was

precious to her, a tangible reminder of her years at Rosings, of her love for Mother Superior, and of the path she had chosen as an aspiring nun.

But to sound an alarm about its having gone missing . . . Adrianna shook her head at the thought of the resulting hue and cry, of the lengthy interrogations Andrew—or even Leith—might conduct.

She would not subject either the clan or herself to that.

Perhaps the necklace would show up again. It wasn't impossible.

And if she were to be honest with herself, there was a part of her that couldn't help but think the necklace's disappearance was fittingly symbolic in a way.

Had she been more steadfast in her resolution to become a nun, would, perhaps, the necklace still be there in her cupboard, nestled among the folds of the white handkerchief? Indeed, would it still be around her neck?

But the truth of it was, in recent weeks she had found herself wavering.

Uncertain.

Filled with longings no nun would ever harbor.

Her body came alive every time she even looked at Leith, and her soul yearned to meet his in the sweetest communion.

Adrianna sighed, stood, and began pacing the length of the room. Her opportunities to see Leith, however, had been few and far between in the fortnight since the incident with the snake. He had given her leave to join them at table for meals but was himself rarely there, preferring, Andrew confided worriedly, to visit the kitchen at odd hours and make a hasty repast of whatever Mistress Betty might have handy.

Adrianna stopped by the bed and absently ran her fingers down the smooth wood of the bedpost. If she could just talk with Leith, perhaps then she could learn why he went to such lengths to keep himself from her. Just talk, that was all she asked . . .

Oh, why was she attempting to fool herself? She wanted to do more than talk. She wanted him to take her in his strong arms, and kiss her until the room whirled giddily around her, and she forgot everything but the hard feel of him, the heady taste of him . . .

There was a hasty knock on her door and then Andrew had poked his head into the room.

"I'm sorry tae disturb ye, Mistress Adrianna," he said anxiously, "but young Hal Gunn has come tae the castle, asking for yer help. He says 'tis urgent."

"I don't remember meeting any Gunns," Adrianna said, frowning in an effort to recall the family. "But I shall be glad to do whatever I can. What is the problem?"

"The Gunns live near Glen Orchy, a two-hour ride from here," Andrew explained. "But they'd heard o' ye and yer healing skills, and that's why Hal rode here. Says his wife, Marjorie, has come tae bed wi' their first bairn but that she's been unable tae birth the child for over a day noo."

Adrianna frowned again, this time in concern. "That seems a long time. But Andrew—"

There was a clatter on the stairs and in the next moment a haggard young man had burst into the room, his gray eyes red-rimmed and framed underneath by purplish half-moons of fatigue.

"Ach, mistress, I apologize for intruding on ye in yer chamber," he said in a tense, shaky voice, "but I couldna wait downstairs another second cooling my heels. Please, can ye no' come right away tae help my poor Marjorie? She's in a very bad way and her mam says there's nothing more *she* can do."

He looked at Adrianna with such raw desperation that it nearly broke her heart to see it. "But—but I know so little about childbirth!'' she said apprehensively. ''I've never helped deliver a child.''

''We ha' no one else tae turn tae,'' Hal Gunn said quietly. ''I'm afraid she'll die, and the bairn as well.''

Adrianna saw the young man's thin shoulders sag in despair, and made up her mind. She looked at Andrew. ''Is there a cart I could borrow?'' she asked.

''Ye'll get a proper carriage, Mistress Adrianna,'' he said firmly, ''and it'll be waiting for ye in the bailey in ten minutes' time.''

Andrew hurried from the room and Adrianna quickly went to the cupboard to take out a sturdy wool cloak—this, an unlooked-for gift from Gracie Ogilvy—and the linen bag containing her supply of herbs.

''I'm ready,'' she told Hal Gunn, and together they made their way downstairs to the great hall where they encountered Maudie, to whom Adrianna explained her abrupt departure.

''Good luck tae ye,'' Maudie said, nodding kindly to the pale young man. ''I'll tell the laird where ye are. He'll wish tae knoo.''

Will he? Adrianna wanted to ask, but did not, only pausing to thank Maudie before she and Hal continued on their way to the courtyard, where, true to his word, Andrew had ordered a comfortable, well-sprung carriage for her immediate use. Ross Sinclair sat on the box outside, as did, to her surprise, Colin, holding the reins in his large, powerful hands.

''Ye dinna mind if I drive ye, Mistress Adrianna?'' Colin said gruffly.

''No, Colin, I'd be glad for it,'' Adrianna replied truthfully, knowing she could trust Colin's abilities handling the horses. She climbed inside the carriage, Hal jumped onto his mount, and then they were clattering off to Glen Orchy. Adrianna clung to the strap as the wheels jolted over rough-hewn roads, her mind worriedly racing ahead to the problems that awaited them.

Marjorie Gunn screamed and doubled over in pain, clutching her enormous belly. "Ye must let me lie down," she pleaded, her voice hoarse from crying out. "I want tae lie down!"

Adrianna held on tighter to the elbow she was gripping, and met the frightened eyes of Hal Gunn who supported his wife's other elbow. Together they managed to keep Marjorie upright, as they had been doing for the last three hours, intermittently coaxing her to take a few steps and to sip at the pungent valerian tea Adrianna had prepared. Hoping her voice didn't betray her own fear, Adrianna said encouragingly, "You must try, Marjorie. Just a little while longer."

Marjorie glanced wildly at Hal, who only nodded and said in a wobbly attempt at firmness, "Mistress Adrianna knoos what's best, love."

"Mam!" Marjorie screamed. "Tell them I want tae lie down! *Mam!*" Her voice rose to an agonized screech as another contraction gripped her.

"Mayhap she could rest on her pallet for just a wee spell, mistress?" Marjorie's mother, Janette, said timidly.

"No," Adrianna said with as much surety as she could muster. "She's not ready yet."

"Sassenach *bizzem! Fasheous taupie!*" Marjorie howled. "Will ye no' let me lie down, ye accursed witch?"

English whore. Troublesome, stupid young woman. At least, Adrianna thought wryly, she had learned enough of the Scottish tongue to translate.

Janette's hands fluttered helplessly in the air. "Oh, mistress, I'm very sorry, I'm sure she doesna knoo what she is saying—"

"I do! I *do* knoo what I'm saying!" Marjorie cried. "I hate ye all!" She twisted her head to glare at her husband. "And most of all, I hate *ye!*"

Hal was aghast. "Ach, lass," he murmured distressfully, "why would ye say such a thing?"

"Because ye're the one that got me intae this wretched predicament, ye bastard! Oooh!" She clutched at her belly again, and when the contraction had passed Adrianna squeezed her elbow and said:

"Walk, Marjorie, walk!"

"I canna!" she wailed. "I'm tired, sae very tired, it's been a night and a day since my pains began. I canna take much more o' this!"

"Walk, Marjorie!" Adrianna snapped, and jerked her forward. To her surprise the other girl, hardly older than herself, obeyed with a whimper. Together she and Hal urged her to slowly hobble around the interior of the small cottage.

A scene of hysterical anguish had greeted Adrianna upon her arrival a few hours ago. Marjorie had been thrashing about on her pallet, her long, lank brown hair plastered to her head and her flushed cheeks stained with tears. Her mother was kneeling next to her with tears streaming down *her* face, clucking ineffectually and trying without success to catch hold of Marjorie's flailing hands.

From what little she knew of stalled labor, Adrianna realized that the most she could hope to do would be to relax the young woman with a strong infusion of valerian root and to promote the babe's journey down the womb by keeping Marjorie upright.

Now, as she and Hal led the whimpering, sobbing Marjorie around the room, Adrianna prayed she had been correct. And half an hour later she was rewarded by hearing Marjorie scream, "Let me down! I've got tae push!"

Quickly Adrianna nodded to Hal and as they lowered

her onto her pallet Adrianna said to Janette, "Bring me clean towels, please, and any spare linens you have!"

"Aye, mistress!" While the older woman hurriedly complied with her request Adrianna knelt by Marjorie's feet. She heard a choked noise and looked up to see Hal standing paralyzed next to the pallet.

"Is—is the bairn coming?" he stammered.

"Yes," Adrianna said with a confidence she did not feel.

"Shouldn't I gae and wait wi' yer men ootside?" he asked, a little wildly.

Adrianna had heard that men rarely stayed by their wives during the actual birthing, and under other circumstances she might have urged him to step outside where Colin and Ross sat, but she could hardly feel that the fluttery, irresolute Janette was an able assistant.

"No!" Adrianna said, more forcefully than she had intended. Then, softening her tone, she added, "I need you to hold Marjorie's hand, Hal! Please!"

Just then Marjorie screamed again. "Hal!" she cried out pitifully. "Dinna leave me, Hal!"

Without another word Hal dropped down next to his wife and gripped her outstretched fingers. "I've got tae push, mistress!" she babbled. "I canna stop it, I *must!*"

"Don't try to stop!" Adrianna urged her. "Do as your body tells you!"

"It tells—me—tae—push!" Marjorie's face was red with exertion and she held on so tightly to Hal's fingers Adrianna was afraid she would crush them. But Hal, bless him, said nothing, only stroked her damp, matted hair from her forehead with his free hand.

"Here, mistress." Tremblingly Janette held out a bundle of towels and linens and Adrianna gratefully accepted them.

A few minutes later Marjorie spread her knees wide, and cried, "Oh, merciful God! Oh! Oh! *Oh!*"

A final, monumental push, and then the babe slid easily from Marjorie's body into the soft linen towel Adrianna cradled. " 'Tis a boy!" she called out, joy flooding through her, and held up the tiny, wriggling body so that Marjorie could view her son for the first time.

The next hour passed in a blur. Young Adrian Gunn, who was apparently none the worse for wear after his arduous passage into the world, needed to suckle at his mother's breast, and then, when his cord had stopped pulsing, it was cut; Marjorie was gently cleaned with damp cloths and a comfrey-leaf compress applied to her tender parts, while she apologized profusely if she had chanced to say anything amiss while the pain had been so bad. Janette served ale and oat cakes and took out a tray to Colin and Ross, who were offering their congratulations to the proud new father. Adrianna smiled to herself as even taciturn Ross was heard to mutter a few words. Then Janette returned inside, smiled apologetically at Adrianna, sank down onto the pallet next to her sleeping daughter, and promptly fell fast asleep as well.

Poor exhausted things, Adrianna thought sympathetically as she sat before the fire, holding the slumbering babe in her arms. She was tired herself, but wouldn't have missed this chance to cuddle baby Adrian for a few quiet minutes before his mother or grandmother woke and claimed him.

She gazed in awed wonder at the button nose, the dark downy hair, the tiny, perfect fingers as he lay utterly relaxed in his linen swaddling cloth. How beautiful he was, this contented little scrap of humanity! And to think that *she* had played some small part in his being here! It humbled her all over again that Marjorie and Hal had insisted on naming the baby after her. *For if it hadna been for ye, Mistress Adrianna,* Hal had said, his gray eyes bright with tears, *well, I dinna like tae think what might ha' happened.*

There had been such radiance on both Hal and Marjorie's faces as they'd watched their son suckling, little fingers splayed on Marjorie's breast, that Adrianna had nearly turned away, feeling that she was witnessing a scene too primal, too intimate for outsiders.

Adrian gave a soft sigh in his sleep and Adrianna gently stroked his cheek with the tip of her forefinger. Now, along with the exhilaration and the satisfaction she had been feeling, came another emotion, dark, sharp, and cruel . . .

Envy.

What would it be like to hold Leith's son like this, to see his fiery dark eyes reproduced in a child of their own making? To look up at Leith and perceive in his face that same radiance? That same . . . love?

Adrianna felt her heart thump in slow, heavy strokes. Just a few short months ago she had been sure that her life's work was that of a nun, safely cloistered within the convent all her days. But now she could think of no greater happiness than to love and be loved, to be a wife, a mother, a part of the greater world with its joys and sorrows large and small.

And at the center of that world was Leith Campbell.

If only . . .

Pain clawed at her heart.

If only Leith loved her.

Adrianna stared, unseeing now, into the serene little face of the babe she cradled at her breast. Tears prickled at the back of her eyes; she was just reaching up a hand to dab at them when there was a gentle knock on the door. "Come in," she called softly, and the door swung open to admit a stranger.

He was of medium height and build, with well-proportioned, fine-boned features, and reddish-blond hair which was cropped short. Unlike the soldierly breeches and shirts Leith favored, or the traditional kilts many others of the clan wore, this man was garbed in the more formal doublet and trunkhose. The cut of his doublet was simple, and rather severe, without padding or decorative slashes, and was of an unrelieved black. Warm blue eyes surveyed her with a mixture of friendliness, curiosity, and admiration. "Ye must be Adrianna, the English lass sae skilled in healing," he said in a pleasant, well-modulated voice.

"I am Adrianna," she acknowledged. "And you are . . . ?"

He smiled and swept off his flat black cap. "Generally I've better manners, but 'tis no' often one sees sae lovely a representation o' the Madonna and child. I'm Ian Martin, at yer service."

"Good even," she responded politely, wondering why he was here at the Gunns' cottage. Her brows creased. Of course, Hal would not have let the man enter unless he trusted him, but still . . .

"Let me allay yer fears," Ian Martin said with a charming smile. "I was in Glen Orchy tae visit another family close by, and heard aboot Marjorie's troubles. I came here directly tae see if there was anything I could do, but I'm happy tae perceive that my services are obviously no' needed."

"Your services?" Adrianna repeated, confused. "You're a physic?"

His smile widened. "Nay, Mistress Adrianna, I'm a minister. O' the Presbyterian persuasion."

"I see," she said, her brow clearing.

"Ye are resting at Inveraray, I understand?"

It was a delicately phrased question. Adrianna merely said "Yes," unwilling to go into further details concerning the intricacies of her situation there.

"I knoo Inveraray well, for I was minister there some time ago."

Adrianna regarded him with greater interest. This must

be the handsome cleric Fiona Grant had spoken of! Perhaps he could tell her more about Leith, and his brother Hugh, and, indeed, all the clan Campbell ...

"Won't you sit down, and join me by the fire?" she asked.

He gave her a keen glance. "Ye dinna mind conversing wi' someone of a different faith, and a minister at that?"

"Do we not believe in the same God?" she returned simply. "That seems to me sufficient common ground."

"Intelligence *and* beauty," he sighed as he took a seat next to hers. "Ye far exceed even yer reputation, ye knoo."

Adrianna ignored the flowery praise. "I wonder, Master Martin, if you might enlighten me about a few things," she began, but was interrupted by the sounds from outside of a horse arriving. There was a low rumble of male voices, and then the door opened and Leith came inside the little cottage, his great height requiring him to duck his head to avoid the beams overhead.

He paused just past the threshold, his gaze moving swiftly from the sleeping figures on the pallet to herself and Ian Martin where they sat before the fire.

"Leith," she said a little breathlessly, afraid she was betraying too openly her pleasure at seeing him. "What are you doing here?"

He smiled humorlessly, his eyes hardening. " 'Tis late, and I was concerned aboot ye."

At Leith's words a warm glow shimmered inside Adrianna. He was concerned about her, worried about her. He had come all this way from Inveraray. Could it be ... that he cared for her? But then his next utterance shattered those rosy hopes, for he went on grimly:

"But I can see that my auld friend Ian Martin is taking good care o' ye."

"Master Martin arrived but minutes before yourself,"

she informed him quickly, feeling flustered yet not knowing quite why.

"Oh, aye?" Leith crossed his arms across his broad chest.

Ian Martin had risen to his feet and now he nodded affably at Leith. "Well met, Leith. It's been quite a while, has it no'?"

"Aye," Leith said, his tone suggesting that he would have been perfectly happy to let further time elapse between encounters. "Yer affair here has prospered, I trust?" he asked Adrianna, glancing at the swathed little bundle she cradled.

"Yes," she answered, blushing as she recalled her earlier fantasy of holding Leith's babe in her arms. "Both mother and son are doing very well indeed."

" 'Tis glad I am," he returned, more gently. "Can ye leave them safely? Are ye ready tae gae home noo?"

Home. Did he realize what he was saying to her? A tremulous smile curved her lips and she nodded.

Just then Marjorie stirred, and woke. She peered incuriously at the two men in her cottage then smiled sleepily at Adrianna who stood, went to her pallet, and, kneeling, carefully placed little Adrian in the warm curve of his mother's arm.

"He's beautiful," Adrianna whispered.

"Aye," Marjorie agreed, staring reverently down at her son. "He is that."

"I'm returning to Inveraray now," Adrianna told her. "If there's anything you or Adrian need, please don't hesitate to send for me."

"Mam will knoo what tae do noo," said Marjorie. "She loves bairns, it's during the birthing that she goes all tae pieces. She told me she would, too," she added reminiscently. Adrianna started to rise but Marjorie caught at her hand. "Thank ye, Mistress Adrianna," she said softly, her heart in her eyes.

"You're welcome," Adrianna whispered back. "I'll send Hal in to you as I go." Marjorie smiled and released her hand, and Adrianna got to her feet. Turning, she saw Leith watching her, his dark eyes hard and inscrutable, and wearily she picked up her cloak and her bag of herbs and went to him. "I'll sleep in the carriage, I think," she said.

"Do that," he answered. Then he took her hand in his and forcibly pulled her from the cottage, leaving her no time at all in which to bid Master Martin a civil farewell.

Leith watched Adrianna from the corner of his eye as together they climbed the stairs up from the great hall. It was late; the castle slept, and their feet whispered softly on the wide stone steps as they ascended. He wasn't tired, but wondered if she was after her ordeal. All throughout the journey to Inveraray, as he had ridden Thunder alongside her carriage, powerful emotions had roiled inside him and now he was as wide awake as if he would never sleep again.

He had been greatly relieved upon his arrival at the Gunns' to find that Colin and Ross had accompanied Adrianna; after all, Glen Orchy was not part of his domain. But then he had gone inside the cottage and come upon a scene which caused his gut to wrench.

There was Adrianna, her lovely features framed by soft firelight; he had been struck by beautiful, how natural she looked, embracing the Gunns' wee bairn with such sweet tenderness . . . and then he had seen Ian Martin seated comfortably at her side, looking for all the world as if he meant to stay there forever. It was a cozy, intimate tableau . . . of what could easily have been mistaken for a wife, a husband, and their child.

Jealousy had raged through him.

And a stinging sorrow, too, for seeing Ian Martin reopened old wounds.

Then, like some uncivilized churl, he had dragged her from the cottage and practically shoved her into the carriage.

He and Adrianna had reached the landing to the second floor, and now both paused. She gazed up at him, her cornflower-blue eyes soft, and tentatively reached out a hand to touch his sleeve.

"Thank you for your escort," she whispered. "I'll bid you good night."

As she began to turn away he came to a sudden decision. "Wait," he said, and when she faced him again he went on: "Will ye come tae my chamber? I've something tae give ye."

"Yes," she answered without hesitation, her expression curious but unafraid.

"Unless ye're fatigued, and would prefer tae retire for the night?" he added, belatedly.

"No. I am refreshed from my nap in the carriage," she assured him, and began walking with him into the east wing where his bedchamber lay. Once there he lit the candles and banked the fire, then went to his desk and pulled open a drawer. He looked to her where she stood near the fireplace. "Ye spent nearly a fortnight in this room, didn't ye?" he said. "Any other woman would ha' gone through every inch o' this desk, but no' ye."

"You're right, I did not," she replied, and went on with a gleam of humor, "But don't think I didn't *consider* it."

No, not his noble, forthright Adrianna! An appreciative half-smile curved Leith's mouth, then faded as he grasped a small object from within the drawer. He took a ragged breath and carried it to her.

"Here," he said, a little roughly. "This belongs tae ye."

"What . . . ?" she breathed, staring at the linked miniatures in her hand. "Why, I remember my father showing this to me when I was a little girl. He told me he was so proud of the likeness." Her eyes rose wonderingly to his. "How did you . . . ?"

"I stole it," he admitted, shame coursing hotly through him. "The night I took ye from yer father's house."

"I see," she murmured.

"I took something else as well," Leith said. He returned to his desk and removed Hugh's Book of Hours from the same drawer, then brought it to Adrianna.

"It is very handsome, and so well-worn I can tell it is precious to its owner." She looked up at him searchingly. "Whose is it?"

"Hugh's," he said with difficulty. "My younger brother. It belonged to him."

Those blue eyes were fixed intently on his; her lovely heart-shaped face was somber. "Will you tell me about him? And the role my father played in his death?"

"Aye." He had to force the word out.

Adrianna went to sit on one of the two high-backed chairs placed around the cherrywood table, and after a brief struggle within himself Leith joined her, seating himself on the second chair.

"Almost eight years ago my brother Hugh went tae fight for the cause o' Queen Mary in Edinburgh," Leith began haltingly, then went on to tell her of the siege, the battle that followed, and Hugh's death and the desecration of his corpse by Adrianna's father Lord Robert.

Leith paused, but she said nothing, keeping her gaze focused steadfastly on his face, and he continued. He described his long wait for vengeance, his journey to Carlisle, his discovery of the miniatures of Adrianna and her mother and, finally, of Hugh's Bible.

And then he stopped. What came next was Adrianna's entrance into the library, and his own abduction of her.

If he were to admit his iniquity in so doing, next would come the inevitable revelation of his intention to send her back to England.

He must say the words. He *must*. Leith closed his eyes for a moment, feeling as if he was about to propel himself from a cliff into a deep, black abyss, then looked at Adrianna and opened his mouth.

Only she interposed. And said quietly, "I can understand why you would hate me."

"Hate ye?" he echoed, stunned. "I dinna hate ye, Adrianna."

"You hated my father," she pointed out, "and with good reason. I am of his blood."

Leith shook his head. He might have felt that way at one time, but no longer. No, now he felt . . . very differently. "Doesna the Bible say no' tae visit the sins o' the father upon the child?"

"That is your mind speaking," she said gently. "Your heart may differ, and if that is the case, I could not blame you. I will not attempt to defend my father's behavior; it was atrocious." Her expression was grave, distant. "How is it that a person can be such a mixture of good and evil? He was a kind father in his way, Leith, and so very devoted to my mother. But . . . I remember he had several glass cabinets in his library, filled with what I thought were curiosities collected on his travels." Her mouth trembled. "Of course a child would not know the truth. But I am not a child now, and I understand; those curiosities, of course, were the heinous spoils of war." Suddenly her face crumpled and she buried it in her hands, her shoulders shaking. "How *could* he?" she whispered.

Leith's heart ached for her. God's blood, but he wanted to hold her, and comfort her, and kiss her sorrow away . . . but the right was not his to claim. "Ach, lass," he whispered raggedly. "I'm sorry."

She raised her head then, tears glistening on her cheeks. "I loved him, Leith," she said softly.

"I knoo ye did, lass," he answered. "And I'm sure he loved ye too."

She smiled a little. "Thank you for saying so."

"I say it because I believe it tae be true." He stood and went to the cupboard where he extracted a handkerchief from one of the drawers, then returned to the table, gave her the handkerchief, and sat down again.

"Thank you," she said again, wiping her face. Then she squared her shoulders and looked up at him resolutely. "Please, you must tell me the rest. What happened after Hugh died? Why has your chapel gone unused for so long?"

All the terrible desolation, the anger and despair, came rushing back, threatening to sweep him away into an ocean of infinite darkness. Leith stared blindly down at the delicate cherry inlay of the tabletop. "I couldna endure it when Hugh was gone from us," he said slowly. "He was sae young, sae full o' life. Why was I here, when Hugh was no'?"

"It is the agony of those who are left behind," Adrianna said softly. "Sometimes those who survive wish that they had died, too."

Leith only nodded. He had felt the guilt all too keenly.

"But you must believe," she went on earnestly, "that Hugh would not wish his fate upon you. I am convinced he would want you to go on with your life, to live your days fully and with joy."

Fully and with joy, Leith thought. *Is it true, Hugh, sweet braithair? Oh, God, could it be true?*

He took a deep breath. "Ian Martin," he said, "was full o' easy words o' condolence, full o' *blether* aboot God's will and how Hugh was in a better place noo. Finally I could stand it no longer and I sent the jackanapes away."

"He must have been quite new to the ministry seven years ago," Adrianna mused. "Perhaps he did not yet know that grief can take many forms, and that for some, compassionate silence can be more healing than an hour's homily, no matter how well intended."

" 'Tis true," Leith agreed soberly, moved. Had he ever known a lass with such wisdom, such empathy . . . such beauty? He added, in an abrupt change of subject, "Perhaps ye didna knoo that our Presbyterian ministers are allowed tae marry, unlike the priests o' yer faith?"

Adrianna's brows crinkled. "No, I didn't know," she said blankly.

"I thought ye might wish tae," he said carefully, "having met Ian Martin."

"Ah! Has he formed an attachment then?" she asked. "Would I have met his intended?"

She spoke with such casual curiosity that Leith felt his heart lift. "Aye," he replied, hardly realizing what he was saying, so intense was his relief. "Nay . . . That is, I dinna knoo."

She looked a trifle confused at his disjointed response, then said tentatively, "About the chapel . . ."

"Aye?" Merciful God, she was lovely. So desirable. And his bed was so tantalizingly close—

"Leith, are you listening to me?" she asked, and he blinked.

"Aye, lass," he said sheepishly. "The chapel."

"Andrew and I have been discussing the plans for May Day festivities next week," she told him. "We agreed that the castle has been long overdue for a proper cleaning, and he seemed pleased when I offered to help organize the servants' efforts while he concentrated on the preparations for the feast."

Leith hid a smile. He could well imagine the harassed Andrew's delight in accepting Adrianna's offer.

"Might we include the chapel as part of the cleaning? I would understand," she added quickly, "if you prefer to leave it untouched."

"Nay, lass, do as ye will," Leith said, thoughtfully.

May Day—the first of May—was a week away.

A week was a long time.

Seven days, seven nights . . .

Leith looked at Adrianna, and smiled now.

He would give himself this week with her, and when the festivities were over, he would tell her what he knew he must. Until then, he promised himself, he would try to live—how had she put it?—yes, fully . . . and with joy.

CHAPTER 11

Giles, the Earl of Westbrook, stared frowningly into the hearth of the great hall, where a small fire smoldered damply. He was wearing a padded wool jerkin over his doublet, and a pair of thick wool stockings underneath his trunkhose, yet he was still cold. And it was nearly May, not the middle of winter!

"Damned drafty excuse for a castle," he muttered viciously under his breath. "Blasted lump of stone!" He shivered in his chair and shouted at the top of his lungs, "Nicholas!"

Moments later a gaunt, balding manservant came scurrying into the great hall. "My—my lord?"

Giles scowled. "Who the devil are you?"

The manservant bowed deeply, and stammered, "I'm—I'm Bernard, my lord. I'm new."

"Who had the blasted temerity to hire you without my permission?"

"N-Nicholas, my lord."

"Indeed?" Giles eyed him with distaste. "And where *is* Nicholas?"

Bernard gave a nervous smile, revealing small, sparse teeth. "Gone, my lord."

"What do you mean, he's gone?" Giles echoed sharply. "He's left to gather more firewood, you mean?"

"Nay, my lord," Bernard replied uneasily. "He's left Crestfield. Said he'd been a full five months without wages and was off to find a better position elsewhere."

"The whoreson!" Giles shouted, jumping to his feet. "Impudent, ungrateful bastard!" He glared at the cowering Bernard. "And why in the name of God did you come here, *knowing* Nicholas hadn't been paid?"

Apologetically Bernard shrugged his bony shoulders. "I—I needed work very badly, my lord," he whispered. "I *hope* you'll pay me! Sometime!"

"A trusting soul, aren't you? How charming!" Giles sneered. "Well, welcome to Crestfield, you fool! Now send Arthur to me!"

Bernard only shook his head helplessly.

"You don't mean to tell me . . ." Giles advanced upon the servant and gripped the shoulders of his shabby doublet. "Has Arthur left as well?"

"Aye, my lord," Bernard whispered miserably. *"And* the cook, the scullery maid, the grooms, and—"

Giles shook him wrathfully. "Who's remaining, you dirty cur? Besides your own wretched, pathetic self?"

"J-jack the steward, my lord, and—and young Peter the gardener," Bernard stammered. Then he brightened, remembering. "And *three* of your lordship's guards!"

Giles released Bernard, shoving him away with a sneer. "How very fortunate for me," he said caustically. "Then I suppose no one's been to the forest to gather more wood for the fire?"

"Nay, my lord," the servant answered apprehensively.

"I been in the storeroom to see if there's something I might prepare for your lordship's supper tonight."

Giles threw himself back into his chair. "Don't leave me in suspense, man," he said with brutal sarcasm. "Is there anything there?"

Bernard cringed. "I—I found a little salted beef, my lord, and some turnips, and thought I would make a pottage."

"A pottage," Giles repeated, his arched brows drawing together ominously.

" 'Tis—'tis a hearty meal, my lord," Bernard offered, wringing his hands anxiously. "One bowl, and you won't be hungry again for ages!"

"Forget the bloody pottage," snapped Giles, "and bring me another bottle of Madeira."

"We—we haven't any more, my lord," Bernard whispered.

Giles stared incredulously at the unhappy servant, clenching his thin fingers on the arms of the chair. That it should come to this! He, the Earl of Westbrook, reduced to such straits! By all the saints, it was not to be borne!

"Ale then!" he said harshly. "I'll take ale!"

Bernard looked relieved. "Aye, my lord," he said. "Right away!" He turned and started to hurry toward the kitchen, when there came upon the door to the great hall a brisk knocking.

"Go see who it is, knave!" Giles bellowed, and Bernard quickly changed his course, tugging open the door to reveal Sir Roger Penroy.

"Good day, Giles," Sir Roger said, ambling into the great hall. "I'm glad to find you at home." There was an affable smile on his round, coarse-featured face but his small mud-colored eyes were cold.

Giles rose hastily to his feet. "Good day to you, Sir Roger," he said, swallowing a sudden lump in his throat as he came forward to meet the older man. "What a delightful surprise. May I offer you some refreshment?"

"A glass of wine, perhaps," Sir Roger said over his shoulder as he strolled past Giles and lowered his heavy bulk into the chair in which Giles had been sitting.

The chair, Giles noted furiously, which was closest to the fire. Aloud he said, "I find ale to be more refreshing this time of day, do not you? Bernard," he smoothly directed the servant, "two tankards of ale, if you please."

"Aye, my lord." Bernard scuttled from the room, and Giles turned to find Sir Roger gazing at him shrewdly with those little piglike eyes.

"All to pieces, are you, my young friend?"

"Not at all," Giles denied loftily. "I've been imbibing a bit too freely of late, and thought it time to alter my habits slightly."

Plump lips smiled. "You can give up the pretense, Giles. Half your servants have come to me, begging for employment and carrying tales of your . . . ah, impecunious circumstances."

Giles shrugged, flushing painfully. "A temporary situation, Sir Roger, I assure you. How are your three charming daughters? I trust they are in good health?"

"They're as fat and ugly as ever," Sir Roger answered coolly, "and will be until the day they die. Let's not play games with each other, Giles. I've come for the money you owe me."

Bernard returned at that moment with the two tankards of ale, one of which he presented to Sir Roger with a servile bow. The other he gave to Giles, sidling close to whisper to his master, "That's all we have, my lord!"

"Thank you, Bernard," Giles said loudly.

Bernard bowed again and quickly retreated from the room.

In the silence that followed, Giles sipped at his ale, his

mind working frantically. Sir Roger, in expectation of marrying Adrianna, had loaned Giles the substantial sum of two hundred pounds. And he in turn had promptly placed a lavish order with the best tailor in Carlisle, putting the money to good use refurbishing his sadly depleted wardrobe. For an earl—especially one newly assuming the dignities of the title—had to look the part, didn't he? And he'd had no choice but to pay the man in advance, for hadn't he impertinently insisted, damn his scurrilous hide, that he wouldn't do the work without it?

But then his faithless sister had disappeared in the middle of the night, whether she'd been stolen away or fled willingly Giles hadn't a clue. All he knew was that he had struck a bargain with Sir Roger and that with Adrianna gone he was no longer able to abide by its terms.

His eyes narrowed, Giles glanced over at Sir Roger, who sat placidly drinking his ale and gazing blandly into the sputtering fire.

Giles was not deceived by Sir Roger's mild demeanor. The man was ruthless in conducting his affairs, and Giles had no doubt that should he be unable to repay Sir Roger, he would shortly find himself rotting in debtors' prison.

Repressing a shudder, Giles forced an amiable smile to his lips. "I'm—I'm certain we can reach an agreement, Sir Roger, that would be mutually satisfactory."

Sir Roger swiveled his head to meet Giles' eyes. "I'm sure we can," he said, and Giles felt his skin crawl at the sinister undertone in that flat, pleasant voice. It was almost with relief that he heard the shouting of his men outside and the sounds of a violent scuffle.

"If you'll excuse me, Sir Roger, I'll just go see what the problem is," he said, putting down his tankard and moving with alacrity toward the door, but was saved the effort when the door burst open and two of his guards dragged in a tall young man who struggled fiercely in their grasp.

"Look what we found, my lord!" Percy said gleefully. "A damned Scotsman, creeping round the castle!"

"I wasna creeping, ye bastard!" the young man shouted, and was promptly thumped by the other guard, Fulk.

"Take him to the authorities in Carlisle," Giles said indifferently. "They'll hang him, I suppose, for trespassing."

"Aye, my lord!" Percy said, and together he and Fulk began to wrest their prisoner back toward the door.

"Wait!" the young Scotsman cried. "I've an important message for the Earl o' Westbrook! It concerns his sister!"

Giles paused and swung around again, suddenly intent. "Now you begin to interest me extraordinarily," he said. "I am the Earl of Westbrook. Who are you, and what message do you bring me?"

"I'm Cedric Murray, o' Glasgow," the Scotsman said, adding defiantly, "And I'll tell ye no more until yer *sumphs* release me!"

Fulk cuffed him again, but Cedric Murray made no sound as he absorbed the blow, his pale lips tightly compressed.

"Very impressive," Giles commented. There was a pregnant silence, and when Cedric remained stubbornly mute Giles impatiently said: "Oh, let him go, you fools, and watch him closely." His men sullenly obeyed and Giles crossed his arms across the padded wool of his jerkin. "Well, Master Murray?"

"I've information aboot yer sister, Arianna," Cedric said. Giles frowned. "Adrianna?"

"Aye, that's it," Cedric confirmed. "She's at Inveraray. I was told ye'd like tae knoo."

"I'm unfamiliar with your godforsaken country," Giles said shortly. "Where the devil is Inveraray? And who told you I'd wish to know this?"

"Inveraray's in the Highlands, a journey o' some three

days from here," answered Cedric. " 'Tis the home o' some laird, I canna remember his name."

Giles pictured some low Scottish noble, barely able to speak the Queen's English, wearing animal furs and a beard that hung down to his knees. "And your informant?" he asked.

"Informant?" Cedric echoed, his brow furrowing. "Ach, ye must mean Mistress Fiona."

Giles saw the blush creep across the Scotsman's ill-favored face and instantly divined the cause. "Who, pray tell, is this Mistress Fiona?"

"Fiona Grant is the bonniest lass in the world, and sae sweet-tempered and kind," Cedric replied, smiling dreamily. "She said she'd come back tae Glasgow as soon as ever she could."

"Yes, yes," Giles said, trying not to gnash his teeth in frustration, "but who is she? How did she come to you with a message for me?"

At Giles' curt questions Cedric seemed to recall his surroundings, for he blinked and said, "Yer sister is held captive at Inveraray, and since Mistress Fiona is as close tae her as a sister, and sae worried for her, she traveled tae Glasgow tae try and find a way tae get a message tae ye. Sae that ye could come after yer sister tae rescue her, dinna ye see?" He stood a little straighter, puffing out his chest. "I was sae much affected by what she'd done for yer sister that 'twas the least I could do tae help poor Mistress Fiona in her distress! And oh," he added, remembering, "Mistress Fiona said that ye'd be sae relieved tae hear o' yer sister's whereaboots that ye'd be glad tae offer her a wee bit o'—ach, how did she term it?—oh, aye, recompense, when ye retrieve Mistress Arianna—I mean, Adrianna—at Inveraray."

So it's like that, is it? Giles thought. He was plainly being asked for payment for services rendered. This Fiona Grant, whatever her motives in alerting him, was obviously a woman of some intelligence and subtlety, for she had chosen her messenger well, the unfortunate dolt. Then Giles stiffened as a suspicious thought occurred to him. "Your tale is a fascinating one," he said slowly to Cedric, "but what assurances do I have that it's true?"

"Ye doubt my word?" The young man started forward angrily, only to be quickly restrained by the guards. "Isna the word of a Scotsman enough for ye?"

"No," Giles drawled, and waited.

After a few minutes of futile struggle, Cedric subsided and at Giles' nod, Fulk and Percy released him. "I ha' a necklace for ye," Cedric said, almost meekly, reaching into the pocket of his muddied breeches. He withdrew from it a golden necklace which he held out to Giles.

The cross and its delicate chain were cool in Giles' palm as he stared triumphantly down at them. Sure enough, it was Adrianna's necklace! For the first time since Sir Roger had intruded with his unwelcome presence, Giles felt hope rising within him.

"I am satisfied that what you say is correct, Master Murray," he said, assuming an expression of deep concern, "and that my poor, sweet sister is being held a captive. But how am I to wrest her from the stronghold where she lies?"

"Oh, Mistress Fiona says she's no' exactly a captive," Cedric answered vaguely. "She's no' kept in a room bound wi' rope, or anything like that."

"I see," Giles said thoughtfully, then went on, more to himself than to anyone present in the room, "But how am I, an Englishman, going to send a party of my men deep into Scotland?"

"I'm not going!" Fulk declared stoutly.

"Aye," Percy put in, "try to make us and you'll find

yourself in need of new guardsmen!" He added as an afterthought, "My lord!"

Giles barely heard them, for he was immersed in contemplation of the problem before him. If he could just get Adrianna back, all his difficulties would be solved! Surely it was worth a try . . . He stroked his chin for some few minutes, then abruptly he turned to Sir Roger, who still sat in his chair, observing the proceedings with his muddy little piglike eyes.

But, Giles saw with mounting excitement, Sir Roger was leaning forward now, and on his round, fleshy face was a distinct look of eagerness.

"Have you a plan?" Sir Roger asked him.

"Yes," Giles lied smoothly. "I've no doubt it will succeed, Sir Roger, and we'll soon have our sweet Adrianna home again where she belongs."

Sir Roger rubbed his plump hands together with lascivious languor. "A gladsome thought," he said, then voluptuously closed his eyes as if picturing a highly agreeable scene. "I've wanted that wench for as long as I can remember." His voice was laced with lustful anticipation and almost dreamy. "She was but a child when my second wife died, and even then I offered to relieve your father of his pecuniary cares by affiancing myself to Adrianna. But he refused, fobbing me off with the transparent lie that 'twas the border raids that so unnerved him he must needs pack that pretty little piece off to a godforsaken nunnery. The old fool!" Sir Roger's ponderous eyelids lifted and he bared his decaying teeth in a smile. "I was delighted to find upon your ascension to the title, my dear Giles, that you were open to reason."

"Indeed, I believe I am generally accounted to be a most reasonable man," Giles concurred. "Now, there's but one small impediment, Sir Roger, and it's something that you can easily pluck from our path . . ."

"How much will you need?" the older man said without hesitation, and inwardly Giles rejoiced. He would think of something. He *had* to.

"A hundred pounds should suffice," he returned casually, already planning to send Bernard into Carlisle for more Madeira and wine.

"Done."

Now Giles permitted himself a wide smile. "Yes, soon we'll have Adrianna back with us," he said, "and you'll be busying yourselves with wedding plans."

"No, we won't," Sir Roger said calmly, and Giles stared at him, his smile wiped from his face.

"What—what do you mean?" He reached for the tankard he'd placed on a small, scarred side table and gulped at his now-tepid ale.

Sir Roger laboriously pushed himself up from his chair. "I mean that I'll have her," he replied. "But I won't marry her, now that she's been among those filthy Scotsmen and engaged in God only knows what kind of degenerate practices."

"Ye bastard!" Cedric Murray shouted, lunging violently for Sir Roger, only to be once again subdued by Percy and Fulk.

"Oh, for heaven's sake," Giles said irascibly, "how can I be expected to carry on a conversation with these foolish outbursts? Take the poor ninny down to the dungeon and lock him up."

"But—but Mistress Fiona said for sure ye'd give me a reward!" Cedric stammered as the guards began to inexorably drag him away.

"Did she?" Giles returned. "Well, we'll make sure you have some of Bernard's excellent pottage then."

"No!" Cedric howled, and for some minutes could be heard shouting desperately for help until finally he'd been

hauled into the still, silent bowels of the castle and his voice was heard no more.

Giles turned to Sir Roger, his eyebrows raised. "I gather he doesn't like pottage."

Sir Roger gave a bark of laughter. "He should consider himself fortunate if you decide to give him *water,*" he remarked. "Well, my young friend, I must be on my way, so allow me to confirm the terms of our new agreement. You bring Adrianna home, and I'll give you the sum of money we originally agreed to in exchange for her hand in marriage. The difference being that this time I'll merely be taking her off your hands." He laughed again.

Giles chuckled fawningly. "Very funny, Sir Roger, very funny indeed."

"So the terms are acceptable to you then?"

"Yes." Giles could barely restrain his glee at the thought of so much money in his coffers.

"You're an odd sort of brother, I must say," Sir Roger commented dispassionately. "Not that it matters to me how I get the wench into my bed. I'll have my man of business call upon you by the end of the week with your hundred pounds. Good day." And with that, he strolled from the great hall, leaving Giles to feverishly ponder just how on earth he could possibly gain access to the distant abode of a savage Highland lord.

Twenty-four hours later Giles was still wondering, and was beginning to think that he might just have to take the hundred pounds and flee the country to escape Sir Roger's wrath, as uncomfortable and irrevocable a course as that might be.

He had been up all night in the library, wasting expensive candles, as he'd riffled frantically among his father's books and maps. But he had found no clues—short of mustering an army of a thousand men brave enough to face the canny, resolute Highlanders—which might suggest a way for his agents to travel safely into Scotland.

"Damn!" Giles muttered, leaning his elbows on his father's immense oak desk and clutching at his disheveled hair. "Damn, damn, *damn!*" Spread out before him was a map of France. Perhaps, he thought desperately, he might make his escape to Paris. He hadn't bothered to learn much French from his tutors, but surely he'd pick it up once he got there . . .

There was a scratch at the door and then Bernard timidly entered the library. "Your pardon, my lord, but there's someone here to see your lordship's sister."

"Well, she's not here, is she?" snapped Giles. "Send whoever it is away."

"Aye, my lord." Bernard obediently began backing away.

"No, wait!" Giles said quickly. "My mind is fuddled; I've had no sleep this night. Send our visitor up to me. Say nothing regarding Adrianna's absence, do you understand?"

"Aye, my lord." Bernard withdrew, and Giles rubbed his aching temples. Christ, but his head did hurt! He was tired to the bone, moreover, and hungry, and in dire need of a bottle of wine . . .

Bernard scratched at the door again and ushered in a humbly dressed man who promptly touched a hand to his forelock.

"Yes, what is it?" Giles said.

"I'm Toby Bridges, my lord," the man said, his rough accent that of a rural commoner. "From Stirling."

The name rang a faint bell. "Stirling?" Giles echoed.

"Aye, my lord, 'tis where Rosings be situated."

Of course! The convent where Adrianna had lived. Giles sat up straighter in the high-backed oak chair. "What can I do for you, my good man?"

"I've a letter for a Mistress Adrianna," Toby Bridges responded. "The good nuns at Rosings helped me when I broke my leg thatching my roof last autumn—'twas a foolish accident, I should never have tried to do it the day after it rains—and when I heard they was needing someone to get a letter over to Carlisle, why, I said I'd do it. It's a long walk, but I was glad to be of service."

"Very good of you, I'm sure," Giles said. He held out his hand. "I'll take the letter. My sister is indisposed at the moment."

Toby Bridges looked at him uncertainly. "The sisters said I was to give the letter directly to Mistress Adrianna."

"But I'm her brother," said Giles. "We're as close as kin can be. I'll take it to her the instant you and I say farewell."

"Well . . ." Toby Bridges said. "Seeing as how you're her brother and all . . . I'm sure there couldn't be no objection . . ."

He reached into his coarse jerkin and pulled out a letter which he placed into Giles' outstretched fingers; Giles restrained himself from ripping it open then and there. "I'll trot over to her bedchamber *tout suite,*" he said, casually putting the letter atop the map of France. "She's suffering from the headache, you see."

"Pity," said Toby Bridges. "My wife gets 'em, too, something awful. She puts a cabbage leaf on her head and vows it works wonders," he added helpfully.

"A cabbage leaf," Giles repeated sarcastically. "I'll be sure and tell my sister you said so."

"Right condescending of you, my lord," Toby Bridges said, pleased. He looked leisurely around the library. "What a lot of books you've got," he commented.

"Yes, haven't I?" Giles held on to his temper with effort.

"I'd never be able to read *half* of them in my lifetime. 'Course, I can't read anyway. But I've got a lot of respect for them that *do.*" He nodded significantly at Giles. "Your lordship, for example. Why, I'm sure you've perused everything in here, haven't you, my lord?"

"Not quite," Giles said. "I'm terribly sorry to break off our charming conversation, but I *am* rather busy . . ."

"Of course you are," Toby Bridges said wisely. "You being a duke and all. All them balls and fancy parties, going hunting and hawking and having the queen come by for a visit. It's a wonder you had time to see *me.*"

"I'm an earl." Giles ground his teeth.

"Oh, aye? I can never keep all you dukes and such straight in my mind. Well, it's a long walk back to Stirling. I'd best be off then."

"Yes," Giles said, "as soon as possible. Have my man give you water on your way out."

"I don't suppose you'd have some ale, my lord?" Toby Bridges asked hopefully.

"No," Giles said curtly. "Good day."

"Good day, my lord," said Toby Bridges, looking a little disappointed as he turned and left the library, punctiliously shutting the door behind him.

The instant he was alone Giles carefully broke open the wafer and devoured the contents of the letter.

He smiled, and read the lines again more slowly, savoring them.

Then he laughed out loud and tore the map of France in two.

Here, thanks to Adrianna herself, was a way to get his men to her—and to get her to come to *him.*

He wondered if she would appreciate the irony.

CHAPTER 12

Leith strode out of the great hall, on his way to the stables, but abruptly halted on the broad stone steps leading down to the bailey. Adrianna had preceded him by some twenty paces and was now handing something—it was made of faded blue cloth—to the itinerant peddler, Patrick Doyle.

"I've mended your shirt, Master Doyle, as I had no money to give you," Adrianna said in her soft voice, "and have kept my side of our bargain."

The red-haired Irishman looked down at his shirt and smiled. "It's beautiful workmanship, mistress," he said. "'Tis rare for a man without a wife to have seams so nicely mended." He turned and tucked the blue shirt into his wagon, then reached more deeply inside and produced a small, cloth-covered cage.

"Here is the songbird you wanted, mistress. He'll give you many hours of pleasure, I'm sure."

Adrianna accepted the cage and slid off the cloth. "I

want but one minute of pleasure from this bird, Master Doyle," she said, pulling up the little wood door of the cage.

"Mistress, he'll escape," protested the Irishman, but Adrianna only smiled.

Leith watched as the small, bright-eyed bird cocked its head at Adrianna. It hopped on its perch, once, twice, and then again, bringing it ever closer to the door which until now had constrained it. The bird looked at Adrianna again, released a sweet trill of notes from its tiny throat, and then with one final little hop it soared up and away into the sky.

Into freedom.

Leith felt his fingers tighten into fists.

Adrianna was *his* songbird, confined in the cage he had made for her.

And tomorrow was May Day.

His time was almost up.

He could scarcely believe a week had gone by so quickly. He had begun joining her at the table in the great hall, and three times each day they had supped together. At first, their conversations were confined to commonplace matters pertaining to castle life.

The much-anticipated arrival of Patrick Doyle and his gaily painted wagon.

The warming weather as spring gave way to summer's promise.

The preparations for the May Day festivities, in which Adrianna was deeply immersed.

Then, unable to resist, Leith had begun seeking her out at other times during the day as well.

He had gone with her to visit little Johnny Ogilvy.

Been there when Mabel, the seamstress, had shyly given Adrianna a gown she had sewn, by way of thanks for her help when her two children had been ill with the ague.

He'd shown her Inveraray's rippling fields of barley and wheat.

Taken her to see Hugh's monument.

She'd smiled, and sighed, and wept quiet tears. Exclaimed in wonder, and asked him countless questions.

Every day she surprised him with her interest in matters great and small, from Johnny's new front teeth to the ways in which crops were harvested. She never forgot a name and had a knack for remembering details that most people would have overlooked or dismissed as insignificant. Leith saw how, one by one, the clan warmed to her, responding to a concern that was so obviously genuine.

Young James, one of the crofter's sons, was especially fond of plum marmalade, and Adrianna had made him some which he repeatedly described in ecstatic terms to anyone who would listen.

She had gathered an apronful of wild dandelions to make a tea that would ease the pain of old Wynn Burns' latest attack of the gout.

No longer was the castle shrouded in dirt and dust; thanks to her untiring efforts and those of the maidservants, it was clean, orderly, and infinitely more comfortable.

Inveraray, he saw now, had badly needed a woman's touch.

And somehow, in her gentle, unobtrusive way, Adrianna was becoming the castle's chatelaine, mistress of his people's hearts.

And what about *his* heart?

It was a path too difficult to travel, trying to articulate his feelings for Adrianna. All he knew was that somehow she had become as necessary to him as the air he breathed or the ground he trod upon.

That she . . . completed him.

Companionship was not a quality he'd ever sought out,

or expected, from a woman. His parents had loved each other, yet had seemed to live almost completely separate lives within their differing bailiwicks; they appeared to have very little in common, and whenever Leith heard them speak together, there was a formality between them which he accepted as a matter of course. It was simply how lairds and their ladies comported themselves.

Leith was surprised, then, when his conversations with Adrianna flowed so comfortably. She was a sensitive and attentive listener, and Leith had found himself telling her things he'd never confided in another soul. She, in turn, listened more than she spoke, but Leith had coaxed her to talk about herself, too. She was strangely reluctant to describe her years at the convent, however, and Leith wondered if it was a part of herself she kept guarded because she was anxious to embrace it again.

He had refused to dwell on that thought, and steered their talk back to more agreeable topics. Had Adrianna noticed how fiercely Rose and Judith, two of the kitchen maids, were competing for Master Doyle's attentions? Mac had learned a winsome new trick; would Adrianna like to see it?

While Leith had permitted himself, for this one week, the gift of her company, he had been careful to spend no time with her where they would be concealed from other people. He didn't trust himself to be alone with her. For every minute they spent together, his desire for her burned ever more hot, ever more fierce . . . He would have sworn he saw a shy, sweet invitation in those cornflower-blue eyes, but he was afraid that if he touched her, he would lose all control and forsake his promise to himself.

And keep her here forever.

Sternly he banished the tempting idea from his mind.

And so the days had flown by.

Quickly Leith walked to the wagon where Adrianna and

the peddler stood. Patrick Doyle had opened a velvet-lined case for her inspection, and she was shaking her head over it.

"Nay, Master Doyle," she said, laughing, "and how do you think I'd pay you for this comely brooch I like so much? Have you more shirts that need mending?"

"I will buy it for you," Leith said.

Adrianna turned, smiling, to look up into his face. "No, no, you must not," she said. "I do not need it, truly."

"Which piece is it?" asked Leith, and the Irishman pointed out a delicate silver brooch amidst the other pretty trinkets. In brilliant contrast to the midnight-black velvet was a pair of intertwined hearts, bound together in eternity by an intricate, cunningly worked spray of roses.

" 'Tis beautiful," Leith said slowly. He withdrew some gold coins from his breeches pocket and laid them on the velvet next to the brooch.

"Nay, my lord, that's far too much," Patrick Doyle exclaimed, even as Adrianna demurred, "Leith, you must not—"

"Hush, lass." Leith picked up the brooch and carefully pinned it to the fabric of her bodice where it met her collarbone. His fingers brushed against warm, bare skin and he felt a flash of shimmering heat pervade his entire body, and the quiver of her own slender form as he softly drew his fingers across the raised line of her collarbone.

"Adrianna," he murmured, gazing into the thickly lashed eyes raised steadily to his. There *was* an invitation in their azure depths; he had not been mistaken in it. *Kiss me,* they seemed to say. *Hold me, and have me . . .*

"Good day!" came a husky, honeyed voice, and Leith, stepping back a pace from Adrianna, swung around to see Fiona Grant and Lisbeth the crofter's wife standing near, each carrying an armload of pine boughs.

"Good day, Fiona," he said, "and tae ye, Lisbeth."

"Good day, laird!" Lisbeth replied, dipping a curtsy. "We've just come in from the woods, and Fiona thought Mistress Adrianna could tell us where this greenery should gae."

"Put it in the great hall, please," Adrianna told her, "by the hearth. Andrew is having the serving boys make wreaths."

"Aye, mistress," Lisbeth said, and would have moved on but for Fiona's hand on her arm.

"A moment, Lisbeth, I wanted tae look at Mistress Adrianna's brooch." She leaned closer, and Leith observed how Adrianna shivered suddenly, despite the warmth of the afternoon.

"'Tis very bonny, Mistress Adrianna," Fiona said, her smile catlike and complacent, "but I would ha' thought ye'd choose a necklace instead. Come then, Lisbeth, let's gae on in tae the great hall."

Fiona sauntered off, followed by Lisbeth, and Leith saw that Adrianna was gazing after Fiona, her brows drawn together in puzzlement.

"What is it, lass?" he asked, and swiftly she turned to him.

" 'Tis nothing," she said, then gave him a smile so bright he was dazzled by it. "Thank you for the beautiful brooch," she said, touching the gleaming silver at her breast. "I will treasure it always."

Leith's own smile was a little sad. "I hope ye do, lass," he said quietly. *And will remember me by it in the long years tae come.*

Their feet flying to the spirited music of the pipers and drummers, children danced in a whirling circle around the enormous, flower-bedecked Maypole that had been raised in the center of the bailey. Wreaths adorned the heads of the girls, and the boys wore green sashes around their waists; all were clad in their best finery, and their faces, arms, and necks had been scrubbed clean in honor of the occasion.

Adrianna, seated on a low wooden dais next to Leith, surveyed the bailey with satisfaction. Andrew had set the grooms to work, and the soil of the keep had been raked until it was clear of refuse and debris. Tables had been set up bearing baskets heaped with small beef and lamb pies, apple pasties, fresh bread, cheese, and butter, as well as flagons of ale, gooseberry wine, and *raspie*—a delicious raspberry cider. Later, when the warm summer sun had set, a splendid feast was to be served in the great hall. There would be stewed capons, baked venison, custard, roasted hazelnuts and chestnuts, leeks, parsnips, peas, and a dish of the exotic potatoes Patrick Doyle had brought with him from Ireland. Strawberries and figs, too, freshly baked gingerbread cakes, and even oranges for all to taste.

She and Andrew had worked hard to make this May Day celebration a special one, and truly everything was going beautifully. People seemed to be enjoying themselves as they wandered about the bailey, laughing, chatting, stopping at the tables for another pasty or a refill for their tankard, many joining the children in the dances and games. Even the weather, Adrianna thought, glancing gratefully up into a cloudless blue sky, had graciously cooperated.

" 'Tis a glorious day," Leith said, breaking into her thoughts.

"Isn't it?" Adrianna turned to him with a smile, her heart skipping a beat at the sight of him. How handsome he was, how magnificent! Today he, like the other men of the clan, wore a kilt, baring his powerful, shapely calves and sturdy knees. The white sleeves of his fine lawn shirt had been rolled back in the gentle heat of the day; more than once Adrianna had caught herself gazing in fascination at the play of muscles in those strong forearms dusted with vigorous black hair. Around his waist he too wore a green sash; his thick, dark hair was unconfined, gleaming richly in the sunlight, and altogether he was every inch the proud, regal Highland laird. For the most part he looked happy and relaxed, yet Adrianna had seen a somber, troubled expression come and go. But he was smiling at her now, and his voice was caressing as he said:

"Ye're very fine today, Adrianna. Isn't that the gown Mabel made for ye? 'Tis most becoming."

Adrianna felt a glow suffuse her at Leith's compliments. "Yes," she replied, a little breathlessly. "Was it not kind of her? And look—" She twisted her head to show him the finely whittled birch comb set in her hair. "This was a gift from Ross. I was so shocked I vow I nearly fainted!"

" 'Tis a handsome piece o' work," Leith remarked. "Why were ye shocked?"

"I was sure Ross disliked me heartily!"

"Nay, lass, Ross is no' one for words, but I knoo he esteems ye," Leith returned, and added lightly, "In fact, I'd say ye made a conquest for yerself."

"Don't be silly," Adrianna retorted, then felt a betraying blush heat her cheeks.

She didn't want Ross as a conquest.

She wanted Leith.

Wanted him . . . Loved him.

She knew it now, had known it for some time.

In retrospect she could see that, even as she had found herself falling in love with Leith, it had been difficult to admit to herself that her desire to be a nun was gone forever. For so long she had been convinced that it was her destiny, but then Leith had come into her life and changed it utterly.

Changed *her*.

Through Leith, with Leith, she had realized the power of her femininity, her own sensual nature.

Thanks to Leith, she had learned so much about the wider world, and how the gifts God had given her—her skills at healing, her desire to help people—could be put to such good use among the clan.

When, during their many conversations in the previous week, he had asked her about her years at Rosings, she had been oddly hesitant to discuss them. She hadn't wanted him to think of her as a nun, for she herself no longer did so.

She wanted him to think of her as a woman.

As *his* woman.

Oh, why did he not look into her eyes and read in them the truth?

Adrianna let out a breath she hadn't even known she was holding, instinctively reaching up to touch the silver brooch she wore.

Then Leith's warm, strong fingers covered her own and he gently carried her hand from her breast to his lips.

"Ye sigh as if yer heart were breaking, lass," he whispered, holding her captive with the intensity of his gaze. "Will ye no' tell me why?"

Adrianna hesitated. Did she dare tell Leith she was in love with him? Surely she was not wrong in thinking that he held some measure of regard for her. Had he not talked with her at meals and sought her out in recent days? Asked for her opinions, listened with every appearance of interest when she spoke? And had he not given her the brooch she had admired, and now cherished?

His dark eyes were warm. Tender.

Adrianna took a deep breath. "Leith," she began, timorous but determined. "Leith, I—"

But she got no further, for suddenly there was a blare

of pipes and Andrew's voice rang out above the noise of the crowd.

" 'Tis time!" he declared loudly. "Time tae crown our queen o' the May!" People quieted expectantly, and Andrew gestured to Maudie, who held a particularly lovely wreath festooned with wildflowers, to come forward.

"As ye all knoo," Andrew went on, "each year we choose from amongst us our queen. No' every lass is eligible. She must be worthy o' the honor we do her. She must be kind, and a diligent worker, sweet in her temperament—"

"And bonny!" someone shouted merrily, and added another vociferously:

"Capable o' many sons!"

There was hearty laughter from among the crowd, and Andrew glared in mock admonishment. "Will ye let me finish, ye rowdy lot?" he said, grinning despite himself. "As I was saying . . . She must be kind and sweet, and pure o' course, for isna she the symbol o' the May Day festival itself? Today, in homage tae the ripeness o' summer—" Andrew grandly flung wide his arms, taking in the sumptuous gaiety of the bailey, the warmth of the day, the brilliant blue beauty of the sky overhead. "—today we celebrate life and love, renewal and rebirth."

"Ach, 'tisn't it lovely how he says it," sighed Judith, the kitchen maid, her eyes dreamy, and good-natured laughter rose up around her.

Andrew turned to Leith. "Laird," he said, with solemn formality now, "we' ha' spoken amongst ourselves, and ha' selected the lass we want tae be our queen."

"Aye?" Leith said in his deep voice. "Bring the crown tae her."

Andrew beckoned to Maudie again, and Adrianna watched in fascination as she moved circuitously through the crowd, a mysterious little smile on her face. Everyone in the bailey was silent, held spellbound by the magic of this age-old ritual.

Finally, Maudie turned, and, holding the wreath up high, paced slowly toward the dais on which Adrianna and Leith sat.

Adrianna's heart began beating hard in her chest. No, they could not mean to ... She was an Englishwoman, after all, an outsider ... And as for being pure, everyone knew she had passed that first night in Inveraray in Leith's chamber; though no one had said anything, she'd known what they must have thought had transpired ... They would certainly choose one of their own, wouldn't they?

Still Maudie approached, smiling broadly now, and Adrianna, feeling giddy, reached over to clutch Leith's hand.

"Did you know about this?" she whispered.

"Nay, lass," he whispered back, "but I admit I'm pleased wi' their choice!"

Maudie stepped onto the dais. Her eyes bright, she stood before Adrianna and said, "We, the clan Campbell, noo crown ye our queen o' the May!" She gently placed the wreath on Adrianna's head and the crowd lustily roared its approval, clapping and shouting her name and stamping their feet.

Adrianna reached up to embrace Maudie, tears stinging her eyes. Was this the clan that had greeted her with such cold, stony suspicion? She could barely remember it, for now, today, they had become her people; they were her friends, her family. "Thank you," she whispered fervently. Then, as Maudie straightened and stepped aside, she looked into the sea of smiling faces and repeated, more loudly this time, "Thank you. Thank you all!" She dabbed at her wet eyes and added tremulously, "I—I'm honored, very much so. I—I hardly know what to say!"

"If ye dinna knoo what tae say, lass," somebody shouted blithely, "ye'd better start the dancing!"

"An excellent idea!" Andrew proclaimed, gesturing to the drummers and pipers who promptly launched into a buoyant, fast-paced song. Children and adults alike swiftly gathered around the Maypole, clasped hands, and stood waiting for her. Shyly Adrianna stood and looked to Leith.

He rose, smiling, and bowed low before her, a king saluting his queen, and Adrianna felt as if her heart was taking wing with happiness.

"Will ye dance wi' me, lass?" Leith said, reaching out his hand.

She placed her fingers in his, and looked up into those glowing, deep-set eyes. Her own, she knew, were naked with the joy she was feeling, and her infinite love for him, but she did not care. She loved Leith Campbell, and let the world know it!

"Aye," she said softly. "Aye, my laird," and then Leith, his hand warm upon hers, led her into the dance.

CHAPTER 13

" 'Twas but a week ago that you escorted me up the stairs," Adrianna said with a reminiscent smile. "When you came to Glen Orchy to bring me home." She glanced at him as they reached the landing. "It seems like a much greater time than that. So much . . . has happened."

"Aye, lass," answered Leith quietly. "It feels that way tae me as well."

They paused, and faced each other in the shadowy half-light of the landing. Adrianna looked back down to the great hall, where all was dark and still, with only the faintly glowing embers in the hearth to illuminate it. " 'Twas a lovely May Day, was it not?" she said, and Leith thought she sounded a little wistful.

"Aye, lass," he said again. His whole being strained toward her, he wanted her so badly he was shaking with his desire, yet he held himself back.

He would not dishonor her.

Or himself.

"Leith," she said tentatively.

"Aye?" He heard the gruffness in his voice but could not prevent it.

"Would you . . . accompany me to my door?"

She was torturing him. In agony Leith gritted his teeth. "Aye."

He turned away from the safety of the east wing, where his bedchamber lay, and walked with her into the west wing.

Into danger.

It seemed to him an eternity before they reached her chamber door.

"Well," he said, "here ye are. I'll wish ye a good night then." He took a step away from her but froze when she touched her fingers to his arm.

"Leith."

"Aye?" he said, very low.

Her eyes were luminescent in the intimate, shadow-filled semidarkness. "Would you . . . kiss me?"

Leith stared at her, feeling all his will, all his reason evaporate. "Do ye knoo what ye're saying?" he said hoarsely.

"Aye," she said, and hesitantly stroked the skin of his forearm. "I do."

Her soft words, her timorous caress were like fire to bone-dry tinder, and the next thing he knew he was holding her in his arms, kissing her as if he would never let her go, parting her lips to his insistent tongue. He groaned, backing her against the wall, and gathered her to him so tightly that she squeaked.

Instantly he raised his head and let her go.

She made a sound that was half a sob, half a laugh, and flung herself against him, twining her arms around his neck.

"Don't stop," she murmured. "Oh, please, don't stop."

His breathing was harsh in his ears. "One more kiss," he told her raggedly, "and I willna be able tae stop this time."

"I don't want you to stop," she whispered, putting a hand between them to lightly rest upon the rigid, demanding length of him.

He nearly exploded at the touch. God's blood, but he would go mad from the wanting of her! Already his fingers were at the soft curves of her breasts, rubbing the hard points of her nipples beneath her bodice. He bent and pressed his mouth to the flesh of her décolletage, then dipped his tongue into the warm, scented valley he found there.

She moaned and Leith grasped the material of her bodice, urgently pulling it lower, uncaring of the laces, conscious only of his need for her. The fabric ripped and he tugged it wide, exposing her breasts to his ravenous gaze. His mouth found a nipple, firm and pink, and he sucked avidly upon it, then felt her hands bury themselves in his hair, pulling his head still closer.

From below, in the great hall, Leith heard the faint noise of one of the dogs, yipping in its sleep, and belatedly he realized that he was on the verge of taking her here, now, against the very wall of the corridor.

He straightened, deliberately tempering his breathing. "Come, lass," he said, opening her door and drawing her inside with him. He closed the door, locked it, and took her to stand before the fireplace, where a small crackling fire sent its pleasant warmth throughout the room.

"I was no' gentle wi' ye before," he said, releasing her hand, "and I crave yer pardon for it."

She looked up into his face, her own flushed, yet serene. "You need not ask my forgiveness," she said. "I find your ... wildness ... quite ... stimulating." The tip of her pink tongue slipped across her upper lip, wetting it, and Leith very nearly lost all his hard-won control.

"I want tae gae slowly this time," he murmured, as much to himself as to her. Her pleasure was to come first; that delight would become his. He reached behind her to pull the delicate birch comb from her hair. Heavy golden locks tumbled free and unhurriedly he slid his fingers down the length of them, following the strands that spilled down across her firm little breasts. Dear God, but she was beautiful! His fingers played teasingly against the sweet flesh laid bare by her torn bodice, cupping the soft swells until she whimpered, then went next to her laces, and carefully now he drew them free of their eyelets.

Her own hands had gone to the side laces of her gown and gently he pushed them away.

"Let me, sweeting," he murmured.

"Am I merely to stand here?" she said, frustrated at her enforced helplessness.

"Aye," he drawled, pressing a lingering kiss to her breast, his tongue toying with a hard, pert nipple, and felt her tremble at it.

"Hurry," she begged, and he denied her with a smile, returning to her side laces as he slowly freed them, one by one, from their eyelets. Then, his heart hammering hard in his chest, languidly he pushed down the sleeves of her gown and stroked his fingers along her bare shoulders, across the hollows at the base of her neck, up the side of her delicate throat where a blue vein throbbed. Her skin was so soft, so radiantly warm, he wanted to know and possess every inch of her, to taste her, take her, and he told her so in a raw, needful undervoice.

"Oh, Leith, yes," she breathed, and then he saw her fingers clench in the exquisite tension of it when he slid her dress down her slim white body, letting it gather in a soft heap around her feet; her petticoats followed, first the one, then the second, and finally the third and the fourth.

Leith knelt before her, amidst the clouds of her petticoats, and slid up the fine linen of her chemise to kiss the firm, silky flesh of her thigh. Her hand came down to grip his hair again, desperately, and he responded by trailing his fingers along the backs of her legs. Her knees began to shake and she murmured "Hurry" once more, but Leith refused to obey, ignoring his own driving desire, the blood pulsing hotly in his veins. Instead, taking his time, he slid her shoes from her feet, unfastened the wool garters just beneath her knees, rolled down her stockings.

Now she wore only her chemise. It was nearly transparent in the glow of the fire and Leith could see the soft shadow of her erect nipples, the dark, alluring triangle between her legs. He could see, too, the rent at the neckline of her chemise; he knew he should feel ashamed at this raw evidence of his urgency but he did not, could not, for his desire was far beyond his own ability to master . . .

"I want ye," he muttered thickly. "I've wanted ye for sae long . . ."

Barely conscious of his own breath coming heavy and heated between parted lips, he raised again the hem of her chemise, drawing it up around her slender thighs, his fingers stroking their rounded white softness. "Oh, Leith," she breathed again, and then he had brought his mouth to the salty-sweet flesh at the core of her. Thinking he might die from the pleasure of it, with his tongue he hungrily explored the soft, moist folds, savoring her, reveling in her, then went unerringly to the rigid little nubbin nestled at the base of her woman's mound. Adrianna gave a low, almost guttural moan, her fingers tightening their grasp upon his hair, and he marveled at the unabashed honesty and naturalness of her response.

His hands clenched upon the smooth, taut flesh of her

behind, Leith kept up his sensual assault, plying her with deliberate, rhythmic strokes of his tongue, and with fierce masculine satisfaction felt the trembling of her legs intensify, heard her soft whimpers grow more frantic; he gripped her hard to steady her and continued with this most intimate of kisses until she convulsed and cried out "Leith! Oh, Leith!" in a keening wail. He rose quickly then, and caught her against him as she shuddered in ecstasy, her body limp against his.

God's blood, but she was lovely, with her thick gold hair swirling about her shoulders, her face sweetly flushed with passion! She had closed her eyes when her release had come, and now she opened them to look up into his face. Lips reddened from his kisses parted in a dazzling smile, and she lifted a white hand to trail shakily down the side of his face.

"Did I hurt you, tugging at your hair so cruelly?" she whispered.

"Nay, lass," he returned, feeling his hardness press with blatant urgency against her belly.

She must have felt it too, for her eyes widened, and as she had before she placed her fingers against his taut shaft. "I want . . . to please you," she said softly, caressing him tentatively through the fabric of his kilt. "Will you . . . show me what to do?"

"Ye're doing beautifully," he said on a groan.

More boldly now, she fondled him, then stunned him by reaching underneath the kilt to the linen of his braies, then inside the slit to the hot hardness there. He groaned again, and gripped her even more tightly against him as her fingers, uncertainly at first and then with greater confidence, stroked him up and down, up and down, then gently cupped the warm globes at the base of his aching shaft.

A few more of her incendiary strokes and he would go

flying over the edge. Leith grasped her wrist and pulled it from underneath his kilt.

"No," she whispered, trying to reach for him again.

"Aye," he growled, then stopped further dissent with a kiss. Lightly his mouth covered hers, his tongue teasing the soft sensitivity of her upper lip, then he withdrew ever so slightly so that there was the merest hairsbreadth between them. She linked her hands behind his neck and tried to draw him to her but he resisted. Deliberately, tauntingly, he let the sizzling tension mount, kissed her again with butterfly delicacy, tantalizing her with the flirt of his tongue, the graze of his teeth, then backed away once more.

Twin pools of sapphire looked up at him, vulnerable and pleading. "Leith," she whispered, "I need you," and then he could hold back no longer. Ravenously he took her mouth with his own and she yielded to him with a gratified sigh, her heavy lids sinking shut, her tongue meeting his own in an ardent give-and-take that left him shaking.

When at last he broke the kiss Adrianna again protested, but he had pulled away only to take her with him to the bed. She sat upon the edge of it and watched, her heart beating hard, as rapidly he disrobed. When he stood before her, naked to her gaze, she could hardly breathe for the sheer masculine splendor of him.

When she had glimpsed him for the first time, in the library at Crestfield, wildly she had thought him to be a god from ancient times. Now, seeing him by the dappled golden light of the fire, that impression was only confirmed as wonderingly she took in the broad, muscled shoulders, the sinewy curves of his strong arms, and the wide chest, dusted with dark hair, which narrowed to lean hips. And at the juncture of those long, powerful legs, springing free from the dark hair there, was the visible proof of his desire for her.

"How beautiful you are," Adrianna whispered in awe, and he smiled a little.

"Men aren't beautiful, women are," he said. *"Ye* are beautiful, Adrianna." He came to her then, and she lay back on the bed next to him, trembling anew with an eagerness that was like a fire in her blood. "Sae very beautiful," he murmured, drawing her chemise up her body and over her head until at last she too was naked before him. There was no thought of modesty, of maidenly propriety violated; she only knew that she wanted Leith, craved his strength and his hardness with every particle of her straining being, basked in the gleaming intensity of his hawklike eyes as they took her in from head to toe.

"Let me touch ye again," he muttered, almost pleadingly, "sae that I can knoo this isna a dream . . ."

Adrianna could only moan her assent as his big warm hands roamed the length of her, from the sensitive tops of her feet, up her legs, framing her waist, circling her tingling breasts. His every caress gratified, yet it tantalized too; every stroke left her wanting more. A burning ache was building inside her, an emptiness that only he could fill, a hunger that only he could satisfy . . .

She clutched at those broad shoulders. "Now," she whispered in her delirium of need, "please . . ." She hardly knew what she was asking of him, only that her body cried out for him.

He smiled again, saying softly, "I can but obey ye, lass," and dipped a hand between her willingly parted legs. She was wet there; unashamedly Adrianna lifted her hips against his fingers, dimly aware of the swift rise and fall of breasts that felt swollen as she panted greedily.

"Aye, lass, aye," Leith murmured. In one graceful motion he had raised himself on top of her and with his knees he nudged her legs wide. She opened to him and with a shudder of excitement felt his hot, smooth hardness

between her thighs. Slowly he pushed himself inside her,
just past the damp folds, then withdrew. Dear God, but
she would go mad with the wanting of him! Desperate,
Adrianna sank her fingers into his muscled buttocks and
pulled him to her, into her again. "Please," she begged
again, and he moved once more, going a little deeper,
and retreated. She looked up and saw that his teeth were
clenched, his expression strained, and in a flash of instinc-
tive feminine wisdom knew that he was exerting an almost
superhuman control. She didn't want him to restrain himself. No! She wanted him to abandon himself to her, just
as she had lost herself in him. So this time, when he moved
gently inside her, she raised her hips to meet him and
thrust hard. His shaft plunged deep; there was a brief
resistance, and then he had buried himself inside her and
their bodies met as closely as two souls ever could.

Leith groaned low in his throat. "I dinna want tae hurt
ye," he muttered, and urgently Adrianna drew her fingers
up the smooth, muscled flesh of his back to grasp his
shoulders again.

"It doesn't hurt," she told him truthfully, and lifted her
head to kiss him, her tongue boldly seeking out his own.
He made a strangled noise and then he was thrusting again,
his movements slow and sure. The needful emptiness was
gone, and now, with each possessive stroke, Adrianna felt
an exquisite, mind-shattering pressure grow, expand,
intensify; heard the harsh rasp of his breathing and gloried
in the sensation of his long hard body against her, with
her, in her. Her eyes locked wonderingly upon Leith's and
as they moved together in a perfect, effortless rhythm,
Adrianna was beyond thought, beyond will, as she felt
herself inexorably propelled once more toward that heavenly precipice . . .

Distantly she heard her soft moans, and his own inarticu-
late, echoing replies. She was close, so close now . . . She

tensed, grabbed wildly at the sheet, at him, and begged, "Don't stop! Oh, do not!"

"I won't," Leith promised, his voice hoarse against her ear. "Oh, aye, sweeting, that's it . . ."

He thrust again and Adrianna cried out as a rush of pleasure poured through her, so intense she thought she might dissolve into pure liquid rapture. Her heart over-flowed and she gasped out to Leith, *"I love you,"* convulsing around him as he moved within her, more swiftly now, the muscles in his arms standing out in sharp relief as he braced his hands on either side of her.

"Aye, lass," he muttered, "aye," then closed his eyes as he found his own release and he shuddered violently, throwing back his head, calling out her name. Tenderly, awash with joy, she drew her fingers down his hard chest, relishing the feel of his warm skin, the vibrant dark hair, and he dazedly opened his eyes again; a moment later, he had withdrawn from her, rolled onto his side, and pulled her against him.

They were both silent as their breathing slowed, calmed, and the world gradually righted itself on its axis again.

Leith lifted up his hand and began playing lazily with a long strand of her hair that curled across her shoulder. He felt utterly replete in body and soul, with each kiss, each caress, each soft moan replaying itself vividly in his mind. Never had he felt such communion, never had he known that he could worship a woman with his body . . . Every sensation had been new, and fresh, every intimate smile an awakening. He had felt as if he was making love for the first time.

Felt as if he was *in* love for the first time.

Passionately, aye, and profoundly.

He had loved her for so long, perhaps even from the first moment they met. She had brought light into his life, where before there had been darkness. She had brought joy and companionship, where before there had been grief and loneliness. But he, ignorant in the ways of the heart, had been unable to put a name to all that he had been feeling for her.

Then she had spoken the simple words *I love you* and they had set him free.

There were no more doubts, no more fears, he thought, exhilarated.

She belonged to him.

There was no question now of her returning to England, for her place was at his side.

Gently Leith took Adrianna's chin in his hand. "Ye must marry me, ye knoo," he said. "I canna let ye gae, lass."

Adrianna's gaze searched his. "Do . . . do you truly wish to marry me?" she whispered.

"Oh, aye." Leith feathered a kiss across her mouth.

"Why?" she asked, and had he been less distracted by the tempting softness of her lips he might have been surprised by her bluntness. "Because ye make me *daffin,*" he muttered. *Because ye make me happy.* Leith kissed her again, more deeply this time. He felt her yield to him, felt her melt against him, and desire flared, hot and urgent, within him again. He stroked his fingers down the warm skin of her throat and to the tight bud of her breast. She gave a soft little moan, wrapped a long, slender leg across him, and Leith, his blood afire, slanted his mouth across hers and promptly lost all interest in further conversation.

CHAPTER 14

A little shyly, Adrianna walked down the steps to the great hall. It was a beautiful day; bright, cheerful sunlight streamed in through the open door that led to the bailey. The long trestle table was full already, and the clan greeted her with smiles and nods as they looked up from their morning meal. Mac capered over to her, his tail wagging furiously, and Adrianna bent to stroke the silky-furred head tilted adoringly up to her.

"Good day," came Leith's voice, deep and velvety. He sat at his place at the head of the table, smiling at her, and Adrianna's heart leaped at the sight of him. How could she think of anything but the extraordinary magic of last night, the manifold ways in which his hands, his mouth, his body had swept her away on a tide of endless rapture?

"Good day," she answered, and felt a blush tinge her cheeks as his warm dark eyes went briefly to her meticulously mended bodice.

"Ye're late, lass," he commented innocently. "Did ye ha' a wee bit o' sewing tae do before ye came down?"

"Aye," she murmured, giving Mac a final pat and continuing on her way to the table. "I could not put it off."

He nodded, and asked, with that same deceptive blandness: "Hungry?"

"Very," she said demurely, taking her seat next to him.

"Aye, I've quite an appetite as well," he rejoined, his voice laden with meaning, and Adrianna felt herself blush all over again.

"Hush, you wretch," she murmured, and took a chunk of the fragrant loaf of freshly baked rye and wheat bread that sat on a wooden board in front of her.

"Ale, Mistress Adrianna?" asked young Stephen, his flagon poised.

"Yes, Stephen, thank you," she said with a smile. When her tankard was full she turned to Leith. "What plans have you for today?"

"Ha' ye forgotten already, lass?" he replied teasingly. "I must gae seek oot that blasted minister Ian Martin and ask him tae perform a service for us."

A service. Adrianna's smile was forced now, as sharp, painful doubts came rushing back into her mind. Oh, how she wished she could feel unalloyed happiness at Leith's playful reminder of their upcoming nuptials! A little mechanically she responded: "Why do you say *blasted*? Do you dislike Master Martin so much?"

"Nay," Leith answered lightly, "he's just a bit too flirtatious for my taste!" At her absent nod his smile faded and he leaned closer to her. His dark eyes were keen, concerned as he said in a low voice, "What is it, lass?"

She didn't even have a chance to begin formulating an answer, for suddenly there was a flurry of horse's hooves outside in the bailey and then, moments later, into the great hall hurried a thin young man with wispy brown hair flying wildly about his face.

"Laird!" he said agitatedly. "Hamish Munro and his men set upon Roderick Fraser while he was hunting in the Moriston woods, and ha' taken him prisoner! Munro swears he's going tae put a knife tae Fraser's throat and end the feud once and for all!"

Leith had already risen to his feet. "Bloody hell!" he said savagely. "We'd all be better off if they slit each other's damned throats!"

"What is it?" Adrianna stood too, looking anxiously into Leith's tense face, and noticing out of the corner of her eye that everyone else had also gotten up from their seats.

" 'Tis a border feud at Strome Ferry," he answered curtly. "If it's allowed tae get oot o' hand, an outright war could result, wi' losses in the hundreds. I must gae."

"Thank ye, laird!" the young man cried in relief.

"Colin," Leith called down the table, "ye and Ross will stay wi' Adrianna?"

"Aye, laird," came the stout reply, and Leith nodded, satisfied.

"Come then, lads," he said to the rest of his men, "it's back we gae tae blasted Strome Ferry!"

Twenty men promptly went filing from the great hall; Leith stayed a moment and turned to Adrianna. "I'm sorry tae leave ye, lass," he said quietly. "But 'tis a matter o' life and death."

"Of course you must go," she said, then caught pleadingly at his hand, uncaring of who would see them thus. "But . . . you will be careful?"

He raised her fingers to his mouth and kissed them. "Aye," he said huskily, "for I've much tae come home tae.'' A brief smile, and then he had released her hand and had gone quickly from the great hall.

Adrianna stood gazing after them, listening as some few minutes later came the sounds of many horses thundering from the keep. She knew Leith would exercise the greatest care for his men's safety, and for himself, too, she devoutly hoped. But what if something went wrong?

She loved him so much; without him she already felt terribly, achingly lonely. Dear God, she would die if anything happened to him, Adrianna thought desperately, reaching up for the comfort of the silver brooch at her breast.

A big gentle hand touched her shoulder and she started.

"Dinna worry, Mistress Adrianna," Colin said in his gruffest voice. His eyes were kind as he added, "The laird will come back tae ye, ye'll see."

Adrianna only nodded, too close to tears to speak.

Adrianna sat on a hard oaken bench and stared unseeingly at the flickering candles on the altar. Had she been in another frame of mind, she might have broken off her reverie to glance with pleasure at the chapel's clean-swept floor, the neatly arranged row of benches, the polished wood of the altar with its fresh array of beeswax candles.

But she did not, for she was deep in thought, as she had been for much of the two long, seemingly endless days that had passed since Leith's departure for Strome Ferry.

Doubts continued to besiege her.

Doubts that kept her from sleeping, from eating, from doing anything but . . . thinking.

Was Leith marrying her because he felt he had to?

Because he had taken her virginity?

Indeed, taken her from her home, and now felt honor-bound to keep her by him as his wife?

Ye must marry me, ye knoo. I canna let ye gae, lass.

There had been no words of love from him, despite all his breathtaking passion, his caresses both tender and fiery that sent her spiraling to the greatest heights of pleasure.

Surely he would have said *I love ye, too* had he returned her feelings for him?

Adrianna's fingers twisted together in her lap.

When she had lain in his arms, when he had been so intimately joined with her, she would have sworn that he loved her, that his body spoke for him words his mouth did not say.

But now, she was not so sure.

Was she only deluding herself because she wanted to believe?

She didn't want him to wed her because of his sense of duty.

She loved him too well, too deeply, to ask him to sacrifice himself in such a manner.

Adrianna lifted her chin resolutely. She would ask him when he returned.

Ask him what his heart held for her.

A dreadful thought tore at her, and involuntarily she clutched at the material of her skirts.

What if he didn't love her, didn't want her as his wife for all the right reasons?

What then?

Adrianna hung her head in despair as a cold, bleak future stretched before her.

Leith was her world, and without him . . .

Without him, the world held nothing for her.

Outside in the hallway, there was a rustling whisper of

slippers, and then Maudie stepped briskly inside the chapel.

"There ye are, lass!" she said. "I've been looking everywhere for ye! 'Twas that pert, lazy Fiona Grant who said ye might be here at prayer." Maudie clicked her tongue in disapproval. "She was sitting on the bailey steps, watching the clouds roll past! I vow, that girl has yet tae do an honest day's work in her life!"

Adrianna rose to her feet. "I've been neglecting my duties, I know," she said apologetically. "And I *did* promise Mistress Betty I'd help her with her strawberry tarts!"

"Never ye mind," said Maudie soothingly. "She's got Rose and Judith wi' her as we speak. But lass, I didna interrupt yer prayers for no reason. There's a carriage come tae the castle, wi' a letter for ye."

"A letter for me?" Adrianna repeated in surprise. "Why, who is it from?"

"I dinna knoo." Maudie's gray brows drew together in a worried frown. "The courier and his two men are Sassenachs, but their carriage is protected by the sign o' the cross."

"They must be agents of the church, then, traveling on some urgent errand," Adrianna said slowly. "Why have they sought *me* out?"

"There's but one way tae find oot," replied the pragmatic Maudie. "Will ye no' come down tae receive them?"

"Oh! Oh, yes, of course," Adrianna answered, her brain whirling. Hastily she followed Maudie out of the chapel and to the great hall, where three men dressed in travel-stained, rather worn doublets, ruffs, and trunk-hose awaited her. Clustered about were numerous clansfolk who stood eyeing the strangers suspiciously, and Adrianna noticed that both Colin and Ross had placed their hands upon the knives in their belts.

She felt a warm surge of gratitude at their protectiveness, and hurried forward to greet the three Englishmen.

"Good day," she said. "May I be of assistance to you, good sirs?"

One of the men, whose greasy salt-and-pepper hair hung lank to his chin, took a step toward her and bowed very low. "I have a letter for a Mistress Adrianna," he said, with a nervous sidelong glance at the scowling Scots who surrounded him and his men. "I come from Stirling."

Stirling! Could it be a missive from her dear Mother Superior? How she had missed her—missed all the sisters! "I am Adrianna," she said eagerly.

The greasy-haired Englishman bowed again, reached past the open buttons at the neck of his doublet, and pulled out a folded sheet of parchment which he had carried tucked against his chest and now held out to Adrianna.

She took it from him, her hands trembling a little, and quickly broke open the wafer, unfolded the letter, and began to read.

My dearest Adrianna,

It is with a heavy heart that I write to tell you that Mother Superior is very ill, and that we have every reason to believe she has not many days left to live. Sometimes her mind wanders, and piteously she asks for you. We are cowards, for we have not found it within ourselves to admit to her that you are gone from here. She takes no comfort from anyone—not from Father Ogden, from her Bible, from ourselves—your presence at her side is her only desire while she remains on this earth.

Can your brother the earl spare you for some few days, and send you to us? We would be eternally grateful, for we

*are convinced that you alone can ease her suffering and
help her in her journey to her heavenly reward.*

God bless you, dear Adrianna, and keep you safe.

						I remain, ever yours,
						Sister Anne

Stunned, Adrianna's eyes filled with tears. Oh, dear God,
no . . . It couldn't be true!

"What is it, lass?" Maudie asked anxiously.

" 'Tis the Mother Superior, at the convent where I lived
for twelve years," Adrianna answered, her voice shaking.
"She's very ill—the sisters say she's dying." Disbelievingly
she glanced again at the letter. But Sister Anne's familiar,
spidery handwriting seemed to scream up at her.

*. . . we have every reason to believe she has not many days left
to live.*

The Englishman said, "Our carriage waits to take you
to Rosings. Will you come, mistress?"

Adrianna stared blindly at the parchment in her hand,
seeing in her imagination Mother's beloved face, her loving gray-blue eyes, her peaceful smile. She heard again the
tenderness in Mother's voice as she had given Adrianna
her cross of gold, saying, *I could not have loved you more had
you been my own daughter. Take my love with you wherever you
go.*

Sorrow, harsh and raw, stabbed at Adrianna.

She had been a babe of five when her real mother had
died, but her childish woe was nothing before the grief
that swamped her now.

Oh, Mother, please, do not die!

Adrianna swayed on her feet, and felt Maudie's steadying
hand at her elbow.

She forced herself to look up from the letter, and met
the intent gaze of the Englishman. "What is your name?"
she asked abruptly.

Once more he bowed, and this time he smiled, displaying blackened, rotting teeth. "Tom Gantrey, mistress, at your service."

"I will go with you to Rosings, Master Gantrey," she said. "Give me but a few minutes in which to prepare myself for travel."

That servile smile widened. "Very well, mistress. And mistress?" he called after her when she'd already turned away.

"Yes?"

"Might my colleagues and me have something to eat? We'd consider it very kind in you."

"Yes, of course," answered Adrianna distractedly. "Mistress Betty, our cook, will see that you are fed."

"Thank ye, mistress," said Tom Gantrey.

Betty marched forward, her expression pugnacious and her plump fists set firmly on her hips. "I'll give them something tae eat, Mistress Adrianna," she declared roundly, "but they're no' coming in my kitchen!"

"Let them eat outside, then, in the bailey," Adrianna said, and went swiftly toward the stairs.

When she had gone, Betty glared at the three Englishmen. "They can ha' cheese and bread, and some ale," she announced brusquely, "but *I'm* no' taking it oot tae them!"

There was a dead silence in the hall.

"*Someone's* got tae do it!" Betty snapped, and added sarcastically, "Or our poor guests might ha' tae gae hungry!"

Another silence, and then:

"I'll do it," a husky voice said graciously. "Ye can give the tray tae me, Mistress Betty."

Everyone turned to stare as Fiona Grant smiled kindly at the English visitors.

* * *

There was a knock on the door, and Adrianna looked up from the little bundle of clothes she'd assembled on the bed. "Come in," she called.

The door opened and Colin stepped inside her chamber, his mouth compressed into a tight line. "May I speak wi' ye, Mistress Adrianna?"

"Yes, Colin, what is it?" Adrianna said, going to the cupboard where she took her nightshift from its shelf.

"I dinna like it," he said abruptly.

Adrianna returned to the bed and added the nightshift to the pile. "What do you mean?" she said, only half attending.

"I dinna knoo." He gave an uneasy shrug. " 'Tis something in my bones. I wish ye'd reconsider."

Adrianna looked up then. "Colin, I *must* go to her. The Mother Superior was so good to me, so kind! I owe her so much!" She bit back a sob. "She's dying, Colin, and she needs me! Perhaps there is something I can do to help her!"

"I do honor tae yer loyalty," Colin said slowly, "but . . . still I canna like it."

"I appreciate your concern, Colin, truly I do," she told him earnestly. "But there's nothing you can say which will prevent me from going to Rosings." She grasped the four corners of the linen sheet on which she'd laid her clothes and her bag of herbs, bringing them together to make a neat bundle which she secured with a narrow length of cloth. She picked up the bundle and went to the door, only to have her way blocked by Colin who stood on the threshold, arms folded across his barrel of a chest, frowning at her.

"Please, Colin," she said, with as much patience as she could summon, "step aside."

"Ye really are going," he said slowly.

"Yes! Yes! As soon as you move!"

"Aye, well, there's no help for it then." He uncrossed his burly arms and reached for her bundle. "Ross and I will come wi' ye," he told her grimly, "as far past the border as we can."

"No," she said quickly. "I won't have you put yourself in such danger."

Colin glared at her. "Mistress Adrianna," he said, carefully, "if ye dinna let me gae wi' ye, ye'll no' get me tae budge from this doorway."

"I *refuse* to have you accompany me!" She stamped her foot. "Get out of my way! Now!"

He said nothing, only stared at her from underneath those bristling black brows.

"God in heaven! Very well! You and Ross may come with me. *Now* will you move?"

"Aye," Colin said heavily, and at last he stepped back so that she could proceed into the hallway. "After ye, Mistress Adrianna."

In the center of the bailey, Tom Gantrey and his two burly companions were hunkered down in the shade cast by their dilapidated carriage. Eagerly they looked up as Fiona approached them bearing a tray.

"Here ye gae," she said dulcetly, crouching down to put the tray onto the ground. "I added some gingerbread cakes as well. Mistress Betty didna want me tae, but I did it when her fat back was turned."

"Thankee, sweetheart," Tom Gantrey said, and Fiona stood watching as the three men fell upon the cheese, bread, cakes, and ale. When they were done, wiping their mouths on the smudged sleeves of their shirts, she said in a pleasant tone:

"My name is Fiona. I believe ye ha' something for me."

"Indeed?" Tom Gantrey said, looking up at her with exaggerated surprise. "Whatever do you mean, sweet-heart?"

Composedly Fiona said, "Money, I'd guess."

Tom Gantrey chuckled. "Oh, you're a funny one! No, I haven't any money for you, my pretty dear. But I *will* give you a kiss if you like!" he added, grinning.

Fiona crouched down next to him, as if reaching out to retrieve the tray, and let him lean close to her. But before he could bring his wet, full-lipped mouth to hers she said softly, "If ye dinna surrender the money the earl gave ye tae pass along tae me, I'll scream . . . very, very loud. My people will come running and I'll tell them ye tried tae take liberties wi' me as I went tae pick up my tray. And then," she concluded calmly, "ye'll be three dead Sasse-nachs."

Tom Gantrey pulled back, paling. "Aye, well, mayhap the earl *did* give me something for ye," he muttered sullenly. He reached into his doublet and withdrew a small leather pouch which jingled as he placed it into her outstretched hand, the gesture concealed by the shelter of their two bodies. Swiftly Fiona slipped the bag into her bodice, and smiled at him, her green eyes very bright.

"Thank ye, Master Gantrey."

"How the blazes did you know?" he asked, with grudging respect. "The earl only said that a girl named Fiona would likely come to us for a reward."

Fiona shrugged. " 'Tis a simple matter o' business. I did something for the earl, and he did something for me."

"You mean by helping him steal away his sister? How does that serve you?"

"I want her oot o' my way," Fiona answered coldly. "And what loving brother wouldna want his sister returned tae him, and reward the person who helped bring it aboot?"

Tom Gantrey laughed. "He wanted her back, all right, but he's no loving brother!"

"What do ye mean?" Fiona said quickly.

He rubbed a hand over his bristly jaw. "Why, he's selling her as a whore to a neighboring baronet, a rich old bastard whose filthy, lecherous ways are the talk of Carlisle."

"Aye?" Fiona breathed, her eyes glittering. "How do ye knoo this?"

"Why, the earl got drunk—more drunk than usual, I should say—one night and told his servant Bernard of his intentions for his sister when he got her back. Bernard's my cousin, and came to me with an offer of work, traveling into Scotland to snatch his master's sister. He being a loose-lipped sort, he told *me* all about it too."

" 'Twas brave o' ye tae come," Fiona remarked.

"Money makes a man brave," Tom Gantrey replied cynically. "So we painted a cross on an old coach, and here we are!"

Fiona laughed. "Aye. Well, I thank ye for the reward . . . and for the glad tidings ye've brought wi' ye, Master Gantrey. I wish ye good journey!" She grasped the empty tray and stood, then strolled leisurely back into the great hall where she was met by a stern-faced Maudie.

"What were ye doing, *blethering* wi' those dirty Sassenachs?" she demanded.

Fiona smiled benignly at her. "As ye say, dear Maudie, 'twas nothing but a bit of idle chatter." She continued on her way to the kitchen, where she deposited the tray on a table, ignoring the fulminating looks of Mistress Betty, and at the earliest opportunity she slipped unnoticed down the steps into the deserted storeroom.

Her hands trembling now in her excitement, Fiona lit a tallow candle, extracted the leather pouch from its hiding place in her bodice, and spilled its contents onto her palm.

Six small gold coins gleamed up at her.

She smiled. It was generous enough.

But wait! There was something else in the pouch! More coins?

Fiona dug her fingers inside the sack.

Onto her palm, amidst the coins, dropped a necklace.

A familiar gold necklace, with its delicate little cross.

Fiona laughed out loud. Apparently Adrianna's brother the earl had a deliciously wicked sense of humor.

Slowly, still smiling, she closed her fingers over the necklace and the coins.

Her plan had far exceeded even her own hopes.

Not only was Adrianna being taken away from Inveraray, but she was headed, all unknowing, straight into a trap as fiendish as any Fiona herself could have devised.

With Adrianna gone, Fiona thought triumphantly, Leith would be welcoming *her* with open arms, and she would finally be able to take her rightful place as mistress of Inveraray.

Oh, it was true what they said.

Revenge made for a sweet dish.

It was a dish she intended to savor for a very, very long time.

The carriage pulled out of the bailey and crossed the drawbridge, the horses' hooves clattering loudly on the massive wood planks. Adrianna waved to the clansfolk until they were mere specks in the distance, glanced once more at Colin and Ross as they rode next to the carriage, then leaned her head against the squabs and closed her eyes, the clan's cries of farewell still ringing sweetly in her ears.

Come back tae us soon, Mistress Adrianna!

Godspeed, mistress!

Fare ye well, Mistress Adrianna!

And Maudie's gravelly voice, rising anxiously above the rest:

The laird needs ye, sweeting, sae come home soon!

Home, Adrianna thought wistfully. If only she had the right to call Inveraray home.

And Leith her laird . . . her love.

CHAPTER 15

From his position at the edge of the Moriston woods, Leith sniffed the air, then angrily clenched his teeth.

Wafting on the warm afternoon breeze was the distinctive scent of boiling oil.

And if his eyes did not deceive him, there on the battlements of Hamish Munro's castle stood a row of archers, their bows at the ready.

The clan Munro was obviously preparing for a battle.

And why not? Leith thought. For behind him in the concealment of the woods were some two hundred men of the clan Fraser, armed to the teeth and ready to risk all to safely bring home their captive leader.

Savagely Leith kicked at a tree root. Damned pigheaded imbeciles, the lot of them!

Four days he'd been at Strome Ferry.

Four long, fruitless days spent attempting to defuse a most volatile situation.

Despite Leith's patient, politely worded requests which

had been relayed by a messenger, Hamish Munro had repeatedly refused him admittance into his stronghold.

Tyrel Fraser, Roderick's younger brother, had had to be forcibly restrained from launching his attack immediately.

And meanwhile, the only place on God's earth that he wanted to be was back in Inveraray, holding Adrianna in his arms!

Leith heard footsteps behind him and turned to see Jock approaching from the Frasers' camp.

"Laird," Jock said nervously, "Tyrel says he'll give ye one hour more before he tells his men tae begin the charge."

"And what else?" said Leith. "Ye've other news, I can tell by the look in yer eyes."

"Aye, laird." Jock hesitated, then blurted, "Tyrel swears he's got Evan MacIntyre and his clan ready tae fight for the Frasers!"

"Mother of a whoreson!" Leith growled. "Let this spread beyond Strome Ferry and the next thing ye knoo we'll ha' the whole bloody Highlands at war!"

Jock nodded miserably. " 'Tis bad, laird, very bad."

Leith bent a steely gaze on Munro's castle, considering his options.

For one, he could have his people join the fight against Hamish Munro. He snorted to himself. Aye, and for what reason? To risk their lives to help stamp out yet another of Munro's petty, rash transgressions?

On the other hand, he could simply stand back and let the Munros and the Frasers conduct their hostilities without *his* involvement.

But could he withdraw and in good conscience allow other clans to become entangled in a petty border dispute that would soon escalate into out-and-out war?

No.

Leith felt rage burning within him, four long, frustrating days' worth of accumulated wrath.

This had gone on long enough.

He had better things to do than idle about in the Moriston woods, cooling his heels while Hamish Munro played him for a fool!

"Stay here," he directed Jock coolly, handing him his dirk and *claid mor,* his heavy broadsword. " 'Tis time I had a wee chat wi' Hamish Munro."

Jock's eyes widened in alarm. "Laird, ye canna gae withoot escort, unarmed!"

" 'Tis our only chance."

"But what can ye do, laird? Munro willna even let down his drawbridge!"

"Aye, he will," Leith said grimly. "Watch a canny Scot at work."

And without a backward glance he set out across the field to Hamish Munro's castle. By not a flicker of the eye, or a hesitation in his step, did he betray his realization that the archers had trained their bows on him. When he reached the edge of the moat over which the drawbridge would extend when it was lowered, he paused.

"Hamish Munro!" he shouted. "Where are ye, man?"

A few minutes later, Munro appeared on the battlements, his long, reddish-brown hair waving in the breeze. "Leith Campbell!" he called back. " 'Tis no use asking me tae wave the white flag, or tae try and coax me intae another o' yer talks o' reconciliation! Things ha' gone too far!"

"I'm here tae request ten minutes o' yer time," Leith said, squinting in the sun as he gazed up at Munro. "I'm alone, as ye can see, and withoot weapons."

Hamish Munro shook his head vigorously. "I'll ha' no more talking! We're readying ourselves for a proper fight!"

"I ask ye tae honor my request," Leith went on inexorably, "because o' the love our clans ha' held for the other, century after century. Can ye deny it, man?"

"Nay, I canna, but—"

"Did no' the Munros and the Campbells fight together under the great Somerled, first Lord o' the Isles? And sit together on the Council o' the Isles?"

"Well . . . aye," admitted Munro uneasily. "But that was then, and—"

"Did no' the Munros and the Campbells struggle as one against that bastard Laird John when he tried tae give away half o' Scotland tae the Sassenachs in order tae secure his own rule?"

"Aye . . . that we did. But—"

"And didna our fathers, yers and mine, swear loyalty one tae the other?"

"Aye, Leith," responded Munro, his expression softening.

"How many times ha' ye and I sat before the fire while our fathers sang *'Craoth nan Ubhal'*?"

" 'The Apple Tree,' " Hamish Munro repeated slowly. "Ach, I ha' no' thought o' that song in many years."

"O apple tree, may God be wi' ye . . ." Leith began, reciting solemnly. "May the moon and the sun be wi' ye . . . May the wind o' the east be wi' ye . . ."

Now Hamish Munro added his voice to Leith's:

"May the great Creator o' the elements be wi' ye . . . May all that ever came be wi' ye . . . May the great Somerled and his band be wi' ye."

There was a poignant silence as Munro stared down at Leith. Then he swiped at his damp eyes and shouted:

"Lower the drawbridge and let Leith Campbell come in!"

Ten minutes later Leith was striding into the bailey, where he was met by the lanky, cadaverous Hamish Munro, who rushed to embrace him.

"It's good tae see ye, man!" he declared, pounding Leith on the back. "Friend o' my youth!"

"Aye, Hamish, aye, that we were," Leith said, smiling. "But let's no' stand aboot in the heat o' the sun, for it blazes fiercely. Will ye no' invite me inside for a tankard o' cold ale?"

Hamish Munro hesitated. "The thing of it is," he confided, "the great hall's in a wee bit o' disarray at present, and—"

"Ach, ye've got Fraser tied up there, ha' ye?" Leith said easily. "Never ye mind, we'll step right around poor auld Roderick, and ha' him watch while we down our tankards."

Munro laughed uproariously. "I *like* it!" he declared. "Come on then, let's gae!"

Leith followed as Munro enthusiastically led the way across the bailey into the cool dimness of his great hall. There in the center of it sat Roderick Fraser, lashed securely to a chair and his mouth stoppered with a dirty linen gag. Some two dozen of Munro's men lounged about the hall, drinking from tankards, their weapons carelessly laid aside.

"Look who's here, Fraser!" Munro shouted gleefully. "My auld friend Leith Campbell, here tae drink tae yer health!"

Fraser's eyes bulged in shock when he saw Leith, and frantically he emitted a series of garbled sounds from behind his gag.

Munro only laughed and called for ale.

"I think ye should let him gae, Hamish," Leith said, "and cease yer preparations for war."

Hamish Munro paused in the act of accepting a tankard from one of his men. "Dinna be a *carlin*, talking like a fearful auld woman!" he retorted. He started to raise his tankard to his mouth, but never completed the gesture, for the next thing he knew he was slammed against the cold stone wall with a powerful hand gripped around his throat like a vise.

"Dinna talk tae me o' *carlins,*" Leith growled from between his gritted teeth. "Ye comport yerself like a spoiled bairn, no' like a proud Highland laird! Ye shame the name o' chieftain, ye foolish bastard!"

Munro only squeaked helplessly in terror, unable to talk for the fingers mercilessly tight about his throat. Instead he feebly flapped his hands in the air, plainly trying to signal to his men.

"If yer lads take a step toward me, or toward Roderick Fraser," Leith warned, "I'll crush yer neck like a wee green twig." He loosened his grasp just enough to permit Munro to croak desperately to his men:

"Dinna move! Dinna move!"

"Tell them tae release Fraser."

"No!" Munro croaked, then quickly changed his mind as the fingers around his neck tightened pitilessly. "Let Fraser gae!" he commanded hoarsely, lowering his hands to his sides.

Leith turned to watch as Munro's men swiftly moved to untie Roderick Fraser and pull the gag from his mouth. The instant he was free Fraser jumped from his chair and rushed to Leith, nearly gibbering in his joy.

"Thank ye! Thank ye, Leith! I *knew* ye were on my side!"

Leith gave him a look of such black contempt that Fraser threw up his arm as if defending himself from a blow.

"I'm on no one's side," Leith snapped. "If it weren't for the innocent lives that would be lost, I'd just as soon let ye two *cairds* ha' at each other and let ye be the instrument o' the other's destruction!" Scowling fiercely, he released Munro and almost flung the red-haired chieftain from him.

Hamish Munro staggered, then righted himself, his

hands at the painful-looking marks on his throat. "Ye tricked me," he said reproachfully to Leith.

"Aye, well, ye ha' wasted four precious days o' my life, ye *fasheous* fool," snarled Leith. "Noo I've something tae say tae ye two, and I suggest ye listen tae me as ye've never listened before in yer life."

Munro and Fraser stood stock-still, eyeing Leith apprehensively. Never before had they seen the laird of the Campbells in such a towering rage.

"I've talked tae ye both, wi' patience and consideration, more times than I care tae count," Leith said slowly. "I've helped ye hammer oot truces, and reminded ye again and again that the border between the clans Munro and Fraser has been established for a hundred years and more, and 'tis eminently fair tae ye both.

"I've grown tired o' talking. Noo I ha' but one promise tae make tae ye. If ye ever again steal a sheep from the other," Leith went on, his voice dangerously soft, "if ye ever take a horse that doesna belong tae ye, or make tae burn the other's crofts, or quarrel over boundaries ... why, I'll come tae both o' yer houses, in the dead o' night when ye're sleeping peacefully, dreaming o' yer ill-gotten gains, and quietly I'll slash yer throats from ear tae ear."

Hamish Munro looked sick, Roderick Fraser swallowed audibly, and a ghastly silence hung over the room like a pall.

"Do ye believe me, Roderick? Hamish?"

"Aye," both men whispered, their faces wiped clean of any color. "Oh, aye."

"Then call off yer damned war!" Leith thundered.

There was another silence as Hamish Munro looked around the great hall, at his men who stood with weapons poised, anywhere but at Roderick Fraser. Finally he shuffled his feet and slowly faced the other chieftain, then muttered, "I will if ye will."

"Agreed," Fraser said, and tentatively extended his hand.

Munro grasped it, then nodded to his men. "Tell the archers tae retire," he called out, "and ha' the fires underneath the oil cauldrons tamped oot. There will be no war!"

Looking more than a little relieved, his men promptly went to do his bidding, and when the hall was cleared Munro said gruffly to Fraser, "I didna wish tae fight wi' ye, ye knoo. Taking ye from the Moriston woods 'twas little more than a prank, dinna ye see."

"Aye, aye, a prank among friends, 'twas very funny," Roderick Fraser responded with a shaky laugh, and added, "Well, Hamish, I must be on my way."

"Aye, o' course ye'd be wanting tae return tae yer people," said Munro politely. "I'll walk ye tae the woods and see ye off. That is, if ye'd like my company?"

"Most kind o' ye," Fraser said with equal politeness, and together the two men set off at a brisk pace.

Leith followed behind them, suppressing a grin. He had the distinct impression that this time, the truce was going to last.

There was a hand at her throat, choking her. Pale blue eyes glittered, a mocking aristocratic voice laughed at her. She couldn't breathe, couldn't move—

The carriage jolted and Adrianna came awake with a gasp.

Her heart pounding, she glanced across to the opposite seat and saw Tom Gantrey watching her with an enigmatic little smile on his swarthy, beard-stubbled face.

"Nightmare, mistress?" he inquired sympathetically.

"Yes . . . no . . . 'twas nothing," she murmured, glancing out the coach for the reassuring sight of Ross and Colin.

There they were, as always, riding alongside, and relief washed over her.

"Would you like to sleep some more, mistress? I'll give you my cloak for a pillow."

"No . . . No, thank you." She tried to smile at him but felt the same unaccountable dislike that had been increasingly troubling her on the three days since they'd set out from Inveraray. It wasn't anything he said, for he had been unfailingly courteous to her. It was just that he sat across from her and . . . watched her.

Watched her constantly, with that mysterious little smile on his full-lipped mouth.

As if she were a bowl of cream, and he a thirsty cat.

She hated falling asleep before him, but in these seventy-two hours of hard traveling had only been able to catch brief, light snatches of respite and was so exhausted that she felt herself powerless to keep her eyes open when the heavy somnolence overcame her.

Her one comfort was that this journey could not last forever. Soon, she prayed, soon they would be at Rosings.

"Have we crossed the border yet?" she asked hopefully.

"Aye, mistress, we passed it some two hours ago, at Flodden."

Flodden! That was but a few hours due north of Stirling!

Eagerly now Adrianna looked out the window, hoping to see familiar landmarks. After some minutes her brow creased and she turned again to Tom Gantrey. "I am not completely sure," she said, "but I believe the carriage is headed to the east. Rosings is to the south."

"The road to Stirling was hit bad by the spring rains, mistress, so we're taking a different route," replied Tom Gantrey.

"I see," Adrianna murmured, and continued to look out the carriage window. Suddenly she saw in the distance a familiar church spire rising high above the woods that surrounded them, and understanding hit her like a cruel blow, threatening to rob her of breath.

She saw again in her mind's eye Sister Anne's letter.

Can your brother the earl spare you for some few days?

The letter had been sent to her at Crestfield. How would the nuns have known that she was no longer there? Somehow, in some way unknown to her, Giles had discovered her whereabouts and had hired the three Englishmen to come for her.

And she, in her shock and dismay at the contents of the letter, had failed to think through the means by which it had been brought to her.

"Colin!" Adrianna screamed, hands clenched about the frame of the window. "That's Carlisle! It's a trap, Colin, a trap!"

She barely had time to see Colin's head whip around before Tom Gantrey was beside her, pushing her forcibly back onto the squabs, one dirty hand pressed hard against her mouth. "Be still, damn you!" he hissed.

But it was too late. Even as she fought frantically against Tom Gantrey's punishing hold, Adrianna caught a glimpse of Colin, his dirk between his teeth, riding hard up against the carriage and flinging himself up onto the driver's box where the other two Englishmen sat.

There were harsh shouts, the sounds of a violent struggle, and then shots rang out.

Adrianna screamed again.

A body—clad in doublet and trunkhose—tumbled off the box, and the carriage immediately slowed its breakneck pace.

"What's happened?" Tom Gantrey shouted. "Kit! What's happened?"

Just then Colin flew past the window and landed with a thump on the grassy tract of the road. Wildly Adrianna jabbed an elbow into Tom Gantrey, unwittingly aiming it at his groin, and when he doubled over in pain, she wrenched herself free and stuck her head out the window.

Thank heavens! Colin had risen to his feet. But behind him, on the side of the road—

Oh, God, no! No!

Ross Sinclair lay unmoving, a hideous red flower blooming below his left shoulder.

"Ross!" Adrianna shrieked in agony, and then, as Colin began running for his mount, she screamed, "Colin, no! Save Ross, and go back for Leith! You can't do this on your own! Leith will know what do!"

"Mistress Adrianna!" Colin howled. "I canna leave ye!"

"You *must!*" she cried out. "Leith will save me!"

And then Tom Gantrey had snatched her back inside, and she could say no more with his hand clamped about her mouth.

"Where's the Scotsman, Kit?" he shouted. "Does he follow us still?"

"Nay!" came the hoarse response from the box. "He dragged his friend's body into the bushes and started riding to the north!"

"Famous!" Tom Gantrey cried. "Keep going, then! We're nearly there!"

"But Oliver's lying dead in the road!" Kit protested.

"I don't give a damn!" Tom Gantrey shouted back. "Keep going, you bastard, or I'll kill you myself!"

The carriage picked up speed again and Adrianna writhed against Tom Gantrey's hold, biting at his fingers and finally managing to catch the flesh of his palm between her teeth.

"Bitch!" He pulled his hand free and then doubled it into a fist which he held close to her head.

Unflinchingly, Adrianna stared into his contorted face.

After what seemed like an eternity but Adrianna knew could only have been a few moments, Tom Gantrey slowly lowered his arm and wiped his bloody palm on the filthy sleeve of his shirt. "Try that again and I'll knock you senseless," he warned. "And carry you into your brother's castle like a sack of coal."

Still keeping her head high, Adrianna continued to stare at him until he sulkily moved from her seat to his own side of the carriage. Then she buried her shaking hands in the folds of her skirt and said as calmly as she could:

"So I was correct. My brother used you to deceive me, and to bring me back to Crestfield."

"Aye, that's right," Tom Gantrey replied, looking more cheerful. "And you fell into our laps like a ripe plum, didn't you?"

She took a deep breath. "What does he want with me?"

"Oh, no, you'll have to wait for the earl to tell you that," Tom Gantrey said, craftily. "I wouldn't want to spoil his surprise."

"It does not matter," Adrianna said loftily. "The Scottish lord to whom I am betrothed will come for me."

A bark of coarse laughter. "You think so, mistress? With your Scottish light o' love a three days' journey away? And three days back to Carlisle?"

"He will come," she said steadfastly, even though her heart was sinking in her breast. With Leith gone to Strome Ferry, it would take even longer for Colin to reach him.

And for Leith to reach her.

"Besides," Tom Gantrey added, grinning, "even if he does get here in a week or so, by the time he does ... Well, let's just say I doubt he'll want anything to do with you." He winked, and Adrianna felt her throat constrict in fear.

"What do you mean?" she asked tensely.

But Tom Gantrey only laughed, and settled himself more comfortably against the squabs.

Still buried amidst her skirts, Adrianna's nails dug painfully into her palms and she shut her eyes to avoid the weight of Tom Gantrey's complacent gaze.

She thought of poor Ross, alone, bleeding his life away on a desolate English road far from home.

She thought of Mother Superior in her narrow little bed at Rosings, calling out for a loved one who would never come.

She thought of Leith, and her passionate love for him, and of a life together that now would likely never be.

Oh, God! Oh, God!

She would have cried aloud, but didn't want the ruffian sitting across from her to witness her anguish.

Instead she sat very still, kept her eyes tightly shut, and felt all hope seep from her soul, leaving only the blackest, darkest despair in its place.

Leith strode blithely into the great hall at Inveraray. God in heaven, but it was good to be home!

His dogs rushed to greet him, tails flying, and Leith glanced about him in satisfaction.

The wood of the long trestle table was clean and polished to a high gloss. His chair at the head of it, and the oaken benches around it, were set neatly in their places.

The stone mantel over the fireplace was free of dust and clutter, and was now adorned with two beautiful sprays of purple and pink heather.

The cobwebs were gone, as were the formerly omnipresent clouds of gray and sandy red dog hair.

The rush mats beneath his feet were fresh and smelled sweetly of herbs.

Everywhere he looked he saw evidence of Adrianna's gentle influence, bringing order and grace to his household.

But where was Adrianna herself?

For five interminable days he'd missed her, wanted her, needed her.

Loved her.

And now he couldn't wait another minute to see her.

"Andrew!" he shouted.

The steward came bustling from the kitchen into the great hall, his plump face wreathed in smiles. "Welcome home, laird! We've been sae worried aboot ye! Did all gae well in Strome Ferry?"

"Aye," replied Leith, "the truce is restored."

" 'Tis excellent news! How did ye—"

"I'll tell ye all aboot it later, but first I want tae find Adrianna," he interrupted. "Where is she? At the crofts, or wi' Betty in the kitchen, mayhap?"

"Why, she's gone, laird."

Leith felt as if the floor had just dissolved beneath him. *"What?"* he roared. "What do ye mean, she's gone?"

Quickly Andrew explained to him the circumstances of Adrianna's departure: the letter, Adrianna's grief and concern at the report it contained, her anxiety to fulfill the old nun's dying wish. "And dinna ye worry, laird," Andrew concluded cheerfully, "Colin and Ross ha' gone wi' Mistress Adrianna. They'll ensure no harm comes tae her."

Leith did not, could not return Andrew's smile. It wasn't that he doubted Colin's ability to watch over Adrianna; he knew the man was as devoted to Adrianna as he was loyal to Leith himself.

It was just that . . .

He couldn't quite put it into words, but . . .

A cold, wet nose thrust itself into his palm, and Leith looked down to see Mac gazing hopefully up at him, his tail wagging back and forth.

"He missed ye, laird," Andrew told him. "He's never quite himself when ye're gone."

Leith bent to scratch the woolly fur between Mac's shoulder blades, and a look of indescribable bliss promptly settled across the dog's expressive features.

"Ye missed me, did ye, ye beggar?" Leith whispered. "Ach, that's what's bothering me, no doubt. I miss her, ye knoo, something fierce." He paused, feeling the full force of his emotions, his desire, his love, roll through him like a much-needed storm after a drought.

Mac licked his arm, and patiently waited for his master to resume his caresses.

CHAPTER 16

Fiona peered through the narrow slit of the window in the tower room, and smiled. There was a full moon tonight, casting a bright spectral glow that couldn't be interpreted as anything other than a fortuitous omen.

The round ripeness of the moon . . .

The full fruition of her plans . . .

Fiona's fingers dipped to the tiny leather pouch nestled between her breasts, then rose to languidly stroke the roundness of her own flesh, bare above the daringly low cut of her bodice.

She was wearing her russet gown tonight.

She wanted to look pretty for Leith.

It was a special evening, after all.

Their long-awaited reunion was nigh.

Fiona whirled in a giddy circle, enjoying the sensuous, rustling sweep of her skirt and petticoats as they rose and fell. Then she glanced for the last time around the tower room. God's mercy, but it was a dismal chamber, with its dilapidated bed and chair, and lopsided old cupboard, and dreary, musty smell. It had been just the right spot for the Sassenach, but *she* would go mad if she had to spend time here involuntarily! No, for someone who liked to roam from place to place, sitting idly here and there, finding some handsome young lad to flirt with and avoiding Mistress Betty's endless harping ... there could be no worse hell than confinement.

Shuddering, Fiona went to the door of the tower room and opened it carefully.

Silence met her.

All was calm and still within the castle.

She'd crept up here as soon as the evening meal had concluded. It had been easy to leave undetected, for the great hall was abuzz with the excitement of Leith's safe return, with all his men unscathed.

Andrew and Mistress Betty had wanted to hastily prepare a feast for them, but Leith had refused. Let Betty serve only the meal she had planned for that evening.

It had been obvious to everyone that Leith, despite his triumph at Strome Ferry, was not in high spirits. His face had been somber, his expression preoccupied.

Of course he was mooning over that bloody golden-haired Sassenach, Fiona thought viciously. With all her queenly airs and graces, and quiet die-away manners that everyone seemed to find so enchanting!

Well, Leith wouldn't repine for long, not if she had her way.

And she *would* have her way.

Once Leith felt Fiona in his arms again, once she had kissed him and stroked him and ridden him to the point of no return ... well, he'd hardly miss Adrianna.

Poor, poor Adrianna.

Almost, Fiona had to feel sorry for her.

But not quite, she thought, smiling again.

And God's mercy, if there was anyone to feel sorry for, it was herself!

Hadn't she spent several long, boring hours cooped up in the tower room, waiting until Andrew had closed up the castle for the night and everyone had gone to sleep?

But, truth to tell, she'd hardly minded, so full was she with her schemes.

Oh, the dresses she'd have, the fine silk petticoats, the dainty shoes, and lovely, lovely jewelry . . .

Fiona left the tower room and tiptoed down the spiral stairs to the hallway of the second floor. She paused again, listening intently. There was only the soft noise of one of Leith's dogs snuffling in its sleep where it lay near the last faint warmth of the hearth.

Fiona frowned. Once she was mistress of Inveraray, she'd get rid of those nasty deerhounds.

She made a mental note of it, then continued padding along in the semidarkness of the hallway to Leith's bedchamber.

He dreamed that Adrianna was beside him, her warm, pliant body nestled intimately close against his own, her heavy hair cascading free. She smiled as he reached out to grasp at her hair, burying his fingers in its silken richness, and brought her inviting mouth closer . . . closer . . .

Knowing fingers slid around his hardening shaft and a sweet voice whispered in his ear, "Aye, that's it . . . Kiss me, my love."

Leith groaned and tightened his arms around her. She felt so solid, so achingly real . . . "Adrianna," he murmured. He'd never had a dream this vivid; it was almost as if he was awake, and Adrianna had come to him, caressing him, giving herself to him . . .

He smiled as soft lips touched his, and drowsily opened his eyes to the gentle light of the waning fire.

But it wasn't his lovely, blue-eyed Adrianna he held against him.

It was Fiona, her brown eyes gleaming voraciously into his own.

With a muffled curse Leith came to full consciousness and shoved Fiona away from him. "What the devil are ye doing here?" he growled, pulling the linen sheet up to his chest, covering the nakedness she had exposed.

Composedly Fiona sat up on the edge of the bed and smoothed the disheveled skirts of her low-necked russet gown. "I missed ye, Leith," she murmured, reaching out a lightly freckled hand to stroke the skin of his shoulder.

He pushed her hand away, scowling. "Sae did my dogs, and ye dinna see them in my bed. Get oot o' my chamber, Fiona."

"But Leith," Fiona said, a tiny crease appearing between her brows, "dinna ye want me noo that the Sassenach is gone?"

"Adrianna is gone, but soon she'll be back," Leith said evenly. "We'll be married the moment we can get Ian Martin here tae perform the service."

"Married?" echoed Fiona, all the sweetness drained from her voice. "Ye're going tae marry the Sassenach *bizzem?*"

In a flash Leith had wrapped his fingers around her wrist. "Dinna ye dare tae call her that!" he said harshly. "Adrianna is tae be my wife, and ye will pay her the respect she deserves!"

Fiona winced. "Ye're hurting me," she complained, and Leith let her go as if her flesh was a substance that repelled him.

"Gae, Fiona," he said stonily.

She did not move. Instead she slowly rubbed at her wrist, and Leith saw that her pretty face held renewed determination. "Leith," she said, "I'm no' withoot my pride, ye knoo. I make my offer only this once."

"I've no interest in anything ye ha' tae offer."

"Noo that Adrianna is gone, ye'll need a woman," Fiona went on stubbornly. "Ye've . . . tasted my wares, and liked them well enough, as I recall."

"How many times do I ha' tae tell ye, Fiona?" Leith snapped. "Adrianna will be returning soon, and will take her place at my side!"

"Nay, she willna," Fiona said, with such absolute confidence that Leith felt his blood run cold.

"What do ye mean?" he said, sitting up, heedless of the sheet falling down about his waist. "What do ye mean, she willna?"

Fiona shrugged, and smiled. "She willna return, Leith, she will never be yer wife."

Before she had time to react, Leith grabbed her from behind, twisting her torso, and pushed her shoulders onto the bed. "Why?" he demanded savagely, staring down at her. "Why will Adrianna no' return? What do ye knoo?"

"Ach, ye're sae handsome when ye're angry," Fiona murmured appreciatively. "Yer eyes flash like fire. Why dinna ye stop talking, Leith, and take me like the Campbell wife I'm destined tae be?"

"Ye'll never be my wife!" he said, his voice harsh with barely controlled violence. "Never! Noo tell me what ye knoo!"

The catlike smile was gone, and now her green eyes glittered menacingly. "I gave ye every opportunity," she hissed. "But ye couldna see that I was right for ye. Right for Inveraray! No, ye lusted after that skinny Sassenach instead! Well, laird—'' She spat the word out contemptuously. "Noo, laird, it's too late! She's back in England amongst her own!"

"We all knoo she's in England!" he rasped. "Why is it too late?"

"Ye're hurting me again!" Fiona cried, and when he loosened his hold she wrenched herself free and stood quickly. Her breasts heaved agitatedly, threatening to spill forth from her bodice, and her face was deadly pale. Her freckles stood out in such sharp relief that she might have looked almost comical were it not for the demonic fury that possessed her.

"It's too late, ye bastard, for she's been taken back tae her brother, the Earl o' Westbrook! He's selling her— like the *bizzem*, the whore, she is!—tae some rich auld Sassenach laird!" Fiona laughed wildly as she stared into Leith's shocked face.

"What, dinna ye believe me, laird?" she cried. With another shriek of a laugh she pulled a small leather pouch from between her breasts and threw it at him with all her might.

It landed silently on the rumpled coverlet near his legs. Feeling oddly numb, Leith reached into the little pouch and gazed down at the golden necklace with its dainty cross that dangled from his fingers.

It was Adrianna's.

Slowly he raised his eyes to Fiona's jeering face.

"*I* did it!" she announced proudly. " 'Twas I that stole the necklace from the Sassenach, then went tae Glasgow and found some poor *clunch* tae gae intae Carlisle and give the earl the necklace wi' a message from me! And it was because o' me," she went on, her husky voice ringing with triumph, "that a carriage came for Adrianna wi' the letter, and took her away no' an hour later!"

"When?" Leith said quietly. There was an ominous roaring in his ears now, and he could barely hear himself speak above that roar. His mind coolly considered the possibility that Fiona was lying, that she'd merely stolen the necklace and in her jealous rage had concocted the story about Adrianna being spirited away to her brother's castle, while meanwhile Adrianna was safely journeying to Rosings. But every instinct he possessed told him that Fiona was telling the truth. "When did the carriage come for Adrianna?"

Fiona tossed her dusky curls. "Why, ye poor bastard, 'twas Wednesday morning, a full two days ago!" she replied tauntingly.

Two days ago.

He was forty-eight hours behind them.

It was a lifetime.

Leith looked again at Adrianna's necklace, and suddenly the icy numbness that had entombed him was shattered by a rush of anger so hot his very bones felt as if they were on fire.

"God's blood!" he roared at the top of his lungs, throwing back the sheet and jumping to his feet. Uncaring of his nakedness before Fiona, who had flattened herself against the wall, he went quickly to his cupboard, pulled out his clothes, and began dressing, even as there was a shout from the great hall and the sound of feet running swiftly up the stairs.

He'd just whipped his shirt over his head and was carelessly tying the laces when his chamber door burst open and in hurtled a dozen of his men who'd been slumbering below. They were all in various states of undress but their dirks and *claid mors* were poised and ready.

"Laird! What is it?" panted Malcolm, barefooted, his carroty hair in wild disarray.

"Ha'—ha' we interrupted something, laird?" Jock's curious glance went to Fiona as slowly he lowered his broadsword.

"Nay, lads, yer arrival is most timely." Leith finished with the laces of his shirt and began pulling on his boots. "Dougal, gae down tae the stables and ha' the grooms make ready mounts for ye, Jock, Malcolm, and myself. Then wake Betty and ha' her quickly gather some provisions. We leave for England within the hour."

"Aye, laird," Dougal said with a nod and immediately ran from the room.

"England, laird?" queried Jock, his narrow face alert. "Does it ha' something tae do wi' Mistress Adrianna?"

"Aye," Leith said grimly. "She's been duped intae going back tae Carlisle, where I ha' every reason tae believe grave danger awaits her."

His men looked stunned.

Just then came the noise of pattering feet and Andrew, still in his white nightshirt, hurried into the chamber. "Laird!" he puffed, the expression on his plump, normally cheerful face one of deep concern. "I passed young Dougal on the stairs, running as if his life depended on it! What's amiss?"

"We're off tae England," Leith informed him crisply. "Ye are tae direct the rest o' the men wi' the care o' Fiona."

"The—the care o' Fiona, laird?" stammered Andrew confusedly. "What do ye mean?"

"She's tae be treated as a prisoner," Leith said, his voice hard. " 'Tis she who created a trap our Adrianna most innocently fell intae."

"What?" gasped Andrew, shocked, and mutely Fiona cowered as several pairs of accusing eyes bored into her.

"She is tae be taken tae the tower room," Leith went on, "where she will remain until my return—*wi' Adrianna*—and I'll then decide what is further tae be done wi' her."

"Nay, laird, no' the tower room!" Fiona whispered, her

green eyes wide, then burst into hysterical sobs. "I—I was hiding there until I came here. I dinna like it there, laird, dinna make me stay there!"

"What could be more fitting?" Leith retorted coldly, reaching into the cupboard for his cloak. Just as he grasped the heavy wool of it, Fiona darted forward and fell at his feet, wailing loudly. "Laird—Leith!" she sobbed. "Dinna do it! *Please!*"

"Get her away from me," Leith snapped, and two of his men quickly moved forward, grabbed her by her arms, and pulled her upright. Still crying convulsively, her feet crumpled beneath her and the men were forced to drag her out of Leith's bedchamber.

When her wails had died away, muffled by the thick stone walls of the tower, Leith went rapidly to his bed, where he bent and picked up the golden necklace.

He paused, and felt his heart wrench painfully in his chest.

Adrianna!

Where was she at this moment? Were Colin and Ross still with her? They couldn't have yet arrived in Carlisle. Was Adrianna well? Or did she know the fate that awaited her at Crestfield, and was even now curled up in raw terror?

He would find her, Leith vowed, no matter what it took, no matter how far he had to go.

He tucked the necklace into his pocket, then turned to Andrew. "Ye're in charge, man. Tell Maudie we've gone tae bring her sweet lamb home."

Andrew nodded somberly. "Aye, laird," he said, and followed behind Leith as he strode toward the chamber door, accompanied by Jock, Malcolm, and the other men. "Good journey, and good luck tae ye!"

Aye, they'd need it, Leith thought grimly when, moments later, he emerged into the bailey. He glanced up at the sky as he hurried toward the stables. About the only piece of luck he'd had this night was that the moon was full, and would allow him the chance to travel without wasting precious hours until dawn. He hoped—nay, he *prayed*— that it was a good omen.

CHAPTER 17

The rickety old carriage pulled up in front of Crestfield and came to a creaking halt on the grassy field that ringed the castle. Adrianna sat frozen in her seat, her heart beating so hard she was sure Tom Gantrey, lounging negligently across from her, could hear the quick frightened thumps. She had been praying this last hour as the carriage barreled relentlessly toward Crestfield. Praying, and asking—no, begging—for a miracle. Miracles *did* happen, didn't they? The Bible was full of miraculous tales! But now that the dreaded moment of arrival had finally come, she was very much afraid that her courage was going to fail her.

"Well, mistress," Tom Gantrey said affably, "you're home at last. And look," he added, "here's your brother the earl come to meet you, and two of his guards! I call *that* a proper homecoming, I do!"

He laughed, but Adrianna said nothing, did not even glance into that swarthy face.

Breathe, she told herself silently, *breathe! Else you'll faint and they really will carry you inside like a sack of coal!*

She lifted her head and waited while one of the guards lowered the steps and opened the door.

"My dear sister," came Giles' suave, aristocratic voice. "What a pleasure it is to see you! Allow me to help you down—and mind those steps, they do not look steady at all."

With punctilious care Giles extended a pale, slim hand and Adrianna's skin crawled as she forced herself to grasp his fingers and carefully maneuvered her descent on small wooden steps that wobbled precariously with her every footfall.

"I apologize for the rude conveyance," said Giles, with an exaggerated sigh, "but one does one's poor best."

Adrianna pulled her hand away and looked up at Giles. Harsh, aging lines of dissipation had scored his thin face even more deeply than when she had seen him last, and on his cheeks was a sickly red flush. She could not help but notice the faint, stale odor of wine that hung about his person.

His richly clothed person, she realized in dazed surprise. Instead of the shabby blue doublet and poorly mended ruff he'd worn before, Giles was now clad in a stiff, blindingly white ruff and a magnificent bright red doublet with extravagantly padded shoulders and laces tipped in gold. A particularly handsome square-cut sapphire dangled from a thick, heavy golden chain around his neck, sparkling brilliantly against its red backdrop. Fine black woolen trunkhose enclosed his slender legs, and on his feet were black calfskin ankle-boots, buttery soft and embellished with ribbon edging of gold velvet.

"You're—you're very fine, Giles," she murmured.

He preened, and ran a proud hand down the luxurious red silk of his doublet. "Yes, am I not? Though I wish I could say the same for you, dear sister. Why, you're looking positively haggard in that provincial's dress."

She was wearing the pretty blue gown Mabel, Inveraray's seamstress, had given her. Adrianna clenched her hands together before her, trying to still their trembling. "It was a long and difficult journey."

"Why?" he said, deliberately pretending to misunderstand her. "Hasn't my friend Master Gantrey treated you well?" He smiled, revealing his yellowed teeth, and from his stance a few paces away from her, Tom Gantrey made a mocking bow in her direction.

Then Giles' pale blue eyes sharpened. "You've only the one man on the box," he said to Tom Gantrey. "Where's the other man—what was his name?"

"Oliver, my lord," supplied Gantrey. "He's dead."

"Dead? How?"

"Mistress Adrianna had two Scottish escorts with her, my lord, and there was a fight but a league from here. We shot one man, but the other killed Oliver and fled back to Scotland, the lily-livered bastard."

It was on the tip of Adrianna's tongue to blurt out a defense of Colin, but even as she opened her mouth she seemed to hear Mother Superior's voice, whispering gently in her ear: *Miracles do not happen, they are made!*

Adrianna blinked and pressed her lips together, insensibly comforted by the remembrance of one of Mother's favorite maxims. And now, now for the first time she felt the tiniest flicker of hope rise within her.

If Tom Gantrey arrogantly assumed that Colin was retreating across the border, why, so much the better for her. The last thing she wanted to do was to alert Giles to the possibility that help, however remote, might be on the way; that would only serve to put him in a panic, and perhaps even prompt him to advance his plans for her, whatever they might be.

" 'Tis just as well," Giles commented. "I didn't bargain for two Scottish savages to deal with, after all."

Again Adrianna resisted the impulse to confront Giles. *Patience, my child,* Mother Superior's voice seemed to softly whisper. *Patience and a steady heart will win the day . . .*

Adrianna swallowed past the cold lump of fear in her throat, and surreptitiously she raised a hand to the silver brooch at her breast. She would not give into despair, she would not!

"How was Oliver killed?" Giles went on interestedly.

"With a dirk, my lord." Tom Gantrey's tone was dispassionate. "But as one as likes to look on the bright side of things, well, 'tis more money for myself and my colleague Kit, isn't it? Splitting two ways is better than three."

He flashed a crooked grin at the driver who was still sitting up on the box, and Giles took the opportunity to hold out his arm to Adrianna.

"Well, dear sister," he said, a little more loudly than seemed necessary, "shall we repair to the great hall for a glass of wine? Master Gantrey, I've no doubt you'll want to tend to your tired horses, so I'll leave you to it."

Tom Gantrey took a step forward and said, "A moment, my lord, before you go in."

"I'm sure it can wait," Giles said imperiously, the red flush on his face intensifying. "I'm terribly thirsty, and I'm certain Adrianna is too. Come, my dear." He grabbed her arm and began hurrying her toward the door of the castle.

"I said a moment." Tom Gantrey's voice was stripped bare of all its easy, servile affability.

Adrianna looked over her shoulder and saw the small, but serviceable-looking pistol he was pointing straight at Giles. Giles turned as well, then froze, glancing frantically at his two hulking guardsmen. They only shrugged helplessly, for high on his box the driver, Kit, was coolly aiming his pistol at them.

"I want the money you owe me," Tom Gantrey said evenly. "Half up front, we agreed, and half on delivery. Well, I went to Scotland and brought your sister back. Now it's your turn, my lord."

"Yes, yes, of course," Giles muttered, his hand clamped so tightly about Adrianna's arm that she nearly cried out from the pain of it. "I'm delighted with the work you've done, Master Gantrey, but the thing of it is . . . It's a trifle awkward, but—well, I'm just a bit overextended at the moment, and—"

"Overextended?" sneered Tom Gantrey. "You mean you spent all your blunt on that fancy rig and your wine cellar!"

"I fail to see how the way in which I disburse my funds is any of your concern," Giles said haughtily.

"It's my concern when you don't pay me, you bastard!"

"How *dare* you, you impertinent upstart?" Giles shouted, releasing Adrianna's arm and taking a hasty step forward. He checked himself when he saw Tom Gantrey's thumb position itself more firmly on the trigger.

"Don't think I won't shoot you just because you're an earl," Tom Gantrey said softly. "I'll gladly put a bullet in that noble heart, strip your corpse of those posh clothes, and sell 'em in the marketplace first thing tomorrow morning. Oh, no, I won't," he corrected himself, laughing derisively. "Tomorrow's Sunday, isn't it? I'll have to wait until Monday."

Giles' voice quavered as he said, "I'll pay you just as soon as I've—I've completed my transaction." He grabbed Adrianna's arm again and she had no doubt that the transaction, whatever it was, involved herself.

"Aye?" Tom Gantrey said skeptically. "And when will this—er, transaction take place?"

"Why, as soon as possible," Giles babbled. "Tonight.

Why not? I've only to send Bernard over with a message, and . . . yes. I'll be able to pay you tonight."

Think! Adrianna screamed silently to herself as waves of frightened panic rolled through her. *What transaction?* Was Giles intending to marry her off to Sir Roger Penroy after all? Her mind reeled at the gruesome thought and she struggled to remain focused.

Whatever the so-called transaction was, she knew she must try to delay it, for every hour brought her miracle closer to her.

And that miracle was Leith.

Gantrey was eyeing Giles consideringly, and then he shook his head. "No, my lord, I don't think so. It's not that I don't trust you"—he bared his blackened teeth in a sarcastic grin—"but I'm not a betting man, you see; I'll take the sure thing any day of the week. So I'll relieve you of that pretty blue pendant you're wearing, and we'll consider ourselves even."

"You're not taking this sapphire!" Giles said in outrage. "Its value is far greater than the paltry sum I owe you!"

"Do you prefer the sapphire or your life?" Gantrey asked pointedly, and smiled as Giles, muttering angrily under his breath, pulled the necklace over his head and threw it at him.

Tom Gantrey caught it neatly, and tucked it inside his doublet. "Thank you, my lord," he said, all politeness again. "Kit and me, we've long talked of traveling to the West Indies—to a place called Barbados—and buying some land to grow sugarcane, as they do there most abundantly. 'Tis a beautiful island, I've heard, where a man may be his own master, and now—" He laughed triumphantly. "Why, now it seems we'll be able to go!"

His gun still aimed at Giles, Tom Gantrey backed away and climbed agilely into the carriage. "Drive, Kit!" he shouted, and as the carriage began to pull away, he tossed out Adrianna's small linen bundle and called, "Mistress Adrianna, I wish you well in your new situation!"

A final mocking laugh, and then the carriage had bowled down the rutted lane, into the forest, and was gone.

"Damned impudent blackguard!" Giles said petulantly, then snapped at Adrianna, "Pick up your things and come inside, then!"

Slowly Adrianna walked the twenty paces to where her bundle lay in the grass. For a single wild moment she thought of trying to run, but knew that Giles' massive guards would bring her to earth within seconds. She stooped and grasped her bundle, and as she did, suddenly an idea sprang to life in her mind.

It was crude, she thought excitedly, taking a deep breath, but it just might work . . .

She straightened and obediently followed Giles into the castle, his two guards close upon her heels. Once inside, she blinked, and as her eyes adjusted to the chilly dimness of the great hall, she saw that there was no furniture left anywhere.

"Giles, what has happened here?" she asked.

He rounded on her with a snarl. "I'll *show* you in just a moment!" he answered curtly, then bellowed, "Bernard!"

A thin, balding manservant hurried from the kitchen into the great hall. "My lord?"

"Bring me a bottle of wine," Giles ordered. "Two glasses."

"No, Giles, I thank you," Adrianna interposed quickly. "Might I have some tea?"

"Good God, how dull," said Giles with a moue of disgust. "Very well."

"Immediately, my lord." Bernard made as if to go, then hesitated uncertainly. "Shall—shall I bring the tray up to the library, my lord?"

"Where else have you been serving me for the past

fortnight, you idiot? Do you wish us to sit here on the floor?"

"N-nay, my lord." A look of abject misery on his hollow-cheeked face, Bernard swiftly left the room.

"Come on then," Giles said to her, "I'm like to catch my death of cold in here," and, with the guards trailing them, led the way up the staircase to the library, where he flung himself into the high-backed oak chair behind their father's massive desk.

But Adrianna paused on the threshold, staring about her in shock. The room was a shambles. The glass-encased cabinets, their contents askew on the shelves, had been pushed without care against one wall to make room for the six-legged elm dais table that previously had sat in the great hall; only five of its original twelve chairs were placed around it. Fully a quarter of their father's collection of books was gone, and the once-plush burgundy velvet curtains framing the casement windows had been torn down and were now draped across a chair.

But it was the hearth that drew her stunned attention most strongly. It was a filthy mess. Charred black remains spilled out of the fireplace onto the floor, and four heaping buckets filled with ashes had yet to be carried away.

Adrianna turned wondering eyes to Giles. "What . . . ?"

"I've no money for fuel," he said, scowling, "I'm down to three servants who are too lazy to retrieve wood from the forest, and this damned castle is cold even in the bloody heat of summer!"

"So you've been burning . . . the furniture?" she said, looking again at the handsome dais table that once had been their mother's pride and joy.

"Yes, I've been burning the furniture," snapped Giles, "and Father's beloved books, *and* using those damned drapes to keep me warm when I sit in here! It's all your fault, you troublesome wench!" he added viciously.

Trying without success to keep her shoes and the hem of her skirts free of the black soot littering the floor, Adrianna walked into the room and sank down on a chair that faced the desk, keeping her bundle securely on her lap. "Why is it my fault, Giles?"

"*You* know, because you ran away—oh, here's the wine, bring it to me first, idiot, *then* give her the tea!" Greedily he accepted the dark-green bottle from Bernard and poured himself a glass of wine which he immediately drank down in one gulp. "You're not serving her tea in that tankard, are you? How stupid *are* you? Don't you know that tea is supposed to be in a cup, not a tankard?"

" 'Tis fine," Adrianna said hastily, taking the tankard the servant held out but now seemed about to withdraw. A tankard was actually far better for her purposes, as it held considerably more liquid than did a cup. It would make her task much easier now . . . "Thank you," she said softly.

A flicker of a grateful smile crossed Bernard's thin face and then he turned to Giles. "Will there be anything else, my lord?"

"No," Giles said, pouring himself another glass, then quickly put the bottle down. "Yes! Go to Sir Roger Penroy and tell him—tell him that his purchase has arrived."

"Right away, my lord." Bernard cast a surreptitious glance at Adrianna, then rapidly bowed himself out of the library.

Adrianna wrapped her chilled fingers around the comforting warmth of the tankard, willing herself to remain calm. What she needed now was information. "Am I the purchase, Giles?" she asked as composedly as she could.

"Aye, dear sister, you are," he resumed pleasantly, his good mood abruptly restored.

"And the . . . transaction is to have me wed to Sir Roger Penroy?"

His grin was an evil mockery of a smile. "I'm devastated to have to inform you that your betrothal has been broken off. But fear not, my dear! Sir Roger, large-minded gentleman that he is, is still willing to have you."

"Have me?" Adrianna's breath caught sharply in her throat as horrified understanding flooded her. "You don't mean . . . ?"

"As his mistress, yes," replied Giles. "To put it less delicately, he's taking you as his whore." He took a long swallow of wine, and reached again for the bottle.

Breathe, breathe! Adrianna reminded herself urgently, and filled her lungs with mind-clearing air. "I . . . see," she murmured. "And . . . he comes for me today?"

Giles nodded cheerfully. "And I do trust he'll have the money he promised me, for there's but ten bottles of wine remaining, and only two of Madeira!"

Adrianna raised her tankard to her lips and sipped at the hot tea. Soon she could begin, but not just now; Giles might become suspicious. "Giles," she said, glad her voice remained steady, "how did you know to send Mother Superior's letter to Inveraray?"

"A woman named Fiona—Fiona something-or-other, I can never remember the names of all these bloody commoners—sent a messenger to me, and 'twas then I learned where you were."

"Fiona Grant," Adrianna said flatly.

"Yes, that's it!" He nodded, pleased.

Fiona. Of course. Briefly Adrianna shut her eyes. It made sense. The voluptuous green-eyed girl had likely hated her from the very moment she'd first entered the great hall at Inveraray. How long ago that seemed . . .

"And what of the letter?" she asked.

"Shortly after the messenger arrived," Giles explained, clearly relishing the chance to relate his triumph, "so did the missive from Rosings. I opened it—in your absence, I thought it best, dear sister—and realized I had the means by which to lead you right back to Crestfield."

"Yes . . . yes, of course," she murmured, then let her head droop forward.

"I was confident you would get into that coach," he went on smugly, "knowing of your saintly devotion to those boring old nuns."

She made no reply to his barb, only closed her eyes and let her chin sag even closer to her chest.

"So I purchased an old coach, and Bernard had a cousin who was willing to earn a few coins, and—Adrianna! Are you attending to me, wench?" Giles' tone was piqued.

As if with an effort, Adrianna slowly raised her head. "Yes, Giles, I'm sorry . . . You were speaking of a messenger, I believe."

"That was five minutes ago!" Then he looked at her more closely, his arched brows drawing together. "What the devil's the matter with you? You look as if you're about to topple off the chair!"

"I—I do feel a trifle unwell," she mumbled apologetically. "Since yesterday's meal I've not quite felt . . ." Still holding the tankard, she covered her mouth with her free hand and made an unladylike retching sound.

"Oh, for heaven's sake, don't spill the contents of your stomach all over the floor. It's bad enough in here already," Giles said irascibly. "Do you wish to lie down in your chamber?"

Adrianna nodded. "Oh, yes, please, Giles," she said faintly. "I'm sure that would help."

"Percy and Fulk will escort you there, *and* stand guard until Sir Roger arrives," he said. "You will be ready, I trust."

Shakily Adrianna rose to her feet, gripping both the tankard and her linen bundle. "Oh, yes," she murmured, then made another retching noise.

"Get out!" Giles barked, and Adrianna, only too glad to obey, lurched awkwardly from the library.

The horses thundered past the hamlet of Ardrossan and into the long, flat valley of Nithsdale. So far so good, Leith told himself. They were making good time. Another day's riding would bring them to Dumfries, which itself was only a day's journey across the border, and into Carlisle by Monday.

Leith thought of Cecily MacBean, who had fed them and given them shelter when they'd stopped in Dumfries on their way from England back to Inveraray. That motherly, keen-eyed dame had quickly recognized Adrianna's goodness, her kindness, whereas he, in all his blind anger and grief over Hugh, had not. Adrianna had merely been a pawn in his game of revenge, his captive and his unholy prize.

But then, slowly, gently, with infinite subtlety, she had shown him how to live again, and to love . . .

And now . . . to win her heart was the prize he sought, his body and soul afire with the longing that consumed him.

Oh, God, where was Adrianna now? How did she fare? It was torture not to know.

His hands tightened convulsively on the reins and Thunder danced sideways, switching his black tail nervously. Leith leaned forward and soothingly patted the sleekly muscled neck; Thunder, reassured, continued his easy, powerful trot. It took all of Leith's self-control not to urge the horse into another gallop, but he'd already been pushing Thunder, and all their horses, as hard as he dared.

Suddenly he spied a small stream some fifty paces away, with trees to shade the horses as they drank. "Jock," he said imperatively, and jerked his chin toward the stream.

Jock nodded, called out to Dougal and Malcolm, and within moments they had all dismounted and their horses were drinking their fill of the cool, refreshing water.

Leith crouched down by the stream, watching them, trying to temper his impatience. Ten minutes, he told himself, ten minutes of rest for the horses and they'd be on their way again . . .

"Laird." Jock held out a chunk of bread and cheese but Leith waved him away. He had no appetite. He was staring into the gaily rippling waters at his feet when abruptly Thunder lifted his head, his velvety nose prickling as if testing a scent that was carried to him on the warm breeze.

Leith raised his head, too, and in the distance he saw a flash of movement. He rose to his feet and, a hand over his eyes to shield them from the sun, looked to the south.

Malcolm came to stand beside him. " 'Tis a horse and rider," he said. "They're coming in our direction."

"Aye," Leith said musingly. "And in some haste." He narrowed his eyes. There was a familiarity to the man's big, stocky shape, and surely . . . surely he knew that large gray gelding as well?

"God's blood, 'tis Colin!" he exclaimed. "What the blazes is he doing here? Why isn't he wi' Adrianna?"

"And where's Ross?" Jock said anxiously.

They all waited tensely for the few—but painfully long—minutes it took for Colin to reach them across the lush green valley.

"Laird!" Colin cried, pulling up his sweating mount, his own breath coming fast. "I didna think tae meet ye on the road! 'Tis a miracle!"

"Is it, man? Why ha' ye left Adrianna?" Leith demanded. "Is Ross still wi' her?"

"She told me tae gae, laird, and I pray I was right tae do sae," Colin answered somberly, dismounting and letting his horse make its way to the stream, where eagerly it drank. Quickly he told Leith and the others what had transpired as he, Adrianna, and Ross had unwittingly neared Carlisle.

"Mother of a whoreson!" Dougal swore bitterly, and Malcolm added in a mournful tone,

"Ach, our poor Ross! Tae be left dying in a Sassenach ditch, wi' neither family nor friends near . . ." His voice broke and he turned away.

"I ha' no doubt he died bravely, like a Scotsman," said Colin unsteadily, then gratefully accepted the wineskin Jock held out to him and took a long swallow of ale. He wiped his mouth with the back of his hand and offered the wineskin to Leith. "I didna hope tae see ye for some days, laird, for I thought ye all tae be in Strome Ferry. Ye concluded yer business quickly then?"

"Aye, and prosperously too," Leith answered absently. He drank from the wineskin and returned it to Jock. "The horses ha' rested. Are ye all ready tae continue?"

"Aye, laird," chorused Dougal and Jock, and Malcolm nodded, his reddish-orange hair flopping across his forehead as a gust of wind caught at it.

Leith looked to Colin. "Will ye ride wi' us?"

"If ye'll ha' me," came the sober response.

"What do ye mean, man? O' course we'll ha' ye if ye're no' too fatigued by yer journey."

" 'Tis no' that," Colin replied. He squared his broad shoulders and met Leith's eyes, his expression strained and serious. "Laird, I can no longer hide the truth from ye," he said quietly. "I ha' played a part in Mistress Adrianna's troubles."

Leith frowned. "We all knoo about the snake ye placed in her bed, Colin, there's no need tae bring it up again."

"Nay, laird, hear me oot." Colin shuffled his big feet, then drew a deep breath. "Do ye recall when we rode oot tae Strome Ferry, the day after the feast celebrating our return tae Inveraray?" At Leith's nod, he went on. "Ye joked wi' me aboot a lass I'd passed the night wi'. I didna ha' the nerve tae tell ye it was Fiona Grant, for 'twas she that had only recently warmed yer bed. She came tae me, laird, full o' sweet words and caresses, and the next I knew . . ." He shrugged. " 'Twas morning, and there she was beside me."

"Ye need no' ha' worried, for by then she and I had parted," Leith commented, gazing at Colin intently. "Gae on, then."

"Laird, I—I was a man bewitched," Colin said, his face flushing a vivid red. "What wi' her soft voice, her sweet kisses, her—her—"

"We all knoo what ye mean," interposed Leith dryly, and Colin nodded jerkily.

" 'Twas easy tae fall in love wi' her, and then she began tae encourage me in my foolish dislike o' Mistress Adrianna. Like a *sumph* I agreed tae find a wood snake and put it in Mistress Adrianna's bed. 'Tis ashamed I am o' what I did, but there's something far worse, laird . . . Ach, would that I had cut oot my damned tongue!" It was an agonized cry from the heart.

"What is it, Colin?" asked Leith, his voice very low.

"Laird, she asked me all aboot Mistress Adrianna, where she came from, the name o' her brother, the castle she lived in . . . I told her everything, all that I knew, time and again until she must ha' burned it utterly intae her memory!"

"And went tae Glasgow," Leith said slowly, "tae find a messenger tae gae tae Adrianna's brother. Aye, it all fits."

"I ha' betrayed ye, laird, sae many times!" Colin said raggedly, hanging his head. "If ever a man deserved banishment, or even death, 'tis I!"

"Nay, Colin, ye deserve compassion, and understanding." Leith went to him and gripped his shoulder. "I will no' say I'm happy at what ye did, but I canna find it within myself tae judge ye too harshly. Ye loved a lass, and felt there was nothing ye wouldna do for her. Well, I love a lass too, and I would walk tae the ends o' the earth for her. Will ye come wi' us, Colin, and help me save Adrianna?"

As if unable to believe his ears, Colin guardedly lifted his head and met Leith's gaze. What he saw there convinced him of the sincerity of Leith's words, for a great smile broke over his craggy face and he reached up his hand to clasp Leith's arm. "Laird, ye couldna keep me away!" he declared. "My fingers are twitching tae gae round the neck o' that damned brother o' hers!"

"No' if I get there first," Leith replied, and swiftly went to his horse.

CHAPTER 18

There was a soft scratching at the open library door, and groggily Giles lifted his head from the desk over which he'd been slumped.

Bernard was there, hovering on the threshold. "Your pardon for disturbing you, my lord," he said nervously, "but Sir Roger Penroy has just this moment arrived."

"What . . . ?" Giles mumbled, rubbing at his bleary eyes. "Oh! Oh, yes, of course. I was merely—merely going over my accounts and I must have . . ." He trailed off and Bernard helpfully offered:

"Fallen asleep, my lord?"

"No!" Giles glared at him. "Not at all, you dolt!" He sat up straight, threw off the burgundy velvet curtain he'd draped about his shoulders, and tugged at his red silk doublet to right it. "You may escort Sir Roger up to me immediately."

"Aye, my lord. Right away."

While Bernard was gone Giles quickly grasped the two

empty wine bottles atop the desk and stowed them in a drawer, then tightened the gold-tipped laces at his chest which had been splayed open. Then, filled with an agreeable sense of anticipation, he leaned back in the chair and linked his fingers across his stomach. His head ached and his mouth had an unpleasantly sour taste to it, but these were minor afflictions, nothing to cavil at, for soon he'd have Adrianna off his hands and Sir Roger's tidy payment *in* them.

He was contemplating whether he would purchase a sapphire to replace the one he'd so ignominiously lost, or would perhaps buy an emerald this time, when Bernard scratched on the door again and ushered in Sir Roger Penroy.

"Sir Roger!" Giles said graciously, rising to his feet. "How delightful to see you!"

As Sir Roger paused just inside the doorway, his little mud-colored eyes leisurely surveyed the library in all its slovenly disarray, then came to rest on Giles, raking him up and down and lingering on the opulent doublet and crisp, snowy ruff. His fleshy lips curved in a small, cynical smile, but he said only: "Good day, Giles. Your manservant here came to me with excellent news. My—ah—purchase is at Crestfield?"

"Yes, Adrianna arrived but a few hours ago," replied Giles breezily. "I thought you'd wish to know without delay."

"Quite right," the older man responded calmly, but Giles didn't miss the eager gleam in those piglike eyes. "My coach waits outside, and my guardsmen as well, in case your sister is . . . a trifle reluctant, shall we say. And, of course, I've something for you, my young friend." He reached into the pocket of his loose-fitting brown wool trunkhose and withdrew a small velvet purse which he held up and jingled enticingly.

Giles stepped out from behind the desk and moved eagerly toward Sir Roger, his hand extended, but stopped abruptly when those meaty fingers dangling the purse went back into the trunkhose pocket.

"Not so fast, Giles," came the flat, pleasant voice. "When you've given the wench to me you'll have your money, and not a moment before."

"Of course," Giles answered, attempting to hide his chagrin. "That's only fair, my dear Sir Roger. Bernard," he called to the servant who had irresolutely remained outside the open door, "kindly bring my sister to the library."

"Aye, my lord." Rapidly Bernard set off down the hallway and Giles, all too conscious of the mortified flush reddening his face, gestured to the chairs set haphazardly around the elm dais table. "Won't you have a seat, Sir Roger?"

"Why, I don't know, Giles," drawled Sir Roger. "Given the state of the room, I'd have to inspect the chair first." He strolled over and peered closely at one, and then another, before finally settling himself into a third, which creaked ominously under his weight.

" 'Tis a fine old elm," he pronounced. "Does it make for good firewood?"

Torn between fury and embarrassment, both of which he struggled to conceal, Giles was still fumbling for an answer when Bernard trotted down the hallway and stuck his head into the library. "Begging your lordship's pardon," he said diffidently, "but there's a slight . . . difficulty in bringing Mistress Adrianna to you."

Giles frowned. "A slight difficulty?"

"Aye, my lord. She's—she's a bit indisposed at the moment."

"She *did* say earlier in the day that she felt unwell," Giles said slowly, "but she assured me 'twas nothing. Do you mean to tell me she's actually ill?"

"Doubtless one of those female ailments," Sir Roger put in knowledgeably. "Both my wives suffered from 'em. 'Tis nothing a few blows to the head won't cure."

"Yes, yes, I'm sure you're right, Sir Roger," Giles said placatingly, then turned again to Bernard. "I daresay that's all it is, then?"

"Could be, my lord," the servant replied doubtfully. "Though Mistress Adrianna did mention something about a custard she'd eaten yesterday."

"Oh, for God's sake . . ." Giles gritted his teeth. "I want to see this . . . this *indisposition* for myself. Sir Roger, pray excuse me."

But the older man was already heaving himself up from his chair. "If you don't mind, Giles," he said blandly, "I will bear you company. You've thrown up just a few too many impediments for me to feel entirely free in my mind that this isn't simply another contrived postponement."

Bernard surprised them both by bursting into nervous laughter. *"Thrown up!* Oh, sir, that's very good!"

"Shut up, fool!" Giles hissed, and, looking abashed, Bernard squeezed himself against the wall of the dank, chilly corridor to let his master and Sir Roger pass.

"I'm confident this is the merest trifle, Sir Roger," Giles said reassuringly as they neared Adrianna's bedchamber, where Percy and Fulk, silent sentinels, stood on either side of the doorway. "She'll be up and about in no time, and—good heavens, what's that smell?"

Expressionlessly Percy opened the door, and as Giles sailed into the chamber his nostrils were assaulted full force with the unmistakable odor of vomit.

"Christ's blood! Adrianna!" he exclaimed in disgust.

Weakly Adrianna lifted her head from the basin set in the crook of her arm. "Oh, Giles," she sighed, then lay back on the bed as if exhausted. "I'm so sorry . . ."

Giles stared at her, horrified. Her face was as white as

chalk, her lips bloodless, and her hair was a tangled mess. There were even, he noticed with a grimace, flecks of vomit amidst the golden strands. His own stomach heaved queasily, and hastily he began to back away.

"Giles!" Adrianna whispered distressfully. "Don't leave me, *please!*"

Giles bumped into Sir Roger's round, solid form, muttered a guttural "Beg pardon!" and quickly left the room. Sir Roger remained stock-still, gazing at Adrianna as if he could not believe the evidence of his own eyes. Then, when Adrianna whimpered piteously and bent over the basin again, Sir Roger uttered a muffled oath, turned on the heel of his expensive cowhide shoe, and fled precipitously from the chamber.

He brushed past Bernard, who, wringing his hands, cautiously approached Adrianna. "Mistress," he whispered, "can I bring you something? A bit of pottage, mayhap?"

Adrianna wiped her mouth with the sheet and murmured feebly, "Might I trouble you for some more tea, perhaps, in that nice tankard? I *think* I could keep it down."

Bernard picked up the tankard that was set on a painted wooden chest drawn close to the bed. "I'll bring it right away, mistress," he promised.

"Thank you," she said in a weary thread of a voice, and closed her eyes. "You're very kind."

" 'Tis a pleasure, mistress," he said, and, true to his word, was back in a quarter of an hour with her tea. "What a ruckus in the great hall!" he commented, setting the steaming tankard atop the chest. "I've never seen Sir Roger so angry. I was sure he'd go off in a fit of apoplexy."

Adrianna cracked open her eyes. "Did he?" she murmured hopefully.

"Nay, mistress, he calmed down after a bit and told Giles he'd come back tomorrow."

Adrianna sighed. "Thank you for the tea, Bernard."

"You're welcome, mistress. I must go now, else his lordship will be wondering where I am." With a quick, nervous smile, Bernard left her chamber, softly closing the door behind him. Someone—probably one of the two guards—turned the key in the lock with a harsh grinding noise.

Adrianna lay quietly in the bed, waiting until she was sure that Bernard was gone from the corridor. Then, stealthily, she reached underneath the coverlet and pulled out her linen pouch of herbs. From the pouch she took a square of fine-meshed linen cloth the size of her palm, and then three small bags.

Passionflower.

Pennyroyal.

Blue cohosh.

All three herbs possessed a variety of healing qualities.

But when taken in combination, and in large doses—in, say, a strong infusion—they were likely to produce nausea and vomiting.

Adrianna smiled despite the wretched turmoil in her stomach, and silently she reached for the tankard of tea.

If anyone had bothered to ask her, she could have predicted that tomorrow she wouldn't be feeling any better at all.

Leith stood in the tall, broad doorway of the barn, staring bleakly out at the driving rain. They had just passed Dumfries when a violent summer storm had erupted, replete with booming thunderclaps, gusting winds and rain, and brilliant lightning strikes piercing the ominously dark sky. Their horses were badly spooked, even the normally steady-tempered Thunder, and they'd been forced to seek refuge on a farm just outside the hamlet.

Mother of a whoreson! Leith thought, clenching his fists

against his tense thighs. To have to stand here idly as crucial minutes ticked by . . . !

There was but one day now between them and Carlisle.

Yet so much could happen in a day . . .

In an hour . . .

Innocence could be lost.

Dreams shattered.

Lives destroyed.

A loud, long roll of thunder seemed to shake the very timbers of the barn, and behind him one of the horses whinnied skittishly.

"Hush noo, lass," came Jock's quiet, calming words. "Hush. I willna let anything harm ye."

If only he could say the same to Adrianna! Leith thought bitterly.

He watched as a young oak tree bent nearly horizontal before a cruel blast of wind, and tried without success to obliterate the memory of Fiona's mocking voice, repeating itself endlessly in his head.

It's too late, ye bastard, for her brother's selling her tae some rich auld Sassenach laird!

He could not, would not think of Adrianna struggling helplessly in the brutal embrace of another, weeping, her cries stopped by a brutal mouth.

No! Dear God, no!

No, he told himself sternly, giving himself a mental shake, instead he would concentrate, focusing all his energies, and peer into the sky, alert to the first sign that the storm was clearing. Summer paroxysms such as these were always brief; ten minutes from now the sun could be shining brightly again and they could resume their journey.

If this was a typical summer storm.

The rain was coming down so hard it looked as if it might last forever.

"Laird." It was Colin, who had come to stand beside him. "She'll be all right."

Leith rounded on him angrily. "How do ye knoo, ye bastard? *Anything* could ha' happened tae her by noo!"

"I'm—I'm sorry, laird," Colin said, backing away a pace. "I didna mean tae add tae yer distress."

"Then dinna come *blethering* tae me wi' yer foolish *clishmaclaver!*" Leith snapped. He jerked away to gaze out into the storm again, his mouth set in a grim line.

Colin continued to stand near him in the doorway, saying nothing, and finally, after some minutes had passed, slowly Leith turned around.

"I'm sorry, Colin," he said with difficulty. "I didna mean tae lash oot at ye. I knoo ye meant well."

"Ye need no' apologize, laird," replied Colin stolidly. "I am yer friend, and will be tae the day I die."

"I thank ye," Leith muttered. He hesitated, then spoke so softly that Colin had to come closer to make out the words. "Colin . . . 'tis unmanly, I knoo . . . but I'm afraid that . . ." Every syllable seemed to be dragged harshly from him, from the depths of an inner hell. "I'm afraid that I'll lose her . . . just like I lost Hugh."

"Nay, laird, nay," Colin answered quietly. "Ye willna lose the lass."

This time Leith looked to him questioningly, his expression one of raw desolation. "How can ye knoo, man? Can ye see intae the future?"

"Laird, I knew when that damned carriage came for Mistress Adrianna that something was amiss," Colin explained earnestly. "I couldna tell ye how I knew, 'twas just a feeling I had, a certainty. I tried tae convince Mistress Adrianna no' tae gae, but she insisted, saying she must try tae help one who had been sae good tae her. Ye knoo how Mistress Adrianna is when she's determined tae help someone, laird!"

"Aye," Leith said, with the ghost of a smile. "I knoo. Ye canna stop her."

"And that's why I tell ye she'll be all right, laird. I feel it . . . here." Colin laid a brawny hand on his chest, above the place where his heart beat.

There was a long, charged silence as the two men stood facing each other, one taut with foreboding and a terrible apprehension, the other almost eerily calm.

Then, at last:

"I pray that ye are right," Leith said gravely, and turned his attention back to the rain and the wind.

He tried to find some solace in what Colin had said, in the sturdy conviction in his tone.

But somehow Fiona's jeering voice kept insinuating itself into his agonized thoughts, taunting him, tormenting him, until he longed to pound his head on the hard wooden wall of the barn in the desperate hope of silencing it.

It's too late, ye bastard!

Too late!

"I'm usually quite an understanding sort, my young friend, but I cannot claim an inexhaustible supply of patience," Sir Roger said stiffly. " 'Tis Monday morning, she's been ill for two days! How can she possibly have anything left in her belly to cast up?"

"It's difficult to believe, isn't it?" Giles rejoined nervously. "One wonders what was in that custard, doesn't one?" He gave a loud, unconvincing laugh and when Sir Roger remained unmoved by his sally he quickly sobered.

"Truly, Sir Roger, her health did seem much improved when last I checked on her," he lied.

"And when was that?"

"Why, not ten minutes ago, just before you graced us with your presence. Would you like a glass of wine, dear sir? I believe you prefer that to ale in the morning. Or some Madeira, perhaps?"

"No," Sir Roger said shortly. "What I want is that wench, Giles, but I'm beginning to think that I shall never have her!"

Giles thought of the money he would owe Sir Roger if their agreement was not satisfactorily concluded, and felt himself breaking into a cold, panicky sweat.

"Worry not, Sir Roger, have her you shall," he said soothingly. "I'm certain that she will be fully recovered by this evening." She *would* be cured of her mysterious ailment, he told himself, smiling confidently for Sir Roger's benefit, or he'd tie her in her chair to keep her upright, and let her puke into her own bodice when Sir Roger wasn't looking! He added smoothly, "Will you not return for her then?"

Sir Roger regarded him from underneath lowering gray brows. "Do I have your word?"

"Of course you do," Giles said expansively. "In fact, why should we not make a celebration of it? Come dine with us tonight, my dear sir, and when you have eaten and drunk your fill, why not enjoy . . . a little sample before you take my sister home?"

Giles watched as Sir Roger mulled over his invitation, and surreptitiously exhaled in relief when a lascivious smile formed on those plump lips.

"Very well then, my young friend. I shall return at . . . shall we say six o'clock?"

"Splendid!" said Giles enthusiastically.

"Need I bring my guardsmen this time? Or will she be . . . amenable?"

"You may be perfectly comfortable leaving them at home, Sir Roger. I promise you, she'll be very amenable." *Even,* Giles thought desperately, *if I have to pour a bottle of my precious wine down her gullet!*

Sir Roger nodded, and had turned to leave when Giles loudly cleared his throat.

"Oh, and Sir Roger?"

The older man slowly swung around. "Yes?"

"Regarding the fare for this evening . . . I'd like to have something special prepared in your honor, three or four courses naturally . . . Perhaps a roast goose, a haunch of venison, fresh olive pie, some marzipan if we can come by it . . . Several wines, of course . . ." He looked expectantly at Sir Roger, who nodded.

"As you will, Giles."

"It meets with your approval, then? Excellent!" Giles rubbed his hands together. "So you wouldn't mind . . . well . . . Some assistance . . . I'm just a trifle beforehand, you see . . ." He paused with great delicacy, then added cheerfully, as if struck by a clever thought, "You may deduct it from my payment, of course!"

Sighing, Sir Roger reached into the pocket of his trunk-hose, extracted the velvet purse, and from it he withdrew three gold coins which he placed in Giles' outstretched hand. "I trust this will tide you over?" he said dryly.

"Indeed yes. I'm all gratitude," Giles said, and grandly accompanied Sir Roger to the door of the great hall. He bowed low, with a flourish worthy of a courtier, and said, "We await your return tonight, dear sir!"

Sir Roger crossed the threshold, then turned once more to Giles. On his round, fleshy face was suddenly an expression so nakedly threatening that Giles felt his gracious smile wilting before it.

"I will say this to you only once, my young friend." Sir Roger's mud-colored eyes were now as cold as ice. "Either I have your sister tonight or you can consider our arrangement terminated. Every pound—every shilling—I have loaned you will immediately come due." He paused, then went on with seeming irrelevance, "I went to London last year, did you know that, Giles?"

"No, Sir Roger," Giles returned, baffled and more than a little afraid.

"Yes, and I went to see a play there, by some playwright whose name I cannot recall. 'Twas called *The Merchant of Venice.* In it a debt is made with a very peculiar surety."

"Yes?" Giles said when Sir Roger appeared to be waiting for some kind of response. "What kind of surety?"

Now Sir Roger smiled, and Giles felt gooseflesh rising on his arms.

"The surety," he said gently, "was a pound of flesh. Don't you think that quite interesting, Giles?"

"Er—quite." Giles ran his tongue across lips that had abruptly gone dry.

"Just so." Sir Roger bowed slightly, said "Good day," and strolled unhurriedly to his waiting carriage.

The horses splashed across the gentle, shallow waters of the River Liddel and Leith felt his heart quicken. The border was just ahead. He glanced over at Colin and saw that his craggy face was serious and intense; so, too, were the faces of the other men.

They were close now, so very close . . .

His tension, his anxiety, sizzling along his nerves, was so great he could barely endure it.

He was just about to press his heels into Thunder's sides, to coax him into a fast gallop, when some instinct made him hold back, made him, instead, draw Thunder to a halt.

The others followed suit.

"What is it, laird?" asked Malcolm worriedly. "Why do we stop?"

Leith held up a hand for silence and looked searchingly

around them. They were in a grassy, lightly wooded area, with lush-leafed trees set apart from each other at goodly distances. Just behind them, the river plashed sweetly, and the gentle twittering of birdsong filled the air. It was a placid, restful scene, and yet . . .

Leith strained his ears.

Yes. There it was.

A weak voice, calling out.

"Laird . . ."

Quickly Leith directed Thunder to a copse of trees more dense than the others that surrounded it. He dismounted and cautiously stepped around the broad trunk of an oak tree, nearly stumbling across a man propped limply up against it.

It was Ross Sinclair.

White-faced, with enormous dark violet circles of fatigue beneath his glazed eyes. And wrapped diagonally across his torso, from shoulder to waist, was a bloodstained bandage he'd fashioned from strips torn off his coarse linen shirt.

"God's blood!" Leith muttered, crouching down, then shouted urgently to the others, " 'Tis Ross! He's alive!"

"Laird," Ross murmured dazedly, then managed a small, effortful smile as Colin, Malcolm, Jock, and Dougal swiftly gathered around him. "Colin . . . ye found the laird . . . I thank God . . ."

Colin gripped the flaccid hand lying against the tree trunk. "Ross, I thought ye were dead," he said, his voice hoarse with anguish. "I wouldna ha' left ye, lad, had I only known . . ."

"I thought I *was* dead," Ross answered. "I didna regain my senses until 'twas near dark."

"The road where ye were shot was an hour's journey by coach tae Carlisle," Colin said wonderingly. "God in heaven, lad, did ye walk all that way here?"

"Ach, it took some time," said Ross. "But just before I passed oot from the bullet in my shoulder, I heard Mistress Adrianna tell ye tae save me and gae back for the laird. Then everything started tae gae black. I remember yer hand on my face, Colin, and hearing ye talk tae me, but I was too far gone from the shock o' the wound tae even open my eyes. And then I heard ye gae."

Colin's eyes were wet with tears. "I'll never forgive myself, lad, never!" he choked out.

Ross curled his fingers around the massive hand still holding his. "Dinna say that, man," he whispered. "I had faith in ye . . . faith that ye all would come back, and sae I managed tae make my way here, tae the place where I thought ye'd most likely cross the border. There was plenty o' water, and I found some berries and mushrooms tae eat, and I waited. Then, when I heard the horses, I took a chance and called oot for ye . . ."

"Ross, ye do the name o' Scotsman proud," Leith said quietly.

The young man turned his head to Leith, wincing a little as he did so. "Thank ye, laird," he whispered, and even through the pain he managed another feeble smile.

"Dougal, take Ross wi' ye on yer horse by easy stages tae Dumfries," Leith directed. "Gae tae Cecily MacBean. She'll knoo how tae tend tae the lad, and she'll send for a physic if one is needed. Take these coins. And when Ross is able tae travel again, buy a horse for him in Dumfries and make yer way back tae Inveraray."

"Aye, laird," Dougal replied stoutly, and Leith asked, "Ross, this plan suits ye?"

"Aye, laird," he whispered, "thank ye. And . . . laird?"

"What is it, lad?"

"I canna recall ever stringing sae many words together at once," he murmured. "Mayhap the bullet has broken a dam."

Leith grinned. "I pity poor Dougal, then. Ye'll be jabbering his ears off all the way tae Inveraray!"

"Aye, he will, if I ha' anything tae do wi' it," Dougal promised fervently.

"Come, lads," Leith said, rising to his feet. "Let's help our brave Scotsman ontae Dougal's horse."

A few minutes later, when Ross was sitting before Dougal, holding himself valiantly erect, he looked to Leith and said a little shakily:

"I canna wait tae come home, laird, tae find ye and Mistress Adrianna safely within the walls of Inveraray once more."

"Aye," Leith said, his voice taut with emotion. "Aye. Fare ye well, then, Ross, Dougal. We must gae noo and make that happen!"

CHAPTER 19

Her back rigidly straight, Adrianna sat silently in an elaborately carved elm chair. She kept her gaze fixed upon the table, where before her was a plate heaped high with food—baked venison seasoned with ginger and pepper, a roasted chicken leg, a mound of leeks and carrots that had been boiled in garlic water—that she had been unable to bring herself to touch despite the fierce demands of her depleted stomach. The soothing, restorative chamomile and mint she'd secretly dosed herself with this afternoon had served to promptly alleviate the nausea of the past forty-eight hours, but had done little for nerves that were now strained to the breaking point.

She felt them twitch nervously when there came the sharp noise of a piece of flame-licked wood snapping in two. A fire was crackling vigorously in the soot-blackened hearth, and at Giles' direction the casement windows had been unlocked and opened a crack to keep the library from becoming too smoky.

To Adrianna's left, at the head of the long six-legged table, sat Giles, who ate and drank copiously but carelessly, spewing crumbs and bits of food unconcernedly across the tabletop as he animatedly entertained his guest with his gay, ceaseless chatter.

And across from her, dressed in a costly black silk doublet slashed with yellow-dyed leather and a large lace-bordered ruff, sat Sir Roger Penroy. Politely he attended to Giles as he too energetically attacked the contents of his plate. Yet time and time again Adrianna sensed his small glittering eyes resting on her with such palpable, avaricious lust that she felt as if he had actually pawed at her with one of those fat repulsive hands. Small wonder, then, that she had no appetite.

". . . and for myself," Giles said thoughtfully, "I find that a balm made with sheep's fat and just a touch of bergamot makes an excellent tonic for the hair. Do not you, dear Sir Roger?"

"Well, Giles, I hardly know," the other man replied in a disgruntled tone, and Adrianna glanced swiftly at the wispy gray strands barely covering his shiny pate.

"I trust you don't think for a moment that your lack of . . . hirsuteness makes you any less masculine," Giles said unctuously. "Why, I've heard that men such as yourself have a greatly expanded capacity for . . ." He looked slyly at Adrianna. "For virility."

Sir Roger chuckled, and under the concealment of the table Adrianna's fingers clenched tightly at her skirts.

Her time was running out.

She had given herself two days, thanks to the herbs that had rendered her so vilely, usefully ill.

But this morning Giles had come to her, and with terms so foul and so explicit as to what he would do with her—do to her—if she failed to make herself presentable for the evening's supper with Sir Roger, had made it abundantly clear that he would brook no further delay.

So she had repaired her appearance as best she could, laboriously combing out her knotted hair, scrubbing at her teeth with a small square of linen, washing her face and neck using a clean basin of water that Bernard had thoughtfully provided.

Then she had sat in a chair near the window, watching as minute by minute the sun inched its way across the summer sky and began to lower itself behind the vivid green line of trees in the distance.

The bright light of day had started to fade, and so had the hope that before had flared with such optimism.

Adrianna knew that Leith would come for her. There was no question of that. It was as certain as the waxing and waning of the moon, the ebb and flow of the earth's tides, the eternal, unending cycle of the seasons.

But . . . would he come too late?

Once Sir Roger had her in his manor, the possibility that Leith could rescue her would grow ever more remote. Unlike Crestfield, which was situated a league or so from the town of Carlisle and was severely short of staff, Sir Roger's prosperous estate was closer to town and was more populated, more patrolled, more securely guarded.

She would be lost to Leith.

And even if he *did* manage to somehow come to her at Sir Roger's manor, would he even want her after tonight?

She would be defiled.

Violated.

Polluted.

An awful, overwhelming sadness pulled at her, so heavily that it was difficult to remain sitting upright.

After tonight, Adrianna told herself, she would be better off dead.

With a painful jolt she recalled the evening when Leith

had spirited her away from this room just a few short months ago. She had thought then that her fate as his captive would be worse than death. Little did she know that she would find not degradation, not suffering, in his magnificent Highland home, but a powerful, life-altering love, as well as a cherished place among a clan that had opened its heart to her. And now, here she was again in her father's library, knowing with every ounce of her being that what awaited her was an unendurable nightmare. How ironic it was! To have come full circle! A hysterical laugh threatened and then just as quickly died in her throat as she considered what she must do.

"Bernard, you may clear the table," Giles said, his peremptory voice breaking into her thoughts, and Adrianna blinked, looking up from her clenched hands to see the servant approaching her from his post near the door.

"Mistress, you haven't had nothing!" Bernard whispered in some concern. "Shall I leave your meal here for a bit?"

"No, I thank you," she murmured absently, and Bernard obediently reached for her plate.

It was heavy, and perhaps he failed to grip it strongly enough, for the plate tilted precariously in his hand and then the chicken leg had slid off onto the table, knocking over her untouched wineglass. Red liquid seeped rapidly across the mellow elm, Sir Roger drew back his chair to avoid the deluge, and Giles shouted angrily at Bernard, "You clumsy fool!"

Amidst all the confusion Adrianna saw her chance. As Bernard fumbled with the grease-laden chicken leg, quickly she reached up and laid her fingers atop the knife that had been set next to her plate, then surreptitiously slid it down onto her lap and hid it amidst the folds of her skirt.

"I'm—I'm dreadful sorry, mistress! Your lordship!" Bernard stammered, managing to finally restore the chicken leg to her plate. He set the wineglass upright and dabbed ineffectually at the pooled wine with the napkin Adrianna gave him.

"Go get some cloths, idiot, to wipe it up!" snapped Giles, and the flustered Bernard, still muttering apologies, scurried out of the room to obey.

In the silence that followed Giles reached for the bottle of wine sitting at his elbow. "May I refill your glass, dear sister?" he asked.

She shook her head.

Giles laughed. "You might want to reconsider," he said archly. " 'Twill help you to enjoy . . . what is to come."

She shot a glance at him and saw that he was smiling so significantly at Sir Roger that his meaning could not be other than patently clear. Adrianna curled her fingers around the reassuring solidity of the knife's wooden handle, and said, lifting her chin, "I thank you, Giles, but no."

He shrugged, and poured more wine into his own glass. "As you will."

Bernard hurried back into the room, bearing several linen cloths which he used to soak up the spilled wine. When he had done, he began stacking Giles' and Sir Roger's empty plates, their forks and knives and napkins, onto a tray. "Shall I bring the nuts and the cheese, my lord?" he asked.

Giles turned to Sir Roger. "It's up to you, my dear sir. Do you wish for the nuts and cheese . . . or dessert?" He winked.

Adrianna's breath caught in her throat as a panicky terror grabbed at her. Once again there could be no mistaking his meaning.

God, give me strength, she prayed desperately. *O please!*

Sir Roger was smiling too, and once again she felt the

weight of that lustful stare. "Why, Giles," he drawled, "I do believe I've a craving for something . . . sweet."

Bernard looked perplexedly at him and then at Giles. "But my lord," he whispered, "we've no cakes to serve tonight, and there wasn't any marzipan in town for love nor money."

"Well, I suppose Sir Roger will have to fend for himself," Giles replied cheerfully, and rose to his feet. "Bernard, you may go now; I'll follow you out."

"Giles, no!" Adrianna whispered. "Pray, do not leave!"

He didn't even look at her, or give any sign that he had heard her agonized plea. Instead he waited until Bernard had bustled from the library, carefully balancing a laden tray, and then he mutely held out his hand. In it Sir Roger placed a plump velvet purse whose contents clinked with a distinctly metallic sound. Gleefully Giles curled his fingers around the purse, even as a satisfied smile curved his thin lips. " 'Tis a pleasure doing business with you, Sir Roger," he said, and nonchalantly sauntered from the room.

No sooner had the door been firmly shut than Sir Roger addressed Adrianna.

"Come here."

It was said in that same flat, pleasant tone, but when Adrianna looked at him she saw that his round, coarse-featured face was red with excitement, and shiny now with perspiration.

Revulsion and a trembling fear shimmied vertiginously through her. She swallowed, and said as firmly as she could, "I will not."

He smiled. "Are you going to make me come after you, my pretty?" She said nothing, only looked at him defiantly as her heart pounded madly in her chest, and watched in dismay as he lumbered to his feet.

"I'll make you pay for this," he said, still smiling, and began to move around the edge of the table toward her.

"You've made me wait, time and time again. I don't like to be kept waiting." His little swinish eyes were hard, gleaming with a carnal greed. "I'm a man accustomed to getting what I want, as those who flout me learn . . . much to their regret."

Jerkily Adrianna stood, the knife still concealed amidst her skirts, and felt herself sway as an icy rush of dizziness surged within her. "Keep away from me," she whispered, gripping the chair back with her free hand for support.

"Feisty, aren't you?" Sir Roger remarked genially. "Well, I'll soon beat that out of you."

The room was tilting crazily beneath her, but Adrianna managed to back away from him, step by step, until finally she came up hard against the cold glass of one of her father's cabinets. Something inside crashed onto a shelf and shattered.

"Don't you *dare* come any closer!" cried Adrianna, hearing in her voice a high, shrill note of panic.

He gave a mocking laugh, continuing to amble toward her with an unnervingly complacent indolence. "And what's to stop me, wench?"

Her breath coming in short, choppy bursts, Adrianna saw that he was but a few arm's lengths from her now. She spasmodically yanked up her arm to show him the knife she gripped so hard her knuckles were white. "I will kill myself!" she said tremulously. "Then you shall never have me!"

He halted, and laughed again, his big belly jiggling raucously. "You won't," he contradicted her pleasantly. "No woman has the courage to do such a thing."

"You think not?" Adrianna panted. "Watch me!" Without hesitation she lowered the knife to her wrist. *Leith,* her mind screamed out, *I love you!* And then the gleaming edge of the knife was at the soft white flesh of her wrist . . .

"No!" Sir Roger bellowed, and as a tiny red ribbon

glimmered brightly on her skin, another voice—a deep, lilting voice, more beloved to her than any other—was shouting hoarsely:

"Adrianna! Dinna do it, lass!"

Stunned, Adrianna threw back her head to see Leith charging into the room, his mighty *claid mor* drawn and its broad, heavy blade pointed directly at Sir Roger.

"Leith!" she cried out, hardly able to believe that he was really, truly here, he had come for her, come for her in time! Her head swam; woozily she sank to her knees and dropped the knife, watching as if in a dream as Sir Roger whipped around with surprising speed and pulled a small, deadly-looking pistol from the pocket of his capacious trunkhose.

"I had a feeling something was going to go wrong tonight!" he snarled. "Stand down, you filthy Scott!"

But Leith didn't stop, only rushed forward with such lightning speed that before the other man could even pull back the trigger he was neatly impaled on the point of Leith's broadsword.

"Ye bastard," Leith growled, "I'd kill ye *twice* if I could," and with a triumphant roar he withdrew his *claid mor*.

Sir Roger gave a choked gurgle, an almost comical look of astonishment on his doughy face, and crumpled with a loud thump onto the floor.

Leith wiped his bloody sword on a cloth Bernard had left on the table and sheathed it, then went quickly to Adrianna, dropping to his knees and gathering her into his arms. "Ach, my little love!" he said raggedly. "Are ye all right?"

"I am now," Adrianna whispered joyfully, reveling in the feel of that rock-hard chest, the muscular arms holding her as if they would never let her go. "Oh, Leith, you're here, you're real!"

"Aye, lass, aye," he muttered, and then he was raining

kisses on her upturned face, on her forehead, her nose, her cheeks, until finally she reached up, buried her fingers in his thick dark hair, and tugged him toward her and his mouth was slanted hotly across hers.

He groaned then, kissing her long and deep, and Adrianna felt the horror, the terrible fear of these last days slip away. There was nothing now but Leith, his strength, his goodness . . . his passion. With a great sigh, Adrianna slid her fingers through his hair, raised them to his face, tenderly drew them along the contours of chiseled cheekbone, firm jaw, powerful neck.

She broke the kiss to murmur, "I was afraid I might never see you again. Once Sir Roger had me locked away in his manor . . ."

Dark eyes looked searchingly into her own, warm and intense. "I would ha' found ye, Adrianna, and saved ye, if I had tae slay a thousand men! Dinna ye knoo I love ye, lass?"

A little shyly, Adrianna rested her hands on his shoulders as she met his gaze. "Do you, Leith? That evening . . . in my bedchamber . . . I told you then what was in my heart, but you did not do the same, and I . . . I was not sure of your feelings for me."

"Ach, I'm a fool!" he said roughly. "That night I loved ye wi' my body, wi' my soul, wi' everything I had; I thought ye knew it, lass."

"But I did!" said Adrianna quickly. "I could tell, Leith, it was magic beyond my wildest dreams! And yet . . ." She hesitated. "Perhaps 'tis because I'm a woman, but I longed to hear you say the words."

"It grieves me that I left ye in ignorance o' my true feelings, lass," he returned somberly. "Will ye give me a chance tae make it up tae ye?"

"You need not apologize—" she began, but he interposed.

"Nay, I wish tae make it up tae ye, ye see. And . . . I think it might take a lifetime or two tae do it properly."

Adrianna's fingers tautened on those broad shoulders. "Leith . . ." she breathed. "What are you saying?"

"I'm saying that I love ye, lass, and that I want ye for my wife, and want ye wi' me forever." His handsome countenance was more serious than she had yet seen it as he went on earnestly: "I didna ask ye properly before; 'twas poorly spoken on my part. Sae noo I'm asking ye humbly, will ye ha' me as yer husband?"

Adrianna gave a glad laugh, and buried her face against his neck, feeling as if she might take wing and float with the wild joy burgeoning inside her. "Yes!" she said rapturously. "Oh, aye, Leith, with all my heart! I do love you so!"

His arms tightened around her. "It's no' just women that like tae hear the words," he said with a shaky laugh. "It gives me great pleasure tae ha' it from ye, lass."

"I'll say it again, many times over," she promised.

"Do that, sweeting," he murmured, pressing a lingering kiss to her lips, then reached up and took hold of her hands that had crept higher to clasp themselves about his neck. "Let me see that poor wrist," he said, and obediently she turned over her hand to show him the thin scarlet line on her skin.

Leith shook his head. "Ach, lass, the image o' ye standing there wi' that knife . . . 'twill haunt my dreams for many years tae come."

" 'Tis naught but a scratch," she told him smilingly. "It will heal."

"Ye'll ha' a scar, ye knoo," he said. "I'm sorry for that."

"It matters not," Adrianna said, and stroked her free hand lovingly down his chest. "What matters is that we are together."

He smiled back at her then, and gently raised her wrist so that his mouth could lightly touch her wound. "Aye, lass, ye're right. Noo, do ye feel well enough tae stand? I mislike kneeling amongst the soot." At her nod, he rose to his feet and drew her up with him. A frown creased his brow as he looked at her more closely and he said, "God's blood, lass, but ye're thin and pale! Were the bloody bastards trying tae starve ye intae submission?"

Adrianna burst out laughing. "Oh, Leith!" she gasped, smiling into his perplexed face. "You'll be so proud of me!"

Swiftly she described to him how she had used the herbs in her pouch to render herself so putridly ill, thereby gaining precious hours. "It was crude," she concluded, "but, I thank God, effective."

"I *am* proud o' ye, lass," Leith said warmly. " 'Twas an act worthy of a Scot!" He led her to one of the elm chairs, and helped her to sit. "But lass," he went on, more soberly, "I canna tell ye how greatly it pains me that ye were forced tae gae through this hell. I should never ha' left ye tae gae tae Strome Ferry!"

Adrianna shook her head. "Do not blame yourself, my love; you only did what was necessary. I've sustained no lasting harm, but ..." Her eyes filled with tears as she looked up at him. "Oh, but Leith ... poor Ross Sinclair! Did Colin find you, and tell you that Ross—Ross died defending me?"

"Aye, Colin did find me, lass," he replied, "but Ross didna die. Despite his injury, the doughty lad found his way tae us where we crossed the border. And ye'll be pleased tae hear that at this very moment he's riding wi' Dougal tae Dumfries, where I ha' no doubt Cecily MacBean will alternately bully and coddle him back tae health in no time!"

"I *am* pleased," Adrianna said softly. "And grateful! To Ross, to Colin, to you ..."

"Ye might tell Colin ye feel that way," Leith told her, and at her inquiring look he explained, " 'Twas he who gave the information tae Fiona Grant aboot yer brother and where ye lived. No' only did Fiona persuade him tae put the snake in yer bedchamber, she wormed from him everything he knew aboot ye as well. Noo he's wracked wi' guilt over the wrong he feels he's done ye."

"She made Colin fall in love with her, didn't she?" Adrianna said compassionately. "Poor besotted Colin! Of course I will tell him I bear him no ill will—and how much I have to thank him for, for if it weren't for his bravery in accompanying me to England, and then in setting off to find you once we knew it was all a trap . . ." A shudder rippled down her spine. "I do not like to think of it."

"Nay, lass, nor do I," Leith said grimly. Then he gave his head a little shake, as if clearing his mind of visions too awful to contemplate, and added, "So ye'll speak tae Colin, then? I knoo a word or two in his ear would do much tae lift the heavy burden he carries."

"Aye, my love, at the first opportunity," Adrianna said, and smiled as he laid a gentle hand on her shoulder.

At that moment Jock came briskly into the room. He saw them both and grinned. "Well met, Mistress Adrianna! I see the laird has been taking good care o' ye, slaying yer dragons?"

"Something like that, Jock," Adrianna said, smiling back at him.

"What's the news?" Leith asked.

"The castle's nearly deserted, laird," reported Jock. "I found merely two great loobies—guardsmen by the look o' them—drunk and asleep in a corner o' the great hall. 'Twas the work of a bairn tae knock their sleepy heads together and tie them up," he added scornfully. "Why are there no people here, Mistress Adrianna?"

"Here's someone," Colin sang out, and entered the library dragging Giles with him, one burly hand firmly gripping the back of Giles' luxurious red silk doublet. The

Earl of Westbrook so greatly resembled a recalcitrant child being taken to task by a stern father that Adrianna might have laughed had it not been for the all too recent memories of Giles' blatant cruelty and avarice.

"He was trying tae escape, but went tae his chamber tae pack first!" Colin said, rolling his eyes. "I found him cramming ruffs intae a valise!"

"Let go of me, you damned Scottish beast!" Giles said furiously, twisting helplessly in the larger man's grasp. "I'll see you hanged!"

Colin ignored him. "Mistress Adrianna!" he said cheerfully. "Ye're a sight for sore eyes! I trust I find ye well?"

"Very well, Colin, I thank you," she replied, dimpling. "And yourself?"

"Much happier noo, Mistress Adrianna. Am I right in thinking this is yer brother here?"

"Yes, Colin," she said, and felt Leith's hand clench on her shoulder.

"I thought sae, there's a wee bit o' family resemblance between ye," said Colin, and continued with unabated affability, "Laird, I'd like tae slash his throat wi' my dirk while I've got him sae close, but if ye wish tae do the honors I'll gladly relinquish him tae ye."

"There's nothing I'd like more, Colin, believe me," Leith said, his voice tense. "My *claid mor* has tasted revenge once tonight, but 'tis hungry still." He gestured to the limp, bloody body of Sir Roger and Giles blanched when he saw it.

"Adrianna!" he said desperately. "I crave your pardon! Do not have me murdered so cold-bloodedly, sweet sister! 'Twas—'twas just that I needed the money, surely you can understand that?"

"No, Giles," Adrianna answered, her voice very low, "I will not pretend that I understand you."

Colin's hand tightened on Giles' doublet and Giles

jerked impotently as he tried without avail to free himself. *"No!"* he wailed. "My dear sister, pray, *pray* do not let them kill me!"

Adrianna raised her gaze to see Leith watching her, his dark, deep-set eyes steady and keen.

"The decision is yers, lass," he said quietly.

She reached up to clasp the warm, strong hand resting on her shoulder. "Leith . . . despite my brother's crimes . . . I cannot find it in my heart to ask that you kill him."

A wry half-smile twisted his lips. "I knew ye couldna, lass, 'tis no' in yer kind nature. Let him gae, Colin."

"Aye, laird," Colin said reluctantly, then gave Giles one last, violent shake and released him.

His thin white fingers tugging convulsively at his doublet to straighten it, Giles took several jerky steps away from the burly Scotsman who glared at him still. "I thank you for your clemency, my saintly sister," he said shrilly, his breath coming fast, "but if you think I'll let you turn me over to the authorities in Carlisle, you're very much mistaken. I'm an *earl,* after all!" His voice rose to a hysterical screech and then, before anyone could stop him, Giles rushed across the library, flung open the casement windows, then hurled himself out onto the balcony and over the stone lip of it.

Adrianna screamed and the men went quickly to the balcony.

"Ach, dear God," she heard Leith mutter, "the poor mad bastard," but could not force herself to rise from her chair to go and see for herself Giles' broken body on the grassy field far below.

Leith, trailed by Colin and Jock, returned inside and he went to Adrianna, crouching next to her chair. "Yer brother is dead, lass," he said, and reached out with his hand to cover her own, which she had clasped tightly together in her lap.

"Yes, I know," she returned somberly. "Leith, I am very sorry, 'tis unsisterly of me to feel this way, but . . . I've little regret at his death. I—I never loved Giles, even as a child."

"He didna deserve yer love, lass," Leith said gruffly, then swiftly rose to his feet at the sounds of a commotion in the hallway and a voice calling out blithely, "Laird, look what I've brought ye!"

Malcolm entered the library with his sword drawn, at the point of it hurrying a cowering Bernard and a tall, homely young man who was spectacularly bedraggled, from his lank matted hair to damp, dirt-encrusted shirt and breeches to boots dull with slimy mud.

Adrianna wrinkled her nose. The tall young stranger also stank to high heaven.

"I made a complete round o' the castle and outbuildings, laird," announced Malcolm. "I found this lad moldering in the dungeon—he's a Scotsman!—and retrieved the key tae his cell from the snoring Sassenachs in the great hall. Then, in the kitchen, I found this one hiding in a cupboard." He indicated Bernard, whose eyes had bugged out at the sight of Sir Roger's lifeless body, with the tip of his sword. "I flushed him oot readily enough."

Leith turned to Adrianna. "Do ye knoo these men, lass?"

She nodded, pointing. "Aye, that's Bernard, a servant. He meant no harm, Leith, and indeed did all he could for me."

"Thank you, mistress!" Bernard said gratefully. " 'Tis very good of you to speak up on my behalf!"

"It is merely the truth," she answered gently.

"You may step aside," Leith told Bernard, and as the servant complied with alacrity, scuttling well away from Malcolm's threatening sword, Leith asked Adrianna, "And the other?"

"I've no idea. I didn't even know Giles *had* someone in the dungeon."

Everyone looked at the filthy, malodorous prisoner.

"Well, lad?" said Leith.

"I'm Cedric Murray, o' Glasgow," came the faltering reply. "I came here on an errand o' mercy, and found myself thrown in the dungeon for my pains!"

Leith sighed. "Fiona Grant sent ye, did she no'?"

The youth's head came up. "Aye," he said eagerly, "do ye knoo her? Did she send ye wi' a message for me?"

Colin snorted rudely. "Ye and I will ha' tae talk, ye poor *sumph.*"

"And after that we'll send ye home, lad," Leith said. "Ye've been punished sufficiently for yer foolishness. Malcolm, are there any horses in the stables?"

"Aye, laird," answered Malcolm, "there's a skinny piebald mare."

"That's my Sheila!" Cedric exclaimed, and Bernard, looking timidly at Leith, put in apologetically, "We'd so little in the larder, your worship, and with the grooms all gone . . . I fed her the best I could."

"I am sure ye did," Leith responded.

Bernard brightened at Leith's lenient tone, and added, "She liked my pottage."

Cedric visibly shuddered, and Adrianna spoke, a little hesitantly.

"Leith, I'm sorry to interrupt, but seeing Bernard has reminded me of something . . ."

"Aye, lass? What is it?"

"I'm terribly hungry," she confessed, her eyes twinkling. "Bernard, is there anything left to eat?"

"Oh, aye, mistress," he assured her. "His lordship had me purchase enough food for ten!"

"Good!" Colin said. "I'm famished!"

"Aye, sae am I," added Malcolm.

"And I suspect young Cedric might like something tae eat that's no' pottage," Leith said, grinning.

"Aye, sir!" Cedric replied vehemently. "Oh, aye!"

Bernard counted around the room. "Supper for six, is it? It won't take me but half an hour, your worship!" he declared.

Leith nodded. "Good enough. We'll keep ye company in the kitchen," he said, "and remove ourselves from this *connached* library!"

" 'Tis been much abused," Colin agreed, looking around him as if for the first time. "Why the devil is there sae much soot on the floor?"

"I'll tell you everything over supper," Adrianna promised, and as the men began trooping out of the room she called out, "Bernard, would you remain behind for a moment?"

He obediently stopped, and came to her, his thin, worn hands laced together at his waist. "Aye, mistress?"

"Bernard, you need to know that your master the earl is dead," she told him.

"Yes, mistress," he said calmly, his eyes going once again to the corpse of Sir Roger.

Adrianna's brows went up. "You don't seem much surprised," she remarked.

"Nay, mistress," he answered, "not with these brave Scotsmen about!" Then he added defiantly, "And I won't say I'm sorry that his lordship is dead, neither!"

"No, nor was I," she admitted candidly. "But Bernard, with the earl gone, there will be no employ for you at Crestfield."

"You won't be staying, mistress?" he asked hopefully, and Adrianna's glance went to Leith, who was perched on the edge of the massive oak desk, one long, booted leg swinging lazily back and forth.

She returned his smile, giddy butterflies swirling in her stomach, then looked to Bernard again. "No, I will not be staying. But as for you . . . Do you have any prospects here in Carlisle? Any family?"

He shook his head, his gaunt face melancholy now. "Nay, mistress, I've neither prospects nor family. There was only my cousin—you know him, mistress, it's Tom Gantrey—and now that he's run off to that barbarous island, well . . ." A mournful little sigh escaped him. "I fear I'm all alone in the world."

"Do not despair, good Bernard," she told him bracingly. "I believe I've a plan that will be much to your liking. Go on to the kitchen, if you please, and hurry with your preparations! We'll discuss my idea after supper!"

"Aye, mistress," he said, looking considerably more cheerful. "And thank you!"

He hurried out, and Adrianna was alone with Leith once more. She rose from her chair and went to him, laying a hand on his arm. "Might I ask a favor, Leith," she said softly, "and then beg a kiss afterwards?"

He caught her hand in his own and raised it to his lips. "The favor is yers if I can grant it, lass, and never think ye need importune me for a kiss!"

She curled her fingers around his, glorying in that warm gaze that was like the golden munificence of the sun. "Must we return directly to Inveraray, my love? There is something yet I must do."

He nodded, his countenance grave. "I had no' forgotten, lass. If ye can bear tae rest one more night in this castle, we'll set oot at dawn."

"Thank you," she answered gratefully, and laid her head on his chest. "With you here, I can endure it," she whispered. "When you are with me, there is nothing I fear."

Swiftly his arms came around her, solid as stone. "Ach, lass, I missed ye," he said, his deep voice a little ragged. "The world wasn't right withoot ye, nor was I. I love ye sae much I hardly ha' the words tae tell ye."

"Oh, Leith, I love you too!" Adrianna said fervently, and stood on tiptoe to raise her lips to his. "Might I have that kiss now?"

He smiled, his eyes alight with a tender fire that thrilled her to the core, and eagerly he complied.

CHAPTER 20

It was noon by the time they reached Rosings. "Sister Anne!" Adrianna called out in a glad voice, sliding from Thunder's back even before Leith could dismount and offer his assistance. Swiftly she hurried along the curving gravel path, which was bordered by low-growing, neatly trimmed hedges of lavender, rosemary, and sage, to the open door of the small, two-story brick convent where a black-clad figure stood stock-still in astonishment.

Leith thrust his leg over the saddle and swung himself to the ground, then handed Thunder's reins to Colin. "Wait here a moment," he instructed, and strode after Adrianna.

She stood on the doorstep in the loving embrace of the plump, diminutive nun, who murmured disjointedly in a high, sweet voice, "Oh, my dearest Adrianna! Thank God you are here! Toby Bridges—one of our local men—kindly took my letter all the way to Crestfield and gave it to your brother, but when we didn't receive a letter from you in return, much less see you here . . . Oh, my dear, we hardly knew what to think!"

" 'Tis a long story," Adrianna said, pulling back to look earnestly into the round, rosy visage of Sister Anne, "but suffice it to say that I came here as quickly as I could. I'm so anxious to see Mother Superior. Is she . . . ?"

"Alas, there has been no improvement," Sister Anne replied, shaking her head. "But she clings tenaciously to life, like the last of a candle that is not quite ready to flicker out. I believe she has been waiting for you, dearest."

"I must go to her," Adrianna murmured, then turned to draw Leith forward when she intercepted the sister's swift curious glance. A becoming pink blush bloomed on her cheeks as she said softly, "Sister, I am proud to present to you my betrothed, the laird Leith Campbell."

Leith ducked his head. "Madam," he said politely, but was unprepared for the spontaneous hug the little nun bestowed on him, though her childlike arms could scarcely reach around him, so short of stature was she.

"Oh, Adrianna, 'tis glorious news!" she cried happily as she let him go. "A Scot, is he? I can tell by that charmingly distinctive accent! And so tall and handsome, too! Child, you've done well for yourself!"

"I am delighted to hear you say so, Sister," Adrianna said diffidently. "I confess I was worried that you might think I had . . . strayed from the fold."

Sister Anne was beaming at her. "Everyone knows you would have made a splendid nun, my dearest, but I think you are eminently suited to be a wife and a mother. Especially with this wonderful man! I vow, I love him already!"

Leith saw Adrianna's cheeks turn even pinker and he smiled down at Sister Anne. "Madam," he said solemnly, "ye are too good."

"Not at all," she denied. "What I am is an excellent

judge of character, young man, and I can see that you're
going to make our darling Adrianna very happy indeed."

He bowed. "I will devote my life tae that goal, madam."

Adrianna clutched his arm. "Sister, may I bring Leith
in with me to see Mother? I so much want her to meet
him!"

"Of course you may," Sister Anne said warmly. "Lord
Campbell, are those your men there on the road?"

"Aye, madam, and will ye no' call me Leith?"

"Thank you, I *will* try, though you are so very large 'twill
seem difficult at first. I will have one of the sisters offer
your men refreshment, and shelter for your horses. Come
now, both of you, let's go inside."

And so saying, she led them into the convent. Leith only
had time to note that it was dim and comfortably cool in
the low-ceilinged hall before half a dozen nuns rushed
toward them, exclaiming softly. Adrianna was affectionately enveloped in black-sleeved arms many times over
before she was able to catch her breath and introduce the
other sisters to him.

There was tall, dignified Sister Alice, Sister Agnes with
a brown complexion and work-roughened hands, Sister
Dorothy who smelled sweetly of lavender water, Sister
Judith with the shy smile, and a few more whose names
he was unable to catch amidst the quiet flurry. All greeted
him as Adrianna's future husband with unconstrained
warmth.

Their unselfish joy in Adrianna's unexpectedly altered
destiny both surprised and moved Leith. It was plain to
see, as the nuns gathered closely around her, that here at
Rosings she was much loved.

A tiny stab of doubt abruptly pricked at him. Was it
wrong of him to take her away from the convent? His heart
told him no, but his intellect was suddenly not so sure.

He had no time to further ponder this troubling question, for Sister Anne quietly but efficiently shooed away the other nuns. "Adrianna and Lord Campbell—Leith—have come to see Mother Superior," she said, and respectfully the sisters drew back.

"This way, if you please," she said to Adrianna and Leith, and began walking down a corridor whose polished wood floor gleamed dully beneath their feet.

"To the chapel, Sister?" questioned Adrianna.

"We converted the chapel into a bedchamber and moved Mother downstairs," answered Sister Anne. " 'Twas easier for us to hear her when she calls out. Now we hold mass in the schoolroom." She paused before a closed door and said soberly, "I fear you will find Mother Superior much changed, my dearest." She pulled open the door and stepped back to let Adrianna and Leith enter.

Ordinarily, Leith thought, pausing briefly on the threshold, this would have been a cheerful chamber, for its large mullion window freely admitted the afternoon's bright sunlight and offered a charming view of the gardens to the back of the house. But the sight of the thin, pallid figure lying motionless in the narrow bed could not but sadden the spirit.

"Mother . . ." Adrianna breathed, going swiftly to the bed and dropping to her knees before it. "Oh, Mother, can you hear me?"

"She sleeps a good deal," Sister Anne told them quietly. "There have been times when she goes an entire day without waking."

Adrianna laid a light hand upon the lined, waxen brow. "Mother," she whispered, "I am here now. I have come to be with you."

The invalid murmured something unintelligible and one of her pale, blue-veined hands lifted slightly from the coverlet, but she did not come to full consciousness.

After a few minutes of waiting, Adrianna rose to her

feet. "I do not wish to disturb her," she whispered to Sister Anne, and as she accompanied the older woman to the door Leith saw that Adrianna's face was stricken, her great blue eyes shimmering with unshed tears.

Once in the hallway, with the door closed behind them, she turned to him and fleetingly touched his arm, as if for comfort. "Oh, Leith, she *is* greatly changed," she said shakily. "She used to be so vibrant, so *alive*... Sister Anne, is there anything I can do? I've brought with me some herbs..."

"Thank you, dearest, but Sister Agnes and Sister Dorothy have tried every herb they know of, every remedy, every treatment... 'Tis the wasting sickness, and even the physic in Stirling said there's nothing to be done for it, that she has remained alive far beyond any normal expectation."

"If Sister Agnes and Sister Dorothy, whose skills greatly exceed my own, have exhausted every avenue," Adrianna said slowly, "then truly there is nothing more to be done."

"I am afraid 'tis true," the little nun said sorrowfully. "Father Ogden administered last rites three days ago. He comes here several times daily, hoping to see Mother when she is awake and lucid."

"Does that not happen often?" asked Adrianna.

"Less and less frequently. She continues to ask for you, my dearest, and always we tell her that you are on your way. It never fails to calm her."

One of the nuns—Sister Alice, Leith recalled, was her name—came toward them along the corridor, her black skirts rustling sibilantly. "Mother sleeps still?" she inquired in a low voice, and when Sister Anne nodded she said, "I will sit with her then, and call you when she wakes. In the meantime, Sister Judith has sent me to inquire if perhaps Adrianna and Lord Campbell would like something to drink or eat?"

" 'Tis an excellent notion; I will take them to the

kitchen," replied Sister Anne. "Thank you, Sister. Come," she urged Leith and Adrianna, "you must be in need of refreshment after your journey," and promptly she ushered them back to the entrance hall and along the corridor into the opposite wing. An open door on the left revealed a glimpse of a schoolroom, where ten or so girls of varying ages sat listening to one of the nuns who was gesturing toward a globe; on the right was a small, cozy library filled with books and pleasantly illuminated by another mullion window that opened onto the back garden.

At the end of the corridor was the kitchen. It was a surprisingly large room, with a vaulted ceiling and two brick-inlaid arches containing twin hearths. There was a brick oven for baking, a long wooden worktable, and along one wall was a pair of deep sinks set side by side. Two tall, wide oak cupboards occupied the length of another wall, their upper shelves displaying trenchers, cups, tankards, a marble mortar and pestle, some saltcellars, and several low, rectangular baskets stacked with knives, forks, spoons, linen napkins, and small bundles of herbs neatly tied with string.

Everything was orderly and immaculately clean, and a delicious scent of baking bread filled the air. At the moment the kitchen was crowded full of Leith's men, who sat around the table with pewter mugs before them and trenchers heaped high with small round loaves of bread whose crusts were dappled with golden-brown oats. In the center of the table was another plate which held a yellow brick of cheese and a knife to cut it with, and next to it stood an earthenware vase filled with pink and white snapdragons.

"I'm afraid we merely have cheese and bread to offer you, and cold perry," Sister Judith said, her smooth forehead wrinkled in distress.

"It all looks—and smells—most appealing, madam,"

Leith said gallantly. "And I'd enjoy a sample o' perry, thank ye."

" 'Tis made from pears and is quite delicious," Adrianna told him, then went to the table and pulled out a sturdy oak bench. "Won't you be seated, laird, and permit me to serve you?"

"Aye, lass, wi' pleasure," he said, and took a seat between Malcolm and Colin. As he ate, and drank the perry which was indeed very good, and talked with the others at the table, Leith noticed that Adrianna was deep in a low-voiced conversation with Sister Anne, who after some five minutes nodded briskly and said, "Yes, of course, my dearest, you would be doing *us* a good turn as well!"

"Thank you, Sister, I knew you would not fail me!" Adrianna said gratefully, then returned to the table and addressed Bernard, who sat shyly at the end, his fingers curled tensely around his mug.

"Bernard," she said, "as I thought, Sister Anne would very much like to have you stay on here at Rosings, and help the sisters in the kitchen and the gardens. You would be paid four shillings a week and receive three meals a day. There is also a small cottage in the back garden where you may stay. What say you? Do you think you would like it here?"

Instead of replying, Bernard, pop-eyed, could only mutely open and close his mouth.

"Ye look like a fish, man," Jock said jovially, slapping him on the back. "Speak, then!"

"Oh, aye, mistress!" Bernard said breathlessly, finding his tongue at last. "Aye, above anything I'd like it! *Thank* you, Mistress Adrianna!" He jumped to his feet and went to Sister Judith, bowing very low before her.

"Sister, where can I begin?" he asked enthusiastically. Sister Judith gave him her shy smile. "Bernard, I do like your zeal. Would you mind chopping vegetables for the evening meal?"

"Aye, Sister! I mean, no! Are you making a pottage? I know how to make quite a good one!"

Adrianna's expression lightened for a moment as she watched Sister Judith lead the beaming Bernard to the root cellar. Then she went to Leith and said softly, "I wish to take a turn about the garden. Would you care to accompany me?"

"Aye, lass, that I would," he said, rising, but added in concern: "But will ye no' ha' something tae drink or eat?"

"Later," she said. "I need to walk." She turned to Sister Anne. "You will come to us the instant Mother awakes, Sister?"

"Of course, dearest," the little nun assured her with a maternal smile. "You two go on and enjoy yourselves. I'm eager to make the acquaintance of Lord Campbell's fine men here."

She sat on the bench Leith had just vacated and reached for a golden loaf of oat bread. "Now," she said animatedly, "I want to hear all about Scotland. What is the food like? Is it true you eat a dish made with the intestines of a sheep?"

Leith smiled a little as he followed Adrianna down the hallway and out into the warmth of the day. Adrianna slipped her arm through his and together they strolled slowly through the well-tended grounds of Rosings.

Leith could not but admire the straight, thriving rows of vegetables, the bright beds of flowers, the assiduously worked herb garden. The sanded path beneath their feet had been planted with wild thyme and water mint, which issued a subtle, agreeable scent when trod upon.

" 'Tis beautiful, this convent," Leith remarked.

"The sisters have labored long and hard to make it so," Adrianna told him. "They believe that without harmonious surroundings, the soul itself cannot truly know inner harmony."

" 'Tis an earthy piece o' wisdom," he said. "Lass, how is it that there's a convent here, and a priest as well? Has no' yer queen declared herself an advocate o' the Protestant cause?"

"Yes, but she's a tolerant monarch," answered Adrianna, "and pockets of Catholicism still exist throughout England. The people of Stirling are tolerant too, and a good many attend Father Ogden's masses."

As Adrianna spoke they passed underneath a bower formed of willow trees, whose graceful branches entwined above their heads, intermingling with fragrant sweetbriars, honeysuckle, and rosemary, and came next onto a small arbor built along the enclosure wall, with climbers of jasmine and musk roses trailing up a crisscrossing wooden latticework. A simply fashioned bench sat near the arbor, invitingly shaded by the capacious branches of a maple tree.

Leith nodded at the bench. "Are ye ready tae rest for a spell, lass?"

Adrianna smiled at him. "Thank you, yes." When they were seated, she went on, "I believe you will like Father Ogden. He is a good man, a brave priest, who taught me a great deal over the years. As have the sisters themselves, who, though they have little money, are rich in their own way."

Her expression was thoughtful, and Leith felt again that small, gnawing doubt in the pit of his stomach. Carefully he said, "Ye enjoyed yer years here then?"

"Yes, indeed!" she replied unhesitatingly. "There was always so much to do, and to learn. The sisters were so good to me, so willing to share their skills and their time. Sister Agnes showed me how to tend a garden, and both she and Sister Dorothy instructed me in the arts of herbs and healing. Sister Judith let me follow her about the kitchen, and assist her when I had learned more. I valued—value—their friendship and their affection very much."

Leith felt his chest tighten in apprehension as she continued, "Yes, 'tis a useful, peaceful existence here at Rosings. Which brings me to a question I want to ask you, Leith."

"Aye?" he said, steeling himself, and conscious of the uneasy rasp in his voice.

"I have been thinking about what to do with Crestfield. If it does not displease you, I would like to sell it, and give the proceeds to the sisters here. It would help them so much!" She was looking at him hopefully, and gruffly he answered:

"Crestfield, and the money it brings, is yers tae do wi' as ye like."

"By law they would be yours . . . when we are married."

He shrugged, and shifted on the bench. Then he remembered something. He dug one of his hands into his pockets and held out his open palm to Adrianna.

"My necklace!" she said softly, gazing wonderingly into his face. "How . . . ?"

"Fiona stole it from yer chamber. Would ye like me tae fasten it round yer neck?" He held his breath; if she said yes, did it mean that she was having second thoughts about leaving her vocation . . . leaving Rosings . . . leaving England?

"Oh, yes, please," she said eagerly, and Leith's heart sank. With fumbling fingers he secured the tiny hook and clasp at the nape of her neck.

"I'm sorry tae be sae tardy in returning it tae ye," he said, a little stiffly. "I'd forgotten it wi' all the excitement at Crestfield."

"Don't apologize!" she exclaimed. "I'm just so happy to have it back! Thank you!" She raised a slim white-fingered hand to touch the delicate cross at her breast, and Leith looked away. Then he felt that same hand upon his arm.

"Leith, my love, what is troubling you?" she asked quietly. "Will you not confide in me?"

He was silent for a while, his gazed fixed blindly on the lovely willow-tree bower. Finally he turned to her and said, with painstaking care, "Am I right tae take ye away from Rosings, lass? Seeing the beauty o' this place, and meeting the nuns who care for ye sae much, I canna help but wonder if ye belong here . . . and if ye still yearn tae be a nun yerself."

She stroked her fingers along his arm, sending icy-hot chills of pleasure curling through him. "It is true that before I met you I was sure I wished to be a nun," she said earnestly. "But as I came to know you . . . to love you . . . I realized that the convent was no longer where I wanted to be. I want to be with you, Leith, and with your people, *in the world*. As fulfilling as it is here, as worthwhile, I don't want to feel like an outsider, cloistered from the joys and sorrows of everyday life."

"Before I met ye," Leith said, his voice low, "I too felt like an outsider, watching as from a distance as my people went aboot their lives."

"But together we transcend that, don't you see?" she said urgently. "Our love unites us, breaks down those barriers!"

"Aye . . ." he muttered. "I knoo it, lass. But what aboot the necklace ye're wearing once more? Is it no' the symbol o' yer intention tae be a nun?"

"In the past it was," she told him, her cornflower-blue eyes searching his intently, "as well as a symbol of my love for Mother Superior, and hers for me. But now its significance has changed, Leith. Now . . . especially that she is so ill . . . it is a cherished token of all that she means to me."

"I see." He took a deep breath, and forced himself to continue giving voice to the questions that tore at him.

"It baffles me as tae why ha' ye spoken sae little o' yer years here at Rosings."

"I was afraid," she answered simply, and when he looked at her sharply she explained, "I knew that I was in love with you. I feared that you would misinterpret my speaking of Rosings as a desire to return."

After a moment he nodded. "And what o' the differences in our religion? It troubles me no', but ye ha' been sae deeply immersed in yer faith . . ."

She smiled. "As I once told Ian Martin, we worship the same God, after all. I will gladly adopt your practices."

"Ye dinna mind?"

"No, I don't," she said steadily.

Longingly he reached out a hand to slide along the length of her golden hair. "Ach, lass, can ye forgive me for my uncertainty?" he asked, hoping desperately to lay his doubts to rest once and for all. "I only want tae do what's best for ye, dinna ye see?"

"Even if it meant sacrificing our future together?"

"Aye," he said, anguished. "Even that."

With a sound that was half a sob, half a laugh, she leaned forward and flung her arms around his neck. "You wonderful, courageous *idiot!* Don't you know how—how *clantie* you make me?"

With her passionate words, the last of his worries were washed away by a sweet, healing wave of relief. He grinned, his own arms sliding tightly around her slender back. "I think ye mean *cantie,* lass."

"I was trying to say *happy,*" she said with as much dignity as she could with her face pressed into his neck.

"Let me show ye how *cantie* ye make me," he whispered, and swiftly sought her mouth with his own. She moaned softly as her lips parted to his questing tongue and pulled him yet more closely to her.

A happiness more pure, more powerful than any he had ever known flooded him. Ah, God, but he was the most fortunate of men!

Lost in a haze of bliss, Leith could not have said how much time had elapsed when the sound of a throat being discreetly cleared nearby jolted them both, and quickly they drew apart.

Sister Anne had poked her head out from within the willow bower. "Forgive my intrusion," she said apologetically, "but Mother Superior has woken, and is most anxious to see you, dearest."

"Oh! Of course!" Her face flushed scarlet, Adrianna stood and, shaking out her skirts, went with a rapid step to Sister Anne. Leith followed, and heard the diminutive nun add:

"Father Ogden is here, too, and was so happy to learn of your presence at Rosings."

"I look forward to seeing him again," Adrianna murmured, and then no more was said as they returned to the house and made their way to Mother Superior's chamber.

Sister Alice was there, seated in a chair placed between the bed and the mullion window, and standing next to her was a slight, white-haired man dressed in the vestments of a priest. "Good day, Father," Adrianna said softly in greeting, glancing at him across the bed, then dropped to her knees and reached for a pale hand that now curled weakly around her fingers.

"Mother, 'tis I," Adrianna whispered, and Leith saw in the sad radiance of her face all the profound tenderness of a daughter looking upon an ailing mother of her own blood.

Gray-blue eyes lifted slowly to the compassionate visage so close to her own. The Mother Superior, Leith thought, would never have been called a pretty woman, yet even ravaged by illness there was a subtle, almost mystical quality to her strongly marked features that rendered her mysteriously beautiful.

"Adrianna ..." The voice was thin, labored, but still there was a joyous affection in it. "You are here ..."

"Yes, Mother, yes." Shimmering tears filled Adrianna's eyes and slipped disregarded down her cheeks. "I'm here."

"I have had ... so many dreams of you, child ... Troubled dreams ... in which danger threatened you ..." The Mother Superior's brows drew together. "I tried to call out to you ... tried to help you ..."

"Oh, but you did, Mother!" Adrianna exclaimed softly. "You *did* help me, I swear it!"

The lined countenance relaxed. "I am ... so glad," she murmured. "You ... look well, child. The brooch you wear ... is very pretty ... and I must confess ... it gives me great pleasure ... to see that you wear my necklace still."

Adrianna glanced over her shoulder at Leith, smiled fleetingly through her tears, and turned back to Mother Superior. "Mother, I have some things to tell you," she said quietly.

"Yes, child," came the tired, but loving voice.

"Crestfield is mine now, and I am planning to sell it. The money I gain from its sale I am giving to Rosings."

"You are ... too generous," Mother Superior protested. "You should ... keep the money for yourself."

"I have no need of it, Mother." Adrianna drew in a deep breath, and continued, "Mother, I am to be married, to a man of great worth and valor."

There was a short silence, and then:

"You are worried ... that you have displeased me," Mother said softly. "I am not ... displeased. I trust you ... utterly and completely ... I know that whatever path ... you have chosen . . . it is the right one for you, child. Your happiness . . . is all that matters to me."

"Thank you, Mother!" Adrianna breathed. "Oh, thank you! My betrothed is here, in the room. Will you meet him?"

"With great joy," answered Mother, and turned her eyes to Leith as gently he approached the bed, then knelt at Adrianna's side.

"Mother, this is the laird Leith Campbell, of Inveraray, Scotland."

"Madam, I am honored tae meet ye," he said, and meant it.

"And I you . . . Lord Campbell," Mother Superior said with the ghost of a smile. "Only a truly remarkable man . . . would have persuaded my darling Adrianna . . . to divert in her chosen course."

"He *is* remarkable, Mother," Adrianna said, and Leith felt humbled by the ringing sincerity in her soft voice. "I love him with all my heart."

A small, wise nod. "I can see it in your eyes," she murmured. "And in your eyes as well, my son."

She coughed suddenly, her thin body wracked by the violent paroxysm, and Sister Alice quickly leaned forward to dab at her mouth with a square of linen.

"Pray excuse me," Mother Superior whispered, then looked around her as if just now noticing that Father Ogden and Sister Anne were in the room. Then her gaze went to Adrianna, and Leith thought he saw a faintly pleading expression there.

"Child," she said slowly, "might I ask . . . a boon of you? If it is too much . . . you need only say so."

"Anything, Mother!" Adrianna answered, her voice trembling.

Tired gray-blue eyes focused first on Father Ogden and then on Leith, and it was as if an unspoken question was conveyed to him. Without hesitation he said: "Aye, madam, it suits me very well."

A faint, satisfied smile curved the pale lips, and urgently Adrianna whispered to him, "What is it? What does Mother want that suits you so well?"

"I believe," Leith told her, "she wishes the priest tae marry us, lass."

"Will you, child?" Mother Superior said quietly. "I would so much ... like to see you wed ... before I am gone."

Tears flowed anew down Adrianna's face. "Yes, of course, Mother," she said tremulously, "but please, do not leave me, Mother! I love you!"

"I love you too, child." With a great effort the old nun lifted her hand and stroked it tenderly along Adrianna's wet cheek. "Do not grieve overmuch ... at my passing, child. I have lived ... a long and rewarding life. 'Tis my time now ... I am not afraid."

Mutely Adrianna grasped Mother's hand and clasped it in both of her own.

"Now that I know ... you are happy ... and loved ... and that the dear sisters here ... will be adequately provided for ... I can go peacefully." She looked up at the priest. "Father ... will you ... perform the service?" Again came that wisp of a smile, this time with a hint of mischief in it. "They kneel already."

Father Ogden smiled. "Yes, Mother, I will."

Ten minutes later, and Leith was repeating with quiet exaltation as he looked deeply into Adrianna's eyes, "Wi' my body I thee worship ... wi' this ring I thee wed ..."

There was a sudden, startled silence. And then Mother Superior, with an unexpected surge of strength, pulled the simple gold band from the fourth finger of her left hand and offered it to Leith.

He smiled at her, slipped the band onto Adrianna's slim

finger, and Sister Anne gave an audible sigh of relief. The ceremony concluded a few moments later; Father Ogden gently closed his Bible, and Leith leaned close to Adrianna and lightly touched his lips to hers, awed by the tenderness, the passion that flowed between them, binding them together as one.

"Ye are my wife," he breathed in wonderment.

"Aye," she whispered, and smiled so luminously that Leith felt dazzled by the brightness of it. "And you are my laird, and my love."

There was another wracking cough, and quickly they turned to look at Mother Superior, whose worn, waxen face was illuminated by a serene smile despite the painful spasm that had just gripped her.

"May God . . . bless you, my children," she whispered to them, and then her eyes began to slowly drift shut. "I am so pleased . . . that you are . . . happy."

"Oh, Mother, I am," Adrianna murmured, an ache in her voice. "So very happy."

"What did I tell you, child?" came the almost inaudible reply, like a tranquil susurration of wind stirring in the trees. "Patience . . . and a steady heart . . . will win the day."

Then the Mother Superior's eyes had shut for the last time, and she breathed no more.

Adrianna sobbed and caught at Leith's hand. "She . . . she looks so peaceful!" she choked out.

"I believe she truly is at peace, lass," he replied softly. Gently he slid an arm about her waist and they both stood.

For several poignant minutes the occupants of the room paid their silent respects to the woman who had been so greatly admired, so greatly loved.

"If you will excuse us," Sister Alice said at last, dabbing at her damp cheeks with a handkerchief, "there are some matters Father Ogden and I need to attend to."

"Yes," Adrianna faltered, "yes, of course. We will leave you to them." After one final, lingering look, she turned away and left the chamber, clinging to Leith's arm. Without a word he led her outside and to the garden again, to the same bench where she had offered him such welcome reassurances of her devotion.

She wept in his arms, and quietly he held her, murmuring nonsense words of comfort into her ear. Presently her sobs subsided, and she looked up, smiling a little through her tears. "You are so good to me, Leith," she said, and laid her head against his shoulder with a long sigh.

"My heart aches for ye, lass," he said gruffly.

She only nodded, and after a while she said, "It *is* beautiful here, Leith, isn't it?"

"Aye, sweeting."

"But somehow, Inveraray is far more lovely in my mind." She sat up and gazed earnestly into his face. "Leith, can we go there as soon as possible? I miss Maudie, and little Johnny Ogilvy, and—oh, everyone! I want to see how poor Ross is healing, and go visit the Gunn baby, and—"

Leith smiled. "And we must see Ian Martin about performing another ceremony, if ye're willing."

"Yes, indeed, that would be lovely! I think Mother would have liked the idea of it very much. Oh, and Leith, I never got a chance to tell you, but Andrew and I have *such* plans for Midsummer Eve!" She stopped short and laughed, and Leith thought he had never heard a sweeter sound in his life. "Oh, my love," she said huskily, "let's go *home!*"

EPILOGUE

Inveraray, Scotland
1581

"Ach, I can scarcely believe that a year has gone by since I conducted yer wedding service, my dear Adrianna," said Ian Martin, leaning back in his chair and comfortably crossing one ankle across the other. "How swiftly time passes!"

Smilingly Adrianna looked up from her mending and cast a quick glance around the bustling great hall. It was early afternoon, and the maidservants and Andrew's serving boys had together scrubbed and scoured and swept and dusted until the hall practically gleamed with a mellow glow. Now the serving boys were seated around the end of the long trestle table, polishing forks and knives for tonight's feast in honor of the anniversary the clan was celebrating.

"I can scarcely believe it myself," she said, then laid

down her mending with a nostalgic sigh. " 'Twas a beautiful ceremony, Ian."

"It was, wasn't it?" he replied cheerfully, and Adrianna's smile widened. She had come to know the minister well during the last year, for he visited regularly to conduct services in Inveraray's chapel. Her suggestion to Leith that perhaps Ian had gained in maturity and wisdom since his early days in the ministry had proved correct, and she had found in him a sensible, agreeable companion. Although, she mused as he blatantly ogled one of the maidservants, he still displayed a lamentable tendency to flirt with all the prettiest girls.

"Ian," she chided him gently, "you're staring at Sheena."

"Aye, well, noo that Colin has cut me oot wi' Judith," he replied unrepentantly, "I've been forced tae move on."

"I'm glad that he's gotten over his *tendre* for Fiona," Adrianna said thoughtfully. "It did take him some months. Even though his mind condemned her for what she was, his heart was slower to follow."

Ian tore his gaze away from the blushing, buxom Sheena to ask, "And how does Fiona fare in Dunadd? She lives wi' her grandmother, does she no'?"

"Yes, and I understand that old Mistress Grant keeps quite a close watch over her." Adrianna paused, then added, "I must admit, Ian, that when Leith banished her from Inveraray, I did not ask for his clemency!"

"Why would ye? She deserved it, and more," Ian said sternly, and then his countenance softened, for staggering toward him was eleven-month-old Hugh, clutching in his chubby fist a bedraggled cloth-stuffed rabbit Mabel had sewed for him.

"How well the lad walks!" he marveled, reaching out his arms. "Come on, then! Ye can do it! Come tae Uncle Ian!"

Little Hugh grinned and gurgled, and with a final lurch he catapulted himself into the minister's arms. He was rewarded with a giddy swoop high into the air and he laughed excitedly.

Adrianna watched her son with loving eyes. He was as fearless as his father, and adventuresome too. Now that he had determinedly pulled himself upright and discovered the joys of ambulation, he was leading them all on a merry chase.

As if to prove the point, Maudie came hurrying into the great hall after her charge. "The scamp!" she said, her proud, indulgent expression belying her scolding tone. "We'd just paused a moment on the bailey steps tae say hello tae Wallace, and the next thing I knew he'd gone tearing intae the hall!"

Adrianna put aside her mending and Ian placed the chuckling baby onto her lap. "I daresay he was only looking for his mama," she murmured, pressing a soft kiss on golden curls that had yet to darken to Leith's rich brown.

"Does that bairn ever stop smiling?" said Andrew affectionately, and Adrianna looked up to see the steward standing before her.

She laughed. "Only when he's hungry, and I scowl too when my belly is empty!"

"Well, yer belly shall be full tonight, lady," Andrew promised. "Mistress Betty has sent me tae inquire if ye'd prefer tae ha' the mutton roasted or made intae a stew?"

"Stew, I think," Adrianna decided. "The laird prefers his mutton that way."

"Aye, lady. Oh, and we've several baskets o' ripe strawberries just come in from the crofts; did ye want them made intae tarts or served simply, wi' some fresh clotted cream?"

"Hmmm . . . You've stumped me there; they each sound delicious. What do you think, Ian?"

"How about both ways?" he proposed, laughing.

"Done!" Andrew declared, and returned to the kitchen, pausing en route to point out to young Stephen a fork that lacked the proper burnish.

Then one of the gardeners stepped inside to ask a question about flowers to decorate the hall, and Mabel came from the solar to display a repair to an elaborately embroidered linen cloth Adrianna wanted to use on the table this evening. Angus Brown, the carpenter, brought in a cunning little chair he'd fashioned for Hugh to use at the feast, over which Adrianna and Maudie exclaimed in delight. Next a milkmaid carried from the kitchen a pale yellow chunk of freshly churned butter for her to sample and approve.

" 'Tis fine, Meg, thank you," Adrianna said, handing her the dish. Suddenly Hugh crowed happily, waving his plump little arms, and Adrianna looked up to see Leith entering from the bailey and striding toward them. Her heart skipped a beat, as it never failed to do whenever she saw him, and she smiled at her handsome husband.

Leith returned that radiant smile with one of his own. God's blood, it hardly seemed possible, but she grew more beautiful every day! He nodded pleasantly at Ian Martin and picked up his grinning son, who leaned forward and bestowed on him a loud, wet kiss. "Thank ye, Hugh," he said, smoothing his hand tenderly over those bright curls. "How fares my lady?" he asked. "Busy wi' yer preparations for the feast?"

"Aye, laird," she answered, and Leith's smile widened as he saw her slender fingers steal to her bosom to caress the silver brooch she always wore. "Everything goes smoothly, I believe."

"I doubt it no'," he said, then, as a familiar heat began pulsing along his veins, he added, "Are ye too busy for me, lass?"

"Never," she said promptly, and rose to her feet.

He gave Hugh to Maudie, captured Adrianna's hand, and murmured, "I need ye upstairs in our chamber, lass. I've an ache that needs tending."

"Leith," she said, laughing and blushing all at once, " 'tis the middle of the afternoon!"

"Oh, gae on then!" Ian put in roguishly. "Else he'll seize ye in his arms and spirit ye away in full sight o' God and man!"

Leith lifted her hand to his lips. "Will ye come, sweeting?"

Those lovely blue eyes were soft as she gazed up into his face. "You know I cannot resist you, Leith," she replied, a little breathlessly.

"Then dinna even try," he said, and in the next moment she was shrieking in surprise as he did pick her up bodily, and held her tight to his chest, his arms securely around her delicate knees and slim, supple back.

" 'Twas an excellent notion, Ian, I thank ye," Leith said. He kissed those rosy lips, and very quietly he told her, "I love ye, lass. I love ye for yer goodness and yer strength, for yer beauty and yer kindness, and each day I thank God that He brought us together, for ye are a prize beyond any reckoning."

"I love you too, Leith," she whispered, and slid her arms caressingly about his neck. "If I am your prize, know that you are my miracle."

He kissed her again, and then, oblivious to the cheers and the applause from the clansfolk in the hall, he carried Adrianna—his wife, his love, his life—away and up the stairs, to the sweet, sensual solitude of their bedchamber.

ABOUT THE AUTHOR

Martine Berne has worked as an English teacher, a public relations assistant, an investment banker, a bartender, and a children's book editor. She has lived in Southern and Northern California, Mexico, New England, New York City, and, most recently, in South Florida, where she and her husband have welcomed into their "pack" Simba, a 95-pound yellow lab, adopted through the Humane Society of Broward County.

*If you enjoyed this stunning debut from Martine Berne,
be sure to look for her next Zebra release . . .*

A PERFECT ROGUE

When a notorious rakehell's racing curricle accidentally
strikes an impoverished governess, angry words
aren't the only things exchanged. Damien, Marquis of
Reston, is shocked to find himself offering the prim
and pretty young woman a position as his sister's companion—and sensible Caroline Smythe is appalled
to find that she's fallen madly in love with the most
infamous—and decidedly seductive—rogue in all
the *ton* . . . .

*AVAILABLE IN BOOKSTORES EVERYWHERE
IN JULY 2000*

Put a Little Romance in Your Life With
Fern Michaels

Put a Little Romance in Your Life With
Janelle Taylor

LOVE STORIES YOU'LL NEVER FORGET . . .
IN ONE FABULOUSLY ROMANTIC NEW LINE

BALLAD ROMANCES

Each month, four new historical series by both beloved and brand-new authors will begin or continue. These linked stories will introduce proud families, reveal ancient promises, and take us down the path to true love. In Ballad, the romance doesn't end with just one book . . .

COMING IN JULY
EVERYWHERE BOOKS ARE SOLD

The Wishing Well Trilogy:
CATHERINE'S WISH, by Joy Reed.
When a woman looks into the wishing well at Honeywell House, she sees the face of the man she will marry.

Titled Texans:
NOBILITY RANCH, by Cynthia Sterling
The three sons of an English earl come to Texas in the 1880s to find their fortunes . . . and lose their hearts.

Irish Blessing:
REILLY'S LAW, by Elizabeth Keys
For an Irish family of shipbuilders, an ancient gift allows them to "see" their perfect mate.

The Acadians:
EMILIE, by Cherie Claire
The daughters of an Acadian exile struggle for new lives in 18th-century Louisiana.